Hou

House of the Waterlily

A Novel of the Ancient Maya World

Kelli Carmean

berghahn
NEW YORK · OXFORD
www.berghahnbooks.com

Published in 2017 by
Berghahn Books
www.berghahnbooks.com

© 2017 Kelli Carmean

Library of Congress Cataloging-in-Publication Data
Names: Carmean, Kelli, 1960- author.
Title: House of the Waterlily : a novel of the ancient Maya world / Kelli
  Carmean.
Description: First edition. | New York : Berghahn Books, 2017.
Identifiers: LCCN 2017030158 (print) | LCCN 2017030563 (ebook) | ISBN
  9781785335501 (ebook) | ISBN 9781785335488 (hardcover : alk. paper) |
  ISBN 9781785335495 (softcover : alk. paper)
Subjects: LCSH: Mayas--Social life and customs--Fiction. |
  Mayas--Civilization--Fiction. | Mayas--History--Fiction. | Mayas--Fiction.
  | GSAFD: Historical fiction.
Classification: LCC PS3603.A75376 (ebook) | LCC PS3603.A75376 H68
2017
  (print) | DDC 813/.6--dc23
LC record available at https://lccn.loc.gov/2017030158

British Library Cataloguing in Publication Data

A catalogue record for this book is available from the British Library

ISBN 978-1-78533-548-8 hardback
ISBN 978-1-78533-549-5 paperback
ISBN 978-1-78533-550-1 ebook

Dedication

For the Maya, past and present.

Contents

Preface

Isn't it a shame we can't converse with the ancients? If we could, I believe we would find that we got many things mostly right about their societies, economies, political organizations, and perhaps even their religious worldviews. Yet it seems that we would also discover an important aspect of the study of ancient worlds that has mostly gone missing: the people themselves. Archaeology is not a discipline that easily engages at the scale of the individual; rather, it is most powerful at the community or the societal scale. Creative writing, however, is well suited to representations at the individual scale that, I believe, contribute to a greater understanding of the whole.

The genesis of what became *House of the Waterlily* was sparked by a student at Eastern Kentucky University, where I teach. After I had regaled my young students with an undoubtedly rousing lecture on the Maya collapse, presenting detailed evidence of its many and varied interacting and contributing factors, a student asked, "But ... what actually happened?" At first I was puzzled. Had he not been listening to what I said? Then I understood: while I was lecturing on the academic causality of the Maya collapse, he had been looking for its human story. At the time I muttered something like "Oh, it must have been terrible ... full of chaos and death!" But once I started thinking about what actually happened at the *human* level, I couldn't stop. My challenge then became how best to render my academic knowledge into an accessible written form offering a sound fictional portrayal of a vitally important and tragic lived human experience. *House of the Waterlily* is the result.

Impetus for writing *House of the Waterlily* also came from Mel Gibson's problematic Hollywood movie *Apocalypto*. Although Gibson, a talented filmmaker, depicted visual elements of the Maya civilization quite well, there was much more that he got wrong. A quick example: time and space and culture in *Apocalypto* are so grossly conflated that we see the Spanish arriving at the height of the Classic period, and the Maya conducting Aztec-scale human sacrifices. Why are these mistakes important? My view is that Gibson deliberately manipulated the evidence with the goal of encouraging viewers to breathe a sigh of relief as Christianity lands on the shores to put the morally bankrupt Maya out of their misery. The problem is that much of the general public who watched *Apocalypto* likely learned everything they think they know about the Maya from it. I offer *House of the Waterlily,* humble though it may be in comparison, as a publicly accessible alternative to *Apocalypto.*

House of the Waterlily is a work of historical fiction. It deliberately does not chronicle one person or family dynasty at one place or one time. Rather, it is an amalgam of archaeological and hieroglyphic material, or has been extrapolated from that material in, I hope, appropriate and probable ways. It takes place in what today is lowland Guatemala. *House of the Waterlily* is fiction, so people and places bear invented names. Centered on the fictional city of Calumook, the story is set at the very end of the Classic Maya Period, in the years around AD 830. Specialist Mayanist readers will recognize the general outline of events occurring toward the end of the occupation of Dos Pilas, but beyond that, *Waterlily* is a deliberate amalgam of Maya life and culture. In the Afterword, I offer some background to help readers place the story in its larger historical, anthropological, and Maya context.

Many of the Maya gods I mention here cannot be proven to have existed in the Classic Period. Rather, they are a mix of historic Yucatec and other, modern interpretations of Classic Period gods. I aimed to animate the Maya cosmos as fully and richly as possible, because the sense of such a cosmos is what is accurate, regardless of time period. Throughout *Waterlily,* I offer a view of what Maya life *could* have been like around AD 830—not what it *was* like.

To bring a sense of the Maya world and yet retain readability, I have used Maya and other indigenous terms sparingly. I have also used Spanish in instances where it has been widely adopted by Maya speakers. I hasten to underscore, however, that the Classic Period ended some 700 years before the Spanish Conquest.

◉◉◉

I offer the following glossary for words with which readers may not be familiar.

Cenote—a natural sinkhole that exposes ground water. Spanish.
Comal—a flat ceramic dish used to cook tortillas. Nahuatl [Aztec language].
Huipil—a woman's tunic-shaped cotton dress woven on a back-strap loom, often with elaborate colors and designs. Nahuatl.
K'uhul Ajaw—Holy Lord of a city-state. The Maya title for divine king.
Mano, metate—traditional stones used to grind maize. Low to the ground, the metate is stationary; the mano is held in both hands. Spanish.
Milpa—slashed and burned from the forest, a milpa is a plot of maize—a cornfield—worked by hand with traditional tools. Nahuatl.
Quetzaltun—in *House of the Waterlily,* the name of a fictional highland city. A quetzal is a large green lowland bird, as well as the currency of Guatemala. Quetzal is Nahuatl; thus it is a word that likely did not exist in AD 830. I use it in *Waterlily* because readers may be familiar with the bird and/or the currency. The Maya equivalent is *k'uk'tuun* or *k'uk'ultuun.*
Sacbe—a raised road or causeway built primarily for regal-ritual processions in cities, and sometimes between them. Yucatec Mayan.
Sajal—the title of a noble member of the Maya court, and often one who governed his or her own subsidiary town or city. Here it refers to a trusted advisor and administrator within the fictional city of Calumook. Interpretation deciphered from Classic Period hieroglyphs and images.
Stela—a freestanding stone monument carved with hieroglyphs and images, usually concerning the history of Maya royalty. The plural is stelae. Latin.

I watched my mother watch the young queen of Lalchich, whose bent legs were properly tucked beneath her red huipil as she knelt on the bench opposite us. I saw my mother take note of the ease in the young queen's voice, the slight flutter of her eyes as she spoke, the quick, subtle flick of her wrist as she ordered her servant to fetch cool chocolate. It was a good flick. It meant business, but it was also a self-conscious one, vaguely uncertain. Would the servant notice it? If not, the young queen might be obliged to repeat her gesture with embarrassment or exaggerated rebuke. Or perhaps that flick held concern—concern that the cool chocolate beverage would arrive in its painted clay pot with a head of froth inadequate for the eminence of such distinguished royal guests as my mother and myself.

"Great Lady of Calumook, allow me again to welcome you most graciously to our humble city, our humble palace," said the young queen. She spoke our proper highborn language, but with the unmistakable undertones of the dialect of this eastern region. "You honor us with your visit, my lady."

"Lady of Lalchich, it is gratitude for your generous reception that rests in my glad heart," replied my mother.

At that our hostess smiled, and as she did even I could see that she did so sincerely. Her narrow lips pulled hard in a tight upward curve to the peaked corners of her mouth. Her slight overbite revealed the long, full stretch of jade inlays in her upper teeth. The flush of her taut cheeks made her appear remarkably jovial for an occasion as weighty as this. Indeed, our hostess's entire face divulged that she was enjoying our visit. I wondered why. Was she eager to do well for her beleaguered people? Did the young queen feel lonely in her almost-empty courtyard? Was it difficult to bear the absence of her kin? Despite the abundant drape of woven curtains, our voices—or rather, my mother's and the queen's voices, as I was not to speak—seemed to echo off the chamber walls.

Enjoyment was not the purpose of our visit. Ours was not some mere social call lacking a precise agenda, and I knew my uncannily guileful mother had already grasped that the young queen of Lalchich would be easy to deceive. It was clear the woman kneeling before us had yet to master the art of the stony mask, the ability to conceal and to misinform at will. A young queen has so much to learn.

The servant appeared and poured the cool chocolate brew into clay cups painted with bright scenes of courtly life. The servant filled my mother's cup, then the cup of her mistress, and finally one for me. As a young maiden with hair down my back who had nothing to say, I was always served last. I watched as my mother raised her cup to her lips and, in the space of that brief trajectory, scrutinized the skill of the master Lalchich vessel painter.

She took a sip and said, "My, how delicious!"

I clasped my own painted clay cup and sipped, disguising the sharp burning sensation that accompanied the recollection that the people of Lalchich add too much chili to this wonderful drink and ruin it along the way, or at least that's what my mother always said. Thickening it slightly with fine-ground white maize was, she maintained, the proper manner in which to prepare cool chocolate, but now I understand that that's just how the people of Calumook preferred it.

I smiled as I set my cup on the carved wooden table at my side. With reluctance, I was forced to agree with my mother: even though these easterners are able to grow such excellent cacao in easy abundance—indeed, we acquire much of our bean as tribute from Lalchich—they really should consider adopting our recipe.

"I regret that my daughter's nose is not as prominent as it might be," my mother said all of a sudden. "It lacks a robust silhouette, but she is attractive nonetheless."

"Oh, yes, she is very lovely," agreed the young queen of Lalchich.

"Indeed, yes," was my mother's noncommittal response.

Then my mother launched into a lengthy discourse detailing the celestial portents of my birth. "Young Lady Winik, She of the House of the Waterlily, was born on 10 Imix."

My astrological compatibility with my prospective Lalchich husband had of course been examined exhaustively more than a year ago. Indeed, only thereafter had it even been possible for the marriage parleys to continue.

"Yes, 10 Imix, a very favorable day," agreed the queen of Lalchich. "A good day for the Crocodile."

"Her heritage could not be more distinguished," my mother said, turning now, I knew, to a recitation of my genealogy, which also featured her own illustrious ancestry.

Neither woman looked in my direction as they spoke. I was relieved that my mother chose merely to summarize our long, renowned, cosmologically divine pedigree rather than narrate it completely. "As you know," she concluded, "my own father was the Honorable K'uhul Ajaw, Holy King of Cenote, Calumook's most loyal and trusted ally. I am the eldest daughter of the first nephew of the deceased K'uhul Ajaw, Holy King of Calumook. Of course I do not need to further elaborate the paternal lineage of our young Lady Winik."

At this my mother's hand rose from her lap to gesture in my direction, her fingers and thumb slightly curled. Several strands of large jade beads were wrapped around her wrist, and one rare gold ring encircled her longest finger. Despite my mother's age, her long, glossed hair was still jet black. It was plaited and folded high in the elaborate style of a royal married woman of Calumook. This heavy coiffure was held aloft by numerous carved and polished bone pins inlaid with tiny bits of luminous shell. My own glossed hair, also intricately plaited, hung maiden-long down my back. My head had elongated well, as had hers. My mother's figure was plump with large sagging breasts, while mine was still the slight form of youth and promise. My mother's almond-shaped eyes were small and dark brown, much like my own, but hers were alert even when they seemed languid. She was always on guard, my mother, even when she pretended not to be. Especially when she pretended not to be.

As she sipped her chocolate I was certain she detested the concoction. She studied the palace chamber in which we sat, her eyes motionless.

The painted clay chocolate cups and the clay frothing pot with its long spout were thin and well made. The low wooden table that separated the Lalchich queen on one side from my mother and me on the other was skillfully carved of dark, rich-grained jungle wood polished to a high sheen. Large engraved wooden chests lined the chamber walls, and several long wooden shelves hung from ceiling beams. The luxurious woven curtains had been drawn open and draped across the bright, painted plaster walls of this formal reception chamber. The draperies' high quality was evident in their lively color, shot through with the vivid red obtained from the tiny crushed bodies of cochineal bugs. Clearly, red was the favored hue of this eastern city. Upon our arrival, as our nuptial entourage had proceeded through their plazas and upon their sacbe, the banners on their temples and palaces and the swinging cloaks of their courtiers all blazed bright red, as did the women's woven huipils, including that worn by the young, smiling queen of Lalchich, seated opposite us on the bench.

I picked up my cup and again we all sipped—or feigned sipping—our cool chocolate.

The ceramic figurines in the wall niches were artfully formed, and their colored imagery was respectable. The jade adorning the person of the young queen was unblemished and rich deep green in hue. Despite its unfortunate overuse of red, the woven cloth of her elaborate huipil was fine-spun. But the mats … the woven reed mats over which our knees hovered seemed to have begun to reveal wear at the spots where feet and ankles came and went and rubbed while sitting. They should have been replaced prior to the formal nuptial visit of such an illustrious queen of such an ancient and emblemed dynasty of a city as recently victorious as our Calumook.

Perhaps the mats had irritated my mother, or perhaps it was the chili in the chocolate, or the unsuitably trusting smile of our hostess, because now she remarked: "I must confess that I am quite relieved to be able to journey to your fine city once more, now that my husband the K'uhul Ajaw, Holy King of Calumook, has graciously restored our good relations."

I believe this remark reflected my mother's sudden desire to remind the young queen of their disparate social ranks. I had not noticed our hostess being anything other than respectful of the difference in their stations, but I had known my mother to perceive insult in the presentation of a fragrant floral bundle.

The queen lowered her gaze and bowed deeply from the waist, displaying proper etiquette at a moment of status chiding such as this. "His Eminence the K'uhul Ajaw of Calumook has been most gracious and generous. I fear we are most unworthy."

"Hmm," my mother murmured.

We all sat, our eyes blank and wary. Our chocolate cups remained properly poised between our fingers, although we sipped no longer.

My mother continued, now annoyed. "Indeed, the recent hostilities, your devastating loss, the terrible humiliation of it, and without doubt the unfortunate consequences, have been so very ... unpleasant."

I had witnessed my mother belittle many nobles, but never before had I seen her denigrate other royals to their face by speaking so blatantly of their disgrace. All present in the reception chamber—my mother, the young queen, one chocolate pot servant, three fan servants, and myself—knew full well that the young queen of Lalchich was as young as she was because my father had captured the prior, older queen's husband in battle and sacrificed him at Calumook. The Lalchich king had fought bravely, it was said. My father clutched his disheveled hair and with a firm heave of his obsidian dagger, severed his head from his neck. Calumook had celebrated. We erected a stela in our plaza to commemorate our resounding victory and Lalchich's crushing defeat. Its glyph band read: "It was Downed, his Flint and his Shield."

That was why the new, young king of Lalchich had ascended the throne and his young principal wife become queen. I imagined his coronation spectacle must have been arranged in haste, as a city must never remain long without a reigning sovereign.

Once, I was told, we had been firm allies, Calumook and Lalchich.

I'm unsure whether anyone could remember precisely why, or even when, our alliance with Lalchich had turned, but our feud had simmered as far back as my memory stretched—which admittedly was not far, then. Raids, ax wars, peace, star wars, counter raids, peace—all occurred, but it was mostly our Calumook that held the advantage. Those days were full of grievances and daggers.

Not long after the sacrifice of the Lalchich king, and the grand Ixchel Moon celebration of my menses—the spectacle during which I acquired the title of Lady—I began fulfilling my obligation to learn the ways of our people. My father required me to attend council and listen as cross-legged men on woven mats conversed in lengthy speeches and self-important discourse. The council included my father's sajal—his chief city administrator and most trusted member of his court—as well as the many lineage heads of Calumook. They were interminable, those councils, and the bright young wings of my Scarlet Macaw companion spirit, which longed to soar on the wild wind, felt instead as though they were bound with an invisible tether. What long, countless recitations I was subjected to—of genealogy, of tedious history, of continuous wounded complaints, of denunciations that could not be endured one moment longer. In the end—in the very end—I am not sure any of it really mattered.

Now, peace was once again restored between the kingdoms of Calumook and Lalchich. As the youngest daughter of the victor's line, and the youngest eligible royal of the House of the Waterlily, my role was to become the flesh-badge of our new and lasting peace. I was to reunite us.

My mother spoke again. "I do regret the increase in your cacao tribute, but I notice your groves are flourishing. They have grown so vast that I do not imagine that even the higher measures would be onerous in the least."

As we approached the city we had traversed a long valley, and my mother had insisted that our route wend through Lalchich's cacao groves. Their groves were bountiful indeed, but even I realized our new demands would not be insignificant. Soon all of Calumook would be able to drink its fill of this delightful brew, thickened as it should be with fine-ground white maize. And as they supped, all of Calumook would love my father even more.

There was nothing the young queen of Lalchich could say in response to such verbal assaults. From the corner of my eye I thought I saw her redden, but she was obliged to remain motionless—kneeling with composure, legs properly tucked above her scarcely worn woven mat—and accept my mother's ugliness with her head so deeply bowed I feared her jade nose ornament might slip from her septum into her chocolate cup.

What I could not have understood, on that long-ago day in that Lalchich palace chamber, was the immense personal grief our young hostess had endured upon the demise of her family. Back then, I did not know how it would feel to witness the slaying of my kin by the victor's sharp blade. Now that I know, I accord that young queen my highest admiration, however long overdue. She refused to collapse before ugliness, and not only was she able to withstand my mother's harsh ridicule of her woe, but through it all she did not let fall a single tear. Perhaps she was not so inexperienced after all.

At the time, I was simply confused. Why would my mother choose to poke the eye of a woman who was one of my potential husband's closest relatives? Second paternal cousins, they were. I knew he was one of the few royal adult Lalchich men my father had not sacrificed—because, you see, I had listened well to those tedious recitations of genealogy and knew the kin web of Lalchich, both its living and its dead.

My mother did not speak for some time. The fan servants, their hands clasped on long wooden handles to which bright parrot feathers were affixed, wafted air about us, performing their long, unhurried motions in silence. Outside in the jungle, the guttural cries of howler monkeys rose in roaring cacophony, then fell silent. My mother was angry. I knew she had not yet determined how she would resolve her anger. She assessed the circumstances, weighing her options, all the while feigning sips of her delicious chili chocolate. Etiquette required that the young queen of Lalchich and I wait in silence.

When my mother spoke again, I recognized the sly stab of deceit in her voice. "My daughter is not as accomplished as many royal young ladies of her pedigree. I am sorry to admit this."

She glanced at me, which was unusual, catching my eye for the briefest of instants because she knew that I knew she had decided to go against my father on the matter of my marriage.

"I don't believe that can possibly be true!" said the queen.

"I'm afraid it is. You see, my daughter, young Lady Winik, has still not succeeded in mastering many of the learned arts required of her station."

"Is her weaving deficient?" the queen of Lalchich asked, surprised but also relieved that mention of the "recent unpleasantness" seemed behind them.

"Her weaving is adequate but lackluster, nothing exceptional," said my mother.

"Ah," said the queen, glancing at my huipil.

"Her skill with flowers is good," my mother said, almost grudgingly, it seemed. "Her celestial knowledge is improving, it is true, but she remains far from able to establish herself as a patroness of the dark cloak. It is her ability to read with eloquence from the codices, however, that I fear remains most lacking. Her oratory can at times be halting and she still tends to cypher with her finger if she encounters a difficult glyph passage. I regret, my lady, if our emissaries have not been fully honest in their portrayal of her talents."

Now it was my face that reddened as humiliation surged through my person.

How could my mother speak such untruths? My assembly of fragrant floral bundles was excellent, and intricate weaving was a skill I had perfected long ago. By then as well, I had also already charted my great lunar orbital discovery with Calumook's master astronomer, a feat acclaimed throughout our city. I felt ashamed that my mother did not value my talents and abilities. Besides, it had been well over a year since I had used my finger to cypher glyphs, and it pained me that she had elected to reveal my embarrassing struggle so publicly.

Even as I began to fathom that my mother must have decided to rebuff the Lalchich nuptial prospect, it hurt that she would choose to do so at my expense. A woman of her stature was not required to state her reasons. My proud mother had always been capricious in her likes and dislikes, this I knew—and she had little concern for those who were destroyed in her wake. Including, it appeared, her own offspring.

"She is still young, your daughter. She has time to amend such bad habits."

"Perhaps, yes."

"Is her tutor working her hard enough?"

"Yes, I believe so."

"With time she can still learn what is necessary. There remains ample opportunity for practice."

My mother murmured something indistinct.

"I am confident she would be able to represent your venerable city with honor in our humble one. I am certain of it."

"Perhaps," said my mother.

"Never would she bring shame upon the House of the Waterlily." Then the young queen turned directly to me and asked, "Lady Winik, do you yourself wish to recite the glyphs less haltingly and never use your finger?"

It seemed as if my fan servant's monotonous motion stopped midair, though I do not believe it really did. All I knew was that the already considerable tension in the chamber became excruciating. Not only had my mother publicly disgraced her own daughter, but now with this shocking enquiry posed by our hostess, the young queen of Lalchich.

It was a dreadful moment. Despite all that has ensued since that long-ago nuptial visit to Lalchich, I remember that my first instinct was to defend myself. I wanted to gesture toward my fine-spun huipil, which I had woven unassisted on my backstrap loom. I wanted to describe its colorful and intricate Waterlily symbolism in detail. I wished the sky were inky black so I might lead them into the courtyard and regale them with accounts of the celestial complexities suspended within the glittering heavens. I wished a codex lay upon the mat, that I might unfold it and read it aloud then and there, in a perfected women's high oratory style, my hand revealing only grace and poise as it gestured in faultless tandem with my words.

Now this shocking query.

The relative making arrangements for a prospective groom was never to speak to a prospective bride. They simply never did, and still do not. My only option was to press my lips together, cast my gaze downward, and pretend I did not hear her words as the battle of pride raged beneath my young stony mask. My mother would be infuriated by the young queen's breach of etiquette, and I did not want her fury to fall upon me as well.

My mother said nothing.

She waited as though by instinct, as a spider might wait for a midge to ensnare itself in her web, as it always does.

"Oh, dear!" cried the young queen, realizing her mistake too late.

Another interminable stretch of silence ensued. True, the long wooden-handled parrot-feathered fans continued in slow and steady motion. And the cochineal-red curtains remained draped back upon the chamber wall, although it seemed that even these objects held their breath in anticipation of the consequences that were sure to follow.

"My honorable lady," said my mother at last, scarcely concealing her venom: "I am afraid Lady Winik and I ... we are still quite ... weary from our long journey. Perhaps we might be offered ... some ... respite?"

"Yes, forgive me, that is most inconsiderate," our hostess blurted, in yet another breach of etiquette. Royalty must never admit error, much less apologize for it—even so egregious an error as a mistake in protocol.

My mother placed her chocolate cup on the carved wooden table, and even the mere thunk of clay as it met polished wood told me she was livid. I was already well aware that she regarded people from Lalchich as barbarians, and this opinion had now become irrefutable, I knew. With that thunk I realized too that the identity of my future husband—a man I hoped to love—and thus the name of my future home would remain elusive for many months to come.

◎◎◎

"But Grandmother, I thought you were in love with Naah Chan?" interrupts my precious Lily Bean. "And he was from our Calumook!"

"Oh yes, my child. You have a sharp memory, and of course both of those things are true." How young this girl seems, and still so naïve in the ways of our people.

"Yes, I knew he was from our Calumook," says Lily Bean. She is justly proud of her memory and of our home, and I smile to recognize it. She has heard me speak the name Naah Chan so often that to her he has become familiar. I smile also at her sweetness.

"But, Lily Bean, you must understand that I was not free to marry Naah Chan." I gaze at her from behind the white film of my aging eyes, knowing I do not want to utter the words that must fall next from my lips. "Just as you will not be free to marry the man you love."

"Why not?" she asks.

"Because you are a daughter of the House of the Waterlily," I say, knowing she has heard these words but still has not grasped their true significance. I sigh and avert my eyes toward the tamped dirt floor of our tiny hut of thatch and pole. I note the sight of my own thigh as it protrudes from below my coarse-spun huipil. I almost do not recognize this thigh. How could I possess a thigh as disagreeable as this? I look back at my granddaughter because I do not wish to contemplate my own sagging skin.

I want this child to know how extraordinary I once was, though now no one sees me as anything more than a shriveled hag.

Youth can never comprehend that such a fate will also be theirs. They cannot see the elderly as anything but old, with their creased cheeks sucking at toothless jaws, and their ugly sagging thighs. Youth cannot grasp that time will foist its burden even on them, on their flesh and also on their spirit. But even that misfortune will come about only if they are fortunate enough to survive. Sturdy enough to endure.

I push myself up from the rough wooden bench, wiping an annoying trickle of sweat from my brow. It is hot even in the shade, even with the good breeze that rustles the leaves of the ceiba far above. Back then, my fan servant cooled my person with slow, repetitive strokes of vivid parrot feathers. Back then, sweat was something I had only ever witnessed upon the unfortunate brow of others.

"Back then, I was of the highest born. Everyone knew the young and beautiful Lady Winik, and royals and nobles strove to be chosen as my husband. Our palace was the seat of the House of the Waterlily, its first stone set thirty-three generations earlier by our ancestor, the revered founder of Calumook." Spoken here, before our pitiful hut, my sudden, grand declaration strikes even me as strange.

Then I gaze at this girl, at Lily Bean.

She is my youngest and favorite grandchild. Her face is perfect; gone is the sour. She lies limp and motionless beside me in the heat, her slight person flopped gracelessly on the shady bench before our hut. Her listless arm dangles to the side. I am close enough to reach out and caress it, but I do not.

"I am of the House of the Waterlily," she repeats, mimicking the strange tone of my pronouncement.

My toothless mouth broadens unbecomingly as I smile at her innocence. Then my smile ceases. She does not understand the burden of our patriline. How can she? No one has taught her our ways.

"My child," I say, holding her youthful gaze with my cloudy one. "The House of the Waterlily has always been the grandest of all." I pause to allow adequate moment for my next words. "You are our future."

◎ ◎ ◎

The grand Ixchel Moon spectacle was not just a celebration to mark the start of my menses; it was also to announce that the youngest daughter of one of the oldest emblemed dynasties of one of the most powerful kingdoms, had come of age. This momentous occasion heralded a time of hurried jostling among my father's peers.

Pride swelled in me as my father officially proclaimed me Lady Winik.

"Beloved people of Calumook, I present to you my youngest daughter! She brings new honor to the House of the Waterlily!" he declared with enthusiasm, with genuine happiness. Because he was so delighted with me, I lifted my chin high. From deep within my chest, my Scarlet Macaw companion spirit spread her bright wings, her magical feathered arms gleaming with joy.

We stood at the pinnacle of our palace.

At that time, I had seldom been present in such an exalted place, and I was nervous as a bat. Long wooden trumpets blared from either side, and in truth they were painfully loud. Nearby the high melodic notes of the turtle shell marimba chimed as the hollow slit log drums beside it produced a low rumble. All eyes roved my person, from my headdress to the tip of my sandals. I was grateful after all that my body servant had fussed and fretted about each detail of my appearance, as indeed I had not understood how penetrating such scrutiny would feel. I was dressed in the new fine-spun huipil I had woven for my own special occasion. Within the design of colored threads at the neckline, I had entwined several rows of small, pale jade beads so that I might seem surrounded by a rich glow. Arranged upon my person were myriad jade ornaments that had been gifted to me since my birth, and on this occasion as well. Indeed, this was the first spectacle in which I had worn the full regalia that accrued to the title of

Lady Winik. I had not realized how heavily it would weigh upon my person.

My father turned to address the crowd assembled in the plaza below; I turned with him. He opened his arms wide.

"She is our future!" he boomed.

And the people of Calumook roared their pleasure.

I stood motionless, my face sealed in a well-rehearsed formal spectacle countenance that revealed nothing. Gazing down upon the commoners in the plaza, I could not help but think they looked as small as ants.

Although I did not meet them at the time of the celebration of my menses, gimlet-eyed nuptial advisors numbered among our honored royal and noble guests. Each of these specialists in esoteric astrology and the computation of celestial calendrics had known well in advance of their arrival that I was born on 10 Imix. This fact was announced again and again, each time with loud blares of trumpets. With each new announcement, the nuptial advisors calculated my numinous compatibility with a wide array of potential husbands. In addition to their shifting and arranging and reckoning of seeds and crystals, the nuptial advisors observed every detail of Calumook. Lest they construe any omen as ill, my father's sajal made certain that not one clay water jar, shade awning, or stray yellow dog was out of place.

In the matter of my marriage, the large number of initial prospects was soon diminished by the substantial bride price. Because I would reside in the city of my future husband, early considerations included painstaking palace reviews by a formal Calumook delegation. My father would never agree to marry me to a man whose city was too impoverished to build a palace of adequate grandeur for his daughter.

The cities whose palaces passed this test sent formal emissaries to Calumook. Granted, most of these were our vassal or allied cities, though it is also true that several places sent emissaries in stealth. These latter places' rulers might consider a shift in allegiance but could never publicly reveal that potential strategy for fear of reprisal.

Those that remained in the running sent official envoys to Calumook to continue formal parleys on the matter of my marriage. First the envoys spoke with our lineage under-advisors in our palace's lowest rooms. Those men sat cross-legged on their woven mats and listened. If they deemed a prospect to hold potential merit, they passed the matter to their over-advisors, higher-ranked men who sat cross-legged on mats in rooms on the second story of our palace. Elsewhere, in other palace chambers, our own gimlet-eyed nuptial specialists reckoned and re-reckoned each prospective husband's birth compatibility with that of my own, 10 Imix. One might imagine such calculations as straightforward procedures with a single possible outcome for each tight cluster of seeds and crystals, but in truth they were far from that. Calculations such as these require interpretation, achieved by celestial channeling through the person of the nuptial specialist. People from Calumook are wise to rely only on the interpretations of specialists from Calumook, which is why we, too, arranged and reckoned our own tight clusters of seeds and crystals.

Having made it through the mid-level rooms, the suitability of a nuptial prospect might finally be considered within the walls of our palace's higher chambers, by cross-legged men upon mat-covered benches in the rooms of my father's sajal. If they withstood his scrutiny, the matter went from there to the king, my father.

To my parents.

Through their own deliberations—and anxiously, I'm certain—my mother and father narrowed the competitors to three. These were Lalchich in the eastern lowlands, Quetzaltun far in the highlands, and Somalx, an independent seaport on the far eastern coast. Each candidate brought advantages and disadvantages, risks and rewards. These were specified in detailed reports submitted by Calumook spies who had augmented the formal inspection tours with their own visits to the three cities. The final list was compiled based on these reports. My parents spoke incessantly of these matters, which was how I knew they loved me.

At the conclusion of it all, my father's sajal sent formal solicitations to the rulers of the three cities: "Send your premier emissaries, as the time to parley in earnest has arrived."

For a short time, my person was revealed for inspection to the emissaries of all three cities. I remember in vivid detail the formal reception at Calumook of the entourage of the emissary of the third brother of the king of Somalx.

As expected, the emissary, upon first appearing at the door of my father's throne room, fell prostrate upon the floor. Behind him hovered his assistants, bowing profusely. These latter men were not required to prostrate themselves because they were not the ones who would converse with my father, the great K'uhul Ajaw of Calumook. At the rear came the gift-bearers, arms brimming with fine-spun cotton mantles and quetzal plumes and jades and finely painted clay vessels to bestow upon the House of the Waterlily. These gifts were required even to continue in parley. Such was my worth that, once the final matrimonial accord was announced, the concluding bride price summation would be an entire staircase full of tall, heaping presentation baskets of cacao beans.

"Greetings, worthy emissary of Somalx!" my father greeted the man. His favorable recognition gave our visitor permission to rise from prostration.

"Great K'uhul Ajaw of the great city of Calumook, I bring you humble greetings from the holy king, K'uhul Ajaw, of Somalx!"

"I thank the K'uhul Ajaw of Somalx for sending his emissary."

"Thank you, kind lord of Calumook, for receiving us."

"You are most welcome here, you are among friends!"

"I am honored by your gracious reception of this humble emissary from the humble seaport of Somalx!"

"Yes, my friend, be at ease."

And so they continued, back and forth, in a long, prescribed sequence of requisite formalities and overstated accolades.

In due course, the emissary settled himself into a kneeling position before my father, who sat cross-legged upon his throne, itself perched high upon a painted stone bench. Carved of stone to resemble a mighty jaguar, the most fierce and powerful creature of the jungle, the image in my father's throne was also that of his companion spirit. My father sat upon a pelt of that same powerful beast, the claws and long tail dangling from the polished stone. An exquisite pair of ear spools—ground very thin from a translucent, milky green-white jade—flared like delicate four-petaled flowers from my father's royal lobes.

Silence prevailed for some time.

My father's dwarf stood motionless beside him, propping his tilted mirror. My father's flywhisk servant shooed away any buzzing insect that might dare alight upon his royal skin. His two fan servants kept the air surrounding his regal person in motion, ensuring he remained comfortable and free of perspiration. As

I've said, trickles of sweat were only for the unfortunate brows of others.

My father frowned. Having never seen him frown quite like that before, I thought he must be pondering with great intensity, via the person of the emissary before him, the nature of my potential husband, and wondering how joyous a marriage his youngest daughter might have with the patron of the man now kneeling before him.

But what my father said was this: "Tell me of your city's prospects. Tell me of your temples and their attendants and their visions. Tell me of your friends and your foes."

In careful rehearsed oratory, the emissary began speaking of these matters in low, measured tones. My father feigned disinterest. For a time he looked instead at his fingernails; then he studied a spot of orange in the jaguar pelt before gazing at his own reflection in his dwarf's tilted mirror.

The emissary spoke of many things, but it was the actual port-of-water he spoke of most. We all knew Somalx was an independent city on the far eastern coast, but beyond that, we knew little.

"The seaport itself," the man explained, "is protected by a shallow lagoon whose waters lapped at a gently rounded beach of white sand. Many tall palms grow along the long edge of the beach, and offer welcome shade."

As he spoke, I thought the place sounded very pleasant.

"Here, in this gentle lagoon," the emissary continued, "our king has pounded wooden posts to construct our wharves. The port of Somalx has many wharves, where our fleet of sea canoes is moored when not out upon the ocean. Other wharves nearby are for the foreign canoes that ply the waves from distant seaports."

Of course it was not only my father who heard this man's description. We all listened—my father's court, his sajal, his friends, his enemies. Of all of us assembled in the throne room that day, only our formal emissaries and official spies had yet made the long journey to that distant place; thus we were all immensely curious.

Why had we never visited?

Calumook had been trading with the port of Somalx for as long as anyone could remember, and all knew that the seaport had prospered greatly of late with the rapid rise of their sea canoe trade. Before this trade expansion, it had not been a place anyone ever considered journeying to. No esteemed K'uhul Ajaw then ruled as sovereign. No grandiose pilgrimage temple towered above its plaza. There was no grand ball court where we might attend a ceremonial match.

All of that had changed. Now, we heard rumors of Somalx and its vast new riches—the delightful tinkle of its multitudes of shiny copper bells, its finger rings of that same shining brown, and even some of the much rarer rings of gold, like the one my mother wore. These and other goods were now shipped in mighty sea canoes from cities several days' paddle south, north as well. The canoes, it was said, were many times larger than the dugouts in which we plied our mighty river and could carry three times as much cargo. They were said to cut with ease, even through large ocean waves, with the combined muscle of twenty-five strong paddlers.

Indeed, my father's sajal had often grumbled about the rise of the sea canoe merchants. "They will steal away our regulars," he warned my father.

My father had always waved away such concerns. "Our regulars are loyal," he would say. "They would never abandon us, a city as grand as ours."

"Times are changing," responded my father's sajal.

"That is true with great certainty," admitted my father, "but not so much that the hallowed name of Calumook has become meaningless. Our trade still thrives along our rivers, and along our overland routes as well."

To that, my father's sajal always said nothing.

The emissary of Somalx had turned to the subject of salt. He was describing how his people simmered ocean water until the liquid disappeared and salt was all that remained. Then they patted the salt into cakes, which they traded to many places.

"And why does the third brother of the king of Somalx wish to unite our families with this marriage?" inquired my father.

"Oh! He has heard of the extraordinary beauty and talent of young Lady Winik," said the emissary, bowing his head.

"Yes, her loveliness is without doubt extraordinary," my father replied. He was waiting—biding time, as he must, while the formalities of prescribed conversation ran their course and some sort of fact became apparent.

It was unusual for an independent city to seek ties with another—this we knew. Moreover, the few places that, like Somalx, had managed to remain separate tended to guard their independence ferociously. For us, it would be risky to ally with a city unaccustomed to such ties. There was danger it would resist our authority. Yet a bond with a wealthy mercantile seaport on the rise could prove most advantageous. It was risk versus reward. This calculus always.

I now realize that a question as direct as the one my father posed to the emissary can sometimes play an important role in the strategy of negotiation. My father was a man who appreciated straightforward responses, which was rare in our world. I once heard him claim that a direct reply was a good measure of the worth of a man.

"Great Ajaw," confided the emissary, lowering his voice and slowing the pace of his speech: "A new power grows to the north."

Intrigued, my father leaned forward. We all leaned forward. One of my father's perfect eyebrows rose into an arch.

"Ah," he said. "Speak to me of this new power in the north."

"It is a power that has the most holy K'uk'ulkan at its center."

We of Calumook, like the people of all other cities, had always held K'uk'ulkan, deity of the feathered serpent, in high esteem. He was an ancient divinity, one we knew and loved. My father's sajal had spoken of the burgeoning cult of K'uk'ulkan, which seemed to grow apace with the rise of the sea canoe merchants.

"We have dedicated a new temple in his honor," the emissary continued.

At this my father tilted his head. "The king of Somalx raised a new temple to K'uk'ulkan?" he asked. He seemed stunned, but I knew he was astute enough to play the innocent.

"The king wrapped a new skin overtop an older temple, my lord."

Of course my father understood that an entirely new temple devoted to any deity was improbable—but who could know? If a prosperous seaport could support a whole fleet of sea canoes by feeding the muscle of twenty-five paddlers for each vessel, who could know what it might be capable of? Particularly now, as so much had changed of late.

My father turned his head and for several long moments contemplated his reflection in his mirror, propped at an angle

by his dwarf; then his gaze crept up to catch the eyes of his sajal. This trusted advisor sat far off to my father's side, listening
always, observing always, but never speaking in the course of
an official parley. Noticing my father's growing agitation, I knew
what he was thinking: How had his spies failed to inform him of
intelligence as important as the raising of a new temple devoted
to this divinity?

As if in answer, the emissary explained, "It is just now finished, my lord, and only at the latest possible juncture did the
king order the stucco to be molded in a decorative form that fa-
vors the glory of the feathered serpent."

"Ah, indeed," said my father.

"He is very powerful in the north, K'uk'ulkan."

"Indeed," said my father again, in a tone that was difficult
to read.

"Indeed," agreed the emissary, hopeful, I think, that all might
still be well with the nuptial negotiations for his patron, the third
brother of the king of Somalx.

"And what thinks the third brother in regard to the motif of
the molded stucco? This new K'uk'ulkan temple? This ... new
power from the north?"

"My lord, the third brother does not so admire this power
from the north."

"No?"

"He wishes to align not with the north, my lord. The third
brother admires those who embrace tradition."

To this my father said nothing. Despite his silence, I knew he
was quickly losing interest in the prospect of aligning with this
seaport—an unpredictable city filled with upstart sea canoe merchants, a city whose impetuous king had so dishonorably bowed
to pressure. Adoption of the trappings of a far-off cult brought by
a group of northern outsiders was something my father would
never tolerate, that I knew for certain.

Looking back, I imagine the doubts and worries that must
have pervaded my father's thoughts:

The third brother, a traditionalist ... this is good. The seaport could bring us remarkable wealth. What dangers might lurk
alongside these shiny new rings? Does our jade no longer suffice?
How could it not? Might the third brother aspire to overthrow
his king-brother and seek my aid? Would I support such an en-

deavor? How powerful have those northerners become? Have we not honored K'uk'ulkan enough? Our canoe trade on our river remains strong—does it not?

At the time, I believed my father simply chose not to marry me into a city—however newly prosperous it might be, however pleasant its lagoon and long lapping beach of white sand—where two brothers might come asunder. It is true that kin-strife is particularly difficult to navigate, and that the Somalx prospect was set aside for this reason. Now, though, I'm uncertain to what extent such peril—my peril—even entered my father's considerations.

2

"Lily Bean, you have grown old enough to understand many things. Very soon we shall observe the Ixchel Moon celebration of your menses, so your formal instruction must now begin."

This little snip of a girl is growing like a fresh shoot of maize, and soon her blossoming buds will be breasts. She is now the one who helps her mother. Hers is the slight, eager form that kneels before the metate in our thatch kitchen, grinding sodden maize kernels into dough with a smooth stone gripped in her hands. It will be lengthy, her dance of the grinding stones— back and forth, back and forth with the swoop and pull of youth. My aging form has grown too old for such dancing.

◎◎◎

I have already informed her mother that we must commence the preparations, and that Lily Bean's puberty celebration must be as grand as we can make it.

"Why so grand?" her mother asked.

"Because with it we shall resurrect my title," I told her. "The time has returned for the House of the Waterlily."

And my daughter asked, "Why, Mother? Why must you always grip the past so hard?"

"Because it is our history, and it is a glorious one."

But she could not grasp this. I deserve the blame, because I did not instruct her as I should have when she was young. Those times were still too dangerous to speak of such things while lying about on shady benches at midday. Fear still silenced me then. It was best I be lowborn like the others.

I tried again.

I told my daughter, "The world has witnessed its destruction, and now we are poised for its renewal. The House of the Waterlily has survived. The burden of time has cycled through."

She looked at me with impatience. Her eyes still shine with vitality, though I sense it will soon begin its wane. Hers remains a world of work: Sweeping our dirt floor with a tied twig broom. Carrying firewood in her tumpline. Coiling simple clay pots. Stirring stew. Grinding maize each morning, although Lily Bean now performs this task. My daughter's hands are like mine, the hands of one who farms milpa—fingernails blunt, callus lines black even when clean. She does not much worry about her patriline.

My daughter pursed her lips and shook her head. She thinks me vain and tedious, and I think her common.

"The House of the Waterlily has atoned," I said. And this I said to my daughter's back as she walked away: "Our time has come once more."

◙◙◙

"Lily Bean, your celebration can not be as splendid as mine, and for that I am sorry. Back then, when I was young and extraordinary, the celebration of my menses occasioned many days of spectacle and feasting. So many fine gifts were lavished at my feet that they reached all the way down the palace stair. I regret our times cannot offer you such splendor."

Still more, I regret that I will not be able to lift my Kalo'mte' grandmother's heirloom jade collar from my frail person and place it upon her young chest. I will not be able to do this because this treasured gift, like so much else, was lost in the upheaval.

Despite the plainness of her celebration, I will say these words: "You are worthy. When all else fails, this you are to remember."

I do not tell my precious granddaughter, youngest scion of the House of the Waterlily, that her education must begin because of my sense of my own rapid diminishment—and because now my aging mind so often wanders to that shadowy remembered world. I urge it to roam only the pleasant memories—of art and learning, fine-spun cloth and jade, fan servants and the clean, glinting water in our pleasure pool, a world in which the high-born did not toil in the dirt of a milpa or conceal their perfect maize-kernel heads with turbans. Yet my mind wanders at will, striking out on trails that lead to unintended destinations. Too often it is drawn back to the terrible times: horror, desperation, bloodshed, and even the memory of my little cousin who, had he lived, could have become the next K'uhul Ajaw of Calumook.

I must tell all of this—all of it—to this most precious child of my lineage while my person still holds the strength. My mind still holds these memories with confidence because it has never allowed me to forget. Not for one day has it allowed me to forget.

Lily Bean cuts through the clutter, the jumble of my thoughts and memories. She asks, "Why won't my Ixchel Moon celebration be as splendid as yours, Grandmother?"

"Because the world has changed so much, that is why."

"But why did it change? Why can't I have lavish gifts piled at my feet?"

I gaze at a dusty row of rafters bearing the load of thatch that is the roof of our hut. In another era, ballgame equipment was hidden from the Hero Twins in the rafters. Those Twins survived many ordeals, as have I—as must Lily Bean. Of course she wants her lavish gifts. What child would not? I too had been eager to receive them. Little could I know then how dear their price would be—dear even for the brilliant radiant glow of the wings of my Scarlet Macaw companion spirit.

"Granddaughter," I say, "why is difficult to know and its telling is long. But even that knowledge must become yours. You are nearing the age when my father, the greatest K'uhul Ajaw of the greatest city of all time, obliged me to learn our ways."

I fall silent. The telling will be so very difficult. Just as my position back then obliged me to learn, it now obliges me to tell.

She rolls to her side, turning her head to look at me and waiting for my raspy voice to continue. I know what she sees—a withered jumble of sagging skin. I see my youthful self, dancing gracefully in heavy jade and fine-spun atop the pinnacle of our palace.

"Grandmother?" she asks, and again I am startled back to now, back to this aged version of my person, away from those grand days and also from the terrible ones.

"Yes, my child, yes." I press my fingers to the corners of my eyes. I rub my temples, note yet again the slackness of my skin. "Where to begin? I know I have told you many stories of our home, Lily Bean, but I must tell you more of our Calumook. We were once—"

"But Grandmother, I have been to Calumook many times. I know it well," she boasts. "It sits nestled within the bend of our mighty river."

Ah, how precious is this child. How she has learned to mimic my pride in our Calumook's siting. I will ignore the impertinence of her interruption. For this child, for our future, I will have patience.

◎◎◎

It was my father who gave me my pet monkey. One morning he appeared in our back palace courtyard carrying it astride his person. He smiled when he saw my gleeful response. I clapped my hands with joy when he plucked it from his shoulder and put it in my arms. I still remember the peculiar feel of its thin furry limbs as it clung to my person. My father tied the animal's leg to the smooth shaft that braced the awning before our chambers. I wove a bright tiny collar for him.

I remember my father as a calm and caring man, or at least in my earliest memories he seemed so as he frolicked with us in the courtyard, or splashed about with us in our pleasure pool. But as I grew older—and he did as well—he became withdrawn. His words seemed less tender than they once had been, and he spent more time in the public chambers at the front of our palace.

Our palace in Calumook was grand. Its front soared three full stories, each having its own long sweep of high vaulted chambers and faced with sturdy columns. An enormous god mask spanned each wide portal, and the tops of the narrower doorways were hung with garlands of cheerful woven bunting. Thick with plaster, the palace was painted in bright colors that caught the sun, making it glow with the power of the gods whose countenances adorned it. Green Waterlily banners lined both sides of our long central staircase, from the highest riser to the very lowest, such that when they fluttered with the breeze, they resembled long slithering serpents.

We were forbidden to play anywhere near the front of the palace. My father became irritated if so much as a peal of childish laughter drifted there on the roaming wind. One day as I sat in our courtyard playing with my monkey, the little creature thing managed to squirm from my grasp. It is true he had gotten loose before, but I had always managed to catch him. That day, though, his strong sinewy legs sprang from step to awning shaft to wall; then he leapt onto the roof and was gone. It happened so fast. I knew from his angle of flight that it was entirely possible he would reappear just above my father's chambers on the palace's third story. I knew I could never let my father come upon my monkey in such a place.

I, too, scrambled up the awning shaft and to the roof of my chamber, and then up onto our palace courtyard wall. Careful to keep my balance, I strode along that long wall to clamber up and over another roof and then another facing it, slowly wending my way through the sprawling maze that composed the private portions of the back palace complex. I had nimbly scrambled like this many times—all palace children had, even though it was forbidden. It is easy when you are young and sprightly and never look down.

At last I sneaked forward and peered around the corner, suddenly finding myself staring at a jade belt dangle worn by my father's sajal. Sour-faced and glowering high above me, he was clutching my pet monkey by the furry scruff of his neck. The skin of my monkey's face was drawn so taut that his eyes were nothing but slits and his little pointy teeth poked from behind flattened lips. His arms were splayed back uselessly because the sajal had grabbed hold of so much scruff. The little collar around his throat had become a tight garrote.

"Don't hurt him!" I cried, deeply anguished at seeing my poor monkey so horribly maltreated.

Before the sound of my cry was gone from the air, my father emerged from his chamber. The K'uhul Ajaw of Calumook was not pleased. When his eyes met mine, his annoyance with me was unmistakable. Already bothered by my presence there, he caught sight of my monkey trapped in the tight fist of his sajal, and his anger mounted fast. As he took in the scene, other men were emerging from palace doorways, cloaked also in their jade and woven finery. After the very briefest of moments, their eyes, devoid of haste, turned to gaze from stony faces at my father.

At the time I did not realize who these men were—as I said, I was young. But as I grew, I came to understand that they were the heads of their lineages, and that our Calumook was composed of many such lineages. Each one had its own audience chamber in our palace, and the colors and patterns of the woven bunting hung above their doorways proclaimed their ancestry. Each lineage took inordinate care to adorn its chamber with fine mats and lush animal pelts, lest anyone regard the lineage as disadvantaged in any way. These men advised and supported my father in council, but they were rivals nonetheless—each of the others and also of my father. Perhaps especially of my father. Though I knew nothing of such things as we stood there on the landing of the palace's third story, the sudden heightened tension in the air told me something was greatly amiss. As if by instinct, I understood my father was being challenged by these men, which explains what happened next.

Without uttering a word, he strode to his sajal, who held my dangling monkey out to him. My father grasped his furry little head, and in one swift motion he twisted the neck of my pet monkey. I cringed at the tiny muffled crack of breaking bone, and my father glared at me as the thing drooped to lifelessness, his scruff still clenched in the cruel fist of the sajal.

In horror, and suddenly fearful of my father, I let out a loud and piercing shriek, then turned and fled down the front palace staircase.

As I descended, bawling, more curious faces poked from doorways to smirk in furtive amusement as the king's young daughter stumbled and sniveled loudly past, tears gushing down her cheeks. I pushed through a well-dressed entourage ascending the staircase, fine ceramic vessels raised in pageantry—and in my wake I heard the commotion as they shattered on the plaster of the steps in an appalling series of crashes. Through my tears, our Waterlily banners were a long, indistinct blur of green. At the bottom of the staircase, my nursemaid seized my arm and smacked her palm across my mouth, then whisked me away in the direction of our back palace courtyard.

As I struggled against my nursemaid's grip, I caught sight of a commoner girl about my age, her pet monkey astride her hip.

She stood at the place where palace stair joined the sacbe. Both monkey and girl stared at me with pitying, unblinking eyes. I knew from the look on their faces that they had witnessed everything that had transpired. In that moment, I envied that common girl. I envied her, standing jadelessly clad in simple coarse-spun garb and ordinariness, overlooked by all in her profound obscurity, her pet monkey safe astride her hip.

◎◎◎

At dusk that evening, my mother's fingers crept slowly around my arm. She squeezed until her fingernails bit my flesh.

"You behaved badly today," she said.

Her voice was low and full of malice. I shuddered at its tenor. Her eyes narrowed as she waited to see how I would respond, but I said nothing, which infuriated her all the more. She turned my person to face hers and scowled at me.

"You have nothing to say?" When I did not answer, she shook me.

"I don't know what to say," I whimpered. "It was an accident. My monkey escaped and Father killed it."

"As well he should have," snapped my mother. "If you are foolish enough to let your monkey get loose, it is no longer yours."

"It *was* still mine!" I protested, as will a child. I was struggling to keep tears from welling up. I did not want her to see me cry.

"No it was not. Don't you see, your father cannot be perceived to lack control over the behavior of his own daughter in his own palace. He had to chastise you, and harshly, right there and that moment. If he had not, he would have appeared weak—dangerously weak." She waited for me to reply, but as I did not, she continued. "When you are in public view," she explained in a tense tone of exasperation, "you must always comport yourself as befits your rank. That is your sole obligation. Only that. Do you understand?" When again I said nothing, again she shook me by the arm.

"Yes," I muttered, "I understand."

"Always!" She almost screamed the word. She wanted more from me.

"Yes, Mother. Always."

"If not, you shame us all!" She had begun to work herself into a state of agitation. "Even worse," she continued, "you shame our ancestors." She uttered the word "shame" with a deep and menacing snarl.

Upon mentioning our ancestors, my mother began hauling me by the arm. Helpless in her inexorable grip, I could not but follow. As I stumbled across the courtyard at her side, her fingernails still biting into my skin, I saw the stern eyes of my kinfolk, who sat tracking each of my stumbling footfalls from the steps of their chambers in the dusk. They too, it seemed, knew of my misbehavior, and they too scowled at me—or at least I imagined they did—from behind stony masks.

She hauled me through the courtyard and down a dark, narrow flight of steps that turned three times. With each turn the light grew dimmer, but she had grabbed a torch on our way, and its leaping orange flame cast strange towering shadows on the tight walls. We reached the landing at the bottom, where many rows of tiny squat compartments were arrayed before us. I knew these to be the crypts where the mortal remains of our illustrious forebears rested for all eternity. This was another place where palace children were forbidden to play, but the older and braver among us had crept all the way down that long winding stair only to race back up, terror in their eyes. I had always lacked the courage to do anything so daring.

Only once, under duress from my playmates, had I even attempted to descend those steps. I had not gotten far when I encountered a dim gloomy recess. From that dark hole peered the grotesque, hardly human, intensely piercing eyes of an enormous painted incense burner. This dreadful visage rendered me motionless, and I imagined it was some Lord of Death lying in wait to trap me in the House of Cigars or Knives. There I remained, staring transfixed into those terrible eyes, until a friend came to my aid and drew me back up the dark stairs.

My mother dragged me past that dim recess, and soon we came to stand at the base of that terrible winding stair. Still she grasped my arm, her unyielding claws still banishing any hope of flight. I stopped struggling against her, and the peculiar sensations of this eerie place began to enclose me. Our shadows loomed frightfully in the tawny dimness. There was the musty smell of decay and of time immemorial. There was the knowledge of what lay within the stone crypts so close. A deep primordial silence crept slowly forward to enfold us.

Ominously, my mother raised a long finger toward a small, dark doorway. The stain of thick copal soot around it marked the chamber within as a shrine room.

Many private palace chambers as well as public ones in front contained ancestral shrines. Every child had been inside such rooms and knew what they were. But this one, here at the dark bottom of this dark winding stair—this shrine room dedicated solely to my ancestors' earthly remains, which lay nearby in their dusty crypts—oh, no, I had never entered that particular darkened doorway. Just the sight of its sooty portal frightened me. I very much did not want to enter that room.

My mother dragged me roughly through it. Before my eyes could adjust to the heavy darkness within, she released her grip—not with a shove, but by allowing her fingers to vanish. To disappear from my arm with no warning. Then she stepped back, she and her bright torch. I believe she released me thusly so that I might encounter this strange room bereft of her touch and her haven of glowing orange light, and that she did so knowing the impact of its extraordinary contents and shadowy unnerving essence would be all the greater.

Silence crept closer, wrapped me tighter within its hush.

Bit by bit, my eyes became accustomed to the gloom. As the objects before me took shape, I found myself staring into the blank black eyes of another enormous ceramic incense burner. This one stood in the center of an engraved wooden table. Bushy, scowling brows arched over its eyes, and the jagged tooth of a giant ocean shark poked menacingly from between its sneering red lips. Its sides were black with soot, and a thick, sweet, smoky scent lingered in the musty dimness. Someone—who?—had burnt vast quantities of copal in this censer not long ago.

As the silence stretched on, a slow chill crept up the bare skin of my legs. I knew we were below the ground and realized it probably came from the dankness of the earth, but the strangeness of this place and my unfamiliar nearness to the revered bones of my ancestors made that chill seem to emanate from somewhere far deeper.

As my sight improved, I made out many unfamiliar objects assembled on the table beside the incense burner. There were several tall, intricately painted vases and elaborate multi-piece figurines modeled from clay. Jade beads filled the bottom half of an enormous oyster, its long red spines curling around the edge. A painted platter held a stack of husk-wrapped portions of maize dough; ripe fruit was heaped high on another. A single polished white stone gleamed from within a massive spiraling ocean conch that was deeply engraved and rubbed bright red with cinnabar. Large leaves of fresh green tobacco drooped from the table, their pungent scent intoxicating in the enclosed space. I saw long, curving obsidian blades and long, straight stingray spines, all so thickly caked with blood that an immediate sensation of corporeal pain surged within my person. Yes: this is precisely where blood is scattered.

My mother studied my reactions as I observed these extraordinary objects. After a time, she pointed that same long finger toward a carved wooden box I had not noticed before.

"Were you aware that inside that box is a piece of bone from every male of your entire patriline?" she whispered. "Even Kalo'mte' bones are inside."

I was unsure whether this was an actual question warranting an actual answer. I certainly did not want to confess that I had not known what rested within that carved wooden box. I also did not want to admit I did not know the significance of the word Kalo'mte', although I supposed it was a title of particular prominence. I thought it prudent to lower my head in quiet reverence and did so. My mother seemed pleased.

Again we stood in silence. The longer we remained so, the more I sensed that my ancestors had joined us in that dark room. How they had managed to pass from their dusty crypts through the thick walls I did not know, but I felt their hallowed presence suspended there beside us. I believe I sensed a *ch'ulel* hovering close at my ear, a spirit still lingering from the earlier blood scattering before the shrine.

"You must never shame the ancestors," my mother whispered.

The malice was gone from her voice, replaced by awe, and from her tone I understood that she too felt the presence of my ancestors. As she spoke, we both gazed intently at that carved wooden box. Then, abruptly, she tilted her head to look directly at me. "They founded our Calumook, you know. Here is where they chose to establish our venerable city, nestled within the bend of our mighty river." As my dazed eyes met her shrewd ones, she continued: "They are our Calumook. Without them we would not be here. Without them our palace would not stand. Without them we would be nothing. You would be nothing."

She paused to allow the meaning of her words to enter my heart. "You would be nothing," she repeated, this time in an even more solemn whisper. "Daughter, beseech our ancestors to absolve you of your shameful actions this day. Plead with them for forgiveness." She urged this of me in low whispered breaths, her voice grave, almost frightened.

This time I knew I could not get away with remaining silent, but by now I had also come to accept that perhaps I truly had shamed us all by behaving as I had that morning on our front palace staircase.

The death of a monkey was nothing compared to what our ancestors had sacrificed on our behalf. They had given so much, worked with such diligence. They had done it for us, their undeserving progeny. Who was I, a tiny worthless speck, to dishonor them in such a disgraceful fashion? Chastened, I began to intone the long and sacred chant of our patriline. They, our ancestors, had handed this chant down to us. They had composed each stanza with great care, inscribing each one in the folding pages of our codices. They had given us this legacy, our history, painted and written within by our own illustrious ancestor scribes. The chant was our most valuable inheritance. It was a recitation that recounted tales and deeds extending far back to ancient, murky epochs when our primordial ancestors lived with the gods themselves. I had heard this chant many times, but until that moment I was unaware that I knew each word and could utter each stanza on my own. Now they rushed forth, fluttering in whispers across my lips as if I had chanted them since my birth; and as the repetitions spilled out one after another, I forgave my father for killing my monkey. When at last I had finished, I did as I was told: with bowed head and meekly humble words, I wholeheartedly sought the forgiveness of my ancestors, staring all the while into the blank, terrifying eyes of that enormous incense burner.

◎◎◎

At the foot of our palace staircase, a broad sacbe stretched southward from our last green Waterlily banner, running straight inland from our mighty river and directly through Calumook. As I grew older, of course I walked our sacbe of my own accord, but my earliest memories are of being carried aloft—by whom I do not recall. Those childhood recollections are full of shouting throngs and loud blaring trumpets, and fright. By the time I reached girlhood, I had grown to love striding over our sacbe, imagining that all the noisy tumult was for me. Then one day it really was, during my Ixchel Moon celebration.

That grand day I strode in my best finery.

Back then I owned many striking huipils, their intricate fine-spun wefts drawn into exact position by my carved bone weaving pin. Many an eventide found me on our courtyard stair, still captivated by the act of transforming skeins into loveliness on my backstrap loom. Even now I can close my eyes and recall the feel of that special Ixchel Moon huipil on my shoulders. And the weight of my jade, its constant pull upon my person—that too I can feel. I recall as well the delightful jangle as I strode across our sacbe for my celebration. It was a sound I had only ever heard emanating from the regalia of the full-grown highborn—but then, of course, the purpose of that day's festivities was to declare me precisely that.

Our sacbe was quite wide, and it curved just a little as it passed through the city's holy precinct. Calumook had temples elsewhere, but that particular precinct had many temples, each dedicated to one of the many gods who gave us their favor. In no other place of Calumook was the scent of copal so constantly present, day and night. When at last we stepped from the sacbe at its farthest end, we stood before one of our grandest temples.

I can still see that temple, row upon row of incense burners lining each of its terraces, each terrace aflutter with a multitude of divinity banners. Beside that temple was our principal ball court, its long, slanting sides bright with aquatic motifs, most prominently our water lilies—stylized green pads and large white-petaled blossoms surrounding golden yellow hearts. As our entourage strode the length of that Calumook sacbe, we paused at each shrine, each temple, each stela and tomb, to offer our veneration. Though the palace was not far from the ball court, the slowness of our passage often made it seem like an endless succession of solemn intonations and wafting copal incense, loudly blaring trumpets and conchs, frequent lavish gifting, and the repeated scattering of our holy blood.

Our sacbe was mostly wide and long, but several narrower ones led to the city villas of the lineage heads of Calumook. Once, our destination had been such a villa—or at least was to become a villa, but on the day of our visit its walls were far from finished, and fresh blocks of white stone still lay on the ground waiting to be hoisted up and mortared into rows. During our procession to this villa, my father's advisors had filled his ears with worry: apparently the villa's proprietor was having considerable difficulty completing it. What I could not then fathom was why that man's troubles should be of any concern to the K'uhul Ajaw of Calumook.

We strode along our sacbe, the great white road of Calumook. The sajal, walking beside my father, said: "Stone workers are becoming more difficult to draw together, my lord. That is the reason for the delay in construction."

"Difficult to draw together," my father repeated, a question in his voice.

"Yes, my lord. It is becoming harder to provide their maize rations. Without adequate maize from the milpa to feed them, the proprietor cannot assemble the necessary stone workers."

Hands clasped behind his back, my father nodded.

We all understood our milpa farmers to be also our stone workers. When they were not making milpa, their labor was often ours, and when it was, we had to sustain them in their toil. We fed them maize and they gave us their sweat. This was how the lineage heads built their grand villas, how my father added a new wing to his palace, or how a ruler might wrap a new skin around a temple.

As the sour-faced sajal prattled on about the maize, the milpa farmers, and the construction delay, I could see my father was growing vexed. He said, "Chaak has not bestowed rain upon us in some time."

"Indeed, my lord," the sajal replied. "That is correct. That seems to be the true basis of the difficulty. Without adequate rain, the maize grows poorly and surplus is reduced. And then it becomes harder to provide for them while they toil."

"Hmm ..." my father murmured.

"Rain has not fallen, and our reservoir is beginning to reveal its sides," the sajal said, his voice low. They walked for a time in silence before the man added, "My lord, the maize harvest is also diminishing because the commoners cannot slash new milpa in the jungle."

"Why can they not do this? Why is it so difficult to slash new milpa?"

"I am not certain, my lord. Perhaps because so many people now live in Calumook that nearby fresh jungle-land is growing scarce."

At this my father unclasped his hands, letting them swing at his sides as he strode; then he clasped them once more behind his back. I don't think he knew what else to do with them.

At this point my father began spending more time at the front of the palace. When he did appear in our back courtyard, he spoke mostly with the other men. In my memory, they stand in small clusters in corners, or on the far side of our pleasure pool. They were far from jovial, those conversations; that much was evident without hearing a word. I wonder, did my father still even notice the beauty of our painted Waterlily blossoms adorning the edges of our pool, or the living water lilies that floated on its clear water? I knew he loved our beautiful lineage blossom—a sacred, regal blossom of water and life—more deeply than anything else. But it seemed that the only things on his mind were maize and stone, stone and maize. He even began leaving Calumook for long stretches to call on our lineage heads at their rural villas. They maintained these villas far from the city because most of our maize was grown in these more distant milpa lands, and because there in the countryside, these men were the rulers, whereas in Calumook it was my father.

I went with him once. He took me with him because, he said, I needed to see how milpa was made, to know how our people in the countryside lived. My mother was not at all pleased about this excursion. I heard them quarrel about it well into the night.

"You cannot take a royal maiden on a long trip into the middle of nowhere like that," my mother declared.

"She will be safe," my father answered. "Our entourage will travel with armed guards. You worry too much."

"It is still too dangerous," she insisted.

"There have been no reports of hostilities nearby for some time. She needs to learn these things."

"She will. There is plenty of time."

"I think there is not so much time."

My mother dismissed this notion. "You worry too much."

"Things are changing."

"Besides," she continued as though he had not spoken, "a K'uhul Ajaw should not deign to appear in the milpas at all. It is not proper. There will be talk." I imagined my mother shaking her head as she said there would be talk. My mother was always concerned with talk. Back then I did not understand her concern, but now I know that talk can be more dangerous than it may appear at first. Her concern was not without merit.

At some point I must have drifted off, but in my slumber I still heard the earnestness in my father's voice. Things are changing, he had said. He had said these words with apprehension, I think, but an apprehension about which he himself was unclear. Though I did not grasp the precise significance of his words, they nonetheless sent a ripple of unease down my spine. My father must have prevailed while I slept, for in the morning I departed with him as he had wished.

Back then, I admit, I never thought about maize. It was always just there when we were hungry. Boiled into a thick porridge and sweetened with vanilla and honey. Fresh tender ears steamed on the cob. Dough stuffed in husks and filled with chili-roasted wildfowl giblets, my favorite tamales. Maize was just always there, always abundant, made delicious by our palace cooks. But when I first saw the puny withering ears in a dusty milpa near that distant rural villa, I began to fathom the source of my father's vexation.

One servant held a wide feather shade over my head while another fanned me, but it was still unbearably hot in the sun-baked milpa, and for a time I wished my mother had prevailed the prior evening, for had she done so I could have been lounging in the cool shade of our courtyard at that very moment. But as I listened to my father converse with the lineage head of that rural villa, I was glad to be at his side, although I'm not fully certain he remembered I was there.

The lineage head was quite pale, and his eyes were somewhat crossed. Such eye crossing was deliberate: back then some considered it attractive, although I never found it so. He had trained his eyes by hanging a bead from his headdress to draw his vision to the center. The crossing did not keep him from walking or performing other tasks. I sometimes wondered why it did not. From time to time he bobbed his head in obeisance to my father, but his words were frank.

"Again this year the rains are late, my lord. If they are like the rains of last year, again the maize will not thrive." We all gazed at the parched stalks as the man spoke. The plants were yellowed and short, and a few did not even reach above my knee. As if on cue, a breeze rustled through them and we listened as the dry stalks rubbed against each other.

My father asked, "Your commoners have made the appropriate observances to keep away the mischief of the *aluxes*?"

"Yes, my lord, they have."

"So it is not they who are the problem?"

"No, my lord, I think it is not."

"And you, you yourself have made certain to perform the ceremonies to Yum Kaax? You have scattered your blood for the Maize God?"

"Yes, my lord, I have done so."

I don't know why my father inquired about the performance of these rituals, as even I could not have failed to notice the shrines at the edge of the milpa and beside the rural villa. Both were well blackened with burnt copal and dark with old blood, so even I knew the response to his queries.

Silence reigned as we stood in the milpa. My sandals were covered in dust, as were my feet and ankles. Never in my entire life had I had such dirty feet before, and these—my own dirty feet—garnered my utmost concern. At that moment a large gray grasshopper jumped onto my foot. I experienced its sharp hasty clutch upon my skin with revulsion, after which it sprang away, startling me so that I let out a small shriek. At this, my father and the cross-eyed lineage head both turned to gaze at me in a questioning manner. After that, I vigilantly kept casting my eyes about my person, as only then did I notice the ground around me was crawling with all manner of unsettling insects.

"What of the swamp?" my father suddenly asked in a hopeful voice. "Are the raised beds within it not in adequate repair? Have they not been cultivated?"

"Yes, my lord, they are in adequate repair. They are cultivated at all times, and they yield well."

"Good, good," my father said.

"Although they yield well, my lord, the harvest still cannot sustain so many mouths. I confess that at times my commoners do not have enough to eat. My lord, some have grown so thin that their bones are like sharp knobs beneath their skin." He said this last bit—the part about the knobby bones—in so very low a voice that I believe he was ashamed.

My father grumbled, in both worry and frustration, I think, but he did not utter comprehensible words.

"They are obliged to slash and burn ever higher up the hillsides, my lord. It has meant the soil high up is getting spare. Even the milpa lands that still retain adequate soil are not allowed to rest."

Again my father grumbled, but this time he formed words: "Why not?" I believe he already knew the answer to this question and wished he did not.

"They must continue farming it, my lord, because there is scarcely any fresh jungle left in which to slash new milpa."

"Too many mouths," my father said. It was a statement, not a question. Then he murmured, "The dirt is tired." Speaking almost to himself, he said, "It is tired and weak from making too much milpa for too long."

"It grows thin as well, my lord. The dirt is sliding down the hills. We see it collect on the upslope of boulders so we know it is sliding from above. We worry that soon there will be nothing but grit and rock up there, and then no maize at all will grow upon it."

Although he could not see them from where we stood, my father gazed in the direction of the hillsides. I recognized deep consternation upon his face. Perhaps he and I were thinking the same thing: if the milpa here on the flatland where we were standing was growing such puny withering ears, then the milpas on the hills must truly be pitiful. I was glad my father did not suggest we go to inspect them.

The lineage head continued: "Our rural villa needs much renovation. I have not been able to build the house for my second son that I pledged years ago. He and his growing family live still with us. So too does my first son and his family—the son that will become head when I am gone. Like the lowborn we are forced to live one atop the other. The plaster on our walls has again not been renewed this year. My commoners cannot quarry stone and build for me when my tribute granaries run so low. I cannot feed their toil. With milpas like these," and here he motioned—in sadness, I believe—to the meager, shrunken ears before us, "there is just too little maize."

Our initial reception at that distant rural villa had been the standard greeting befitting the arrival of an entourage of our rank: a fine feast with music and oratory and copal burning. But in fact I had expected something a little, well … *grander* from what they called a villa. The presentation had seemed small and underwhelming. Still, I realized, I had only begun to think this after the cross-eyed man himself admitted his difficulties.

He continued: "My lord, the tumplines of firewood we are required to chop and carry to Calumook … It is becoming more challenging. The wood is so much farther away. It is difficult to make milpa and also to chop firewood. And to quarry stone for the needs of my own villa … It has all become too demanding."

At this my father stiffened.

The man bowed his head as he murmured, "I cannot turn over as much maize this season, my lord. Nor my assigned cotton measure. It cannot be accomplished, my lord. The firewood measure will be difficult, but that I will be able to manage."

I admit that I experienced an immediate surge of resentment as the man said this, and I think my father did too: I saw him bristle and was certain he was about to rebuke the insubordinate lineage head. But then he just turned away from us both. He reached out to pensively stroke a puny, shriveled ear on one of the many thirsty stalks surrounding us, and said nothing.

◙ ◙ ◙

Around the time I became Lady Winik, the baby who would turn into my favorite cousin was born. He was the eldest son of my father's youngest brother.

Perhaps the pain of my own head shaping was so immense that I have put it from my mind, but a strange ache in my own skull accompanies my memory of the day they fixed a wooden press to my cousin's head. It was his maternal uncle who did it.

He laid a thin wooden slat on the fresh bone at the brow of this tiny infant not even a month old and lashed it down with soft deerskin that ran around the back of the child's head. At first I giggled because my cousin looked a bit silly in his wooden hat, but then the uncle cinched the deerskin tight, and soon thereafter the fussing began. I thought the man might loosen the thing a bit to relieve the discomfort, but he did not. Instead, he took up an engraved stingray spine, and in a flash had run its sharp tip straight through both my cousin's tender earlobes, which only increased his hurting. The uncle chanted as he did all of this.

Of course I had seen wooden presses like these many times by then and knew what they were for, though in truth it was the first earlobe piercing I'd witnessed. While I understood that we shaped our soft young skulls in this fashion, this was the first time I'd seen firsthand the immediate consequences of the tight cinching on someone I was already coming to love.

"Why are you making him howl?" I asked.

"So that like your own, his head will resemble a precious kernel of young maize," replied my cousin's mother. The uncle slid two tiny jade ear spools into the bleeding holes of his lobes.

"But it pains him," I protested, even as my hand rose of its own accord to finger the jade spools suspended within my own lobes.

"Yes, and it hurt you too, but he will not remember the pain, as now you do not."

I must still have appeared skeptical because she added, "It is our way to do this, in exaltation of the Maize God. He is our cherished patron. By remaking our heads in his glorious image, we reveal to him the depth of our love. We express our appreciation of his ancient sacrifice in our own persons."

"But perhaps the Maize God does not require this one tiny skull to be shaped like a kernel."

"Oh, but he does."

"How do you know?"

"We know."

I consoled my little cousin as best I could. I must have succeeded in distracting him a little, because after several days he ceased to howl with such intensity. But then they cinched the lashes tighter, and again he howled. Since then, I have witnessed this practice so often that I have, like my elders back then, become inured to the suffering. But this first time was admittedly as agonizing for me as it was for him, and I think it is why I came to love my little cousin with such fervor. I may also have loved him so much without my pet monkey I felt a bit lonesome and needful of a special friend. In any case, as my little cousin grew I carried him around with me, astride my hip, as much as I was allowed.

◎◎◎

After celebrating our homecoming from that rural villa, my father returned to his chambers in the front of the palace, and I did not see much of him. I was playing with my little cousin in our courtyard when word came that my father had decided to make a grand announcement that evening. We were to prepare ourselves forthwith to witness the spectacle that would accompany his message.

That happened a lot, back then. We, the royal family, along with the many nobles of my father's court, would be summoned, often at short notice, to witness a dedication or ceremony or spectacle of some sort, or attend yet another grand feast. I rushed to comply—perhaps because I had only just become Lady Winik and my full participation was still a novelty, I was still quite eager to appear in my finery. My mother, however, like many others, would object when such summonses came. I overheard their grumbled complaints about the increasing demands on their time and sometimes, having noticed many whose girth had expanded considerably, wondered what a lot of them had to do other than lie about and nap.

Later that evening, in my proper place on the second-story landing of the palace, I stood with my cousin straddling my hip. His head, only just liberated from that hurtful press, had taken the beautiful form of a young maize kernel. Now that the painful shaping was over, he was his sweet-tempered self again. I remember I was wearing a new huipil that I had created with an asymmetrical linking of water lily blossoms and ceiba leaves at the neckline, and I was proud of it. Beside me stood other women, all of them draped in finery as lovely as mine. Indeed, there must have been hundreds of highborn standing on those landings— all of us, the men as well, swathed in many lengths of fine-spun cotton. While it is true that we noblewomen did the handiwork of weaving on our own backstrap looms, it was the obligation of female commoners to supply us with the fine-spun skeins. As required, those cotton skeins regularly appeared in heaping baskets at our courtyard door, where they were tallied. Gazing upon the profusion of finery, I recollected the words of that cross-eyed lineage head in that dusty rural milpa. The lower cotton measure he had told my father of might mean fewer heaping baskets of skeins at our door. I confess that as this thought crossed my mind, I prized my new huipil all the more.

I was grateful the sun was low and it was not hot as we waited through the pomp and pageantry: the pounding of the hollow slit log drums, the dancing and the pre-announcements, the thick, black, billowing smoke of copal, the loud blare of the trumpets and the chimes of the turtle shell marimba, and then more pounding of the hollow slit log drums. I recall that as we waited, a tight cluster of dark clouds hung on the far western horizon, blocking a bit of the bright red orb of the setting sun and casting a strange gloaming light over the god masks of our palace. In that extraordinary dusk—half day and half night on the cusp of the departure of the Sun Lord K'inich Ajaw from the Skyworld—it was as if the masks themselves burst into animation, their eyes gleaming and their teeth lustrous in the twilight. From atop the staircase I looked at the commoners crowded below in the plaza. Once more they appeared small and insignificant like tiny ants, this time roving about in eventide.

At last the ocean conchs sounded the deep swelling roar that always announced the appearance of the K'uhul Ajaw of Calumook. My father emerged as if from nowhere, framed by the darkening entryway to the middle room at the top of our palace. There he stood, the K'uhul Ajaw of Calumook—our direct link, our holy channel to the immense and the dangerous, to the fickle, powerful, unknowable cosmic realm.

Oh, he was striking. A massive jaguar pelt was draped across his shoulder so as to accentuate my father's intricate chest tattoos. Two great paws of that enormous jungle beast dangled at his flanks, their sharp and menacing claws fully extended. My father wore a tall headdress of resplendent green quetzal streamers, and his feet were bound in the high-backed sandals reserved only for spectacle. He strode to the edge of the landing, his motions stirring the rich jangle of jade. That jangle is a sound we love dearly because it comes to us from the realm of our ancestors. It is how their voices, their wise words, reach our earthly ears. The rich jangle of jade was how we knew they had come to be with us that evening—our ancestors, standing in benefaction beside my father at the pinnacle of our palace.

Clasped within my father's mighty hand was our Manikin Scepter, carved from one magnificent stone. The likeness of K'awil, our sacred god of abundance, graced its top, and his long serpent foot wrapped down its polished stone handle. Among our many important scepters, this one was supreme. Beyond the jaguar pelt, beyond the quetzal streamer headdress, beyond even the sweet jangle of jade, the Manikin Scepter was the most essential insignia of my father's divine right to rule. My father, the great K'uhul Ajaw of Calumook, clasped this vital object in his perfect hand, positioned before his perfect chest.

As his gaze swept the crowd, a roar of appreciation arose from all of Calumook. My father paused for dramatic effect, and then swept his muscular arms grandly up from his sides to stretch them wide. As he did, the roar from the crowd below swelled louder, and my heart felt like it would burst with pride.

When at last my father spoke, it was in the splendid, booming, formalized speech that was only ever uttered by the K'uhul Ajaw of Calumook from the pinnacle of our palace.

"I pronounce here, on this most grand, this most auspicious day of 9 Baktun, 19 Katun, 14 Tun, 13 Uinal, 19 Kin, 7 Chen, 6 Cauac, that I will gift maize from my palace granaries! I will gift it for you, my children of Calumook! I gift it today, 9.19.14.13.19, 7 Chen 6 Cauac, for the construction of a magnificent new edifice! This edifice will be the grandest, the most superb place of worship ever constructed in honor of mighty Chaak! Great God of Rain! We, his humble children of Calumook, will venerate him, love him in this most humble fashion! He will witness the depth of Calumook's affection! He—our faithful patron—will love us above all others! In gratitude for our gift, he will bless us with his generosity! He will bestow upon us his plentiful liquid! His rain, his moisture! He will pour it forth from the Skyworld for us, his devoted children of Calumook!"

Below, the tiny ants in the eventide plaza roared their approval. They roared their appreciation and their affection for my father, and their gratitude for all he did for them. Amidst the clamor, I thought I detected a fresh gleam of pride, of deep conviction, in my father's eye. Of course he was proud—he was the K'uhul Ajaw of Calumook. He was vital to every one of us. He commanded on behalf of us all! His countless efforts and sacrifices would bring rain to all of us—even the puny, withered ears in that distant, dusty milpa.

Then I noticed his gleaming eye shift to the far western horizon and read the sudden relief that my father took from what he saw: strong red rays shooting from the enormous glowing orb of K'inich Ajaw, rays that bravely battled their way past a dark, stormy cluster of clouds. Holding Calumook's Manikin Scepter in one hand, he reached the other—his holy royal arm, his holy royal hand—toward the horizon. His hand reached toward that stormy western sky as if to grasp those hopeful clouds in the palm of his holy royal hand, and bring them to us.

◎◎◎

I first laid eyes on Naah Chan during Calumook's lengthy preparations for the dedication of my father's new Chaak temple.

Our city had been abuzz for months, with countless laborers coming and going. All of Calumook, it seemed, was hard at work. I found it a cheerful diversion from the staid life of our back palace courtyard—at least, it was when I was permitted to leave that confined space. In truth, I was wearying of splashing about in our pleasure pool or lounging in the shade of an awning. Even my intricate weaving of fine-spun garb was starting to become repetitive. In those days, I was grateful whenever I was permitted to roam, particularly when it was at my father's side.

"Stride with me," he said one morning.

I wonder if he ever understood how much I enjoyed my excursions with him. Of course I never spoke of such to him. I think he must have discerned my affection, however, in the swiftness with which I leapt from my position of repose in the shade. Every time I was unconcerned about where we went, but even as we departed our courtyard, I knew our outing would bring us to monitor the progress of my father's new Chaak temple. Indeed, each one of our forays of late had been for this precise purpose. Sometimes as we strode toward that rising temple I wondered how the stores in our palace maize granaries fared: you see, I often pondered over our visit to that dusty milpa and the sight of that stunted, desiccated maize—and my father's glumness during the trip. But on this morning as we departed our courtyard, neither of us spoke of maize, or of palace granaries, or of rain, and for that I was grateful.

All I knew was that work was everywhere.

As we strode the jungle trail toward our stone quarry, we encountered a steady stream of laborers on their long, meandering trek back into the city. They bent far forward, each straining to haul a single weighty cut stone block, tumplines taut against their foreheads, their skin glistening with sweat. When we arrived at the quarry, we stood on its edge and peered down. From all directions came the bright tap-tap of sharp chisels biting stone. It was an odd, incessant din, as tallies of rough stones gave way, chip by chip, to tallies of fine cut blocks. One long line of laborers wound down into the quarry from its east, tumplines empty and sagging, as another trailed up its far western side, tumplines heaving. Deep within the quarry plodded others, perhaps many hundreds. They moved in slow, monotonous, predictable configurations.

From where we stood at the quarry's edge, I was reminded of the view from the top of our palace of the ants in the plaza below. Now, as I observed them in their toil, these ants resembled the ones that cut and carry enormous green leaf burdens, swaying them aloft as they creep along the ground. We played with them as children—leafcutter ants, they are called—poking them with sticks to momentarily disrupt their long and orderly lines, after which they regrouped in their methodical laboring manner. We had attempted to dislodge the little green cuttings from their tight black pincers, but the tiny creatures always clung tenaciously to their minuscule possessions, refusing to surrender them. From my perch at the quarry's edge, our Calumook laborers truly did resemble tireless, persistent crews of leafcutter ants.

After the stone was placed, my father's new Chaak temple would become riotous with brightly painted plaster. I had seen our master mural painter's plan for the interior walls of the inner sanctuary; I'd also seen the design of our master stucco sculptor, for the vast panel would wrap the sanctuary's entire exterior. That stucco panel would depict our ancestral founder, Calumook's initial king and its most brilliant architectural genius. That initial king would be passing our Manikin Scepter to my father, thus marking him as his direct descendant. My devoted father, portrayed as a beautiful and perfect infant, was to be cradled in the loving arms of Chaak, patron god of Calumook, bringer of rain, bringer of life. Elaborate water lilies framed the entire scene.

To make the plaster and stucco, our laborers—our leafcutter ants—collected stone chip debris and crumbling chunks of poor quality rock, and burned it. Vast amounts of firewood were needed to build fires hot enough to burn stone, and tall stacks of logs circled the entire bottom edge of the quarry. During those long months of construction, our licking flames devoured innumerable jungle trees while thick black smoke darkened the brightness of day. My father and I watched as they pounded the cooled stone into beautiful white lime powder, and then heaped it into woven reed baskets to be tumplined to the construction site. There, other leafcutter ants stirred in water to make a paste that was smeared on the stone walls and floors, then sculpted and polished, polished and sculpted, until smooth. There was so much to building, back then.

A group of laborers had begun their midmorning repast along the quarry's back rim. Squatting in course-spun loincloths, they swiped maize porridge from gourd bowls with their fingers, eating it with tiny bites of green chilies for flavor. The shift that would soon replace them would bring more swipes of fingers, and thus more maize porridge passing through the lips of more laborers. Almost against my will, I considered our palace granaries. This time I thought also of our jungle trees, transformed into countless tall stacks of firewood.

All this labor was overseen by my father's sajal, the sour-faced man against whom I still harbored a grudge because of my monkey. He stood some distance from us, also at the quarry's edge, speaking with a group of noblemen whom I recognized as lineage heads. Despite the distance between us, in my opinion that sour-faced man was still much too close.

As if reading my thoughts, my father said, "You must trust him, Daughter. My sajal is the most loyal of everyone at Calumook."

He said this just as his sajal turned and began walking in our direction, so I did not have the chance to offer a response. In any case I believe one was not desired.

As he neared, my father, called out to him in a cheery voice, "How goes the toil?"

"It goes well, my lord," the sajal called back, also with light-ness—jollity, even—in his tone.

"Excellent, excellent," my father said, pleased, as the sajal came to stand at his side. "And the stone—it remains hardy?" my father asked.

"Indeed it remains quite hardy, my lord, even at depth."

"Excellent news." Then they were silent for a time as we all observed the intricate comings and goings along the twisting trails in the quarry below. The ringing tap-tap of chisels filled the morning air, as did clouds of dust from the breaking stone. Thick black smoke of scorching stone also hung in the air, as did the low, monotonous crush and grind of burnt stone upon the metate. I found it all so marvelous, this grand scene in the quarry below as the many diverse parts and pieces of my father's new temple took slow and measured shape.

My father spoke: "And the timing, how goes the timing?"

"All remains on schedule, my lord. Our dedication specta-cle will indeed be reached on 10.0.0.0.0," the sajal answered. "Of that I am confident."

My father was delighted with this news. As he and the sajal launched into a lengthy discussion of the details of construc-tion and the timing of the spectacle, I realized that I too was delighted, for of course I recognized that Long Count date was a Katun ending and therefore warranted a grand celebration in its own right. But to combine a Katun ending with the dedica-tion of a new Chaak temple at the same gala event? I had not before known of my father's intention to stage a double specta-cle, but now that I did, I thought his plan was nothing less than brilliant. A full entourage from Lalchich would be in attendance at an event of such magnitude, as would one from Quetzaltun and each of our other allied, vassal, or puppet cities. I realized too that I would need to begin considering the design of a huipil even more extravagant than the one I had been envisioning. The feasting and music and dancing, the new finery, the ceremonies and the grand ball game pageantry—all this would last many long and wonderful days. Perhaps my father would again declare an entire month of festivities. We would doubtless be exhausted by the end of it. And slumber? Slumber could happen later. Oh yes, such a magnificent double spectacle would be spoken of for many years to come, and I was delighted about the increased standing that would accrue to my father, whose mood of late was again deteriorating.

My father and the sajal seemed to have concluded their discussion, and my father turned back to me. "Daughter, let us stride to the site of the rising temple."

"Yes," I agreed, "let us visit it."

"I will find you there," the sajal called over his shoulder as he walked away. I thought this a very rude action, as protocol required everyone to refrain from leave-taking until my father dismissed them. I supposed it was testimony of their friendship that his sajal did not, and it occurred to me that I might have been mistaken as to the true nature of this sour-faced man.

My father proposed we take a longer route, one that wound through the commoner neighborhoods of Calumook. The unexpected passage of royalty always caused disruption, but like my father I enjoyed these long meanderings because in comparison to the staid life in our back palace courtyard, there was always much afoot in the neighborhoods.

"Take my arm," my father said, offering it to me, and I took it with a concealed smile. I so enjoyed walking arm in arm, close at my father's side.

We followed a narrow, winding trail that, once it neared the city, was lined on either side with vendors. Ceramic vessels—mostly simple cooking jars, eating bowls, and open, wide-mouthed work basins—were laid out on lengths of coarse-spun cloth. Basket makers displayed wares woven of reed and rush, cane and vine, in myriad sizes and shapes and plaits and coils, some bright with patterns and dyes. There were a leather worker and a shell crafter, and the joined boxes and benches and carved stools of a good carpenter lay arranged in rows. There were a gourd painter and an old woman who whittled wooden figurines. There was the mano and metate maker, his wares under inspection by what appeared to be a very shrewd customer.

"What do you think of all this, Daughter?"

"All of what, Father?"

"All this trade?"

"Oh, I think it is quite enjoyable," I said.

"Ah, yes, that it is indeed—enjoyable. Other than that what do you think? What part of it should we get, do you suppose? For our use at the palace?"

"I'm not sure what you mean, Father. We are given such goods as tribute. It is brought to our courtyard door." I did not remark that tribute was not accompanied by the exciting din and flurry or the rousing stir of haggling that occurred along these neighborhood trails.

Next we came upon an obsidian knapper who had creatively arranged his shiny black knives and spear points in an appealing array. Farther on, a barber trimmed a client's hair as her assistant sweet-oiled and plaited the hair of another. Close by, a tattooist was at work concocting an imaginative design in soot along the length of his client's arm.

"Yes, our allotted tribute, to be sure, that indeed we acquire," my father acknowledged. "But, Daughter, should we not also take an additional bite? Are we not owed this? Without Calumook, founded by our Waterlily ancestor thirty-three generations ago, there would be no one to trade with, would there. Without us, the basket maker we just passed would not easily be able to exchange her basket for someone else's carved wooden stool. Is that not so?"

I did not answer straightaway. I wanted to consider my father's words, lest he think my mind capable only of trivial notions. I regretted that my previous comment had been about enjoyment, believing he would consider it childish. Without doubt, his world had very little to do with amusement lately.

"We take an additional bite from the vendors along our sacbe, do we not?" I asked.

"Yes, Daughter, that is correct. And if they petition us to build a formal stall beside our sacbe, they owe us an additional measure of cacao beans. Does this seem reasonable to you?"

We continued walking as we spoke, all the while noting the many goods and services—chipped obsidian and wooden boxes, haircuts and tattoos—and all the bustle and barter that attended this commerce. What a contrast with our sacbe, where the marketing was much more sedate than on this simple neighborhood trail.

I said, "The sacbe vendors trade mostly with those on palace business, so yes, I believe the palace should bite decisively from them."

"Hmmm," my father said in a neutral tone. I believe he was at least somewhat pleased with my response, although he did not say so. But then he continued to press for an exact response to his actual question. "But, Daughter, should we also take a bite from these simple vendors?" He motioned to either side of the trail. "From those who lay out their garments of threadbare coarse-spun and their little trinkets along these humble trails? Should the palace also bite here, Daughter? That is my question."

There was a sandal maker measuring a man's foot to determine the length of the leather crosspiece at the instep. Women from nearby communities had hauled their woven textiles to Calumook, as sometimes women like to dress in something unusual. Interspersed among them were sellers of steaming savory tamales, salted fish, and sweet honeycomb, and of grilled fish and dog stew. Rich, mouthwatering aromas wafted from braziers heated by glowing embers.

Just then my father paused to peer toward the smoldering coals in one such brazier. As he did, the cook quickly snatched up a hot skewer of grilled meat and presented it to him, head bowed in deference. My father accepted the steaming skewer, nibbled delicately, and then exclaimed loudly, "My how delicious!"

As he spoke he waved the skewer aloft about him in grand fashion. The cook, delighted, beamed. The other watching faces beamed as well. He was such a man of the people, my father. The people of Calumook loved him.

As we continued on, my father now spoke in a confidential tone. "You realize, Daughter, the only thing separating us from them is our blood."

At the time I could do nothing more than agree with him, but I now know there is so much more that separates the high-born from the low—so many obligations of proper behavior that set us apart. It takes an entire lifetime to learn what is required to fulfill our enormous responsibilities to our people, our ancestors, and our gods. I now understand what is meant by the saying "from those to whom much is given, much is expected." The difference in our blood is only the start of it. I believe my father said what he did at that moment because he was feeling generous in spirit. That is what comes of being a man of the people.

The familiar, distinctive calls of the market reverberated around us as we walked. Each cry hawked this fare or that, these wares or those, a particular service or another, all amidst excited hubbub and haggling. Pyramids of stacked tomatoes, the hard and green ones as well as the soft, ripe, and red. Orange and green chilies heaped in their own little piles; delicate yellow squash blossoms placed in cheerful arrangements. The bustle and bargaining, the din and barter. Though I knew the proper attitude for someone of my position was disdain for such base commoner displays, and part of me duly felt it. But another part deemed it all exceedingly thrilling, and in that I believe I resembled my father greatly.

Still unsure how to respond to his query, I tried to pose it back to him, though in a pondering manner. "On the trails, our bites would need to be very small, Father. I think it might be difficult to take such small bites from such small people, do you not agree?"

"Hmm. That may be the case," he said.

"I wonder too, if we tried to bite on the neighborhood trails, whether people might stop marketing on the trails and trade elsewhere instead. Try to hide it from us. That might not be good. Might it be so?"

"Hiding their marketing from us does not sound good. I agree with you, Daughter. That is an astute observation." When he said this last part I had to turn my head because I could not keep a smile from spreading across my face.

As my father's partially constructed temple came into view, we observed another long, meandering line of men and stone, this time ascending—leafcutter ants slowly picking their way upward on the temple itself. Masons toiled on its scaffolds, positioning cut blocks in thick mortar in neat rows and tracing exact horizontal lines using a taut string. Others pieced together a mighty puzzle of mosaic stones that, once assembled and mortared in place, would be the most impressive Chaak mask the world had ever seen. I marveled at it all: the craftsmanship, the sheer and vast quantity of stone, the enormous mounds of white lime powder, the endless mass of sweat and motion and careful organization it took to accomplish such a feat of construction.

We had arrived at the work site from a rear trail. My father wanted to check on the progress at the front, where the edifice would face the sacbe, so we rounded the corner toward the rising temple facade. It was then that I first saw Naah Chan. Only later would I learn his name, of course. At the time he was only a strong, compelling form bent deep at the waist, one knee to the ground, working almost astride his stela commission. The medium-spun loincloth he wore was that of a high-skilled craftsman, not an elite. His hair was well coiffed, although many strands that had fallen loose as he toiled hung along the edges of his face.

Rounding the temple from its rear, my father and I came upon Naah Chan from behind, and thus I was able to note the movement of his strong back muscles as they shifted beneath his skin. It was as if I had been seized by a shaman's incantation and rendered powerless to avert my gaze from this enthralling person. Perhaps the intensity of his pose attracted me as well; it reminded me of how I felt when I assembled fragrant floral bundles. Those long, pensive mornings alone at the cutting table surrounded by color and texture and delightfully pungent perfumes encouraged such quiet reflection that I failed to perceive the world around me.

That was Naah Chan. When commoners knew my father was close, they ceased all activity and stood silent, hands clasped, eyes cast downward. But Naah Chan was kneeling there so engrossed in his task that he failed to notice the hush that had fallen all around him. Instead, he continued the quiet transfer of his precise design calculations to an enormous white slab of fine-grained stone. This very stone would become my father's magnificent new stela near the grand façade of his magnificent new temple. A long white furl of bark paper lay at his side, held flat with smooth black pebbles. Wholly absorbed, he consulted the drawing on that furl, looking back and forth as he studied and measured.

Later, I learned that this man, this Naah Chan, had only just become Calumook's master stela carver. He had been elevated to this lofty position due to his talent, but also because so many of our highborn stela carvers had died in combat or been sacrificed in our recent wars with the Lalchich. In truth, Calumook was fortunate to have discovered such a talented carver hidden within its own ranks.

My father's sajal, who had walked the sacbe and was waiting for us near the front of the rising temple, moved angrily to rebuke this insolent young carver for his misconduct, but my father motioned him away. You see, my father had a deeply inquisitive nature and took much delight in the direct observation of things. He wanted to see for himself, without disrupting the work in progress, the initial stages of what surely would become the most magnificent of all his many stelae. I believe as well that my father wanted to ascertain the level of his new master carver's craftsmanship unimpeded by tedious protocol. He stole up behind Naah Chan and peered over his shoulder. Still arm in arm with my father, I too peered over that same strong and alluring shoulder. What we saw being conveyed from the bark paper furl to the flat white stone was nothing short of remarkable.

3

Some months after our visit to Lalchich, my mother and I undertook the long journey to Quetzaltun. It was again the matter of my marriage that prompted our trip to that cold and distant highland city.

The mountainous path our litter carriers trod was rough and jagged. In places it twisted tightly back and forth, and our carriers had to maneuver around immense boulders. We were jostled about all day, and Quetzaltun was so distant that it took five full days to get there. By then I knew that it was usually the side of the aspiring husband that dispatched a prospective nuptial entourage, which then had to endure the rigors of travel to the city of the would-be bride. Thus, with each new jolt of my litter, I found my mother's insistence on making tremendous effort to reach this remote place increasingly unfathomable. The prospective groom was the second son of the K'uhul Ajaw of Quetzaltun, a city with which my father had become closely allied only recently. It was a sizable gamble to consider marrying me to a place with unproven loyalty. At the time, I was still naive enough to believe my mother had insisted on traveling there in order to assess Quetzaltun's trustworthiness.

Despite the jostling, I managed to notice the peculiarities of our twisting route. Ever up into the highlands it wound, and it was like no land I had ever visited. I was born in the warm, humid jungle lowlands, a good place where we are embraced by thick green jungle and wake to the crescendo of howler monkeys. The backdrop of life is different for the unfortunate folk of Quetzaltun.

We traversed an extraordinary forest filled with trees I had never seen before. So very unlike the flat, broad leaves of our jungle foliage, they were tall and narrow, with tight clusters of sharp, long leaves. Our route carried us through an astonishing landscape of gray crags and deep gorges through which torrents of fast white water plunged far below. As we climbed farther into those highlands, it sometimes felt as if we were penetrating the clouds themselves, and on a few occasions the mist enfolded us and we lost sight of the land entirely. In all my life I had never felt so cold.

When at last we arrived at Quetzaltun, I was shivering, even under my layers of cloth and fur. I found shivering to be a most unpleasant sensation; my teeth chattered so uncontrollably that the incessant vibrations penetrated my skull. Perhaps that constant chattering of my teeth accounts for the profound disappointment that colored my first impression of the city. The palace and all other prominent buildings were built of long wooden planks hewn from the tall timbers I had seen growing in their unfamiliar forests. Unlike ours, their chambers were not graced with soaring corbeled stone vaults but were squat and square, with low, flat ceilings and walls of wood. I was struck with an immediate sense of claustrophobia.

Constructed on low earthen foundations, their wooden temples were likewise small and stubby compared to ours at Calumook. As at Calumook, however, enormous incense burners circled their temples, and the familiar scent of burning copal hung in the air. I was grateful for that fleeting sense of familiarity.

While it is true that I enjoyed the distinct flavors of Quetzaltun cuisine, I was taken aback by their choice of venue for the feast: it was held inside their ball court. Lowlanders never feasted in such places, but these highlanders unfurled their feasting mats right down the very center of the playing alley as though it were entirely normal—and there we sat upon our cushions and ate and ate. And against this unusual backdrop—little more than rough stone slabs upon the alley's low earthen berms—the peculiar notes of friction drums of many sizes came from all around. I gathered then that this particular kind of drum this was their preferred musical instrument.

Despite our peculiar backdrop, the highlanders were graciously generous with their praise as well as their cuisine.

"Lady of Calumook, welcome to our humble city!" the Lady of Quetzaltun said. "We are pleased you undertook such a long and arduous journey to visit us." As she spoke, she presented my mother with a pair of carved jade ear spools.

"Lady of Quetzaltun, gratitude rests deep in my heart for your kind and gracious welcome, for your fine greeting." As my mother spoke, she presented the queen—an older, grizzled woman—with a spondylus shell pendant, its gleaming white interior intricately carved. Such was a common pattern of official gift exchange, you see, initiated at the first formal feast.

Our hostess greeted me as well. "Young Lady Winik, you are also gladly welcomed here. Please make yourself truly at ease." Of course by then I knew these to be the standard predictabilities of formal greetings. Making myself at ease would be truly far from easy.

The following morning our retinue toured the city again. Once more, disappointment lay in wait around each corner. When finally we halted to formally review the stone stelae that dedicated their temples, I experienced a surge of humiliation on behalf of the unfortunate royal personages whose carved likenesses I saw. The quality of the workmanship was mediocre at best, and the stelae were fashioned from very thin stone that was weak, uneven, and yellow-veined. Even I could see how poorly executed the lines and figures were, and how the carver's careless chisel had failed to smooth the rough corners of the glyphs. It seemed that no one had even tried to buff and polish the stone's surface to a high sheen. Its entire effect was one of dull lifelessness, whereas it should have evoked the extraordinary celestial rock forests our royal stelae were intended to resemble.

Standing before those wretched monuments that felt like the final disappointment in a long string of disappointing days, I experienced an immense swell of homesickness. At that moment I dearly missed Calumook—the fine steamy warmth of our jungle, the familiarity of my own high-ceilinged chamber, and the jolly comfort of my little cousin astride my hip. The sad sight of those stelae also reminded me of how much I missed Naah Chan. They reminded me of how much I would ache to see him after I departed Calumook as a married woman and we could never again meet behind our green curtain of jungle vines.

Yes, by then we had begun to meet in secret, but that is a story for another time.

I had told myself I would not think about the inevitable day of our parting until it was upon us, but now, on this cold, disappointing day, standing before those pathetic stelae in that cold, disappointing city, I was unable to keep the sadness from intruding. I felt as if a heavy shadow hung in the sky above me, threatening the optimism of even my Scarlet Macaw companion spirit.

This was not my customary disposition, and my mother, who seldom missed anything, noticed my melancholy. Later, after our official tour had concluded and we were alone in our chamber, she spoke to me with surprising kindness.

"Be assured, Daughter, if it is decided you are to wed the second prince, there will be an expert stela carver in your permanent entourage." That was all she ever said, at least within my hearing, in acknowledgment of how lacking that highland city truly was.

At that point, I had not met any of the three men I might marry. I had, however, already fallen in love with Naah Chan, and people newly in love too often fail to think before they speak. So I committed a grave error. "Mother," I asked, "do you think our new master carver that goes by the name of Naah Chan might be the one to accompany my entourage?"

The scarcely perceptible hesitation in my mother's hand as she raised it to right some strands that had strayed from her coiffure told me of my blunder. No, she did not turn and glare at me. No, she did not interrogate me about how I came to know the name of Calumook's new master stela carver. What she said was this: "I should never have allowed you to accompany your father so much." She said these words in such an even tone that a shiver suddenly rippled up my already-cold spine.

◎◎◎

The soles of my feet feel like bony knobs as I totter in through the door of our hut. As I totter back out, I cradle a large bundle in my gnarled hands. The time has come to retrieve this old family heirloom from the dusty thatch where I hid it some time ago.

"What is that, Grandmother?"

I do not answer. Instead, I begin unwrapping this precious treasure. I do not hurry. One fold of dusty fine-spun after another,

I unwrap. I turn, I unwrap, I bare another inner fold to the light. How I cherish the luxurious feel of fine-spun as it brushes against my skin. These old callused fingers—fingers that have gripped too much—still recall the feel of fine-spun. In quiet murmurs, I intone the ritual chant required upon bringing such objects into daylight. It has been so long since I last chanted such phrases, but still I recall each word. Fold after fold, I open and I chant, chant and open, and then it is there, unwrapped at last. I have not seen this marvelous thing since I myself wrapped it in preparation for its long concealment, tied to the dusty rafters of our hut.

Then, with unrestrained pride, I raise up my father's magnificent quetzal streamer headdress.

First there is only silence, but then in a whisper of astonishment, Lily Bean exclaims, "Grandmother!"

And I beam at her, joy sparkling in my eyes despite their cloudiness and their weeping.

It seems an eternity since I held such splendor. Memories rush back. I remember my father, the pinnacle of our palace, the ancient Iguana sentry who directed me to the patch of plaster on the bench. With admiration and with reverence, I stroke the long, upright, shimmering green tail streamers. My fingers trace the path of the long graceful droop at the top of each plume. Miraculously, even after so much loss, these plumes retain their grandeur. I pick up the headdress and move it about in my hands, and the streamer tips bob and dance, bob and dance, still alive after all the misery and carnage that has transpired around them.

When at last I can speak, my words also come in awed whisper: "Is it not exquisite?"

"Grandmother, where did you get this?" Lily Bean still cannot believe what she is seeing. Nor, almost, can I.

"This belonged to my father—your great-grandfather. He was one of the finest K'uhul Ajaw of Calumook." A sudden tear—of love? sadness? regret?—escapes the corner of my eye.

Lily Bean gently runs her youthful, precious hands up the long streamers, careful not to stroke them the wrong way. She is smart, my little progeny; she knows instinctively how to treat such an opulent thing. It is in the blood that such knowledge resides.

"Why have you not shown this to me before?" she asks.

"I had to hide it lest it be stolen. That is also a story I will tell you, but now I want to tell you of the time I myself saw mound after mound of resplendent quetzal plumes just like these, up there in that cold highland city. As I tell you, Lily Bean, think of this, the glory of this," I say, gesturing to my father's magnificent headdress, now resting on my lap.

◎◎◎

As we settled into that highland city, I truly could not comprehend how the poor people of Quetzaltun could live in that cold and cloudy land. How could they worship their gods and ancestors in such squat and trivial wooden temples? Carve such pitiful stelae? How could they bear existence within the confines of such low wooden chambers? To be sure, I had yet to grasp why my mother had been so eager to travel here. Up to that point, all I knew about this highland place was that it was an abundant source of quetzal plumes, like those in my father's magnificent headdress.

In this cold and cloudy land, I learned that feathers and streamers from the quetzal bird were part of the tribute paid to lineage heads by their commoner kin, who were obligated to deliver ten wrapped bunches of streamers each month. They caught the green birds in vast nets strung across the cold forest, plucking four streamers from each quetzal that became caught in the net. After this they set the birds once more to flight, as one must never kill a quetzal on penalty of death. Only if the bird fell from the sky of its own accord would a finder be permitted to pluck every last one of their brilliant plumes. I was glad for this small mercy because without their warm feather coverings these birds would never have managed to survive in the cold.

Upon delivery to Quetzaltun, the plumes remained under armed guard in a storeroom deep within the palace. My mother and I had been in that highland city for some time before we were finally invited to visit within. The room's few windows were small and high up in the walls. They were the kind of windows one latched shut from the inside. From the thickness of the walls and the heavy strength of the wooden door, I understood even before we passed through it that extravagant wealth rested within.

The room was sealed, so when I entered, the stale air reeked of something I had never before smelled. The odor was earthy and ripe, and I recall with certainty that I did not find it agreeable.

The room was inky as night until the guards unbolted the latches and threw open the wooden shutters of the high windows.

As my eyes began adjusting to the dim light, I could make out a low outline starting not two paces from where I stood. As the light grew less shadowy the shape grew clearer, and all of a sudden I understood what I was seeing: a giant heaping mass of green quetzal tail streamers. Of course I had seen such streamers many times, but never so many at once, and never not assembled into a royal headdress. At that moment, in that dark and malodorous inner palace storeroom, I finally grasped why my mother wanted to travel here, why she might want to marry me into this cold, miserable highland city. Even as this realization was taking shape in my mind, my sight penetrated deeper into the room, and I grasped that behind this mound was another, and another behind it. I turned my head, and on the other side of the room I saw yet more mounds, though these were red—the red of the shorter breast feathers of this same stunning flying highland creature— and white, like its short white under-tail feathers, and still other mounds were the green of the quetzal's short green chest-feathers. Taking in the vastness of this hoard of feathers, I could not help but wonder how many exquisite birds had been plucked to provide us with our headdresses.

No one had spoken since we entered the room and the guards flung back the shutters. I'm unsure why; no one had bid us not to speak. But as I surveyed the vast wealth lying before us, inside my person that silence merged with a deep, raw craving that pervaded my viscera. Strange though it may sound, as of course we do not eat plumes, it was as if I could taste their richness, this abundance, that immense fortune in my watering mouth.

I knew my mother tasted that same rich flavor, that same raw craving, because she said, "The K'uhul Ajaw of Calumook and I are most pleased that our friendship has deepened."

She said this only after we had walked back out, past that heavy door and into the strong sunlight. I remember squinting hard against the sudden glare, shielding my eyes with my hand against the bright sun. I also remember the sounds of the wooden shutters slamming shut on those high windows, and of wooden bolts being thrown from inside, and how they all but drowned out her words.

Only much later in our visit did I understand another advantage of a union between Calumook and Quetzaltun. The longer we remained in that cold city, my mother, in her own slyly ingratiating manner, began to pay prying, ambiguous compliments to the highborn denizens of Quetzaltun, in regard to the jade ornaments they wore on their persons.

"How bright the hue of that particular green," she might remark as her eye roamed over a pair of jade ear spools.

"How unusual, that deep golden vein that streaks through the beads of this bracelet," she told a courtier.

"Even though that green is dark and dull, as befits your station, it still has good substance," she pointed out to a palace servant, a meek, older female who stood obediently, head lowered, as my mother inspected her pendant—possibly a gift acknowledging a lifetime of loyal service—by lifting it from the woman's chest and turning it in her hand.

"My, but your wrist beads have such extraordinary specks of black in them, do they not?" she said to a young woman in the court of the Quetzaltun king. Thus did I figure out for myself that my mother was so intensely inquisitive about the jade from this highland city that she could almost not restrain herself.

Cornered, the woman asked, "Would young Lady Winik and your Majesty perhaps deign to visit our most humble jade workshop?" Of course my mother responded with the appropriately formal, fawningly hesitant affirmative.

We departed the main courtyard through a small wooden door in its back wall. Our guide was a plain, shy woman many years older than I, but still much younger than my mother. She was slight of build and light of foot, and her hand trailed the wall as she led us through a long narrow passage. She paused on the topmost step of a short flight that ran toward a small lower courtyard of the palace complex. Pressing open the courtyard's wooden door, she said, "This is where many of my paternal cousins live and work."

"And your father is … ?" My mother asked as we descended the first step.

"He is the fourth son of the king's nephew."

Thus, within the span of time it took to descend those few steps, my mother had calculated this woman's genealogical position. Thereafter she proceeded to ignore our hostess-guide and concentrate her attention on our whereabouts.

The courtyard was surrounded on all sides by low wooden buildings with low wooden doors, and many broad wooden steps rose up to the front of each building. As at Calumook, glyphs were carved upon the risers—apparently by the same clumsy hand that had chiseled this city's wretched stelae. A wide awning was stretched at the sunlit edge of the courtyard. I had come to appreciate that even here in the highland cold, shade could be desired by late midday. Tucked into the awning's shadow were at least a dozen men, some young, some much older. I cannot say they were hard at work, as in fact they were not. These were elite artisans, surrounded by chisels and hammer stones and engravers of various sizes and shapes. Several rope-handled wooden boxes holding more crafting tools lay nearby. Rough cobbles of raw jade tumbled from coarse-spun sacks. From others there spilled many different kinds of ornaments in various stages of completion. We could see ear spools of several styles in their early stages, each matching pair with its own distinctive cutout pattern beginning to take form. We observed many still uncompleted jade pendants of various sizes and shapes, as well as a long looping string of half-finished beads that lay beside its abrading stone, still in need of much grinding until smooth.

My mother walked into the shade of that awning, and I followed her. We peered at the efforts of the nearest man, who was now napping with his head drooping at an angle that made my neck ache. "What are you engraving?" she demanded, without so much as a greeting or token honorific thrown in for pleasantness, much less any recognition that she had interrupted his midday slumber. Her behavior did not surprise me. As I've said, my mother had already reckoned everyone's genealogical position and thus knew that this man and the others in this royal artisan workshop were of far lower rank than she.

The startled man shook off his drowsiness, and then hoisted his ample person to kneeling before he spoke. "My lady, this piece will be a belt dangle."

"A belt dangle," repeated my mother.

"Yes, my lady. I am making it in preparation for the grand nuptials of the second prince."

My mother did not react to this presumptuousness, but my own gut leapt at it. I could not say whether this betokened alarm or an odd sense of anticipation.

Her attention still directed not at the man but at the hard green stone, my mother asked, "Have your superiors performed the proper engraving rites to bless this piece?"

"Yes, my lady," he answered, "The proper rites were performed for its heat treating as well."

Holding out her hand, my mother commanded, "Let me see it."

The man placed his unfinished belt dangle into her palm without argument. She let it rest there for several long moments to assess its heft, then slid her fingers over its surface, evaluating its grain and texture. Then my audacious mother lifted the piece to the sky, her eyes narrowing as she scrutinized the translucence of the green. The fine craftsman had already roughed out its general dangle shape, which was to be a long, thin form like that of an ear of maize. He had begun the engraving as well: the profile figure of a royal man, standing tall in full regalia. Even though the glyph outlines were little more than shallow scratches in their current state, I could see that the figure was to depict the second prince—a man I had yet to encounter. I remember peering at those scratches with a strange curiosity.

◙◙◙

I'm unsure why, but this time my mother chose to leave me in our chambers while she and the queen of Quetzaltun sipped cool chocolate and conversed privately on the matter of my marriage.

As my mother had denied me free access to the courtyard, I was left to while away my time closed up in our chamber, which I had to admit was warm and cozy with its snug hide door and small brazier of glowing embers. I passed the tedium either by sleeping, or having my body servant groom my person, or playing board games with the mid-ranking noblewoman who showed us the jade workshop, who I had since discovered was as dull as a toad.

After several days of tiresome inactivity, my mother at last drew my formal presentation huipil from my wooden traveling trunk. After an entire morning of near endless preening, I was led to the royal reception chamber to meet the second prince.

"I present Lady Winik, she of the House of the Waterlily!" my mother announced, in a tone of proud formality.

I stood framed by the entrance portal, my eyes cast down as was proper for a young prospective bride. Even with lowered sight, I knew all eyes of the royal family of Quetzaltun—as well as those of all the courtiers of this highland place—were inspecting my entire person. As trained and practiced, I began to tread with slow, elegant dignity. Toe first, heel last, one soundless foot followed by the other, in measured stride. My eyes were on the floorboards, but my peripheral vision was alert to each detail of my new surrounding as I advanced sedately through the hushed room.

By this time, I confess, I had become accustomed to wood.

As you might expect, it was everywhere in the palace. Here in the innermost royal chambers, enormous timbered panels carved into elaborate painted screens divided the space into somewhat separate rooms yet also allowed for ample airiness, so that the chambers felt at once spacious and snug. Thick woven reed mats and piles of soft animal furs cushioned both the floor and a bench that ran along the entire edge of the long room. Intricately carved wooden tables and stools and chests stood all about, bright with paint. Long, plush woven curtains hung over the doorjambs. I found their color appealing: rather than the strident cochineal red or quiet Waterlily green of the emblazoned draperies in Lalchich and Calumook, they were of a brilliant green hue that alluded to the city's namesake bird. In a corner of the room, a long horizontal pole hung suspended from ceiling beams, and upon it perched a pair of captive quetzals. This was the first and only time I saw one so close. Their talons were tied with cords, and their long tail streamers curled far forward, reaching a distance far longer than the length of my own arm. I remember thinking how sad it was that these two magnificent flying jungle creatures would never again soar the skies above a tall and towering ceiba. As if in response to my just concern, each bird cawed out one long, shrill solitary cry. Their strange, eerie, echoed complaints seemed somehow portentous, although in a manner I was unable to decipher.

Many large braziers warmed the chamber. Embers aglow, they lined the far back wall, attended by stony-faced palace cooks grilling thick slabs of venison. Reaching this advanced juncture in the matter of my marriage was cause for celebration, so after the initial formal introduction of the prospective spouses, we would partake of a sumptuous feast, making contented gluttons of ourselves. Despite my nervousness and my wish to comport myself as befit my station, I admit that my mouth watered at the delicious aroma. I have always preferred venison above all other meats.

I made my way through the gauntlet of inquisitive eyes and took my place beside my mother, who I noticed was wearing what seemed an overabundance of jade ornaments, none of which I recognized. I tucked my heels beneath my legs, one knee tight against the other. Then I waited. My obligation during such formal occasions was always to wait silently and patiently until I had my mother's consent to do or say anything. I was strictly forbidden to cast my gaze upon the second prince of Quetzaltun without her permission. He sat with legs crossed on a cushioned bench just across the room from me, but regardless of his relative nearness I was not to look at him. By now, though I had long felt his eyes roaming unhindered over my entire person, observing each detail, watching my every movement.

It seemed an eternity before my mother gestured, graceful fingers curled, and said, "Prince Aj Took', He of Flint, here is my humble daughter, Lady Winik. We have journeyed far to make your generous acquaintance." With that I lifted my face and met the eyes of the man who might become my husband.

He was staring right at me. By then I had learned that this was the way of highlanders in general, who tended not to follow the eye contact etiquette customary among us lowlanders. By this point, in fact, I had learned much about these highlanders. Life here was wholly unlike life in the lowlands, but it was not, I had discovered, uncivilized. Their life fit their land. Their stelae were of poor quality because their stone was. For that same reason they also lacked high, vaulted ceilings, but strong timber they had aplenty. Having already feasted several times in their low ball court, I had come to acknowledge that food could taste good even in such an odd setting. I was even used to their lack of eye contact etiquette—or more precisely, their unique eye contact etiquette.

Because Prince Aj Took', He of Flint, was staring so unabashedly, it was impossible for me not to notice that one of his eyes wandered about in his head as if untethered to the other. I had already observed that unlike the men of Calumook, the men of Quetzaltun did not pluck the black hairs that sprouted from their chin and upper lip. Coupled with this was the unfortunate fact that the second prince's jaw was quite weak. I almost turned away in revulsion just looking at the bottom half of his face. By then, I had figured out that my mother's intention all along had been to marry me to this Quetzaltun highlander, whereas my father wanted me to reunite us with Lalchich. At that moment, however, in that wooden palace chamber in Quetzaltun, it struck me as cruel that my mother had made no effort to prepare me in advance for the disagreeable appearance of second prince. She had already met him—that I knew. I sometimes wonder whether she had deliberately kept the knowledge of his unsightliness from me, or whether his appearance was in fact immaterial to her calculations in the matter of my marriage. As it was, it took all my fortitude not to shrink from the sight of this man. I was glad that etiquette demanded I cast my gaze downward.

"Most fair and righteous Lady Winik," murmured the second prince in the customary exaggerated formal greeting.

To this day I remember the timbre of his voice. It carried their peculiar highlander accent but was deep and smooth and melodious nonetheless, presenting a surprising contradiction to the outward appearance of his person.

"Prince Aj Took', He of Flint, I am most honored," I murmured in the compulsory return greeting.

"Lady Winik, I thank you from deep within, for making the long and difficult journey to visit our humble city," he said, and again I experienced the unexpected pleasantness of his voice. "I believe it is probable that from your perspective, Quetzaltun is a place that would take getting used to, is that not so?"

I had no choice but to respond to his direct question. "My lord," I said with proper courtesy, "the journey was indeed long, that is quite true. And yes, it is also quite true that your city was strange at first, but now it does not seem as strange as when I first arrived."

"Ah yes, Lady Winik," he said, nodding, "it is indeed true that time accustoms us to many things." For a time he did not speak further, so neither did I.

"And what of the cold?" he eventually inquired.

"Prince Aj Took', the palace is very cozy."

"Ah yes, Lady Winik, the temperature indoors is indeed agreeably pleasant," he said, nodding, his voice as warm as the outside air was cold.

I nodded as well and hoped I seemed agreeable, but because his words did not again form a direct question, it would have been improper for me to speak; thus I remained silent for the rest of that long day. During the remaining formalities of the initial prospective spousal introductions, I said nothing. During the ceremonial feast in which we gorged ourselves on grilled venison, I said nothing. During the subsequent genealogical recitations and lengthy discussions of our numinous compatibility, I said nothing. Not one word.

Earlier, before my long hush following his agreement in regard to the temperature of the palace, I had already sensed tension mounting in the chamber within every kneeling woman and every cross-legged man. Keenly observing Prince Aj Took' and myself from their woven reed mats and sitting cushions in the grand wooden palace of Quetzaltun, they were searching for even the slightest sign of what our estimation, each of the other, might be—whether there had arisen between us any tiny spark of appeal, or at least whether there had not arisen, on either of our parts, a dislike that could blight the furtherance of our nuptial parleys. For you see, I did have some say in the matter of my marriage. Brides have the option of negating a prospective spouse, but we must never do so publicly, or too many times, or without strong, just cause; else we risk the disapproval of our illustrious kin both living and dead.

◙◙◙

Toward the end of our stay, my mother and I journeyed to the principal jade quarry of Quetzaltun. The treacherous path was even more jolting than the one that had brought us to this highland city, which was why such a visit had not been on our original itinerary. An excursion had been arranged once my mother expressed her wish to see it.

Our carriers bore us in tiny litters that allowed for negotiation of such steep, narrow, winding, rocky footpaths. Huddled beneath many layers of heavy furs, I was nonetheless shivering again, and for a time I wished my mother had chosen to leave me in my warm palace chamber, even if it meant playing more board games with that dull noblewoman. Burrowed deep in my furs, I was fascinated by the guards. There were so many of them. Some stood beside the path in full view, but others were hidden behind trees and boulders, attempting, it seemed, to blend into the landscape. While I cannot be certain, as I only observed them from afar. Suspicion hung in the air as thick as the mist that obscured the valleys below, and I sensed that some might have been tasked with surveillance of the others.

Like so much else on that trip, the jade quarry was at first a disappointment. Never had I imagined such a glorious stone could have such an inglorious origin. The quarry was little more than a long stretch of cliffs and some haphazard clumps of rough boulders alongside a rocky ravine. Guards stood watch over this place as well. They carried long atlatls and the long, polished wooden shafts of sharp, stone-tipped spears, as had the guards on the trail. Protruding from each guard's loincloth was the long, carved wooden handle of an obsidian dagger.

As we neared the ravine, I was surprised to recognize the second prince of Quetzaltun among a group of men standing at its entrance. I had not been informed that He of Flint was to be our guide. To be sure, I was seldom informed of much.

While the others fell back at our approach, He of Flint stepped forward and waited as our litters neared. When mine was lowered, he reached out his hand to assist my exit from its cramped wooden seat. This surprised me. I believe most prospective husbands would first have fussed over my mother in an obsequious effort to gain her favor. He did not. It was there, before the entrance to that rocky ravine, that I decided I could perhaps become fond of the second prince, even if he was unattractive to behold.

"Lady Winik," he said, "I bid you welcome." Even here, in this stark and doubtful land, his voice was melodious.

"Thank you," I murmured.

"Please, watch your step. This rocky ground is apt to turn an ankle," he cautioned.

"Thank you," I said again, taking his proffered arm.

He led me to a swept section of flat ground, released my arm with a brief amicable bow, and went to retrieve my mother from her litter. As they approached, I thought she seemed oddly pleased to have her arm through his, and she appeared to be trying to carry her person in a youthful fashion. As I noticed these flirtations, an unexpected jealousy arose within my person. Servants appeared with cool water, and I recall its bright sweetness as it trickled down my dry throat. As I drank, I thought it most considerate that this man had anticipated that we would be parched after such a strenuous journey and, without wasting breath to inquire whether we desired cool water, had ordered it be poured.

We sipped while servants unfurled a woven mat and laid brimming platters upon it. One of the culinary specialties of these highlanders was diced ripe tomato and fresh red chili sauce over beans, adorned with fresh-cut avocado slices. I found the combination of green and red very appealing; of course one eats with the eyes as well as the mouth. Once they discovered I was partial to this particular dish, they served it with each meal—even here, upon this mat near the entrance to the rocky ravine. After we dined, we rested a bit, but before long my mother wanted to see what she had come to see.

"Please reveal this place to us," she said to the prince.

"Of course, my lady," he answered, offering an arm to each of us to assist our graceful rise.

He led us along a narrow path hugging the edge of the long ravine. "Keep your persons leaning always inward toward the hill," he advised, which I did perhaps more than was actually necessary, not daring to peer over my shoulder and down the steep slope. I was glad it was sheltering me from the chill wind, and as the sun shone on my person, I grew pleasantly warm as we continued along that narrow path.

As we approached its end, a group of laborers stepped back from their boulders. The second prince stepped toward them and rubbed his hands across the surface of several large boulders, reviewing both their rough and their smooth sections. At last the prince called to us: "Here is an excellent example! You can see the rough jade, right here, and feel it also, exceptionally well in this one."

I followed my mother over to his excellent boulder. We looked where he indicated we should look, and then touched what he pointed at for us to touch: rough little patches of raw jade that were visible within the much rougher gray background of the boulder. Then the second prince picked up a large rock from the ground. "Watch," he said, smiling.

With both hands he raised the rock high above his head and brought it down hard upon the boulder. Looking back, I admit I did not know what to expect. I supposed the rock would just hit the boulder with a dull and dusty thud, so when it bounced back into the air I was surprised.

"Oh!" I said.

With the rock poised in midair between both hands, the second prince smiled at me. "Yes," he said, "a boulder that contains a good amount of jade will repel what strikes it."

"Oh," I said again and smiled back at him, more out of astonishment than anything else.

He did it again, brought his rock down hard upon the boulder, and again it sprang into the air. As I watched it rebound, I noticed a resemblance to the balls of our ball game, which were made of hard rubber tapped from our rubber trees—though of course I knew the rock was not rubber.

"Would you like to try?" he asked, holding out the rock to me.

I confess that in that moment I was not sure what to do. His offer was wholly unanticipated. Indeed, everything about this entire journey to Quetzaltun was unexpected, and so very different from everything in Calumook—including that odd flush of jealousy when my mother had flirted with him. Watching him with the rock, I realized I was growing fond of this unappealing man, this Prince Aj Took', He of Flint, and now he had unexpectedly offered me the rock. I very much wanted to take that rock. And I wanted our hands to touch as I took it from him, just to feel how his person might feel. I also wanted hold the rock because it seemed that bouncing it on the boulder with my own hands would be a remarkable sensation, something I had never experienced. But I didn't know if I should.

Amidst these many odd and unfamiliar emotions, I looked instinctively to my mother for guidance. Even as I did I wished I had not. While I did not want to be in need of her in any way, I also did not want to incur her wrath. Flushed of embarrassment at having sought her permission in the company of the prince, I did not know whether or not I should accept that rock from his hands and bang it against the boulder for myself. I was so young, back then.

Meanwhile, my mother was as though entranced by the boulder itself. It took a moment for her to even notice my ambivalence, and when she did she only shrugged. I decided that was all the permission I needed and took the rock from Prince Aj Took', clasping it tight. Never before had I held such a raw thing in my hands. Making no effort to conceal my eagerness, I raised it high above my head and brought it down hard on the exact spot where the prince's blow had struck. As my hands and the rock bounced high in the air like a rubber ball and the unexpected sensation of that rebound reverberated up my arms, I could not contain my delight, which spread across my face.

"Is it not splendid?" the second prince asked, smiling also.

"Oh yes," I agreed, "it is quite splendid!"

We were both still looking at the boulder. "Do it again," he urged.

And I did. Again, our faces—blatantly unmasked—shone with delight, but this time we looked at one another. I think that both he and I were pleased that I had been bold enough to grasp that rock in the first place, even though our hands never touched.

◎◎◎

As our tiny litters jostled back down the steep winding footpath and the narrow ravine full of rough jade boulders receded behind us, I gazed out over a broad, open highland vista. The sight of an open vista was not something we had in Calumook or, truth be told, anywhere in the lowlands. I found it offered opportunity for deep reflection.

Without doubt I was thinking of the second prince. He of Flint was engaging and adventurous, unlike so many of the lethargic aristocrats that peopled our courts. His city was made of wood, wood from timbers with long sharp foliage that grew tall in cold, cloud-draped forests. His face was disagreeable, but the rest of his person was not displeasing, and the resonating beauty of his voice still hung in my ears. "Is it not splendid?" he had asked. I was also feeling rather proud to have been so bold up there with the rock and boulder. Would I have dared to take the rock if I had been in Calumook? Who was I here—or who might was not there? I had never before imagined even the existence of such a question. Exposed again outside the protection of that rocky ravine, I burrowed into my furs as the chill wind buffeted me. Again I considered the coldness of this place, and its contrast to the lush easy warmth of our jungle lowlands. I believe it was my longing for that warmth, as well as my boldness with the rock, the feel of soft fur against my skin, and the sound of the voice of He of Flint, the second prince of Quetzaltun, that drew the image of Naah Chan to my thoughts.

The first time we kissed it was only in a dream, but it is that kiss, not those precious, rare real ones that came later, that flutters most in my memory.

I waited for him along the narrow trail I knew he would take to Calumook's stone quarry, taking an enormous risk by going to such a place alone. Even as I knew I was dreaming, I knew I was being daring, which is why I hid behind a curtain of green vines hanging from the limb of a ceiba. As I waited, my nostrils flared with anticipation, and with the musty scent of this wild and earthy place.

I heard his approach before I saw him. He was whistling a low tune—which tune it was remains uncertain because dreams play tricks on us, as does memory—but I know he was whistling because he stopped mid-tune when I stepped from behind those vines.

Standing very still, we gazed at one another for a long moment. Each was taking careful measure of the other: our intentions, the dangers, the prospects. There we stood, he on the trail and I in the jungle, and also beyond these places in the world and within our hearts. Then, with calm composure, he stepped off the trail and into the jungle, and clasped my arm. I feel his touch even now, firm but gentle, at the place just above my elbow. Drawing me back with him into the shadows, he sought my mouth with his, kissing me with his full intention. A warm flush of desire surged within me.

Then I awoke with a start, my eyes jerking open to stare in dismay at the woven curtain against the wall of my palace chamber. Gone was the wild musty scent of earth, the lush green vines, the quiet stillness of that shadowy jungle ceiba. In their stead was the lingering smell of grilled duck from the evening repast. The softness of the woven mat beneath me seemed lonesome compared to the dream of Naah Chan's gentle touch upon my arm, the feel of his lips pressed against my own.

But the matter of my marriage had nothing to do with Naah Chan, Both of us knew this with certainty. I might indeed have a say in whether my husband would be this engaging and melodious-voiced yet ill-favored highlander, or the cousin of the young queen of Lalchich, a man I had not met. But he could never be the new master stela carver of Calumook, however skilled, however talented, however newly prosperous. That could never happen.

I reflected on the mounds of quetzal plumes that gave this highland city its name, and the fact that it had boulder upon well-guarded boulder of rich jade, as well as a rear palace complex teeming with noble artisans who had little to do besides turn out fine crafted ornaments. These two things—plumes and jade— were valuable everywhere in the world. As our litters lurched back down the rocky slope toward that sprawling wooden palace, I knew my mother would push for my marriage to Quetzal-tun's second prince, whereas my father preferred I marry into the royal line of Lalchich to seal that wayward city's return as a loyal, subordinate ally. And even as I pondered the complexities of my marital prospects, all I wanted was run far away with Naah Chan.

4

Cenote town had arisen from a seed planted by my father's grandfather's nephew, so the king of Cenote was ours. Unlike the lords of our conquered towns, and at times even our allied ones, our Cenote puppet was never in need of a reminder of loyalty, and my father's dealings with him and his court were always conducted smoothly.

Our ancestor had seeded Cenote to ensure Calumook's unencumbered access to its hallowed water for all eternity. It was, after all, our city's foremost entryway to Xibalba, the Underworld. That watery portal lies still and quiet. From its damp cliffs the sacred substance of Chaak seeps and trickles. Its delicate ferns embody his power to command life. It was there, deep beneath the tranquil surface of our revered cenote, namesake of our seeded town, that our lineage first emerged. Water lilies, the visual living memory of our origin path, float upon its still surface. There they lie, pads as large and round as the biggest painted platters. There they lie, the whitest of white flowers with yellow-gold centers as bright as the shining face of K'inich Ajaw. It is from the water lily roots that float on this glistening surface—the long roots that rise from the deep primordial ancestral muck—that our herbalists concoct our mind-expanding brews. We came from this watery world, so we render offerings back to this place. We offer copal, prized jade, finely painted ceramics, and even human life itself—the precious maize dough that sustains the gods who made us.

The visit to Cenote town of which I now speak occurred some months after my return from Quetzaltun. The matter of my marriage had not yet been decided, or perhaps it was just still unannounced. Surely no one had discussed it with me. I had been serving as Lady Winik for some time, and it was in that esteemed capacity that I journeyed to Cenote. Indeed, my presence as Lady Winik of Calumook was now required at every formal event. I had not yet attended enough of these to weary of their grandness.

We arrived at Cenote atop our finest ornamental litters, by way of the long sacbe that joined our two cities: Calumook and Cenote, linked in the physical world as well as the cosmic. After he had seeded Cenote, as evidence of our close affinity our illustrious architect ancestor sponsored the sacbe's construction and designed its two magnificent decorative arches, one at each end. The building of the sacbe and of its two arches earned my architect ancestor two new stanzas in our patriline chant.

Did I mention that I was present when those linking sacbe and arch stanzas were first chanted in public? It was during my very first formal appearance as Lady Winik outside of Calumook. Why these stanzas had taken so long to compose I do not know, but I accept that creations as significant as patriline stanzas have their own particular pace of divine unfolding. They were also first chanted in Cenote.

I was giddy with excitement. Their unveiling was timed to coincide with the rite of apotheosis—the moment at which a deceased relative transforms from remembered ancestor to anonymous deified ancestor residing in the realm of the gods. This was not the apotheosis of the ancestor who had seeded Cenote and built the linking sacbe and arches twelve generations earlier. That ancestor had been deified long ago, and as I said, the pace of divine unfolding was not mine to comprehend. Rather, this rite of apotheosis was for a Cenote ancestor who had died two generations earlier. People referred to him as the Kalo'mte', a title I still did not fully comprehend.

We stood beside the crypt of my soon-to-be deified paternal Kalo'mte' ancestor, on the lowest level of the Cenote palace. Sweet copal smoke filled the air. I watched as my paternal uncle intoned our patriline in a low chant. Stone by stone, he slowly removed the crypt's cover in cadence with his recitation. He raised an ornate painted bowl, from which he grasped several generous pinches of powdery red cinnabar, our metaphoric blood of gods and ancestors. Still chanting, he sprinkled it within the crypt. Then he reached in, took hold of our ancestor's skull, and drew it from its place of rest. The memory of that skull has never left me. Despite all that has happened, that vision holds as much power as it would if it had emerged from the crypt this very morning. A dusting of bright powdery red lay upon its smooth white surface. My ancestor's skull had empty, cavernous eyes. When my uncle picked it up its toothless jaw suddenly opened wide, and a dusty jumble of jade beads rattled out of it.

I gasped. Though I did not know quite what to expect in the course of a rite of apotheosis, I had not anticipated that I'd be seeing jade beads suddenly tumble from a gaping toothless jaw. At once, however, I understood my gasp was unpropitious, because under his breath, a different uncle commanded, "Silence!" Moments later, in a mean and ominous whisper, he added, "If all goes as intended, young Lady Winik, you will consider yourself fortunate to be buried with a mouth full of jade beads"

I turned to look at him, and I think he understood from the honest, searching appeal in my eyes that I needed some sort of explanation. He whispered, this time with a bit more kindness, "My child, if you have no jade beads, what will you have to offer as passage through Xibalba?"

He uttered those words with a strange sense of pity. I knew that overall he was angry with me and his words were a rebuke, but now I think they were also intended as an uncanny forewarning of sorts—that he himself was far from certain that all would go as intended. What did this mean? At the time, I was far too young to grasp the full portent of my uncle's gloomy words, but later, much later, after all that happened, I pondered them many times, for without doubt nothing went as intended.

I grant that in my dotage, my memory often bends and folds upon itself. At times my mind certainly does flit and flutter around my uncle's prophetic words. Had he foreseen what lay ahead? Might it all have been unpreventable? My memory sweeps to my father. It sweeps to Naah Chan, and then back it sweeps to the red cinnabar skull of my Kalo'mte' ancestor, and the sudden jumble of his falling jade beads. I remember tiny bursts of dust as they fell on the earth of his crypt. His toothless jaw had guarded what he needed for his passage through Xibalba. I can almost feel the hardness, the cool smoothness, of jade beads against my own tongue. From somewhere vague and distant, I can almost hear the chanting of our patriline.

Oh yes, the chanting of our patriline. The new stanzas. I was lost for a moment. Now I recall I was telling the story of the new stanzas composed in honor of my architect ancestor who built the long linking sacbe and the magnificent arches. Yes, now I remember. Yes, I was there in Cenote town when those stanzas were first chanted in public, at the rite of apotheosis of my Ka-lo'mte' ancestor.

Many lines in those stanzas heralded my ancestor as a visionary. It had taken keen architectural acumen to imagine building such a long linking sacbe, let alone such magnificent ceremonial archways at either end—one at Calumook and the other at Cenote.

Once my father's new Chaak temple was completed and dedicated, he too could be expected to earn a new stanza in our patriline chant. If it was as grand as my father intended, he might earn two stanzas, perhaps more. Those stanzas would be composed by his descendants—by our descendants, scions of the House of the Waterlily—and thus his accomplishments on our behalf would live forever. I understood my father's great ambition for his new Chaak temple: he aspired for it to compare well with our ancestor's architectural acumen. More likely than not, as he monitored the slow progress of his temple, my father had begun composing in his mind the lyrics of praise he hoped one day might be chanted. I believe that as he strode along our sacbe, he envisioned that not-yet-born Waterlily scribe, stylus poised in an elite, practiced hand. The scribe would touch stylus to paper and exalt my humble father's astounding accomplishment in perfectly inked glyphs, effusively lauding the genius of his outstanding talent and his enormous generosity to the people of Calumook. As he strode on our sacbe and studied, striding and fretting and counting the days, I imagine my father envisioned the most extravagant of all these extravagant stanzas, possibly describing the elegance and imposing grandeur of the single enormous mosaic mask that had yet to take form—though it most surely would—atop his temple's lofty summit. That one final mask of Chaak would be the paramount achievement of my father's entire life. That mask, that temple, would be akin to our architect ancestor's magnificent arches.

"But, Grandmother, I have never seen the arches of which you speak. Where are they?" I see puzzlement and consternation on her perfect face. "Why have you not brought me to see them?"

As I look at this child and her young face looks back at me from the depths of innocence, I regret that that such a face must soon learn the art of falsifying its true countenance. Then I shut my eyes against the bittersweet memory of those arches, my ancestor architect's utmost masterpieces. How precise their alignment with the rising of the Venus star. How impeccable their symmetry. How eager the young Lady Winik, who had fallen to her knees that long-ago day before the Cenote arch to intone the proper passages of our patriline chant, including its two new stanzas—and then scatter my royal blood upon its base.

"Lily Bean ..." I begin, but then I fall silent. I cannot hide the truth, the horrible truth of the end of Calumook and our world, from this child much longer. Knowing this, I open my eyes and my gaze creeps back to fall upon the last of our patriline. She is our greatest hope for our future, and I feel even older than I am.

"Lily Bean, You have not seen the arches because they no longer stand." I look away as my anger begins to simmer. "They are nothing but weedy piles of rubble. They mock us, those weedy piles, they mock us with our own humiliation. And to further disgrace the House of the Waterlily, a great many of our beautiful carved arch stones were looted and used as adornments before lowborn hovels to mock and insult us. May the hearts of those thieves be eaten and shat out by vermin!" At this I spit, a despicable gesture unbecoming of my rank. Then I am ashamed of myself, of how I have let slide the conventions of proper elite comportment. I watch my spittle sink into the earth like rain, my spittle like the gift of Chaak, a gift he never gave.

◉◉◉

After that day's last rite of scattering, I stood composing myself and then climbed back onto my ornate wooden litter. Moving out of the cool shadow of Cenote's grand arch, our entourage proceeded toward their ceremonial ball court.

I sat on the tiered bench behind my father's, looking out at center court with my little cousin nestled at my side. My mother, who did not approve of my bond with the child, warned that if he fussed I would have to leave and would be forbidden to return for the remainder of the game. I was not worried, as I knew my cousin's disposition was so sweet that he rarely fussed, or at least, not when was astride my hip.

By that time I had attended many ball games at many ball courts, but the grand ceremonial court at Cenote was unique among them because its northern end opened onto a dark hollow that led to the cenote cleft deep in the earth. Through that watery cleft, one entered Xibalba.

My father was in a jolly mood that day. He raised his arm and waved it grandly about in his poised, regal fashion. "Greetings! I offer you our salutations as your humble visiting competitor!" he called to the lineage heads of Cenote as they gathered on the tiers of the rival side of the court.

"Greetings! We welcome you, great K'uhul Ajaw of Calumook! We welcome you with our salutations as your humble hosting competitor!" they called back.

They bandied such jovial calls several more times in the prescribed manner until the puppet king of Cenote swept onto the playing alley. Like my father, he was clad in striking ballgame finery. He strode to my father and stood before him, and then announced, in the requisite formal manner and at full volume: "In honor of your visit, my lord, I present this humble token of our humble city."

Clasping a tall, narrow, cylindrical vase, he proffered it to my father. Painted with skill in orange and white and deep red, its polished surface revealed many superb, well-proportioned glyph panels framing lively action scenes. My father accepted the ceremonial gift vase with a grand show of humility, admiring it for a moment and then raising it aloft for all to see. It depicted my father as a champion ball player in the full vigor of youth, swathed in royal sporting regalia. Cenote's master vessel painter had captured him in full action, sliding daringly on his knee just moments before striking the ball. Our puppet king, appropriately the diminutive painted figure, did little but stand in awe of my father. Bowing to our Cenote puppet, my father said, "My deepest appreciation for your gracious hospitality, and for this splendid gift." Then he raised it even higher into the air, this time to loud and raucous cheers.

My mother seemed anxious that day. She was quieter than usual, and several times her fingers crept to her many ornaments, ensuring they were properly positioned. An odd tension creased her brow, and I noticed her eyes dart furtively around more than was typical. These observations I likely arrived at only later, in retrospect, as I puzzled back through all the deceit she must have wrought prior to that Cenote ball game.

The spectators crowding the official elevated tiers were royalty and nobles of assorted rank, men and women who had arrived in their own ballgame finery, borne also upon wooden litters from city villas or nearby towns. All wore much jade, which they had chosen with heightened prudence that day by calculating the proscriptions applying to their own ornamentation relative to the grandeur of my father's. True, they always did this, for even if they happened to possess more or better jade, no one was permitted to openly outshine the K'uhul Ajaw of Calumook. But on this particular day they had selected their ornamentation with especial prudence because ball games always entailed ferocious gambling.

"I wager one jade ear spool that no player falls!" cried a noble.

"I wager three arm-long strands of jade beads and the fine-spun on my back that there will be two falls on the Cenote team!" cried another noble from Calumook.

"I wager that a Calumook player will hit the central marker with an elbow thrust in the first round!" taunted another. "If he does, I shall claim one jade ornament from each person present!"

The crowd sneered. "And if he does not?"

"If he does not, I shall give away every jade ornament on my person!"

And so it went, back and forth, each wager duly recorded on bark paper codices, one kept by Cenote's official scribe and the other by Calumook's.

My father made more bets than anyone else, for he loved this game dearly. Because he wore more jade than anyone else, he had more to bet. My mother did not seek to hinder his extravagant wagering, which I later realized was an additional sign that something was amiss.

I was also enjoying myself that fine day. The sun was warm but not too hot, and a light breeze freshened the air. I was beginning to feel confident in my new position as Lady Winik. Best of all, a sprinkling of rain had fallen just yesterday afternoon, offering hope that Chaak had begun to respond to my father's supplications. At long last, following much pounding of hollow slit log drums and blaring of wooden trumpets, the competing teams paraded onto the court. My enjoyment was soon to end: moments thereafter I would feel as if a sharp spike had been thrust into my chest.

Each team had four players in uniforms that bore the colored insignia of their respective cities. The two teams emerged from opposite ends of the court, moving swiftly in rhythm with the pounding drums. As the players marched before the tiered benches the crowd leapt to its feet, and from it surged a tremendous roar. The fans pumped their fists and cried out the chants of Cenote and of Calumook, waving the pennants of their cities as the antagonism of rivalry flushed their faces.

The players were heavily painted, and thick leather protectors shielded their torsos, knees, and elbows. Each player also wore a tightly fastened feather headdress low across his forehead. Despite these trappings, I could not have mistaken the person of Naah Chan for any other player. When I recognized him my hand flew to my mouth, and a sudden cry escaped my lips. My father was wholly engaged in bellowing the Calumook team-song with fast-rising enthusiasm and did not notice my cry. But my baby cousin heard it and swiveled his tiny, wobbly head to peer at me. My mother most certainly noticed it, for a sly smile crept onto the only part of her face I could see: the very corner of her mouth. It was then that I began to realize the extent of her deviousness.

Of course Naah Chan was a ball player, and a fine one. Most men played ball back then, though very few played in formal settings. Rather, they played on the simple dirt ball courts that most commoner neighborhoods built for their own recreation and amusement. Very few participated in contests between cities—supernaturally charged competitions in which the players acquired creation-era personas, and in which much was at stake. Players in lofty ceremonial settings such as these were hand-selected from an elite cadre of royal or noble youth, to be trained and expertly hardened by demanding palace coaches. Naah Chan unquestionably was not among this cadre. Yes, he was an athlete in his prime who regularly vanquished his rivals on the simple recreational courts of Calumook, but so vast was the gap between us that he could never have played on the rarefied Cenote court where the earthly reenactment of the sacred struggle of good and evil was staged.

Silent tears began to trickle down my cheeks.

Around and around the court they strode, each player's feet pounding the central playing alley in rhythm with the loud beating of the hollow slit log drums. From time to time a player raised an occasional arrogant fist into the air or crouched low, mimicking the stealth of a night-stalking otherworldly jaguar on the prowl. Naah Chan did not search me out within the crowd as he marched past, although he must have known I would be present and seated somewhere near my father. Why did he not seek me out? I think he did not want to jeopardize my position with even the merest glance. Every spectator scrutinized each player's face, probing for signs of weakness or knowledge of their fate. I think Naah Chan also knew that surviving the ordeal that lay ahead would require more strength, more concentration, more strategy than he had ever devoted to his play. He did not need the added emotional burden of the horrified expression that undoubtedly was openly showing on my face, a face now streaming with tears. I was fortunate that everyone around me gazed only forward, so that no one observed my disgrace.

Even as tears streaked my cheeks, I knew it was disgraceful of me to publicly reveal such raw emotion.

As I wept, I was careful to keep my person motionless. I refrained from shifting my gaze toward the far end of the court, toward its open northern end, toward that dark watery cleft in the earth. In that cenote, the corpses of the vanquished would be thrown into the joyous embrace of the Lords of Xibalba—the Lords of Death. I also refrained from looking at the carved and painted motifs that ran along the sides of the playing court, illustrating the spectacular decapitation of the vanquished, even though only moments earlier I had observed those motifs with no particular emotion. I squeezed my eyes shut to keep from foreseeing such a fate for Naah Chan, but it was as if those images pursued me, as if the torrents of blood from those severed heads threatened to drench my person, as if the sprouting vines were slithering over the skin of my neck to strangle me. I had never considered our practice of sacrificing the losing team to be wrong, but then again, I had never before been in love with a player who might himself be one of the vanquished.

Yes! Death was necessary for rebirth, for the resurrection of the Maize God. Yes! The celestial forces of good and evil must always struggle. Yes! There must be sacrifice so the fiery orb of K'inich Ajaw could remain in motion through the sky. It was blood that sustained the gods, the gods that made us, and that cause maize to sprout from deep in the watery cleft in the earth. We feed the gods so that they will feed us. I knew all of this, accepted all of this, but every last fiber of my being rejected any notion that it should be the sacrifice of Naah Chan that preserved our ancient pact with the gods and kept our world intact. Yet, as if to counter my own will, I could no longer keep from peering with horror and trepidation toward the court's northern end. As I beheld its distant, hovering cenote gloom, my heart beat with such ferocity I felt as if my chest would rupture, flinging all my rosy, ripe viscera like carrion to the vultures. In that instant I despised my wicked mother with a passion far greater than I could ever have imagined.

As highest ranking male and a former champion player, my father raised the hard rubber ball high above his kingly head and held it there dramatically clasped within his mighty royal hands. He chanted for many long moments as priests roved about him with their small clay bowls of smoking copal. And then my father hurled the ball down against the plaster of center court.

That loud slap of hard rubber on plaster resonated throughout that deep cleft in the earth. There, at the dark watery entrance to the underworld, the Lords of Xibalba pricked up their ears.

The sound reminded them anew of Hun-Hunahpu, father of the Hero Twins. It was he and his brother Seven Hunter who were the first ball players, back in the primordial mists of creation-time. It was he, Hun-Hunahpu, and his brother Seven Hunter who accepted that first invitation sent by the Lords of the Underworld.

Come play ball with us!

Thus Hun-Hunahpu and his brother Seven Hunter had journeyed through the cleft to Xibalba to play ball with the Lords of Death. And it was Hun-Hunahpu and his brother Seven Hunter who lost the game, because that time evil triumphed over good.

They were sacrificed by the Lords of Death, and the decapitated head of Hun-Hunahpu was hung in a tree like a gourd. Hanging in a tree, the gourd-head of Hun-Hunahpu then spit in the palm of Little One, a daughter of Xibalba, impregnating her. Little One, her belly large and round, journeyed through the earth cleft and up to this world, where she gave birth to the twins Hunter and Jaguar Deer. Little One and their grandmother hid the ball-game equipment of the twins' father and uncle, so that they might never be summoned to die in Xibalba. But the twins discovered it concealed amidst the dusty roof thatch of their hut, took it out, and began to play ball. It was then that the Lords of Xibalba again heard the loud slap of hard rubber on plaster and pricked up their ears.

Come play ball with us!

The twins, too, answered the invitation from the Lords of Death and journeyed through the earthen cleft. Once below, they underwent many terrible ordeals: a River of Blood, a House of Darkness, a House of Knives, a House of Cold, a House of Jaguars, a House of Bats. But the twins survived. They survived these trials in order to play ball, like their father and uncle, against the Lords of Xibalba. But this time, finally, after desperate struggles, the forces of good prevailed over those of evil, and it was the Lords of Night who were vanquished. Yet the victorious Hero Twins—our generous, beloved heroes, Hunter and Jaguar Deer—chose to sacrifice their own persons. They gave their lives for us. They jumped into the blazing flames for us—for us! And having jumped into the raging fire, they were resurrected and rose high into the glittering heavens to become Venus and the Sun. The decapitated head of their father, Hun-Hunahpu, still hanging in a tree like a gourd, was also resurrected and became the Maize God, the god who gives us sustenance. We eat, thanks to his generous sacrifice in that very first ball game in Xibalba.

Our team grabbed control of the ball. Our player used his chest to spin and fling the ball to our second player, and then Naah Chan got it and used his elbow to drive the ball downcourt into Cenote territory—a particularly skillful move that stirred me with a sudden flash of pride—before the ball was intercepted by a Cenote player who bounced it back past the center marker and into our territory again. Then a quick, sudden knee slide by Calu-mook regained the ball and bounced it back down court, whereupon Cenote sped in and on bent knee sent it toward the other end. It went like that for hours, it seemed, back and forth, down and up, one player twisting and jumping to propel the ball from his rival's reach with an elbow thrust, another player sliding on his knee to send the ball to another player, who used his hip. All the while my father, bellowing and bellowing, was oblivious to the distress his daughter was suffering behind him. All the while my anxious mother followed the play, her eyes narrowed to slits. The tension of it all was too much for my little cousin, as he began to fuss after all. I fled my seat in relief, for I too could bear no more.

Once I cleared the spectator tiers I ran with my baby cousin toward the far end of the court—the southern end that faced away from that shadowy hollow and its deep watery chasm. I shoved my way through the throng of commoners that stood, jostling and straining, to watch the competition. I wove past the drunks who had again over-imbibed our free-flowing balché, a fermented tree bark drink brewed for this important ceremonial occasion. Those not stumbling around were on their knees, heads hanging, retching vilely. Some lay motionless, splayed upon the ground in their stupor, damp gourd cups still clasped in drunken hands. As I fled, I chanted. I chanted to Ixchel, patron goddess of the moon, to safeguard the life of my beloved Naah Chan. I chanted as well for all the faith and courage that could be mustered from within the colored wings of my Scarlet Macaw companion spirit.

When at last I found a quiet nook behind the ball court, I soothed my little cousin. Soon his eyelids began to droop. I tucked his head beneath my chin, and his tiny person collapsed in peaceful slumber against my chest. I sat with my back against the wall of the outer court. It was still warm from the day. With my eyes closed, I followed the course of the game. I experienced each cheering crescendo as a tightening fist within my gut as players from one team and then the other made good moves or bad. Through it all, the crowd bellowed.

"Calumook!" they bellowed.

"Cenote!" they bellowed.

I cringed each time I heard the loud slap of hard rubber against plaster, wondering whether this time it would be the forces of good or those of evil that prevailed in the world. I heard the thud of hard rubber against leather torso protectors. I heard the bellowing and more bellowing, and the pounding of the hollow slit log drums never seemed to cease.

Despite the turmoil that raged all about, or perhaps because of it, I slept. It was a timeless, dreamless sleep that did not provide respite. I awoke from that hazy place when my little cousin squirmed against my chest, a sign of life I took as hopeful. The pounding of the drums had ceased. Like a madwoman, I dashed to where I could survey the playing court and the four decapitated bodies that lay sprawled on the bloody ground amidst the eerie dancing glow of torchlight at the northern end of the ball court. Naah Chan was not among them.

◎◎◎

The Lalchich raid came some days after the ballgame. We were still in Cenote, resting after all the excitement, still recounting the exhilarating highlights of the game, still recuperating beneath the shade of awnings. The raid was wholly unexpected. None of our spies had reported the approach of friend or foe. Usually we might be able to glean some sense, however vague, of impending danger, but as my father had become fond of saying, the concept of normalcy was growing more elusive lately.

We killed or captured the invading warriors with ease. Still, my father was furious at their treachery. "The Lalchich are fools!" he roared, his fine humor from our victory in the ballgame now extinguished.

"They are fools!" echoed our Cenote puppet.

"Like cowards they strike us here, at this pitiful defenseless town," my father continued. "They are too weak-willed to risk a direct attack on our great city!"

"How could they imagine they could prevail?" our Cenote host said indignantly, choosing to ignore my father's slight.

"This new king of Lalchich does not know his place," my father muttered, incensed. "I see they have left me no recourse but to teach them another lesson in loyalty. They must be forced to learn the meaning of respect. I shall go against them in ax battle once more. I shall return with a long ropeful of captives! Then I will save them for the dedication spectacle of my new Chaak temple. Until it is ready, I will torture them all every day until they beg for mercy! They will suffer for their insolence."

The palace at Cenote was elegant, but it was also quite small, so despite our deliberate attempts to keep our distance from my father's rage, we could not but overhear his irate words and heated vows of retribution.

I certainly heard them. And as I listened I grew more anxious—for my father, but also for the future, however dimly I perceived it; and yes, also in regard to the matter of my marriage. All I knew from the loud, bitter tone of my father's voice was that he was enraged at the treacherous Lalchich, who had dared turn on him, the "slovenly ingrate upstarts"—words that echoed through the walls of the Cenote palace. Again! So soon! And so cravenly, after he had made such a generous overture to them, extending a genuinely open, loving hand of reconciliation by offering his youngest daughter! I admit, I was confused by the part about offering his youngest daughter. Was it even possible he was still unaware of how my mother had behaved toward their young queen? Did he not realize it had been his own principal wife who, of her own accord, had in essence ended the prospect of my marriage into the royal lineage of Lalchich? Did my father not know this? I had simply assumed that the prospect of my marriage to Lalchich was no longer an option. Had I been mistaken? Even in my confusion, I was deeply relieved to learn that he considered my role essential.

Again my father thundered, "How could they fail to recognize how I have honored them by even considering giving them my daughter! Sharing with them our esteemed Waterlily blood and heritage? A dynasty of thirty-three generations! Thirty-three generations!"

"Ingrates!" boomed the Cenote lord.

"The upstarts!" my father railed. Even through walls of stone and plaster, I could sense his contempt.

"And they dare create their own emblem glyph!" spat the lord.

The usage of such special glyphs was carefully controlled—extremely so. At least, it had been. This man, our Cenote host, was of course obliged to use our Waterlily emblem glyph, as were all our puppets. Only fully separate dynasties had the right to create separate emblem glyphs. As a conquered vassal, Lalchich was also required to use our Waterlily emblem. That they had created their own did not bode well for our renewed reunion.

Lalchich's new emblem glyph was only the most recent in a series of problems troubling my father. Calumook spies had informed him of the existence of the new glyph soon after the return of my nuptial entourage. Possibly my mother's rebuke had something to do with its creation, but my father seemed unaware of this. In the accounts we heard of what was afoot in Lalchich, the stelae carvers of that eastern lowland city had begun chiseling their despicable new emblem—some stupid leaf symbol or another—on every stone surface about the place. Whenever my father spoke of it, he ended up shouting: "How dare they provoke me like this?"

Listening through the walls, I was distressed that our Cenote puppet had chosen to remind my father of this emblem glyph situation. It was like poking a jaguar with a stick. By now I had endured enough council meetings to see that this Cenote puppet was trying to ingratiate himself with my father, to demonstrate that his loyalty surpassed that of all others. Why would he grovel so? One conceivable reason was a wish to increase his quota of tribute redistribution. Perhaps he wanted also to acquire some new jade ornaments. Our Cenote host surely knew—as did everyone, for it had been announced from the palace pinnacle—that Quetzaltun was a contender in the matter of my marriage, and he surely must also have known—again, like everyone—that Quetzaltun controlled a rich source of jade. Our puppet could have ingratiated himself with my father for any number of reasons. Back then, there was bribery and blackmail, feign and feint. There was treachery from within and treachery from without. Even then, my heart still went out to my father above all, at perplexing moments such as these.

Our spies also brought reports that the Lalchich stelae carvers had been busy chiseling in other ways, so that the appearance of many of the new stelae defied tradition. Rather than depicting the divine royal genealogies that upstarts did not have, their stelae boasted imagery of great triumphs in war—something they did have, and were having more and more. They even chiseled long, ornamental nose bars on their royal figures, following a new artistic trend from the north. Further, the square frames of certain day-sign glyphs were a new style adopted from the north, rather than the perfect, time-honored oval of our lowlands.

"These northern styles are unwelcome here," my father had responded to this news. "They are tawdry. Our artistic traditions are grander, older, vastly superior. Those northerners should be emulating us, not us emulating them."

I also learned something new through the walls of that Cenote palace: my father meant to combine the sacrifice spectacle of the captured Lalchich raiders with the coronation ceremony of a new puppet at Cenote. You see, the ball game pitting Calumook against Cenote had been but one small event in a larger assortment of official state amusements. The coronation was the real reason we had come.

We needed a new puppet at Cenote because my father intended to install our current puppet on the throne of one of his distant vassal towns, whose weak king had been unable to quell an uprising in his region. We had even heard about a peasant rabble managing to advance to the very throne—the literal seat of power—and vandalize it, smashing it to pieces.

How that thorny situation too had vexed my father of late, prompting the emergence of another of his litanies: "As if I don't have enough on my platter here at Calumook, I have to worry about protecting the thrones of my vassals! Why can't they deal with their own problems?"

"You must command them to," was my mother's response to this particular litany. "One. You must allow just one of them to fall. Then the others will understand."

◎◎◎

Three bound captives—naked, bruised, and beaten, lips flayed— were dragged before us. We stood on the main landing before the main temple of Cenote, which made up a wing of the palace. Behind us loomed the temple doorway, a sculpted gaping orifice with fierce painted fangs. This was a divine maw ready to receive sacred human flesh. Flesh born of maize dough, to be transformed back into maize dough. Sustenance for the gods. For the gods that made us.

As the true ruler of Cenote, the K'uhul Ajaw of Calumook stood at the very center of the maw of this massive otherworldly fanged creature, this entrance to the underworld. My father's feet were wide apart and his legs strong. His antagonistic stance showed he did not fear the Lords of Death. It was he, the K'uhul Ajaw of Calumook, who kept our world in order. It was he, the

K'uhul Ajaw of Calumook, whose ritually scattered blood also fed the gods. To his side stood our Cenote puppet—the current one, as the new one had not yet been coronated. The rest of us, including the full court of Cenote as well as the royal and noble members of our Calumook entourage, perhaps some fifty in all, stood to the rear.

The assistants who led the Lalchich captives before the K'uhul Ajaw knew their task. The lowest ranking captive was hauled forward and forced to kneel facing that fierce painted maw. Incense burners behind the doorway produced black copal smoke that poured from between the rows of hungry fangs. The assistants paused, looking to my father. The K'uhul Ajaw of Calumook stabbed his arm skyward.

"Begin!" he roared.

And they began.

With a stinging switch, they whipped his back until blood coursed down his skin. The captive winced but did not cry out. The crowd jeered. They tied his hands to a wooden log and extracted each fingernail one by one as blood pooled at the base of the wooden log. The captive cried out. The crowd jeered. With a club they inflicted brutal blows upon his person; I heard the muffled cracks of ribs and bone. The captive cried out. The crowd jeered.

"Behold the despicable animals of Lalchich!" my father taunted.

And the crowd—which had followed each whip of the stinging switch, each drawing out of a fingernail, each thud of the brutal club—again jeered the now barely-conscious captive. An assistant threw a gourd of cold water in his face, and he revived enough to scream in agony.

"Ha! He cries!" my father bellowed. He was pleased. "The warriors of Calumook would never cry out like women," my father boasted. "Their flesh has been hardened to stone!"

He said this last word—stone—in glee. He said it also in angry mockery of all three of the naked, humiliated, brave, flayed-lip captives, one near death before us in front of those fierce painted fangs. I could not see my father's eyes—he never took them off the bloody writhing sight before him—but I could sense his mounting frenzy. He was drinking deep of his revenge. Within him seemed to roil a viciousness I had never before witnessed, and with each horrendous scream of agony, I became ever more aware—ever more fearful—of my father's capacity for cruelty, which showed little sign of abating.

I too was angry at the Lalchich.

I might have married into their royal family. I would have been a loyal and devoted patron of their fair city, would have loved and cherished their people as my own. I would have woven and worn their cochineal red with affection and pride. Yet despite the generosity we showed to them, they returned our kindness with a raid? They were the ones at fault. Damage caused by my mother's rebuke could have been mended, I was certain. They had been too hasty, much too hasty, to turn against us in this fashion. Their treachery was a personal insult to my father, to myself, to all our long line of Waterlily ancestors ... an insult to all the virtuous and honorable people of Calumook! It could not go unanswered.

"Death to the people of Lalchich!" someone behind me shouted.

"Death to the upstarts!" someone beside me yelled.

"Death to the traitors!"

My father wanted the same, I was sure, because upon his gesture to the assistants, they dragged the captive up and into that fierce fanged maw. Once there, they forced him to his knees, although in truth the man was by then so spent that in reality he collapsed without a struggle. As an assistant held him in position, my father towered above, his stance still wide, still antagonistic. His flushed, manic face shifted agitatedly between the captive at his knees and the angry, jeering crowd.

I do not recall whether my father had held the obsidian dagger all along or only picked it up a moment ago, but now he raised the glinting, glistening, perfectly chipped black blade high over the treacherous captive from Lalchich. Mesmerized, I could not look away from either the glint or the glisten. I thought of the young Lalchich king thrust too early onto the throne, who had miscalculated so terribly by attempting such a raid. Youths are always so eager to earn a stanza in their patriline chant or have a victory stela carved in their honor that too often they are willing to take risks they should not.

As if in a trance, chanting in a resonant drone, my father touched the tip of his glistening black blade to the tender hollow on his panting victim's neck, into which it soon would plunge.

Copal smoke billowing, my father, the great K'uhul Ajaw of Calumook, called to the sky, "In the name of the Maize God, for your generous sacrifice, I offer this blood—the water of creation! I offer you this head, like the gift of Hun-Hunahpu that hung like a gourd from a Xibalba tree! Here, for you, is your gourd-head! Here, for you, is your maize dough! I offer you this precious ear! This I gift I give to you! For your divine sustenance!"

"For the bounty of the milpa!" someone behind me yelled.

"For the bounty of the milpa!" someone yelled beside me.

Still I stared in awe at the glint and the glisten of that black dagger. My memory leapt back to the day I had stood in that dusty rural milpa with my father. The tragedy of those puny withering ears. The hard dryness of the dirt around me. The tiny kernels of delicate maize, struggling with thirst deep within their parched, browning husks. We were formed of maize dough. The gods formed us. Maize was our sustenance, our life! We must give ourselves as maize dough back to the gods. Thus I too shouted out: "For the bounty of the milpa!"

And with a renewed beating of the hollow slit log drums, the K'uhul Ajaw of Calumook lifted that black glistening blade and plunged it deep into the maize-flesh of the captive's neck. My father twisted the dagger and pulled it toward him with one strong motion, and the sacred gourd-head fell free of its earthly tether. There stood my father, clutching that dripping gourd-head by its despicable Lalchich hair in one hand and his dripping red-black dagger in the other.

The crowd was roaring. Chanting priests circled with their bowls of billowing copal. My father stepped to the edge of that divine maw and fed those hungry fangs, smearing them with the rich red liquid of creation. Then my father tied this bloody thing to his belt, and there it hung by its own disheveled hair, among his many jade dangles. They clanged, jade against jade, jade against gourd-head, jade against sacred maize dough flesh, as without haste my father leapt and swirled, sang and danced the sacred dance of sacrifice.

We knew the Maize God heard that clanging. We knew he hearkened to those heavy wet thuds, took pleasure in the lilt of my father's praise-song of remembrance, his prayer-song of gratitude. He, the resurrected Hun-Hunahpu, flared his nostrils at the aroma of our sweet copal. He, the resurrected Hun-Hunahpu, tasted the taste of the sacred red liquid of creation. He knew we were grateful. He knew we recognized his precious heartfelt sacrifice, his generous, willing head hung in a tree like a gourd. Of the spittle he spat into the palm of Little One. We were fulfilling our sacred debt. From our acts in the Cenote temple maw, the Maize God knew we loved him.

5

My father brooded after our return from Cenote. For almost an entire month he did not appear even once in our courtyard, and I missed his presence. I ached for those times—they seemed so long ago—that he had teased and tussled with us, though of course I had long since grown far too old to romp about with my father like that.

But one morning he came to rescue me from what was becoming boredom and tedious confinement in our back palace courtyard. "Stride with me, Daughter," he said. "I desire your company."

With my little cousin straddling my hip, I walked beside him with constrained delight but also with a certain trepidation because, you see, I remembered all that had transpired in that Cenote maw. But now my father had ceased to be that frenzied and frightening man with the obsidian dagger; he was simply my father, and for that I was grateful.

We strode in silence for a while, and then he asked, "Daughter, how do you fare?"

"I fare well, my lord."

"Good, good," he mumbled, and we continued along in silence a while longer. There was only one direction we were likely to head in—that of his new Chaak temple, to monitor the progress.

While it may seem odd, but my father seldom inquired how I fared. I believe he truly did wish to know how I fared, and wished that I fare always well, but his world was so demanding and complicated compared to mine that it was not uncommon that he forgot to inquire. Thus I was pleased that day when he did.

"And what is your estimation in regard to He of Flint, second prince of Quetzaltun?"

My father's question was so abrupt and unexpected that I was uncertain how to respond. He had never queried me on the matter of my marriage before. Of course my mother had never asked my opinion on anything of the sort either, but that was not surprising.

My silence must have seemed long. Again my father spoke: "Does he please you, Daughter?"

"He of Flint is most kind, my lord."

"Most kind," my father repeated, and I knew by his tone that he was unconvinced by my choice of phrase.

"Indeed, he is quite kind," I said, and because I was unable to muster any commentary beyond such an inanity, I felt rather dim-witted and embarrassed in front of my father. Frustrated by my own self, I hardly knew what else to say, because what I had said was in fact my estimation of the man. I recalled our exciting banging of rocks against those jade-streaked boulders in that high ravine, and the man's smile when I experienced the delightful rebound for myself. His melodious voice—without question I remembered that. And a certain fleeting fondness, a certain jealousy, yes, I remember that as well, but never would I speak of such things to my father.

"He is clever," I said at last. "And quite amusing," I added, wishing I had not, as I realized how ridiculous this last comment must seem. I believe my father had not experienced amusement in so long that even the notion of it had grown foreign to him.

"Your mother wishes you to marry the second prince," my father said, his tone even.

Of course I had known for some time that this was my mother's wish, as the brilliant gleam Quetzaltun jade brought to her eye was unmistakable. Since our return from Cenote after Lalchich had reestablished itself as our bitter enemy with its ill-conceived raid, I had surmised that my marriage to that highland city was now very nearly certain. But by then I had also learned how difficult it is to predict what might be decided when men sit cross-legged on woven mats in high palace chambers.

"Yes, my lord, I do know that is her wish."

"Do you care for that highland place?"

"It is quite cold there," I confessed, knowing my father also disliked the cold. We were similar in that way, he and I.

"Indeed, it is cold there," he agreed. I thought I detected a shiver move through his person.

"Their palace is of wood."

"Yes, Daughter, it is of wood."

We continued striding in silence for some time, and I shifted my little cousin to my other hip. Now he was on the side closest to my father, who reached out to ruffle his hair, upon which the infant swiveled his head around and grinned at my father. My father grinned back. He gave a chubby little cheek a squeeze and uttered a few nonsensical words. Then he rubbed my cousin's nose with his own, and all three of us tossed back our heads and laughed. We laughed because this day was bright and this tiny child so delightful, and I laughed because the frenzied king had left my father and I was at my father's side. I do not recall a more pleasant moment than that morning when the three of us strode our sacbe and laughed.

Still in that jovial mood, we arrived at the site where my father's new Chaak temple continued its steady rise. As I've said, new temples were rarely truly new. My father's temple was new only in the sense that a bigger, more grandiose skin was being wrapped around a smaller, older temple. Of course ancestral accomplishment must always be respected, but it was also true that people still tended to speak of such constructions as if they were new. In fact, it was my great-great-great grandfather who had built the temple now being wrapped. His temple was said to house an even smaller, earlier one that had likewise been wrapped with a new skin. The smallest temple was reputed to be the very one built at the founding of Calumook by our ancestral lineage head of the House of the Waterlily. Our original ancestor bundles had been laid inside its sanctuary, and the font of our Waterlily power and divine favor dwelt in its stones and mortar. This earliest buried temple was infused with the essence of the holy mountain where our first ancestor-shaman scattered his blood to the Maize God. Our dynasty spanned thirty-three generations. The continuity of our Waterlily heritage now accrued to my father, and its burden rested upon his shoulders.

Together, my father and I stood observing anew the flurry and bustle of construction. I had not visited this spot for some time, and clearly much progress had been made.

"Daughter, regard the summit … a mere forty courses of stone are lacking," he said, not looking at me but gazing instead toward the top of his rising temple. His voice had a dreamy quality. He did not speak again for some time, and I supposed he was again envisioning its grand dedication spectacle.

It would take place on 10.0.0.0.0. It would be there, precisely there upon that lofty summit that he would stand, legs wide and commanding. He would be dazzling in his heavy jade regalia, his leather high-backed sandals, his tall quetzal streamer headdress, his Manikin Scepter clasped before his strong, tattooed chest. He would appear ethereal up there amidst the billowing copal. The mighty ocean conchs would roar, and the mighty pounding of the hollow slit log drums would resound about him. That moment, atop his finished temple, would be the fulfillment of everything our ancestors had expected of him.

I was imagining his grand moment with him. I would be beside him on that lofty summit. "Yes, only forty courses still lacking," I said, nodding my head in agreement with his calculations, even though I had no means of judging.

I did know, however, that our spies had only just brought home some distressing intelligence. It concerned recent events at Becilna, the city of our close and longtime ally. It seemed the Becilna king had decided that he too would build a grand new temple. Not only had the quarrying already commenced, we learned, but he had managed to wrest a very large supply of cut stone from his lineage heads. If the lineage heads of Becilna were anything like those of Calumook, which I suspected they were, then procuring this stone was a significant feat.

As we had long known, the honorable, emblemed dynasty of Becilna had a strong king. In their youth, that king and my father had been teammates—ball players on the same elite squad. The two young men had developed an exceptionally close camaraderie because each was so adept at anticipating the moves of the other. As a pair they had been all but unstoppable, leaping and sliding, turning and twisting, and bouncing that hard rubber ball to many resounding victories. I knew it saddened my father greatly that he and his erstwhile friend now seemed at odds.

But beyond his sorrow, what did this mean?

It meant we now faced the troubling prospect that the Becilna temple might be dedicated before ours. Our ally, the strong king of Becilna, might steal the thunder of my father's precisely timed spectacle. Might Becilna also have scheduled a grand 10 Baktun, 0 Katun, 0 Tun, 0 Uinal, 0 Kin dedication? Given the pace of its temple's construction, that date was not out of the question. If they were also planning a double spectacle, attendees would be at a premium. Guests would have to choose. Which city's spectacle would they opt for—Becilna's or Calumook's? What if they did not come to us? What if the Becilna temple was more impressive than ours? I wondered if our spies had managed to glimpse any of their construction plans—perhaps the creative strategy for their stucco panels, or the pattern envisioned for mosaic masks. Such documents were well guarded, so I suspected they had not.

My father, my cousin, and I stood on our sacbe surrounded by the flurry and bustle of wrapping a temple with new skin. As I watched this marvel unfold, I realized that such hubbub must have prevailed at this very place many times in our long and glorious past. A shiver ran down my spine: my earlier royal Waterlily ancestors must have stood exactly here—here—monitoring the labor of earlier leafcutter ants, their tumplines taut against sweating brows. I could not recall the number of generations in the Becilna dynasty. Members of their patriline would have likewise overseen great flurry and bustle along their sacbe, but I could not fathom any way in which their line could have been as long or as glorious as ours. That was impossible.

My father continued: "And after that, Daughter, we will mortar-in the mosaic stones, and soon after we will begin the molding of the stucco panel. Then the painting, of course—but that could go quite fast … if the pigments are prepared well in advance … and then the stelae must be ready … and then the feast …"

At that I turned to look at him and discovered he was no longer conversing with me, but speaking to himself—or to some vision or likeness of himself—as he gazed skyward toward the still-invisible summit of his glorious future, a future to match his glorious past.

At mention of his stelae my mind leapt to Naah Chan, whom I had not seen since that awful day when his head was so gravely endangered at the Cenote ball court. I tried to discern his person amidst all the flurry and bustle before my father's rising temple, but instead I caught sight, not unexpectedly, of my father's sajal. Again he was off to one side of the temple, conferring with a group of lineage heads.

I now knew these men—their names and their titles, their ancestral genealogies, their current associates and adversaries. They were the heads of the many noble lineages that together composed highborn Calumook. Their lineages—as well as the individuals within them—were all ranked relative to one another, and all well below our own Waterlily lineage. My father's sajal was responsible for supervising the delivery of tribute from each lineage each month. Specific counts of quarried and cut construction stone were a critical part of this tribute. It appeared that the king of Becilna had successfully exacted quantities of stone from his own lineage heads in excess of their agreed-upon tribute quota. Only a very strong king would make such a daring move.

I supposed our sajal's conference at the side of our rising temple concerned stone, particularly the status and timing of the delivery of what might well be those remaining forty courses.

Let me see ... hmm, yes, this month our accountants have recorded the conveyance of twenty cut stone blocks from you, my father's sajal was perhaps saying, consulting a sequence of bar and dot ciphers in his tabulation codex.

And from you, he might say, nodding politely but with undeniable authority at a different lineage head.

As well as from you, he could indicate with a nod to yet another. *We are appreciative of your promptness.*

From you, however ... hmm, let me double check. Yes, my tally reveals your delivery is short by ten blocks. I can assure you that our accountants do not make errors in their reckoning. After saying this, I imagined, my father's sajal would stare at the delinquent lineage head, his sour face blank although its stony edges brimmed with deliberate and threatening condescension.

It was all about labor and stone. That was how all the truly impressive buildings rose back then: labor and stone. Today this art is all but lost. No one builds great buildings. No one can meet the maize requirements of feeding the long lines of leafcutter ants needed to quarry and haul. Carvers no longer carve like that or mold stucco like that. Back then, though, buildings rose from the bright tap-tap of hundreds of chisels clutched in tight fists, and a multitude of tumplines taut against sweating brows. All this was kept in motion by kinship obligations and tribute quotas, all overseen by the lineage heads. The duration of the sweating depended on lineage rank; the current building needs of my father and the lineage heads; and the strength of their love for my father, and of his for them in return. Yes, of course it was about quotas, but even more it was about love. Our lineage heads demonstrated their love for my father through generosity with the sweat of their leafcutter ants. In return my father demonstrated his love for them with gifts of jade and quetzal streamers and cacao beans.

That was why it was impossible to tell my father the truth. I could not confess that I found He of Flint, second prince of Quetzaltun, however melodious of voice and clever he may be, unappealing to the eye, and that the latter had become my strong and prevailing assessment. You see, I knew my father needed the jade trapped inside those boulders in that dusty highland ravine, and the mounds of quetzal streamers lying in that dark malodorous storehouse—not for himself, but as gifts to the lineage heads of Calumook. If he succeeded in keeping them content, then the bright tap-tap of chisels and the heave of tumplines would continue apace. And when all was over, my father would revel in the completion of his new Chaak temple as his grand vision of himself atop that lofty summit came to pass. Speed was now even more of essence, not just to meet the 10.0.0.0.0 Katun ending, but also to finish before the completion of the rival Becilna temple.

How could I tell my father that although I had briefly felt otherwise back in that dusty ravine, I now shrank from the thought of the second prince's hands roving over my person? Too much was at stake to reveal this truth.

Should I have sought to conceal my repulsion, agreed to marry Him of Flint for the sake of my father? Should I have surrendered my person in that way? Such are the questions I ponder even now. I still wonder whether everything might have turned out differently if, while striding our sacbe that fine day, I had lied and told my father I loved the second prince of Quetzaltun. Might that one, small, selfless act have been able to prevent all that followed? Could I have saved us?

◎◎◎

Soon thereafter I learned we would travel to Somalx. I was surprised when my mother told me of this, as because I had long supposed this far eastern seaport had been removed from consideration in the matter of my marriage. I imagined it my father had removed it on account of their K'uk'ulkan temple and their regard for that power from the north, which my father disdained and the king of Somalx adored. But as I've said, much can change when men sit cross-legged upon mats in high palace chambers.

I cannot be certain, but my hunch is that Somalx was again in play because by then my father's suspicions had been confirmed. Such was my mother's skill at misdirection that until then, he had remained unaware of my mother's discourteous comportment in Lalchich during our nuptial parley with its young queen.

Now he would also have realized that her behavior had played a role in the Lalchich raid on our Cenote puppet. Of course my father had known she favored Quetzaltun from the beginning. I knew my father to be by and large an agreeable man, but he was also prone to bad temper when someone—in this case, my greedy mother—pushed too far. In a fit of ire, he sent a dispatch to Quetzaltun informing the king that He of Flint was no longer under consideration in the matter of my marriage.

Thus we were to journey to Somalx. Indeed, our intended trip was announced with fanfare sufficient to lend the impression that this beloved and prosperous seaport had always and forever been our preferred partner in the matter of my marriage. Such were the strategies devised upon the woven reed mats. Back then I blamed my mother for all this, but in truth perhaps we were all becoming reckless.

◎◎◎

I knew we were nearing the coast when I caught the scent of salt hanging in the air. It swung against me without warning, just as a woven curtain strikes your face if you are careless entering a doorway. Soon I also heard the coast—the low rumble of the mighty ocean, a vast watery world I would come to know as immense and unfathomable. When at last I stood atop a steep, jagged cliff to behold its blue-green expanse with my own eyes, I wished never to stop gazing out upon its vastness. In truth, it was nothing short of breathtaking.

The complete royal court of Somalx turned out in their finery to receive our nuptial entourage. They lined the access route on both sides, with their commoners standing in several rows behind them. To reach their city we had to pass through guarded walls, entering by a small but thick wooden door. I knew that some cities had fortifications, but these were the first such defenses I had seen. As we crossed from outside to in, I wondered what it must be like to feel such immediate fear that one would ring one's entire city with tall stone. Once inside, however, I could not comprehend why they would bother ringing it at all, for despite the tales I had heard of this prosperous seaport, it seemed to contain very little wealth. Their palace was of stone but was a mere single story high, and flat and squat at that. Their temples were also very small, smaller even than those of Quetzaltun. As I had in that highland city, in Somalx I missed the true beauty of stone temples soaring skyward. Perhaps because I had observed the construction techniques at my father's rising Chaak temple, I noticed the strange crookedness of the Somalx temples, the poor masonry skills causing most courses to run askew, and the crude chisel-work on the stone itself. My overall impression of the city was that its buildings had been erected overnight, with little concern for their appearance.

Despite the underwhelming physical expression of Somalx, its denizens welcomed us lavishly.

Salutations! blared the long wooden trumpets. Salutations! thumped the hollow slit log drums. Salutations! chimed the turtle shell marimba. And after we had rested from our long journey for a night and a day, the entire royal court and the fine people of the seaport of Somalx fêted and fed us with enormous hospitality.

Fish, fish, fish. That was what they served us most: fish. They had so many different kinds. Some had skin that shimmered like bright rainbows; others had strange popping eyes sitting atop their flattened heads. Different sorts of hard-shelled creatures that fastened themselves to the black shore rocks, those we ate as well. Thrusting a sharp flint between the shells, the Somalx cooks would extract raw little gobbets that slid down our throats soon thereafter. Those were tasty, but the fish were absolutely delicious. Of course I had eaten fish many times, but only our river fish. These now seemed bland in comparison to sea fish. Somalx fishermen hauled them straight from the ocean and tossed them, still thrashing, onto glowing coals in braziers where they would sizzle for a moment—just long enough to allow a delightful aroma to waft toward my nostrils—and then appear right before me, steaming on a platter. The palace cooks were experts at flavoring and spiced much of their fare with a light dusting of ground dried chili. It was utterly delicious. Even if I had not taken a liking to the third brother of the king of Somalx, I might have wanted to marry into this place for the sake of the sea fish alone.

"Lady Winik," said the queen sister of Somalx during one repast, "would you care for another grilled fish?" Her smile as she asked this conveyed that she was genuinely pleased that I so enjoyed their cuisine.

"Oh no," I said, "I am so satisfied I could not eat another." This is what one is supposed to say in response to such an inquiry.

"I am delighted you appreciate our cookery," she said.

"Oh, it is very tasty."

"Please, do have another!"

"Oh, I couldn't."

"I don't believe you've yet tried our two-eyes-on-top-of-head fish. Perhaps you might like to taste it?"

"Oh, another time, perhaps. Really, I am simply bursting."

"It is so fresh just now!"

"Well ..."

This is the protocol, you see: you must refuse three times.

"Fish servant!" the queen sister called, and soon another steaming fish lay before me. This time two strange eyes stared up at me from my platter.

My mother ate as much as I did—possibly even more. It was hard to tell, as she was more adept at concealing her enthusiasm.

I suppose I should not exaggerate the prevalence of fish: we ate meats as well, such as grilled manatee, a strong, dark meat that was less to my liking. Many times I had seen these fat, bulbous creatures lolling about in the lagoon. I was surprised so many of them were still alive, as they were so easily harpooned. Occasionally we ate venison or tepezcuintle while at Somalx, but it seemed we ate these mostly as side dishes, or mixed with other ingredients to stretch the meat. Thinking back, I believe that as at Calumook, wild-hunted game was becoming scarce for everyone everywhere, even for the highborn. I guess the sea fish were more abundant, which was why we could devour as many as we pleased.

Much of their art—in particular, their bright wall murals and painted stucco sculptures—was in honor of Chak Way Xook, a fish god and the patron deity of fishermen. Yes, Calumook knew this god, but here at Somalx his stature was heightened. I could certainly appreciate that people sought his favor so that he would continue to provide delicious bounty from the vast watery depths. Here in this coastal city, it was the Chak Way Xook temple where they made their many offerings, hung their best woven banners, and burned copal in soot-black incense burners.

Somalx faced a beautiful lagoon. I walked its long white beach, watching its gentle lapping waves until my skin reddened because I had foolishly dismissed my shade servant. In amusement I watched tiny pale crabs scurrying sideways across the hard, wet sand. I chased them hither and thither but was never able to catch them. I gazed endlessly at the orange and purple starfish that clung to the sides of the shallow pools at the rocky headlands. I held a conch against my ear and listened to the sound of the sea. I collected colored shells until I held so many they fell from my hands. I stood in the white frothy waves and felt them surge against my knees. When they retreated, the rush of gurgling water grabbed the sand beneath my feet. It tickled, and I laughed.

One morning as I strolled along the far end of the lagoon, I caught the distant sound of human voices. I was walking the beach with a royal brother and sister whose company I enjoyed. Neither of them seemed interested in the voices, but I had not previously noticed the activity far at the back of the beach, so I turned to look. The voices came from men toiling on a long, high strip of land separating the beach from the low scrub of the coastal jungle. Alongside these men, enormous, impenetrable gray piles of gnarled driftwood twisted oddly aloft as a smoldering fire filled the air around them with black soot. Seeming to be Somalx leafcutter ants, oddly similar in nature to our own in Calumook, the men were bent over peculiar-looking ceramic pots set over the fire—peculiar because they looked, at least from a distance, like a long line of little creatures standing on tiptoe and holding hands. I had never seen such pots before. Nearby was a large white mound, so white the sun glared from it. I observed these laborers and their toil with only middling interest. I was undoubtedly curious about what they were doing, but the lagoon and the beach and the blue-green ocean beyond drew my attention like the constant tug of waves.

"What is in those pots?" I asked my companions.

"Saltwater," replied the sister.

"Saltwater? Why put saltwater in pots when there's plenty enough in the sea?" I asked, gesturing to the lagoon behind me, and the vastness beyond it.

"They are boiling it, my lady, so that the water vanishes, leaving only the salt behind," explained the brother.

"Ah," I said, losing curiosity, as salt was a dull thing.

The brother continued: "They pat it into cakes and wrap the cakes in leaves. These men are fed for their toil by our merchants, who then carry the many cakes to many places." As I watched them from a distance, I could now discern the outline of numerous stacks that must have been leaf-wrapped salt cakes. As I watched, I reflected that in this way, the ants of Somalx and those of Calumook were dissimilar, as ours were fed not by merchants but by our nobles. I also observed that Calumook had far fewer merchants than did Somalx.

Perhaps wanting to appear erudite as well, the sister asked, "Have you seen our sea canoes, my lady? They are so large that twenty-five men dip their paddles. That is how we trade salt cakes to so many places, and bring back other goods in exchange."

Of course I had seen their sea canoes. I had seen them bobbing out in the lagoon, tied with rough gray ropes to gray, sunbleached wharves. A visit to the wharves had been one of the first official outings for my mother and me. Their canoes were large indeed, and Somalx had many of them. Back then I did not fully comprehend the true importance of their fleet, or of their salt. I did not comprehend such things because our world had not yet fallen apart; thus the matter of my marriage still seemed vitally important. So did the wonderful adventure I was living, making many new and delightful discoveries on that far eastern coast.

I turned back toward the lagoon to gaze again at the vast blue-green ocean beyond. Again I giggled at the tickle of the gurgling sand beneath my feet as I waded far out into the lagoon. It was so wonderful to go without sandals! At home in Calumook, outside our courtyard, we were never to be seen without our sandals, but here even the king of Somalx went barefoot, except on formal occasions. Because he did, so did we.

I even submerged myself in the ocean, that vast endless expanse reaching all the way to the bending edge of the horizon. The waves tugged with such urgency, luring me deeper and deeper with each strong pull. Indeed, with one such tug I bent my knees and dipped my person all the way down into it. Unlike the people of Somalx, I did not know how to swim, so I was careful not to go out of my depth. The water splashed in my face and the salt stung my eyes, making me blink and blink. I even put my whole head under the surface, despite knowing my body servant would not be pleased.

It was all so extraordinary and new, and the coast and the palm trees and the constant cooling breeze and the sparkling, glinting blue-green ocean were all so beautiful, even if the walled city itself was not. And the delicious seafood, that too was new, as were the people of Somalx, who were different as well but not at all disagreeably so. I confess that these days at Somalx were the first time I had felt truly relaxed since my Ixchel Moon spectacle. It may seem strange because I was still so young, but only when I frolicked there on the coast did I realize that the strain of increasing royal obligation had in fact begun to weigh upon my person.

Why was I permitted such freedom at Somalx?

As at Quetzaltun, my mother chose to drink cool chocolate and discuss the matter of my marriage with the queen of Somalx without me present. I suppose she had wearied of me by then. Her failed attempt to behead Naah Chan at the ball game had likely caused her deep humiliation. Also, I suspect, her disagreement with my father on the matter of my prospective husband had upset the fragile nature of their relations. In any case, she spent as little time in my presence as possible, and I cannot say this disappointed me. In the highlands she had chosen to lock me up with that dull Quetzaltun noblewoman, but here at Somalx she did not impose such a companion on me. I was not about to question this unanticipated gift, and even now I don't know why she extended me such freedom. Since then, however, I have wondered whether she might have secretly hoped I would drown in that blue-green ocean. She knew it was dangerous, and she also knew I was drawn to it.

My mother nosed about this seaport city without shame. She inspected its wharves and even entered the temple to Ek' Chuaj, patron god of merchants. Much like the temple to Chak Way Xook, the patron of fishermen, it seemed only fitting that merchants have their own guardian too; clearly, many in this seaport gained their livelihood from trade.

My mother examined the Somalx storehouses as well. Unlike those of the cold highland city of Quetzaltun, they held not a single quetzal plume. Instead, they housed row after row of rough sacks brimming with loose salt, and clunky piles of spiny red oyster shells sorted according to size and color. I loved to watch the Somalx sea divers hold their breath and plunge deep to pry these red shells from the reef with strong flint knives. We had many such red spiny oyster shells at Calumook, and one day as I watched a diver surface, clasping one such large and lovely shell in his dripping hand, it occurred to me that because highborn everywhere exchanged so very many things—jade, quetzal plumes, cacao, salt, spiny red oyster shells—we relied on one another far more than we realized. I wonder, if we had known back then that the fall of one city would destroy our entire web, we would have comported ourselves any differently.

I suspect the rulers of Somalx did not realize their seaport was our final prospect in the matter of my marriage. If they had, I doubt they would have been as tolerant of my haughty mother, who behaved as though she held the upper hand when in reality she held nothing of the sort. As I've said, my mother gave me leave to do as I would, so I was free to frolic. I was doing just that, bobbing far out at sea in a canoe, when a squall approached as if out of nowhere.

As soon as my paddlers noticed the storm mounting in the distance, they gripped their wooden handles and pointed the bow of our canoe toward shore. I had commanded them to paddle me far out into the open ocean, where I was exhilarated by the slow rise and fall of the swell. For that reason they faced quite a long row back to safety.

Darkness devoured the horizon as the storm bore down upon us. The wind whipped the waves into a fury and white froth foamed along their ridges. The bright blue-green of the sparkling ocean had given way to menacing black. Salt spray shot from the churning water and stung my face, and I squeezed my trembling person as far into the bottom of that little wooden vessel as I could manage. With each strong stroke of the paddles I felt the lunge of our canoe. Even though sometimes I felt it slide sideways across the waves, we lunged mostly forward, slicing through the waves with the power of each stroke. Hard rain beat down on my person while frigid water sloshed about me in the bottom of the canoe. And as the storm rocked our vessel, heaving and rolling it across the fitful rising swells, I muttered prayer after prayer to Huracan, and also to the one-legged lightning god, Ah Peku, Coyopa, and Imix the Crocodile, and any other sky or weather deity that dwelt anywhere near this dangerous watery world. As these muttered petitions passed my lips, I found I missed my mother tremendously, although I'm doubtful she would have offered me much comfort, were she huddled with me at the bottom of this boat. She would be livid to discover the predicament I had gotten myself into.

I did not perish in that sudden squall. The moon goddess Ixchel was still quite young in the sky, still just commencing her gibbous phase as the erratic fledgling Rabbit waxed round and bold in her arms. I too was still young, so she did not call for me that stormy day. Though I cannot know, I believe it was Crocodile who answered my supplications and kept our canoe from plunging to the watery depths of that blue-green ocean.

Imix, the Crocodile, is my patron because I was born on his day. Ours is the opening day of the almanac. And as a creature of the aquatic world he is close with the water lily, so we are connected in two ways. On that first almanac day, when the gods wished to form the earth, they commanded Crocodile to rise from the watery depths. From deep below he swam, carrying up wet mud and muck to form the earth. Just like on that opening almanac day, Crocodile swam from deep below to the surface, and from there he sought our floundering canoe. He swam up to save me. Upon finding our canoe besieged by the wild frothy waves, he smacked his mighty tail down on the menacing water. He did this to let me know I could stop being so frightened because he had risen from the depths to come to my rescue.

Whack! went his rough tail. Whack! Although seeming to emanate from the Skyworld, those sounds from aloft were really just the echoes of the smack of his massive tail against the tense low clouds. Whack! the echo came again. It was Crocodile.

Then he dove back under the churning salty water and rose up beneath our canoe. I know this because I felt a sudden surge, followed by many other strong surges as I huddled on the bottom of the canoe. Those surges were Crocodile, nudging us with the rough skin of his rutted back. He did this many times. He was there, nudging us to shore and to safety. Because of him, our canoe did not go under. Because of him, I lived.

After being tossed about in that tempest, I found my fascination for saltwater adventure was satisfied. For the remainder of our stay in Somalx, I chose not to wander far from our chambers. I permitted my body servant to groom away the damage done by sand, salt, and sun, as well the emotional stir occasioned by my brush with a violent watery death. Once more I relished the feel of the carved comb as my body servant drew it through my long black hair, applying a rich and fragrant palm oil unguent to each strand, restoring its gloss. Though I appreciated this attention to my person, I felt oddly broken and retreated into a self-imposed docility.

After I had spent several days recovering, the third brother of the king came without warning to visit. I was surprised to hear his voice calling to me through the portal to my chamber.

We had already met, he and I, here in Somalx. Our first meeting was formal, much like the one where the entire seated court at Quetzaltun observed my official entrance into the royal audience chamber. Unlike at Quetzaltun, however, at our first meeting my prospective groom, the third brother, chose to speak with me for a long while.

He had asked, "Do you hold with the theory that it is the force of our great lunar orb which governs the tides?"

Failing to understand this question, I had responded with a polite smile and hollow verbal formalities.

"Oh, yes, of course. Living far inland you may not know what is meant by the word tide. Is that so?"

His question seemed harmless, and I agreed that I did not recognize the word.

"The tides," he explained, "happen where the ocean meets the land, which here is at the sandy beach."

"Ah, yes," I said.

"You have stood on the part of the sand, right next to the water, where it is hard and wet?"

"Yes, my lord, I have stood on that part."

"Then perhaps you have noticed that at times the water flows far inland, and other times it ebbs away, back toward the blue-green vastness. Then it flows toward land, then it ebbs away, and so on and again forever. That is what is meant by the tides."

"Ah, yes," I said. Up to then I would not have been able to describe this phenomenon, but now that he was speaking of it I knew I had indeed noticed it.

"One must stand still on that hard wet sand a long time to observe its effect," he said.

I nodded, making a polite sound that indicated I was listening.

"The passage of an entire day is ideal," he continued. "Do you believe it could be due to the pull of our goddess Ixchel, the great lunar orb that commands the tides?"

Along with the third brother, the entire court of Somalx had awaited my reply. Not knowing how to respond, I thought he might be was testing my intelligence. I decided I would test his as well. I may not have known anything about tides, but I did know about celestial matters, including even the fickle lunar orbital cycles.

After pausing long enough that those present might believe me flummoxed, I said, "Hmm ... let me consider. How predictable are the reach and the ebb?"

He paused before answering. "Quite predictable," he said. "Yes, they seem in point of fact very predictable, even though they are shifting as well."

"Hmm," I said again. "In what manner are they predictable? In what manner are they shifting? Do they associate with the daylight passage of K'inich Ajaw as he exits his earth cave and re-enters again in the west?"

"No, the tides do not associate with K'inich Ajaw."

"K'inich Kakmo? Do they follow the flight of the Solar Macaw?"

"No, they do not."

"Then they also do not shadow the trail of Ah Ciliz, the god of solar eclipses?"

"No, I do not believe they do," said the third brother.

"Then, yes," I reasoned, "it could be the great goddess Ixchel that commands them. Perhaps your astronomers might consider charting the maximum reach and the maximum ebb and comparing them with her cycles? You could bid them to pound even-notched wooden markers into the sand at even intervals perpendicular to the water. Then you would be able to measure the movement of the tides with the waxing and the waning of her bright orb. I think the results would be interesting as well as instructive to your inquiry."

◎◎◎

As I've said, the unexpected visit of the third brother following my ordeal at sea was unusual. Being surrounded by servants engaged in their customary tasks, we were not truly alone; nevertheless, his visit to my chamber was improper. Had my mother been present she would have flown into a rant, but she was not (and never did I tell her), and as long as my visitor stood far outside my portal, I decided to deem his visit proper enough.

"Are you well, Lady Winik?" he called, his voice full of concern.

I did not answer right away because of course I had not expected to hear this question, any question, from outside my portal, least of all coming from him. Then I called back, "Yes, I am well."

"Are you recovered?"

"Yes, well recovered," I called back. Then I said, "thank you for your kindness."

This brief exchange now over, I supposed he would depart. Coming to inquire as to my condition could merely have been a proper expression of hospitality. But he did not depart.

"I was very distressed to hear the news," he said. "I made certain your paddlers were severely punished for their poor judgment."

I did not respond to this, in part due to my own chagrin, but also out of regret. I was the one who had ordered the paddlers out so far. I did so because I craved the exhilaration of bobbing in the vastness of that blue-green ocean. It was not only the favor of Imix but also their skill and strength that had saved my life. Royalty, however, must never admit to mistakes in judgment. It was customary that our underlings pay the price.

After a moment the third brother spoke: "You know, Lady Winik, I find it troubling that our weather shamans report an increased tally of these sudden storms. We don't quite know what to make of this reckoning. What might it mean?"

I smiled, knowing the third brother could not see me because I sat within my chamber and he stood outside it. I smiled because this topic of conversation reminded me of my father—intensely curious about the ways of things. I smiled as well because I believed this man recognized my intelligence. I believe he had been impressed by my logical conversational capacity in regard to the tides and the cycles of our lunar orb. Now he sought my opinion in regard to the sudden storms.

Perhaps his question was rhetorical, but I was intrigued because I had recently experienced the overwhelming power of a squall out on the ocean. "How many have there been this year?" I inquired.

"This storm makes the tenth," he said, distress evident in his voice.

"Ten!" I exclaimed. It was a truly impressive tally.

And it truly frightened me. Ten such storms? Upon my grateful return to shore I had witnessed the results of its tremendous strength firsthand. It had flung down limbs and yanked up entire trees, their bare, twisted roots and fractured pieces forming a new, impenetrable jumble of wreckage. The storm had hurled one wharf into the air but left the one beside it unscathed. A capricious wind that had only to extend a finger to reduce a whole wharf to tiny gray splinters was a terrifying thing. And because the gales had ripped up long lengths of the wooden boardwalks that traversed the sodden marshland, our passage from beach to lagoon and on to Somalx was onerous, though of course I was borne in a litter and spared the worst. Water was everywhere. Even far inland it sat in stagnant brackish puddles, flotsam drifting about in slow loops in filthy dark liquid. Beholding such destruction, such appalling wreckage, I was no longer certain I wished to live in any seaport, despite the deliciousness of their fish.

"With the storms come floods," he continued. "Our zapote and avocado orchards are ruined, and the winds carry off the ducks and turkeys in our pens. Even the wild deer are damaged. The floods overrun our milpas, and the maize cannot flourish as it ought when its roots drink the briny water. So much maize is spoiled, in the milpa and sometimes even in the granaries. Our commoners have little to eat in the aftermath of such terrible tempests. Sometimes even the highborn suffer."

His observation reminded me of my visit with my father to the dusty milpa at that rural villa. Concern for the commoners, both my father and the third brother had concern for the commoners and their milpas—for adequate sustenance for all of us. I smiled to know it. Studying my face in my mirror, I detected within my own smoky reflection the rise of the corners of my lips. They rose only a little, but it was enough. In the privacy of this chamber, where I was not obliged to wear the stony mask of concealment, I found I liked the smoky reflection of my own smiling face. Or perhaps it was the third brother of Somalx that I liked, and he was what was making me smile.

My body servant continued to comb the fragrant palm oil unguent through my hair. Next she would trim and shape the nails of my fingers and toes, smoothing the roughness from them. She had already applied a soothing balm to my sun-reddened skin. As silence fell between the third brother and myself, my mind wandered to my father's maize granaries, and I began to consider how all of us—the highborn, our leafcutter ants, my body servant, even myself—were fed. If those maize stores were the true foundation of my father's new temple—of our entire palace life—then it was the maize stores of Somalx that fed the salt workers and the canoe paddlers so that merchants could trade. Here too, maize was the true foundation of wealth. Parched milpas and flooding brackish milpas were important to us all, not just to the commoners with their calloused hands and coarsespun attire who scraped and bowed when we passed. I glanced again at my reflection: My face had lost its smile, and a furrow had appeared upon my brow.

"What might it mean?" the third brother asked again. "Why so many storms? We offer as we ought at our temples, but still so many."

"Might it be the K'uk'ulkan temple?"

I had not intended to say these words. It was as though they escaped from my mouth of their own accord and hung there awkwardly in the air. My reflection in the mirror peered back at me with surprise. The ways of flower assembly and of the glittering heavens and perhaps even of tides—of such things I was knowledgeable. But the ways of kings and their shifting alliances and the erratic favor of their supernatural patrons—of such complicated matters I had little understanding. If he had heard my query, I believe my father would not have been pleased.

The third brother was silent. He was silent so long I supposed I had offended him. But now that my query had been raised, it seemed plausible that Somalx's new and intimate association with K'uk'ulkan—his new temple—might indeed play a role in provoking the storms. How could it not? This high worship of K'uk'ulkan was new to us here. It came from the north. What of our more traditional gods? Gods tend toward the jealous, of that I was certain.

So I said, "Oh, but there would be other signs if your new temple was truly the reason." And then I uttered a delightful little laugh, understanding even as I did that it would negate my own intelligence, which is precisely why I did it. Indeed, it swung our conversation back to where it had been, without the third brother saying a word.

I have often brooded over that moment. If I had believed more deeply in myself, if I had been less concerned with pleasing the third brother, if I hadn't negated the solid explanation that I myself had put forth, might it all have turned out otherwise? Might the third brother have convinced his king to cease worship of K'uk'ulkan and return to honoring our old gods? If that had happened, so very many things might have been different.

I was so young. So foolish. Still I had so much to learn. At that moment in Somalx I was simply grateful I had not met a watery death. I was also glad I had realized, without a shred of doubt that I wanted to marry the man who spoke to me from outside my chamber door. The third brother had asked me a question to which he himself did not know the answer. Although I was unable to enlighten him on the matter, I was delighted he inquired at all.

I believe he asked because the increase in storms troubled him greatly. It troubled me as well. Once my surprise at his unorthodox visit had passed, I was happy he had come. I liked it that he stood several paces from the portal of my chamber, as it would have been improper for us to see one another without my mother present. But conversing around a corner like that? There was no fixed rule that said it could not be done, so you see, I learned that he was the sort of man who respected rules but also knew how to bend them, just as our voices bent around the portal of my chamber.

Yes, I found the third brother of the king of Somalx very appealing and would tell my father so. From our formal presentation, I knew his face and person were attractive. His temperament was both pleasant and inquisitive, and he respected my opinion. I also now understood how he felt about rules and about nature. Moreover, I had seen my own smile in my smoky reflection—that was how I knew I would like to marry this man, despite the terrible storms in his seaport.

I know you will be wondering about my love for Naah Chan, so I will tell you. Even though I knew I wanted to marry the third brother, that did not mean I had fallen out of love with Naah Chan. Ours was a world apart.

◎◎◎

First the gods made the beasts of the jungle, but they could not speak and thus were unsatisfactory. Then the gods made humans out of mud. Soft and formless, they dissolved with the floods. After that the gods made humans out of wood, but they lacked souls or minds and could not praise their makers or call them by name, so they were beaten into splinters. But after the sacrifice of the Hero Twins—Hunter and Jaguar Deer—the gods made humans out of maize dough. From maize dough the gods shaped us so flawlessly that we were able to see the future, as the gods themselves see the future. Because we were perfect, we were not humble. We did not feel obliged to praise the gods or call them by name. We did not offer them sustenance. Because of this, the gods grew displeased with their creation. To make us imperfect, they caused a dense mist to descend before our eyes and render our vision blurry and indistinct, so that we would be humble before our makers.

That is why humans are unable to see the future. Because of that mist, none of us could predict the abysmal fate awaiting us that morning as we set out on our return journey to Calumook.

Our nuptial entourage was of normal proportion for a visit of this nature to a place as distant as Somalx. Its size and composition had proven satisfactory on our visits to Lalchich and Quetzaltun to discuss the matter of my marriage.

At the head of our entourage two low-ranking noblemen strode abreast, bearing our bright, woven banners on long wooden poles. Our green banner held the Calumook emblem glyph, which of course featured our Waterlily insignia. The second banner was blue and bore the watery glyphs of Chaak, the divine patron god most beloved by our people. They hung hopeful and expectant, our beautiful banners, ready to lead us homeward. As my mother and I inspected the proper placement of the banners at our fore in the knowledge that Calumook lay only a three days' journey hence, my thoughts raced ahead of my person. I wondered whether my father's new Chaak temple had indeed continued its steady progress. I hoped he had not grown so distracted by his hatred of the treacherous Lalchich—or the rivalry of the Becilna king, or his anger with my mother—that he had neglected to properly oversee his grand undertaking.

I was eager to stride our sacbe at my father's side once more, my cousin again on my hip. I wondered how long it would be before the tiny boy took his first tentative steps, and hoped they would occur before my impending marriage parted us. As my father and I strode arm in arm, he would inquire about my estimation of the third brother of the king of Somalx. We would speak in low, intimate tones. I would not only recount the story of our visit, and tell of the tasty sea fish and the mighty blue-green ocean, though I'd neglect to mention I'd almost drowned at sea. I would also truthfully tell him my estimation of my prospective seaport husband. My father would be pleased that I was pleased. I would delight him to no end by telling him how much this man from Somalx reminded me of him. Together we would bask in the knowledge that the matter of my marriage could now be successfully and happily concluded.

We would halt before the rising temple site. I would gasp and he would be overjoyed at my reaction. He would describe the many labors that had been accomplished in my absence, and I would marvel at the progress. I would commend my father on its swift pace and agree that soon his majestic vision would be fulfilled atop its lofty summit. I smiled at these warm thoughts.

These warm thoughts brought others. They ushered in my longing for Naah Chan—the feel of his hand as it clasped my arm, his lips as they pressed against mine, the sweet smell of his breath. Ever since I had all but lost him at the Cenote ball game, I had had only one precious occasion to slip from our palace courtyard and meet him behind our curtain of green vine. I had nearly wept when at last he appeared upon the dark trail, then stepped from it. Despite the beauty and novelty that Somalx had to offer—and my fondness for the third prince—I also realized that the moment of my ultimate departure from Calumook was imminent. I would be leaving my home forever. I longed for our return journey to be finished already, to once more see my father and my little cousin and also Naah Chan. But of course our entourage was only just assembling in preparation for a formal departure spectacle presented by Somalx.

Behind the banner-bearers stood several nobles of higher rank—a hand-selected few of our royal court. Some of them were our advisors: some for numerology, some for divination, others for assisting our selection of fine souvenirs, and others for assessing the kind, quality, and quantity of gifts and bride price we received. Also among them were our own scribes. These well-trained, elite men had sat, stylus poised, cut conch shell inkpots at their knee, transcribing each word of our formal parleys into their folded paper codices. At all times, all these individuals remained watchful, ears alert to any secrets floating on the air, any gossip whispered behind a hand, any other intelligence that might be garnered from the place and folk where we journeyed.

Behind the members of the royal court came my litter, which traveled just behind the much grander litter of my mother. Behind our litters strode lower-ranked nobles, then our personal assistants and body servants. Behind those people strode our many other servants, who now, for the journey, were used as porters to bear homeward the many wooden trunks that held our clothing and ornaments and gifts, as well as adequate provisions for the entire entourage to consume en route.

Armed men surrounded us on all sides. These brave warriors of Calumook carried obsidian-edged club, and round, painted rawhide shields strapped to their forearms. Sharp daggers were tucked in loincloths. Across their backs their atlatls hung at the ready, and their strong hands clasped the long, polished wooden shafts of their spears. Their eyes combed the jungle on either side of the trail.

The journey between Calumook and Somalx would take several days, so we pitched camp along the way. As always, our vigilant warriors kept careful watch, especially at night while the sun passed through the earth cave. To this day I fail to comprehend how our Lalchich adversaries succeeded in penetrating our defenses. I still do not understand how they discovered our whereabouts on that jungle trail. How did they know where to find us? Our entourage had not disclosed the day of our departure to a single living creature at Somalx, for fear a foreign prying ear might wish to know it. Our diviners had shaken and sorted and interpreted their seeds and crystals again and again, and none had foreseen ill fortune. But as I've said, the dense mist of the gods descended—even before the gimlet eyes of our numinous experts—because there are many futures that humans are not intended to know.

I woke to the heavy thud of a footfall outside my tent. I was alarmed, for no soul from Calumook would ever dare stomp anywhere near the nighttime tent of the sleeping Lady Winik. Moments later a dagger plunged through the taut cloth of the tent, slashing and tearing it, and I bolted upright on my sleeping mat. A hand seized my arm with a grip as tight and unyielding as a boa snake, and hauled me through the slash in my tent. Outside, another boa-snake hand clamped onto my other arm.

"Hey hey!" gloated the owners of these hands, pleased with their catch.

The day had not yet dawned, so all was black except for the flaming torch a third Lalchich warrior cast near my face. I winced at the heat and sudden light.

As they recognized Lady Winik, they called "Hey hey!" with still greater delight.

The third man grabbed my chin in his calloused paw and yanked it back to the torchlight. Then he squeezed until I cried out in pain, and they all laughed, those dogs of Lalchich. By that time other warriors had also hauled my mother from her tent some distance away. They had begun parading her about in a most undignified fashion, loudly chanting their vile Lalchich capture-song.

A fourth warrior now appeared, and this one too gloated, "Hey hey!" when he recognized the rare prize they had just plucked. He smiled wide in his gladness, that dog, and I saw the long row of turquoise inlays in his teeth—a sight I would see many times, and one I will never forget. Still smiling, he glanced back at his chanting comrades marching my mother about, and realized that we, over here, were unwatched.

"This one I take now," he said, and those warriors of Lalchich dragged me into the jungle and threw me to the ground.

Of course I kicked and flailed my arms, but there were six of them. Six! I could do little but twist my head to grab with my teeth the hand that sought to stifle my screams. When I found its flesh I bit into it with all the muscle of my jaw, but that hand became a fist that struck my face and thrust the back of my head into the dirt of the jungle. When I opened my mouth to wail, a gag was shoved into it. It ripped at the tender corners of my mouth, pinning my head and keeping my cries low and guttural.

The warrior with turquoise in his teeth was the lieutenant of this war party. This became apparent as he took his place above me, between my splayed legs. He stood there in his haughtiness, staring straight down upon my face. Such a man would never have looked so directly at Lady Winik, but here he was dominant, and his frank stare underscored that truth more than did his haughty stance. Although he was a round-headed lowborn, he wore large jade ear spools in his lobes, and there within his eager, lusty smile shone those turquoise inlays. Staring back at him, I knew I could do nothing other than submit to this round-headed man, here on the dirt of this dank jungle. To submit to all these dogs of Lalchich.

After the lieutenant went, they took me one by one. When each was done, their circle shifted to seize my legs and pin my arms anew, and my gagged cries became pitiful whimpers as their appalling circle proceeded around me.

"Ah ha ha, what a tiny stalk," one of them laughed.

"Okay, okay, my turn now," one said hastily.

"Ah ha ha, what a pathetic little grunter that one is," one of them sneered.

As if suspended in a haze, I heard this transpire around me. I smelled the odor of dank earth, of blood, the reek of treachery, the salty stink of semen, the stench of Lalchich sweat. Even as agony gripped the soft private place between my legs, I knew there was nothing I could do but submit.

When at last they had finished, they dragged me by the hair like a dirty limp rag to the circle of torchlight and flung me in. Other warriors were there, all flush with their own prizes. My mother was there. She too had been transformed into a dirty limp rag, as had all the women in our entourage. In the days ahead they raped us many times, those dogs of Lalchich, as we stumbled with rough ropes around our necks, naked and humiliated, lips flayed, bodies bruised and battered, along the trail to the city that might once have been my home.

6

I am silent. I sit motionless on our bench. I have stunned even myself with the brutality of these memories. The flaying of my lips with that Lalchich flint persists as long, bulging streaks of shining white on my mouth. I trace their suffering with the tips of my fingers. Even after all this time, the remembered image of those turquoise inlays evokes anew the terror that has lurked within my heart for so long. I caress these smooth, protruding streaks that have now become a part of me. I remember the harsh slice of their flint, the taste of my own hot blood rushing onto my howling tongue, the unremitting clench of that rough rope round my neck. An old surge of agony throbs at that soft place between my legs, now as dry and withered as the rest of me.

I have frightened my cherished Lily Bean, my most precious granddaughter. In silence, I observe her fright from the corner of my eye. Am I telling this child too much? Perhaps she need not know all these details—these particular details—of my life. Of back then. But this daughter of the House of the Waterlily must learn to abide many things. She will be asked to bear more than she ought. While it is true that times are safer, that marauding men in search of prey no longer roam the jungle with such impunity, still they prowl. She must know. Take the proper precautions. She must understand my life—our life. All of it, the glories as well as the afflictions. Like me, she must be able to endure the burdens of a daughter of the House of the Waterlily.

I turn my head to look at her. Her eyes are alert and fearful, as indeed they should be. I close my eyes to her innocence. She will have to hear worse. I hope she has the fortitude to listen and also to forgive. To comprehend the depth of all that was lost. For now, though, I will give this child respite by telling her also of our wisdom and sophistication, so that she understands what she must regain. She must not think us savages.

◎◎◎

We were clean then, much cleaner than now. Back then, I entered the sweat bath each day with my mother and older sisters and the other Waterlily women. It was our custom to bathe our persons before dressing to take our evening repast. Moonlight and torch-light glinted from the still surface of our pleasure pool, and fragrant floral bundles were arranged wherever our gaze may alight.

The sweat bath was a series of low rooms that ran along the short back edge of our courtyard. We had the luxury of morning slumber until our chambers grew so warm that even the most vigorous fanning by our fan servants could not keep us from sweating. Only then did we emerge. Cool, sweetened water was soon brought, and we would drink and wake while lounging in the shade of the awnings. We chatted and nibbled a few morsels, and then, after our body servants dressed us for the day, we went to study or read or to practice our chosen arts, or to stroll or stride or confer in regard to the endless matters that required our attention. After the sun passed its zenith, we would again nibble a few morsels and nap in the shade. Then, upon waking anew, we would proceed to the sweat bath.

As we entered its antechamber, we dropped our day huipils on the floor and entered unclothed through a low passage. An attendant opened and shut the low wooden door to keep the steam trapped inside. As we women sat in our rooms, so men sat in adjacent rooms. We could hear their muted voices in idle conversation.

Water tipped over hot rocks gave off a delightful hiss as vapor swirled in the dim air. Chanting, we tossed fresh herbs on the rocks, and soon the air was infused with a soothing, curative, purifying aroma. We would fill our lungs with curative air. You see, our sweat baths were not only for cleansing our persons but for cleansing our spirits as well.

Once we had basked and lounged and let the cares of the day melt from our persons, our massage servants entered and began their work. They rubbed our muscles until they relaxed, scraped sweat from our skin with a hard cut reed to extract the impurities from our pores, and shampooed our scalps with a soothing fragrant unguent concocted from ferns, then soaked our tresses with nutritious palm oil until our hair gleamed. They did this gladly, our servants, as it was in everyone's interest that our royal persons remain hale and hearty, as well as exquisite in appearance for our public spectacles.

By the time we departed the steam room and returned to the antechamber, our soiled day huipils were gone, and upon the bench lay fresh, formal fine-spun huipils, ready for the evening ahead.

There was an antechamber on the men's side as well. It was larger, however, because not only did they find their soiled day attire removed and their fresh evening finery on the bench after their bathing was finished, but they were also greeted by the palace concubines. I imagine those lovelies sitting, or perhaps reclining, patient in wait. Just as we could hear their muffled voices in idle conversation, so too could we hear our menfolk's bawdy merriment.

"Ah ha-ha, you have a fast stalk today!" said a male voice.

"Ah ha-ha you have a slow one!" laughed another.

The sound of a woman laughing and cooing.

"Hey, what's wrong, don't you know what to do with it?" taunted a male voice.

"Ah, let him be," said a father's voice, "this is his first time, wait till he gets some practice."

"That one there, she's a sweet new one, isn't she?"

"That one over there's my favorite—come here and stroke my stalk!"

Again the sound of a woman, laughing and cooing.

"Oh, look at him go now!" said a male voice.

"Eh, done so soon?"

We amused ourselves by eavesdropping on their bawdiness, their grunting, their lewd taunting of one another. Some women thought they could identify their husbands' voices and would remark on what inept lovers they were—lazy, unable to last, unable to arouse—and how they knew nothing about pleasuring their wives. Having begun bathing with these women when I was very young, I knew nothing of such things at first, but as I grew I listened more keenly, both to what I heard through the wall and to the ribald chatter, which was how I learned what men and women do together to make babies and for merriment. I was relieved, however, that my mother never chose to take part in such vulgarities. As I reflect on that fact now, I am confused as to why she did not, for she was never one to hold back her opinion on any subject.

◎◎◎

I never entered the men's sweat baths, but I imagine their antechamber was similar to ours in that fragrant floral bundles adorned its wall niches. Often it was my own fragrant floral assemblies that rested within those niches.

I assembled most of my bundles using my favorite pink- and purple-blossomed orchids, with an occasional white accent flower. My other floral bundles contained yellow orchids with orange accents, or hard red spiky bromeliads with their tufts of variegated greenery, and showy red poinsettias too. By far, my finest large assemblies were the dramatic floor arrays of tall heliconia stems with their red and yellow beak-blossoms. I recall them in such detail because fragrant flower assembly was one of the highborn female arts I studied as a girl.

Our arts were many, and I partook joyfully in their study. Astronomy was a favorite of mine. In this particular art I could have earned renown, for even before I became Lady Winik I had assisted in discerning a new lunar cycle within the glittering night sky.

For months my eyes had roved the night from our dark rooftop observatory under the tutelage of Calumook's master astronomer. We were actually observing a different celestial phenomenon, but so often something new is discovered when it is least expected, as was the case when we recognized a new pattern of the most unpredictable of celestial phenomena: our moon, that erratic Rabbit that bounds across both inky night and the daytime sky. It was essential that we study the lunar cycle so that no spectacle was ever scheduled on a day when the moon would be eaten by its shadow.

Already we had lain for some time upon the woven mats of the dark rooftop. At dawn from this rooftop, in alignment with a building across the plaza, we had long since learned K'inich Ajaw's more knowable passage: sunrise occurred above the southern door at winter solstice, above the northern door at midsummer, and above the middle door at equinoxes.

My lunar discovery occurred several months after we had been taught the sacred knowledge hidden within the constellation called Orion.

"There, observe," instructed Calumook's master astronomer. "There, along the center of this crossed star group resides a line of three bright stars. Can you discern them?" I could not see his face, but I knew from his voice that our eager astronomy teacher was filled with happy expectation.

"Yes, yes we can," I answered, along with my fellow stargazing students, reclined on the mats beside me.

"Excellent," he said. "Describe them to me."

Our teacher was wise to keep asking us questions, because lying on mats in the middle of the dark night was conducive to allowing one's eyelids droop until they shut, so that slumber overcame study. I admit this happened often at first, but soon I became accustomed to napping during the day and was able to recline, without fear of heavy eyelids, and observe the jump and play of those lively celestial bodies. It was then that our teacher, a kind-hearted man of whom I grew quite fond, regaled us with sacred stories.

He towered beside us on the dim rooftop, enfolded by the long dark cloak that was his official astronomer garb. His hair was pulled back into a long, thin, graying tail. "Those three bright stars are the three glowing stones of our original hearth of creation," our teacher continued. Pride swelled in his voice—not his own pride in possessing such knowledge, but rather pride in the beauty of the knowledge itself.

Gazing up into that dark dome night after night, I began to sense, in the stillness and the roar of cicadas, the varying depths of the glittering stars. That indeed they did not all lie on one single plane, but were staggered within the darkness in thirteen distinct layers. Careful scrutiny of those twinkling bodies revealed that each layer drew from another without haste, gliding alone, spinning without assistance, but always in concert with the others. The realization of this truth, this celestial grandeur, stirred me profoundly. With my own eyes I could observe the slow shifting of the tiny orbs traveling across our dark vault, often at a measured pace but sometimes as if hurled by a strong, invisible hand. At times this hand was angry, at others it was contented, but it was always fickle. From these orbs' passage we deciphered sacred messages, omens, the auspicious timing for our actions, all embedded within this boundless symphony of sparkling motion.

To be sure, I was so intrigued by the depth and breadth of the knowledge our astronomy teacher revealed to us upon that dark rooftop that for a time I believed I might like to live the quiet life of an astronomer, don for myself the dark cloak. I indisputably had the aptitude for such a calling. Sometimes still, I gaze into the glittering heavens and imagine how different my life would have been had I claimed the dark cloak. But I knew that life was not what my father intended for my future. As his youngest and most beautiful daughter, I had always known my life would be part of Calumook's nuptial strategies. Had I been a middle daughter, or homely, or lacking in grace and talent, I might have been able to live a humble and happy life on those dark rooftops.

"Yes, there they hang, the three glowing hearthstones," Calumook's dark cloak continued, turning toward us. His silhouette blotted out the brilliance of the stars behind him, and the blackness obscured the features of his face.

"Do any of you know who placed these three glowing stones? And the significance of the timing of their placement?"

I knew. I hesitated for a few moments, lest the dark cloak or my reclining peers think me haughty, and then, trying to keep the delight from my voice, I said: "Itzamnaaj set the hearthstones, the Hearthstones of Creation. When he set them he put our Long Count in forward motion." After a brief pause, I continued: "Then he revealed to us how to reckon the passage of time. And Itzamnaaj also taught us how to write, so that our history could be merged with time."

In those days, our stelae most often portrayed the Long Count, which marked truly important passages of time. They recorded lineage births and kingly ascensions, marriages and temple dedications, and war deaths and victories, always in concert with the long passage of time. As Itzamnaaj had instructed, our histories should always be remembered.

But now? Now the Long Count is being forgotten, because stelae are no longer erected. It will be lost because master carvers no longer tap sharp chisels, and divine kings no longer ascend thrones. Ours is becoming a disremembered past.

The dark cloak crossed the brightness of the starry dome to stand before my reclining figure. You see, even in the dimness, our astronomy teacher recognized the timbre of my voice. Impressed, he said, "Yes, my good young lady, that is correct." At that moment I wished my father had been present on that dark rooftop. I was certain he would have been delighted I knew the answer.

But Itzamnaaj's setting of the Hearthstones of Creation had nothing to do with the tracking of lunar cycles, which was where I made my greatest contribution, up on that dark rooftop.

I stop telling my story. The joy of my rousing astronomical discovery fades, and I feel my face grow solemn. I wish I had never begun recounting this lunar cycle tale, when all it does is remind me of my own decline. The poignancy strikes me fast, like a sharp blow to my person. I recall that the cycle I helped discover and chart in neat glyphs on a paper codex on our rooftop observatory was that of a deep twilight waning crescent moon. A vanishingly thin curving sliver of white was all that was visible of our Rabbit moon. It was the goddess in her most aged incarnation, as grandmother Ixchel's inverted jar was emptied of its final drops of water, its youth, its fertility—the very last drops of its life. What I had charted so long ago was the timing of my own death.

◎◎◎

The death of my grandmother was sorrowful, but her funeral was splendid. Perhaps this was because that tiny, ancient woman, my father's mother, had become venerable while still alive. Long before she died, she became unable to walk on her own, so two attendants carried her about on a wooden litter. That her legs no longer functioned did not prevent her from roaming all of Calumook, conveying her desires to her carriers via blunt commands. Despite the frailness of her person, her demeanor remained robust, and no one would have dared suggest she consider a rest.

My most vivid memory of her is at the Ixchel Moon celebration of my menses, where she sat silently observing every detail of the long entire spectacle. Part of the ritual bid me to go my grandmother and kneel before her, which I did. I recall wondering as I knelt there whether her jade bead cape might weigh too heavily on her person, for her tiny shoulders hunched far forward and her scrawny neck curved back from her chest at an odd angle. But then one corner of her old and wrinkled mouth rose in a loving smile as she lifted an engraved collar of heirloom jade from her person and placed it around my neck. The transfer of this piece was clearly a special moment of climax, for the music ceased and a hush fell over the entire palace. I had seen this unusual collar on the person of my grandmother many times, so I was not unfamiliar with the piece, but still I recall the extraordinary sensation of the heirloom resting on my chest. The sensation was substantial, but it was not due to the weight of the jade alone. Rather, it was as if the formal ritual transfer of that specific treasured ornament now marked me in some vague fashion, connecting my life with hers anew.

Then my grandmother's thin, gnarled fingers clasped my chin. I remember my surprise at the strength still contained within that hand as she raised my face to hers. Her old, cloudy eyes looked straight into my shiny, youthful ones. Her other knobby hand brushed a stray strand of hair from my face. Although I was so young and could not then have voiced it, I wonder now whether my grandmother's extraordinary touch—the gentleness of one hand in marked contrast with the strength of the other—might not have been her truest gift to me.

Her ancient lips smiled, revealing toothless jaws, and she said: "You are worthy. My dearest young Lady Winik, when all else fails, this you are to remember."

These unexpected words startled me—I believe my grandmother was not supposed to have said them, and thus I did not know of a proper formal reply I could have memorized. But she seemed unperturbed by this; revealing the expanse of gums once more in a smile, she bid I stand by gently raising the gnarled hand that clasped my chin.

Her funeral was the first at which I heard the word Kalo'mte', or at least the first time I was old enough to inquire as to its meaning. Kalo'mte' is a title bestowed upon a supreme war captain—someone who has demonstrated a superiority strategic capacity and the ability to organize complex battle tactics. It is conferred on someone who is able to keep calm in the face of pitched combat.

That, I learned, was my grandmother.

As befit a woman of such standing, her funeral was, as I've said, grand—but purposely not as grand as those of kings. Her tomb was hollowed into the second-story landing of our palace. I do not believe our architects had ever envisioned a tomb being dug in that place, but it seemed fitting to lay her bones in that prominent location, near the chambers in which she had strategized with other captains of Calumook. Later, when I asked my mother whether digging into the palace landing like that might have angered our ancestors, she responded: "How could the palace architects have predicted a Kalo'mte' would rise in our midst? They would be pleased to know such a person is entombed within."

The hollow slit log drums sounded, the long wooden trumpets blared, the turtle shell marimba chimed its high-pitched notes, and the ocean conch roared.

The funeral entourage proceeded to position itself around the open tomb of Calumook's Kalo'mte'. Peering into that tomb, I was surprised to see it was little more than a hole burrowed into rubble. A few cut stones had been wedged along the sides of the hole, and six newly placed stone steps offered access. We knew these stones were new, you see, because the mortar was still white and moist, its fresh, bright scent unmistakable.

Once we had taken our places, my grandmother's corpse emerged from a palace chamber. Arranged on a grand wooden funerary divan, it appeared so small and insignificant that it was hard to believe this tiny woman had led, much less won, essential battles. While she lived, two carriers had conveyed her litter from place to place with ease, but her divan was so weighty that four strong men, one at each corner, were needed to carry it into the tomb.

All around us, women wailed. Their slow ululations, trilling sobs, and ritual sighs mounted to fill the air. Earlier my mother had explained that here, at the funeral of my grandmother, I would be permitted to sob. At first I could not believe this was true, given the relentlessness of my recent training in the art of the stony mask. It seemed extraordinary that I should be permitted—encouraged, even—to remove it during a spectacle. I looked in disbelief at my mother.

"All of Calumook loved our Kalo'mte' deeply," she said

"I am allowed to cry?"

"Only then and only there. Beside the tomb. And only while the women are wailing. Yes. It would be good if you cried—but not too much. Do not scrunch up your face."

So I cried with the wailing women, trying not to scrunch up my face. I'm not certain I succeeded. It felt peculiar to let tears stream so freely over my cheeks. I was glad for the wails that rose and fell behind me, as they encouraged my sorrow. I cried, and as tears trickled over my lips I tasted their salt, a flavor I still recall because that was the first time I lost someone I loved. Although I was still too young to understand her life as Kalo'mte', I had come to know my grandmother as a kind and compassionate woman, and to understand that she loved me deeply. Never again would her gnarled fingers clasp my chin or brush a stray hair from my face. Never again would I hear her words of faith in me. Already I missed her; thus I wept.

Soon the wailing gave way to the muted notes of our patriline chant, sung in low voices by people who now stood amidst the musicians, and behind the wailing women, there on our palace's second landing.

As my father's mother, she was not born of our patriline, yet her dedication to the House of the Waterlily was so steadfast, and without doubt her Kalo'mte' status so extraordinary, that she had long ago become part of it. If our world had not fallen, a patriline stanza would surely have been composed in her honor, to tell of her many battles, her bravery, and her remarkable triumphs.

When the chanting ended, the wailing arose again, followed by more chanting of our patriline.

In the course of this second round of chanting, the Calumook mortuary priest bid us one by one to approach a wooden table that held my grandmother's offerings. While it is true that many of those offerings may have resembled pots and plates, funeral ritual rendered them much more than painted clay, actually transforming those vessels into living beings who themselves became sustenance for the gods.

As each of us approached, the mortuary priest selected a specific offering and placed it in our hands. As each of us descended the steps, an attendant indicated where to lay each one. The proper ritual placement of offerings was crucial, as a mistake could jeopardize the outcome of my grandmother's passage through Xibalba by impeding her progress and dooming her to reside forever with the Lords of Death. If she remained there, my grandmother would never be able to take her place as an ancestor who could intervene with the gods on our behalf. So you see, much was at stake in the precision and the accuracy of every funerary detail. Even the fragrant floral bundle I assembled for her tomb had to be blessed by death ritual, one beautiful blossom at a time.

A tall stack of kindling stood beside the tomb. Within its dry tinder I made out the light brown of pine, the twisted aromatic wood from which copal seeped, and the dark forest wood of the sacred ceiba. The mortuary assistant touched his flaming torch to the stack, igniting a roaring blaze from which long, loud bursts of fiery sparks leapt, flashing brilliance into the darkness that had grown around us.

This is what we did against that fiery, flickering backdrop:

My father placed a pot atop her head. It was painted in many bright colors, and the images and glyphs bore her name and titles. My paternal uncle placed a bowl filled with smoldering copal near her right hand on the wooden divan. As my father's principal wife, my mother placed a spiny red oyster shell over the spot where her legs met. My paternal aunt placed a bowl of maize kernels on the floor of the tomb, and I placed a squash-filled bowl beside it. A different uncle placed a ceramic bowl of jade beads near her left hand, on top of the divan, then opened her jaw and slipped a few beads inside. My oldest brother placed a bowl of obsidian blades near her feet on the divan. My uncle struck white chert with a hammerstone. The spark was lightening and the strike a thunderclap, and the chips remained as they fell, an offering on the floor of the tomb. The mortuary assistant placed a hollow clay whistle on the divan near her knees, then sprinkled red cinnabar powder over her corpse.

My grandmother entered the watery road of death by canoe. Her White-Flower-Thing paddled to Xibalba, realm of the Lords of Death. Like the struggles of Hunter and Jaguar Deer, her journey through Xibalba was fraught with danger. But like the Hero Twins, she did not remain in Xibalba but was resurrected, raised from the earth cleft along the trunk of the sacred ceiba. Her White-Flower-Thing now resides in a land of plenty, shaded by the leafy limbs of the sacred ceiba, the tree of life that rises from the Hearthstones of Creation.

Later, we came here to scatter our blood before the tomb-shrine of our revered ancestor, my Kalo'mte' grandmother of Calumook. As supplicants, we scattered our blood to gain her favor, piercing our royal flesh in a trance with the sharp tip of the stingray spine, and the obsidian lancet like the sting of a scorpion.

Pain is our offering. Blood is our offering.

My mother and I and other royal women let our blood from our tongues and from the soft tender lobes of our ears. My father and other royal men let their blood from the loose flesh at the tips of their stalks. Here, before this tomb-shrine on the second story of our palace, we let our lifeblood. Far below in the plaza, commoners scattered theirs.

Drums and trumpets sound in this world, and we hear them in our trance. Our red drops saturate white paper in a painted clay bowl. We lay the red-drop paper on embers, and our offerings and our supplications rise within its smoke. In that smoky haze a portal opens to reveal our Vision Serpent, from whose gaping maw our Kalo'mte' emerges. Far below in the plaza, the commoners lay their own red-scattered offerings in censers and petition their own ancestors through the Vision Serpent portal we have opened.

For my father, I believe it was the deified first founder of the House of the Waterlily who typically emerged from the Vision Serpent's gaping maw. For me, when I drew the thorn-studded rope across my tongue, it was always my grandmother who appeared—our beloved Kalo'mte' of Calumook. She wore her jade bead cape, and her shoulders hunched forward under its weight. Sometimes I think I saw one hazy corner of her loving mouth rise as her cloudy eyes peered into mine.

"A supreme war captain? My grandmother was a supreme war captain?" I asked my mother several days after the funeral. She and I were weaving on our backstrap looms in the shade of our courtyard awning.

"Oh yes, she was Kalo'mte'. Of that you can be certain."

"But she was so gentle," I said. "It is odd she could wage war."

"Yes, Winik, that is true. But as you grow, you will learn that one can be many things. One can be gentle at home but fierce when it is necessary, as so often is the case."

I pondered this contradiction. You are worthy, my grandmother had said as I knelt before her. I had been so young, too young to understand how obligation might press with such force that to retain even a semblance of gentleness was itself a feat.

"She was a good woman," my mother said.

Some moments after she said this, she laid her hand upon my arm. Seldom did my mother touch me, and when she did, rarer still was it with softness. It did not last long, that touch, for she quickly moved her hand back to her weaving. In my dotage, sometimes I reflect on that moment. I have come to believe that my mother may have missed our Kalo'mte' as much as did I, perhaps much more. I also now know that the death of someone you love can change the way you walk in the world.

◎◎◎

Fragrant floral assembly was a learned art that brought me boundless pleasure. Immersing myself in the starry heavens also brought bliss, though of a somewhat different nature. I enjoyed floral assembly because it was immediate, something of the senses and not just the intellect.

Once our daily flower tribute had arrived in baskets at our courtyard door, I was usually the first to stand before the cutting table.

Well before I took up my blade, I lifted each flower by its stem, turning it bit by bit, scrutinizing its color, inspecting the composition of its cascading bract or petal whorl structure. I plunged my nose into each blossom. Often I was finishing an assembly before the other women even entered the room. I may be mistaken, but never did I sense that they held my early bird nature against me; rather, I believe they simply did not care as much about floral bundles, so the beauty of mine meant little to them.

As I've said, it was bundles such as these that adorned our world, including the long woven mat of our evening repast. Those evenings were always pleasant occasions.

Following our sweat bath, our body servants dressed us in finery and coiffed our hair with plaits and loops and engraved bone pins and, yes, fragrant flowers. Then we gathered in our courtyard near the pleasure pool to sip cool chocolate, nibble on tidbits from painted platters, and chat with courtiers who had arrived from other palace courtyards and beyond. It was a gay time. During our evening repast we could relax and revel in the sweetness of life, and our world seemed full of contentment.

My father always appeared last, and soon thereafter began the feasting.

By then, dusk had fallen and our torches flickered orange. Servants had positioned small cushions along the edges of our dining mat, my father's cushion always at its head. Our nobles lined the sides, each positioned according to rank. Musicians played in the shadows.

Our servants placed platter after sumptuous painted platter before us on the mat. Avocado and grilled venison, tamales stuffed with roasted tapir, tepezcuintle stew, and braised iguana. Blue chili-dusted maize fungus in a folded duck egg omelet. Bowls of honey-sweetened maize with vanilla and annatto. Fire-roasted tomatoes. Juicy slices of papaya and zapote, pitaya and guava. The sight and smell of the platters of culinary delights amidst our beautiful fragrant floral bundles rushed water to our mouths.

My gaze shifts to Lily Bean, my precious lineage child, and I pause my recollections. There she sits, listening on the bench. She is regarding me strangely. The look on her face seems one of confusion, I think. Or perhaps it reflects woe that her evening repasts have never neared this level of culinary refinement. Her meals—and mine, now—seldom consist of much beyond an earthenware bowl of stewed dog. Perhaps it is cruel to speak of such delicacies.

"What worries you, my child?"

"Grandmother, you know we still have blossoms. They hang from the vines and branches of the jungle. You can still assemble fragrant floral bundles. In the morning I will go and cut some for you."

I silently contemplate this truth as seen through the simple eyes of this child. Then, hoping I do not crush her—for it is clear she does not understand the role of our floral bundles—I say, "Yes, Lily Bean, yes. Flowers still abound in the jungle, so yes, there are flowers. But it is not the same. Who would admire my skill of assembly? Who is there to appreciate the complex visual and aromatic aesthetics of my expert selections? Our doleful evening repasts are just a clump of barely washed souls in coarse-spun, hunched around the hearth. If I glimpsed a fragrant floral bundle amidst all that misery, I believe it would send me sobbing. You see, it all died with Calumook."

◎◎◎

The sources of my father's pride were many: his Kalo'mte' mother, his jaguar throne, my skill with fragrant floral bundles. His greatest pride, however, lay in his dwarf. He was proud because dwarfs were rare in any court, and his court had a living one, not just a likeness carved of wood, to prop up his mirror. My father was also proud of his dwarf because he had stolen it as a young warrior; thus the squat half-man was also a flesh-badge of my father's prowess in war.

For both of these reasons, I suppose, my father bade his dwarf dance with him at spectacles. Although there were many such occasions, the one that stands out in my memory is the performance in the spectacle in which my father announced the construction of his new Chaak temple.

After reaching his arm toward the dark clouds on the glowing western horizon, my father began the stately dance that celebrated the resurrection of the Maize God. An enormous back-rack appeared, quetzal streamers springing from it like the bold rays of K'inich Ajaw. Of course he already wore his magnificent quetzal streamer headdress. The K'uhul Ajaw of Calumook knew precisely how to quiver his head to achieve the dramatic bob and dance of its tall, drooping tips.

Raising his arms, he bent his knees. He turned his head and waited while Calumook's principal orator, enfolded by his fine-spun green cloak, strode to stand near my father. The orator spoke only after the awed silence following the last jangle of my father's jade had dissolved into the gloaming. Trumpets blared, and my father turned his head to the other side, crossing his arm before his magnificent chest. Again the orator spoke, narrating the story of the death and resurrection of Hunter and Jaguar Deer. Another blare of trumpets, and with another low jangle of jade, my father struck another pose, raising his other arm. His voice rose in a patient crescendo to a high falsetto. As a trained singer, he knew how to breathe and how to keep a long note steady. He knew how to make his voice burst forth with sudden strength, and then clap his hands to accentuate the silence that followed. He knew when to rise on perfect prancing toes, when to shift his arms. All these motions were flawless, nimble, and precise despite the weight of jade, and they were performed in tempo with his singing, and also with the narrative of the green-cloaked orator, who continued the long account of the Maize God.

Then my father's dwarf appeared. He wore a mask, a grotesque of clay-hardened cloth painted with vulgar eyes and a strange grimacing mouth. There were holes at those same places. From his mouth hung a fat smoldering cigar, which must have had considerable potency for such a diminutive creature. Despite the mask, his identity as my father's ugly half-man was unmistakable.

Stubby arms wide, the dwarf began twirling. From his trance-like movements we knew his demeanor of the staid creature that propped up my father's mirror was much altered. Meanwhile my elegant, poised father danced the stately, regal dance of the Maize God as the counterpart to his dwarf, who danced awkwardly, jerkily, in his impersonation of darkness and evil. The dwarf also sang in falsetto, although his was shrill and off-key. Long hours of practice together had resulted in this perfection.

Then my father's falsetto switched key, and we heard the cries of a newborn, just now resurrected. He turned from us, and when he turned swiftly back we saw he had donned a jade mask with slanting slits cut into its pale translucent green. His transformation into the infant Maize God was complete. Behind the slits, my father's eyes glimmered.

From his side, my father swung a turtle shell polished to a brilliant sheen. A bird talon appeared, black and craggy with age. Thunderclaps descended the staircase as he struck talon against turtle shell, then paused for dramatic effect. He raised the talon, pointing it at the red setting sun and the cluster of dark clouds on the western horizon. That cluster seemed to have grown angrier, more swollen than before. Indeed, the air had become cloying and tight.

Again he struck, and the thunderclaps came. Again he waited, pointing his craggy talon, beckoning forth the rain. He tore the mask from his face and again I recognized my father, his countenance so contorted it seemed scarcely human. As he struck the shell with increasing haste, up rose a mighty din and amidst that din and the gloaming stood the Maize God, now fully grown. The ugly half-man continued to spin around him. The grotesque mask, his dreadful form, his shrill falsetto, his monotonous spinning: these made the Maize God seem all the more beautiful.

As I've said, my father bid his dwarf prop the mirror because of his rarity, and also because of his status as a flesh-badge. This mirror was itself another source of pride—a marvelous mosaic of tiny pyrite pieces that stretched almost the dwarf's entire wing-span. Sometimes I wondered if that ugly little man ever grew drowsy, with his stubby arms always outstretched to steady this weighty thing at the perfect angle so that my father could gaze into its mystic ring.

Have I told you of the fascination my father's mirror held for me? My own mirror, and indeed all our regular mirrors were of polished hematite. They were fine and reflected our images well, but they were nothing compared to the one owned by my father and propped up by his dwarf.

What did he see, my father?

No one but the K'uhul Ajaw of Calumook was ever to gaze within this magical loop of reflection upon reflection. When it was not in use in the stubby arms of his dwarf, it was hidden beneath an abundant drape of fine-spun.

What did he see, my father?

All I ever saw was the mirror's back, itself a mystic circle of polished slate inlaid with fragments of bright shell. Around its edge ran glyphs that few were permitted to read. I was not among those few.

In truth, I do not know what my father saw when he gazed into his mirror. His own visage must have shone back as hundreds of refracted images of the K'uhul Ajaw. Perhaps it was clarity he sought, clarity within that bedlam of strange ethereal phantas-magorias staring back from some distant conjured realm. As I've said, the gods cast mist before our once-perfect eyes so we cannot know the future, but we seek to know it nonetheless. I believe that is what my father sought in those reflections upon reflec-tions, that abundance of mosaic likenesses. Through this round and shimmering portal, he sought entry to the realm of godly knowledge. Little could any of us have predicted that our world would soon shatter into countless shining calamitous pieces—as would my father's mosaic pyrite mirror, the one propped at a per-fect angle by his dwarf.

7

Only later—and much too late—did we learn that the construction of the Becilna king's new temple was not as advanced as we had feared. Was it our suspicious nature that led us astray? I knew my father's anger toward the Becilna king had been simmering, as erstwhile friend gradually converted to newfound enemy. Or, maybe we had purposely been led to believe its temple construction was more advanced than it was. Perhaps outright lies had been told to us in an effort to unsteady my father's hand, to encourage a misstep. As I chafed in brutal Lalchich bondage, I remained uncertain which account seemed more probable. Perhaps each of us remembers those times differently. Our accounts have been altered with each retelling. Some versions may be half-truths, some sheer fabrications; meanwhile our own notions of certainty bend and twist, and at the same time become more resolutely etched in our minds.

Besides, there was so much deception in those days, so much intrigue. Rumor and innuendo lay in wait behind each tree, and error was inevitable. If in fact sound decisions were not made, then we could hardly have expected them to issue from those whose vision was obscured by the impenetrable mist.

Least of all my father. Of all people, how could he have been expected to make good judgments? He must have been livid, so overcome with distress for my well-being that it is understandable he may have erred. Perhaps his error had been to overplay his hand with our lineage heads.

"You shall obtain it," he may have demanded of his sajal. "They must quarry faster," he may have demanded. "Faster! I will have my stone!"

It cannot be denied that my father had become preoccupied with his Chaak temple. How could he not have been obsessed with completing it in advance of the most crucial spectacle of his entire life? The spectacle that had grown into a triple ritual—a spectacle of all spectacles. It would dedicate his grand new temple, commemorate the 10.0.0.0.0 Katun ending, and occasion the sacrifice of ropefuls of Lalchich elite, thus putting them once more in their place. Surely my father would have grown agitated at any prospect of a slackened construction pace, especially one slower than that of the rival Becilna temple.

As for our relations with the Becilna king and his court, they continued cordially—at least, as evidenced by the stony masked faces in attendance during our respective generous and hospitable visits—and would not, could not, abate.

Had the pace of construction of my father's temple slackened?

If so, then his grand vision of himself standing boldly atop its lofty summit, basking in ancestral glory and Chaak's abundant rain, must have triumphed over his senses. I admit my father may have tended toward vanity.

Had the work of our Calumook leafcutter ants indeed slowed?

If so, had it slowed because their lineage heads whispered in their ears that it should? Had the lineage heads managed to divert more than their allotted share of cut stone, despite the vigilant eye of my father's sajal? What of those bar-and-dot tallies in his tribute codex? Might they be in error?

I recall that on the day when I first saw Naah Chan, I had first observed the sajal speaking with the Calumook lineage heads to the side of my father's slow-rising temple. Twenty thousand times I have reconsidered what their discussion might have entailed.

There was one lineage head who may not have been able to muster adequate labor. He was round-headed and rumored to be the weakest of the lot, only a mere shred above nobility and thus unreliable. Two other lineage heads may have been dragging their feet, but not because they lacked the maize or the labor or the stone. In fact, they wanted to see my father fail.

They wanted to see my father fail?

Every time I considered this possibility, I experienced it as a blow to my own person, a dagger plunged into my heart. After all my father had done for them, after all his lavish gifts and his love, how could they want him to fail? I could not then fathom why our own Calumook lineage heads might wish for such a terrible thing. But now, with age and after twenty thousand reconsiderations, I have grown familiar with the nature of rivalry—the pushing and the pulling, the pretense, and the constant yearning for higher status that threatens to betray our very souls.

My father would have pushed back. As I've said, when pressed he had a temper. He would have demanded what he felt was his due. Was he strong enough to do this? Was he as strong as the Becilna king? Perhaps this time his demands really did exceed the balance of his lavish gifts and his love.

Perhaps they even exceeded the possible. Collecting tribute has long been a challenging undertaking. It can be difficult to gauge what highborn can take from leafcutter ants and how much those ants can provide. Of course they are wont to claim inability to yield what we demand, but now that I have toiled in a dusty milpa I know that providence is fickle, and just one harvest can lead to considerable change. It is the scattering of our royal blood that maintains the maize in its divine cycle, so the ants are indebted to us for every finger-swipe of maize-gruel that passes their lips. Confused, I waver, not knowing what to believe or which side to take now that I have lived both sides, highborn as well as ant.

Trying to order my thoughts, I consider again what may have transpired in that last tumultuous stretch of days.

Perhaps one lineage head, in an act of outright defiance, had responded thusly to the sajal's exacting demands for stone:

"My city villa is of more significance to me than the new Waterlily temple. My commoners will quarry stone for me first. Two seasons hence they will quarry for you, but for now they quarry for me, for the glory of our ancestors—not of yours."

My father would have been incensed, had the sajal told him of such insolence. But had such insolence in fact been expressed? It is impossible to know; it feels as though my thoughts spin upon themselves. What if the intelligence from Becilna regarding the pace of their construction was in error? Or exaggerated? Had the pace of my father's temple construction indeed slackened? Nothing was as it seemed, back then. Everyone had secrets to conceal. Therein lay the danger: We expended so much effort fighting threats that did not exist that we were ill-prepared to combat the ones that did.

◎◎◎

I know from experience that the fates of captives are difficult to predict. Sometimes they are treated well; other times they are tortured severely every day but allowed—or rather, required—to stay alive for years. Sometimes they are sacrificed without delay. That was my mother's fate, once we arrived at Lalchich.

Word of our capture had reached the city long before the victorious war party paused to prepare their triumphant entry. The morning was cool, and clouds hung low in the jungle canopy as we slumped, disheveled, on the jungle dirt with rough Lalchich rope around our necks. We watched our captors tidy and preen, readying themselves for the raucous cheering and loud praise of their valor that would soon ensue. We heard the pounding of their hollow slit log drums, the blaring of their wooden trumpets, the chiming of their turtle shell marimbas long before we were paraded around—bound, bloody, and naked, flayed lips scabbing over—and forced down onto our knees at the foot of their palace stair.

Then the music ceased and the formal captive review began.

"And this one? Who is this vile woman?" called out the red-cloaked Lalchich orator.

Of course they already knew our identities, as runners had informed the city of our capture soon after it occurred. No, these reviews, these queries, were not about our names: they were meant to publicly humiliate us. The loud roll call and the feigned surprise at our identities. The contrived roar of scorn at each mocking recital of our titles. The derisive laughter at our cries, our pleas, our disheveled royal persons. All Lalchich knew of our entrenched rivalry. They knew as well that our city had spurned theirs in the matter of my marriage. On this grand day they would have their revenge.

At the top of the palace stair, the young queen stood at the side of the young king. The black jaguar pelt slung over his shoulders shimmered, its weighty paws dangling in midair. His chest was muscular, and intricate tattoos circled his arms and torso. Heavy jade regalia covered both their persons. Their faces gazed stonily down from atop of the mighty Lalchich stair, feigning aloof disinterest in the tumult far below. As each of our names was bellowed out, attendants grabbed our hair and wrenched our faces to look up that staircase. My strongest recollection from the moment when my face was thusly wrenched is the sight of the cochineal-red banners lining both sides of that grand stair.

The young queen's visage remained stony, showing that she had matured since that day when my mother and I sat in her chamber sipping chili-infused chocolate from her painted clay cups. Despite the stoniness, however, I detected a slight expression of poignant satisfaction on the young queen's face when her eyes met those of my mother as my mother's title was bellowed and her face wrenched to look up that red-bannered stair.

As if some silent order had been given, my mother was separated from the rest of our pitiful, ragged group and jostled further up that stair. I am convinced she had known her fate from the start, because at the time of our capture—as we knelt on the dirt like dirty, limp rags with the rough rope wound about our necks—she apologized for scheming to kill the ball player Naah Chan and for trying to force my father's hand in the matter of my marriage. She confessed these missteps amid dreadful sobs, holding me tightly against her person until the Lalchich ripped us asunder. Even from her position two captives down from me on the rope, she continued her confessions. So miserably did she bawl about how badly she had wronged me, how selfish she had been, how she had betrayed her maternal duty to me, that I called back to her to affirm that I forgave her for not loving me well enough.

Was this true? Did I forgive her? When I called to her down the rope, I meant mostly to ease her woe. But now? Now I think I told her that because I did not want death to part us on bitter terms.

It may sound strange, but I don't believe my mother bore the young queen of Lalchich any rancor, even when they pried her jaws apart until her blood flowed in long red streams down that Lalchich palace stair.

◎◎◎

I languished long in their brutal bondage, not knowing how many days or months were passing. I faced each dawn with a sense of doom. The new day could be my last, or it could be only the next agonizing day in a lifetime of torture. And tortured I was. They ripped out both of my thumbnails, each on a separate occasion. They broke my forearm, only to send their bonesetter to mend it later. I think they intended to break it again. Of course my lips had been flayed when they first bound us round the neck with their rough rope.

Many times I saw the young queen and her husband, the K'uhul Ajaw of Lalchich, always at a distance, always towering high above, the wife clad in a fine-spun cochineal-red huipil and her husband wearing a cloak of similar hue that swung freely when not draped with his shimmering black jaguar pelt.

I also saw the round-headed lieutenant of that warrior party, the one with the turquoise inlays—the one who raped me first in the dank dirt. Once I heard him speak to his king. His voice was thick and harsh, and he had the unschooled accent of Lalchich. By eavesdropping on my gossiping guards, I came to understand that he was the head of a recently ascendant Lalchich lineage, and that his skill in combat was swiftly propelling him up through the warrior ranks. Never in my captivity did I lay eyes on the man who might have become my husband. At least, if I did, I was not aware of it.

During one of my many humiliating exposures before that palace stair, I caught sight of what must have been Lalchich's master stela carver beneath a shade tree next to the palace. A furl of white paper on the ground by his knee was held in place with smooth black pebbles. He was in that same low crouch in which I had observed Naah Chan so many times. The stela carver in the Lalchich shade shifted back and forth between paper and stone, paper and stone, his movements so familiar that tears sprang to my eyes. I supposed my captors believed their taunts and jeers had once again succeeded in letting lose my tears. On most days that was true, but on that day it was not.

On each outing to the staircase I searched for that master stela carver. My eyes longed to rest upon something familiar, something comforting. In this Lalchich stranger I found a crumb of solace. Like Naah Chan, this man was an artist able to unite history and beauty on sacred stone, even if it was Lalchich history, Lalchich stone.

With each outing to the staircase, I also thought of my Ka-lo'mte' grandmother. She might have been required to endure torture by an enemy, I speculated—perhaps even by the Lalchich. At the memory of my grandmother, my emotions raced back to my Ixchel Moon celebration and the feel of her one strong hand gripping my chin in such contrast to the other, gentle one that brushed the hair from my face.

At that moment of contact, I did not yet understand the contradictory nature of my grandmother's hands. A child cannot be expected to understand things of maturity. As a youth, I could not know the importance of cultivating the ability to hold two deeply opposing natures within one being. But in my Lalchich cell, I came to believe she had intended her gnarly touch as an unspoken message to assist in my survival. To know that even a frail old woman like my grandmother retained the capacity to manage such opposite natures—to be both gentle and strong, soft and hard—offered enormous comfort. As if by instinct, I knew I had to hide the gentle part of my being and summon all my strength to the fore. My Scarlet Macaw companion spirit was with me. She wrapped me in her bright protective wings, and I concealed my gentleness deep within them.

There was also a young Lalchich commoner, a girl who brought me food. How did a mere girl provide succor? By giving me a single, fleeting look in which I recognized deep anguish over my condition. In her anguish she reminded me of a very similar girl—the young Calumook commoner who had stood in witness at the base of our palace stair when my father killed my monkey. Even the lowborn, it seems, have the capacity for empathy.

Once while on their Lalchich stair, I peered toward that shade tree and saw the Lalchich sajal standing beside the master carver. The men were gesturing toward the stela being chiseled, discussing the carving before them without haste or emotion. While they were much too far for me to see its content or overhear their words, I imagined it was us. Many of Calumook's stelae recounted our grandest victories and the public humiliation and sacrifice of captured elites that followed. It seemed only reasonable that the stelae of Lalchich would do likewise. Probably my mother's name and title glyphs were already there, carved in stone along with our Calumook emblem glyph. Perhaps that master carver had chiseled my own glyphs onto his stone just this very morning. Perhaps he had done so because on this day, this very day, I was to perish on that red-bannered Lalchich staircase, whereupon my death would take its place as part of the history of this foreign land.

But death did not come for me that day on their stair.

Several days thereafter, a ruckus ensued outside the small, windowless room where I was held. That room was a hidden place, located off a tiny back courtyard deep within the palace's labyrinthine halls. First I heard muffled shouts, then some scuffling, then several moments of urgent whispering that stopped abruptly.

Then I heard nothing.

I knew something had happened in the tiny hidden courtyard but had no idea what, and I was afraid to look. You see, I had learned that if I was a meek and docile captive, the guards abused me less. I had grown so desperate that I believed that if I never saw them, they might forget I was there. Just poking my head out to see into the tiny courtyard had prompted vicious beatings. It was better to stay silent, let them carouse and gamble, nap and gossip.

So I did not move. I cowered in the depths of my darkest corner.

The still air was heavy in my small, close room. Off in the jungle the toucans had ceased their low guttural croaks, and even the endless drone of the cicadas had fallen mute. I waited, afraid even to twitch, afraid to open my eyes.

"Lady Winik," whispered a voice. It was a man's voice, harsh and low, and its tone held urgency and trepidation. "Lady Winik," it whispered again.

I didn't move. It was a trick. My guards sometimes played cruel tricks on me to break the tedium of the day. When I responded to their pranks with hopefulness, they would roar with amusement.

"Lady Winik."

No, I thought, this time it was not the guards. Something was different about the words the voice had just spoken. Only then did I realize I had not been called Lady Winik in some time. I had been called Whore of Calumook and Peasant of Calumook and Calumook Filth, but no one here had ever called me by my rightful name and title. Only then, cowering in my dark Lalchich cell, naked and bruised, dried blood and dirt thick upon my per-

son, did I begin to grasp how far my emotions had truly fallen—
so far that I had begun to accept my captor's image of myself, so
far that I had failed to recognize my own name.

My first, most powerful desire was to remain hidden in the
relative safety of my dark cell, for it was only when I was wrested
through its portal that suffering ensued. I dreaded that portal, that
terrible rectangle of vacant space, the colored paint of the jambs
at which my fingers scrabbled as I tried, but always failed, to prevent my departure. I dreaded the bright daylight and grimaced
at the sight of that tiny back courtyard through which my guards
dragged me, upon order of the Lalchich king or queen, to be flung
at the foot of their palace stair for another viewing, another round
of humiliation. Cowering in my dark cell, I realized the abuse
had been perpetrated not just upon my lips and fingernails and
bones and elsewhere on my person, but also on my very spirit,
deep at its core.

So disoriented was I that in truth, I was no longer certain
who lay captive in that dark cell. Desperately fearing for the survival of my soul, I had bidden my Scarlet Macaw companion
spirit to invent a new creature. We named her Lady Macaw. Lady
Macaw's stony face became my stony face. My person became her
person, and hers was the one who accepted my pain. And as the
days stretched onward, the generous Lady Macaw stood valiantly
in the stead of Lady Winik on that Lalchich stair. I hid within her,
deep within her Macaw's colorful plumage. It shielded me, that
plumage. Down her thick curving beak, I watched as my thumbnails were wrenched from her gnarled talons. It was she who
cawed and cried, not I. I was not there. But even so, during the
passage of those agonizing days and months—even when hidden
by her bright feathers—I knew that the generous spirit wings of
my faithful Scarlet Macaw companion were beginning to falter,
and that even brave Lady Macaw could not endure forever.

"Lady Winik?" the voice whispered again.

This time I detected in it a quality of uncertainty, of doubt as
to whether I was here at all. Perhaps the wrong span of the palace
wall had been scaled. Perhaps reports that I still lived had been
faulty intelligence. Or perhaps they had arrived too late to this
hidden back courtyard.

I heard muffled voices and quiet shifting movements, and
all of a sudden I feared that whoever was in that courtyard might

depart. The intensity of this new fear surpassed my dread of peering around my painted portal, that terrible rectangle of space.

In the end I did peer around it, and my disbelieving eyes beheld the longed-for sight of my own Calumook warriors. But even as relief surged through my person, so too did trepidation, since what I saw could be just another wicked hoax perpetrated by my captors, who soon would shriek with delight at its success. For a moment I shut my eyes. When I reopened them, the men were still crouched in the courtyard with their distinctive, hearteningly familiar Calumook warrior hairstyle and tattoos, and at last I began to trust that they might truly be my people—brave warriors sent to my rescue by my beloved father, the great K'uhul Ajaw of Calumook. Hot tears of relief began to slide down my wretched filthy cheeks as I stared at their handsome forms, low and stealthy, with lethal swords and strong bows at the ready.

◎◎◎

News of the fall of the Becilna king came on the heels of my return to Calumook. Grateful as we were for my homecoming, the spectacle for its celebration was canceled on account of the unsettling news.

I feigned disappointment at the cancellation, believing that my father wished wholeheartedly to publicly honor my safe return. In truth, however, after my ordeal I was eager simply to convalesce in my chamber—a long familiar place that now seemed strangely plush—while my body servant repaired the many assaults upon my person. For a while even our palace courtyard felt too open and unprotected. It took some time before I wanted even to sit on the steps to my own chamber. An entire month passed before I felt I had recovered enough to carry my little cousin— who had grown large in my absence—astride my hip again.

Soon thereafter, I felt able to slip out under cover of night to meet Naah Chan at our ceiba, behind our curtain of green vines. At first I was fearful of even his kind and gentle touch, and I shrank from him. He was patient. He waited as I collected myself, and then I reached out to rest my shaking hand on his arm. He was my friend, my only friend. With surprising tenderness, he lifted my hands and just barely brushed his lips across the angry red scars on my thumbs, those aching places where there should have been nails. It felt as if his breath alone touched those hurting places, and with such quiet witnessing compassion that tears welled up again. These he kissed as well—the tears of relief flooding down my face. It was then, in my moment of greatest need, that I discovered within this person a profound humanity I had not even realized one could possess. For that I loved him all the more.

◎◎◎

I would have thought the news of the fall of the Becilna king would bring my father immense joy, but it did not. Instead he withdrew even more to the rooms at the front of the palace, where he deliberated with his sajal and with Calumook's lineage heads. He also conferred with the many emissaries of the vast royal and noble cousinhood that formed the web of our world, many of whom paid rushed, unexpected visits to one another. Much seemed amiss, although I was not then certain why the fall of one king, the fall of one city, should cause such deep consternation.

During those days my father seldom appeared at the evening repasts beside our courtyard's torch-lit pleasure pool. When he did, his demeanor was strained. Gone was the jocular, easy-going man who had sat at the head of our woven feasting mat. Hiding my own anguish, I tried to lighten his mood by laying my most attractive fragrant floral bundle on the mat near his cushion, but he did not seem to notice it. Of course I was far too old to cuddle on his lap as once I had, but I admit there were moments when I wished I could do precisely that. Instead I was obliged, as the highborn, unmarried adult woman I had become, to sit in my proper place many cushions removed from him. I longed for a return to those simpler days when we strode our sacbe arm in arm, chatting happily, each delighting in the presence of the other, but those times seemed long ago. Although I took tremendous comfort from the tenderness of Naah Chan, I discovered that there is no substitute for the affection of a loving father. It was a great disappointment that I did not receive it.

The second time I was at all in close proximity to my father after my return, I was summoned to appear in a front palace chamber, where I was bid—yet again—to recount each detail of my time in brutal Lalchich bondage. The men—my father among them—sat cross-legged upon their woven mats and benches, listening in flinty silence as I told my long and frightful tale. After I finished the harrowing account, their questioning began. They interrogated me fiercely, it seemed, and I became confused, for somehow it appeared they failed to grasp that I had been kept in a dark, guarded cell in a tiny back palace courtyard and thus simply had nothing to offer in response to their endless queries about the palace, its inhabitants, their defenses and storehouses, or other puzzling matters. In this I believe I only added to my father's burden.

One evening, as we sat on the twilit steps of our courtyard several days after the departure of our last visiting dignitary, we received a message instructing us to assemble in our finery early the next morning at the palace's front. This time, I too, grumbled at the inconvenience, as in truth I was not yet fully recovered from my ordeal; also, the primping required prior to an early spectacle intruded on our slumber.

The next morning, however, we stood in our customary places. The hollow slit log drums pounded and the loud wooden trumpets blared and the high-pitched marimba chimed and the ocean conch roared, and then my father appeared at the top of our staircase. Jade-draped and regal as always, he wore his jaguar pelt about his shoulders and his tall quetzal streamer headdress. Beside the K'uhul Ajaw of Calumook stood his ceremonial battle spear—a tall, polished wooden staff tipped by an enormous flint chipped with great skill into a likeness of Ek' Chuaj, the black god of war, with his sharp scorpion tail curled in menace.

I was surprised when our master astronomer appeared from one of the rooms and stood near my father. I smiled to see his dark cloak sweep round his legs once more. In the crook of his arm he cradled a thick, well-used codex. This man, my kind-hearted teacher who taught me all I knew about the glittering heavens, looked exhausted. Even at the dawn of those mornings after we had observed and charted the dance of the celestial bodies all the long night, I had never seen him look as haggard as he did now, standing beside my father atop our palace stair.

My astronomy training had concluded when my nuptial activities commenced, so I had not seen this man in some time. Still, as I gazed at my former teacher I was surprised to discover that the memory of our dark rooftop sojourns together roused within me a swell of nostalgia. I smiled at the sight of the long graying tail of hair hanging down his back. I had once thought that thin, unkempt tail unattractive but soon came to consider it endearing. I tried to catch his eye, but he did not look around. I imagine he felt nervous in this unfamiliar public setting so profoundly dissimilar to his usual dark rooftop quiet. So much had happened since those nights.

As I watched the two men standing side by side, my benevolent teacher—so wise and learned in his humble black cloak, with his unobtrusive demeanor—seemed out of place beside my father's flamboyant glory and many luxurious trappings of royal extravagance. Observing the two men's contradictory existences, I experienced sudden, deep confusion about which world—which male figure—I was drawn to more, my father's or my teacher's. At the same time I realized that I no longer had any choice, if I had ever had one at all, of a world I might prefer. Nonetheless, there I stood, as commanded: the just-returned Lady Winik, properly positioned in my jade regalia and finery with my cousin on my hip. The commoners of Calumook, tiny as ants, were assembled in the plaza far below.

After the trumpets and other musical din of spectacle had dissipated into the rosy break of day, my father raised his arm and cried: "Children of Calumook! The Venus star once again shines his bright face in our dawn sky!"

In obedient, awkward haste, our astronomer held aloft the thick codex he had been holding in the crook of his elbow. I had heard him speak many times of this particular book and had even once been allowed to peer within its painted pages. It was the codex that charted the movement of Venus as the morning star—its invisibility at superior conjunction, its visibility as evening star, and invisibility again at inferior conjunction. Together we had studied this cycle, I at my teacher's side.

After a brief pause, my father continued, "It is our Hero Twin that arrives to shine so brightly upon us!"

A less-than-enthusiastic roar rose from the sleepy crowd, in the plaza and as well from the highborn upon the palace steps, but my father did not seem to notice the lack of fervor.

"The Venus star brings us his message," my father cried. "It heralds a call to arms! I beseech our bravest Calumook warriors—prepare your shields! Collect your swords! Ready your atlatls and assemble your spears"—at this my father shook his ceremonial spear with its eccentric flint tip—"for the time has come to let our mighty ax fall upon our enemy Becilna!"

The momentary pause in the clamor from the commoners in the plaza below was nearly imperceptible. Stony of visage, the highborn stood looking down upon them. They looked at us, we at them, each of us seeking to contain the astonishment we all felt. Might we still be deep in slumber in our cozy chambers, upon our soft woven mats? Could we all be dreaming that my father had just spoken these words? I stole a quick glance at my kindhearted astronomy teacher, seeking some sort of guidance, but I could not pierce the enigmatic expression on the haggard face of our black cloak. Both men now stood with their arms pointing eastward to the appearance of the Venus star above the dawn horizon. Although both were gazing at the same distant object, the contrast between my father and our astronomer was nothing short of stark.

Everyone in Calumook—indeed, every creature for leagues in all directions—knew of the fall of the Becilna king. By then this news had rippled to every corner of the world. He died bravely, it was said, obsidian-edged sword in hand.

Everyone was also aware of the brutal Lalchich attack on our innocent entourage as we returned home from an innocuous marriage parley at Somalx. Everyone knew that my mother—my father's kind and loving principal wife, the Greatest Queen of Calumook, a gracious woman of splendor and royal pedigree and high esteem—had been put to death by the treacherous Lalchich. They knew that the king's youngest and most beautiful daughter—their own beloved Lady Winik—had been viciously tortured on their loathsome red-bannered stair. They were upstarts and ingrates. They had dared to invent their own, despicable, emblem glyph.

They had started all of this! They had had the temerity to snub our royal entourage, and in a most ill-bred fashion had refused to marry our cherished, beloved Lady Winik. It was an insult and an outrage! Such effrontery must not go unanswered.

All this was now being said, so why were we about to engage in a star war against Becilna?

I knew why. Most did, I suspect. Still, not one stonily masked face revealed it. No, we all knew to keep all emotion from the surface, to conceal our knowledge of everything. We also knew we were to slowly turn our reverent gaze to the dawn horizon, from whither glowed Venus the morning star, our beloved Hero Twin in his celestial and resurrected guise.

Why war with Becilna? Because Becilna had become easy prey. Our erstwhile friend and ally had a palace filled with cacao and jade and granaries stocked with maize. Now that the king was gone, its storehouses would be guarded by a ragtag troop of unproven warriors of the loyal but unorganized lineage of the Pretender to the Becilna throne.

Becilna also had stone, lots of stone. Fine, cut stone that would be laid out in long, neat, ready rows, block upon block, beside their rising temple. Mounds of white lime mortar powder would stand ready beside the cut stone blocks. If we did not take Becilna, a different city would.

My own visage stony and unmoving, I felt intense heat begin to mount from deep within the center of my chest. Standing motionless and unreadable, I could feel my face begin to flush. How could my father make such a crass, opportunistic bid for Becilna when our real enemy was the brutal Lalchich? The brave party of Calumook warriors who rescued me from my terrible dark cell had assured me that my father was already planning a mighty ax war against the city of my captors, and that he had vowed not to rest until he crushed it like a beetle into the dirt. I knew final preparations for that epic battle had begun the moment our capture had become known. And now, so soon, my father had forgotten my torment? Forgotten my humiliation? The cruelly twisted, bleeding jaw of my mother, honored queen of our proud city? A sudden ache surged from beneath the hard scabs on my captive's lips as the memory of that sharp Lalchich flint sliced once more through their pinkness. I brushed my thumbs with my forefingers, and throbs of renewed pain surged through my arms. From deep in my marrow I recalled the slow, purposeful agony with which my forearm had been broken. It felt as if my blood had begun to drip anew, right here on our own green-bannered palace stair. Even as I stood upon the landing, I found myself ever more confused with what was said and what I saw, with what I knew and what I only thought I knew.

◙◙◙

Our battle against Becilna was a rousing triumph. The ragtag warrior-guards had indeed fallen with little resistance before the might of the victorious Calumook ax. For an entire month, lines of defeated Becilna leafcutter ants bent by heavy tumplines wound their slow, monotonous way into our city. Bulging burdens appeared at our palace—both its front and its back—and our storehouses and granaries swelled. Not only goods but slaves, too, arrived from Becilna. Under laden tumplines they trod to the homes of Calumook warriors who had answered my father's call to arms, and proceeded to toil and sweat for their new masters. My father's temple was far from forgotten: tumplines of cut stone blocks and baskets of white lime powder lay piled at its foot. And after casting off their burdens, those Becilna ants scaled its rising sides to labor on its glorious, nearly finished façade.

Celebration was in the air.

My father presented his lineage heads with an impromptu round of lavish gifts, opened his newly replenished granaries, and ordered grand feasts for all in our proud city. Music and sweet honey and chicha flowed like our mighty river, and commoner and highborn alike swaggered and staggered in glee and gluttony. The demoralized players of Becilna faced off against those of triumphant Calumook in a hurriedly arranged ball game. As expected, it was the pitiful, already conquered men who found themselves on their knees with sharp blades at their necks as the forces of good vanquished those of evil.

In haste and as required, Naah Chan had taken up his chisel to carve a new stela. It would depict my father's success in the war against our enemy Becilna: how their humiliated king had died at my father's own hand, and how tribute would pour into our triumphant city for generations. This stela was to be erected in front of my father's new Chaak temple on 10.0.0.0.0. First a temple dedication, then a Katun ending, and now a great victory in war to be commemorated! Yes, Calumook now had three momentous occasions to celebrate. What had already been planned as a spectacle of spectacles had become even grander, and our great victory over Becilna was sure to warrant its own proud stanza in our fast-lengthening patriline chant.

These were heady times. I watched my father as he watched Naah Chan tap his chisel. From time to time, a smile broke through the stony mask of his royal visage. My father was joyful! At last he was joyful. Even Chaak had sent more little tastes of rain to let us know he was delighted with my father's recent decisions about his rising temple. Calumook was thriving. Our future was assured. Night after night we feasted, pale moonlight and orange torchlight glinting from the surface of our pleasure pool, the sweet fragrance of victory and floral bundles aloft on the warm and blissful air.

◎◎◎

It is not difficult to grasp how the warriors of Lalchich were able to penetrate our defenses amid such jubilation. It was as if people—everyone, someone, my father's sajal?—had forgotten the treachery of these sly, brutal enemies.

They struck in the darkness before dawn. Bare feet padded silently from the blackness of the jungle onto our unguarded sacbe. Two noiseless columns of trained warriors moved through the hushed, moonless night past our shadowy ball court and the craggy silhouette of my father's rising temple. Their soundless feet headed straight to two places. One was the back courtyard that led to where we slumbered, curled up on our soft mats on our benches in our quiet painted chambers. The second warrior column slithered up our grand palace staircase. In my mind's eye I see the low, steady line of inky forms gliding skyward like vultures on the smooth air of night. Unsuspecting, groggy guards at both places woke to find obsidian daggers plunged deep within their chests.

I awakened to a dreadful commotion. It rapidly rose to a crescendo more hideous than anything I had ever heard, as the victory cries of the warriors of Lalchich resounded from the very center of our palace courtyard.

They touched torch-flame to our awnings and curtains, causing thick black smoke to force us from our chambers, clutching at our throats for air. I too stood bent at the waist, coughing with the rest of my kin, as those despicable Lalchich dogs watched with pleasure in the light of the flickering flames. Within the center of our courtyard they stood, laughing at our humiliation, and I knew they were anticipating the joy and riches that would soon be theirs.

When they came at us with clubs, mayhem ensued. I grabbed my little cousin, who was scarcely roused from his sleep, and ran, a raucous blur of orange flames, shrieks, smoke, and war whoops on either side of me. Amidst the turmoil, no one noticed me speeding through the courtyard and down the winding steps that led to my ancestors' crypts. When my hand plunged into emptiness, I knew as if by instinct to squeeze deep within the tiny recess on the stair, the one with the grotesque painted incense burner with the great blank eyes.

I wedged myself against its far wall, the tiny person of my cousin clutched tight in my arms. Panting, I shut my eyes but could not escape the tumultuous sounds of the fearsome acts I knew were occurring just paces beyond the top of the dark, winding stair. I heard it all: the breaking of bone, the roar of flames, the thudding of clubs, the chaotic screams of terror, the brutally thwarted footfalls of escapees. They were so close, these sounds—closer than a mere stone's throw.

My little cousin had awakened now. Innocent amidst the great tragedy unfolding just there in our courtyard—in all of Calumook—he stared into my own panicked eyes, for a moment uncertain. But then, only just visibly in the dim shadowy light, he smiled.

Beyond our hiding place the mayhem continued unabated. As strange as it seems, my cousin and I both drifted into an uneasy, blank slumber through it all. I do not know how long I slept.

I awoke with a start to new shouts and cries. As my gaze met the unfamiliar wall of plaster before me in the recess, the terrors of the previous night returned. Thin shafts of daylight shone down the winding steps. Those scant beams did lighten our tiny recess, but we would only be seen if someone peered straight into the dimness. As if by a miracle, the ceramic incense burner at the fore remained in its upright position. Still I marvel at how it had not been smashed into a thousand painted shards when I scrambled past it the previous night.

As we huddled in the dark recess, I recalled my childhood fear of that painted countenance, that day my playmates had dared me to descend those dark stairs. It had gripped me with such terror on that long-ago day that at last a friend had had to come to my rescue by dragging me back up into the courtyard. At the base of those winding stairs lay the crypts of my ancestors. As I remembered their presence, it seemed as if the dusty bones within had begun to recite the low tones of our patriline chant.

In silence I chanted with them and spoke with them our ancient revered words, and found those words brought great comfort. Animated by my ancestors, I envisioned the fearsome features of that mighty incense burner striking against our evil assailants. So formidable a visage would, I hoped, repel even the most ruthless of Lalchich warriors. Huddled behind that incense burner, I felt it had become my brave defender.

But a loud voice abruptly disturbed my newfound sense of safety. "Bring them!" it demanded.

It was a Lalchich voice. I had come to know their harsh accent well—and loathe it utterly—during my brutal captivity. A knot began to form in my gut at the sound of it.

"Line them up!" the voice demanded.

I heard the struggle of scuffling feet. Then came the loud and bitter wailing of my kin. Little by little it grew, and within its strains I could identify the terrified cries of my older brothers and their wives. I knew they clutched their children, whose diminutive voices also wailed. These sounds all came from the far side of our courtyard, near our pleasure pool.

It suddenly struck me that I knew that Lalchich voice. It was one I had never expected to ever hear again. It belonged to that round-headed Lalchich lieutenant—the one with the turquoise tooth inlays. The one who raped me first on the dank dirt of the jungle.

"Who is here?" he demanded. "Name them."

The next voice was also one I did not expect to hear, at least not in apparently willing response to the round-headed Lalchich lieutenant's query. As my father's sajal began naming my kinspeople, individuals with whom he had worked a lifetime, my heart lost its spirit. I stared straight ahead as that familiar Calumook voice did as commanded. But as the familiar names tolled off, I realized it was not a reluctant voice I was hearing from within my tiny recess. No, it was an agreeable, confident voice, one that spoke with a quiet edge of satisfaction. Sitting with my back against the wall of my dim, dusty hiding place, I came to fathom the depth of my father's betrayal by a man he had known all his life and trusted completely.

I heard the sajal's deliberate recital of names and royal titles through a strange and distant haze. After each name was called out, muted sounds of thrashing and struggling ensued as a Lalchich warrior strangled the person. From my ever hazier distance, I heard the sorrowful rising tones of our Calumook ritual wail. Those plaintive cries of grief caused my skin to shiver; emotion rose in my chest, and tears streamed steadily down my cheeks. I sang with them my own silent lamentations. I sang with them, suffering with them the anguish and the misery of each being whose voice would never again speak in this world. I sang in silence with them until their lamentations ceased, one by one, replaced by the splash and gurgle of finality as each corpse was thrown like rubbish into our pleasure pool. Still my mind can make out each slow sway of each lifeless person, weighted still by their jade. Still my mind follows their slow descent through the dark watery world, through the long tangled stems of water lilies, into the waiting arms of the Lords of Death. Lastly they settle— royal limb upon jumbled royal limb—motionless on the bottom.

At the sound of my name I all but leapt. "Lady Winik is not accounted for," declared my father's sajal.

"Where is she?" boomed the angry voice of that round-headed lieutenant.

"I have not seen her."

"Where is she?" he boomed again, this time to his warriors. "You did not allow her to escape, did you?"

A low muttering of negative responses came from the mouths of those Lalchich dogs. I could envision that disagreeable band, hunched in unruly clumps around our pleasure pool. They would be squatting there, ugly Lalchich warrior hairstyles and despicable body tattoos, while the last breaths of air escaped from the lungs of my kinspeople. I could almost see it bubbling to the surface, those last tiny remnants of precious life releasing into nothingness.

Perhaps because my heart had again begun to pound against my chest, my little cousin awoke. He had slept soundly through the night—the horrible calling out of names, the guttural chokes, the wailing and the wet splashes of death—but now he was wide awake and looking right at me with his clear, beautiful eyes.

He was also hungry and soon began to fuss and fidget. I tried to distract him by wiggling my forefinger up and down—a little game he loved—but this time he wanted nothing to do with it.

"Silence!" roared my father's sajal. And all around him was silence.

Moments later, I detected the slow, controlled tread of sandaled feet as they crossed the courtyard. These sounds of stealth were moving in our direction.

"What do you hear?" called the round-headed Lalchich lieutenant, who must have remained at the edge of the pleasure pool with his men.

My father's sajal must have raised an arm to beckon silence, as there was no further sound except for the quiet fussing of my little cousin, there in our tiny hidden recess along the winding stair.

Now, with insistence, I wiggled my finger before his face. I grinned with desperation into his eyes, but with a grumble he batted away my finger. I held him tight to my person to cuddle him into happiness, whispering into his ear an endless string of only just audible tenderness, his head now tucked beneath my chin. I cupped a hand over his mouth, but he did not like it there and made him fuss all the more. As he squirmed and twisted within my grasp, I felt his warm urine seep around my belly. Upon that sensation, at that frightful moment, I lost control over my person and released my urine, too.

The stealthy footfalls of my father's sajal grew closer.

I called upon my ancestors in the dusty crypts below. I called upon my beloved Kalo'mte' grandmother to shield us with her strength. I implored the painted incense burner that guarded our tiny recess with its grotesque face to protect us. I pleaded to Ixchel, the ever cherished goddess of the moon. I don't remember what happened next. The only thing I cannot forget is the sound of a tiny muffled crack emanating from somewhere below my chin. It might have come from the general direction of the sweet-tempered cousin whom I loved so dearly and cuddled so close. Then silence reigned again.

My father's sajal must also have perceived that silence, for his footfalls ceased their slow approach. I imagine that sour-faced man standing several paces away from the first step of that winding stair. He sniffs like a wild jungle beast, nostrils flaring, hoping to catch the fresh scent of Lady Winik's royal urine on the air. His eyes dart and hunt, attempting to distinguish any tiny movement. I do not know how he fails to hear the pounding of my heart.

All around the courtyard and the palace, the din of pillage and spiteful glee soon arose. The round-headed lieutenant must

157

have turned his warriors loose. Their Lalchich accents faded in and out of my hearing. Sometimes I think it was because they had moved back and forth to some distant location, but other times I think it was I who journeyed elsewhere, wandering lost in strange emotionless circles, even though my cramped form was still hunched in the tiny recess. I held my cousin tight in my arms, even as his small person grew cold and rigid.

When again I awoke, both darkness and silence had fallen. I remained motionless for some time in that tiny recess. But at last—numb, dazed—I left my little cousin's lifeless corpse behind and crawled forward bit by bit, infant-like, on my knees and hands. Without a sound I moved the incense burner to the side and slid from the recess, and when I looked back upon that object's visage, I saw it as nothing more powerful than painted clay. Despite the dimness at the top of the stair, it was obvious there were no sentries. I supposed they were all off in a drunken victory stupor. I saw not a soul as I slipped out the palace courtyard door, stepped like a sleepwalker through an exposed strip of glimmering moonlight, and then melted into the darkest edge of the darkest jungle.

8

It was dark but I ran.

I was starving and reeked of urine. I was numb, distraught; my limbs were stiff from long hours squeezed in the tiny recess, but still I ran. I knew not where I ran, but I ran. Even in shock, even in despair, I knew I must put as much distance as I could between myself and the dangers of our dying Calumook. I zigged and zagged from the trail to try to confuse any dog or person tracking my footfalls. I skittered furtively into trackless jungle wilds where I could never retrace my path. As I ran and ran in the darkness I prayed no evil root or creeping Xibalba vine would grab at my ankle and tumble me to the earth. The sharp stink that pervaded my person, now sticky with sweat, did not overcome the grim fragrance of fear oozing from my own form. That fear was its own cloying self, bound to my skin like a strong invisible wrapper.

As I ran I implored Yum Kaax: "Yum Kaax! Send forth no wild prowling jungle beast! If one be already astir, do not let its nostrils catch my scent on the moonlit air!"

As I ran I pressed my hands over my ears.

I pressed them tight to halt the wails of my kinspeople, but even deep in the inky jungle their lamentations followed my every step. Their helpless cries reached me all the way from their still and watery graves. The appalling reality of that tiny muffled crack from beneath my chin pursued me as well. These sounds stole through the narrow cracks between my fingers, slid beneath the narrow curved hollows at my wrists. My kinspeople were gone. I knew the appalling fate of beleaguered Calumook. Even now, my home, the ancient and glorious city of my Waterlily ancestors—was still undergoing its obliteration. It would be utterly demolished, razed, and uprooted.

I had thought the rules of life did not apply to me—to the beautiful Lady Winik. I would exist in a state of grace and, unlike others, enjoy a life devoid of loss and pain. How mistaken I had been. Memories of my Lalchich captivity reverberated anew like a scourging inside my skull. I was startled by their latent ferocity. As I ran, I recalled the covenant I had made with myself while in their brutal bondage. Alone in my tiny cell, I had convinced myself that if I survived my ordeal, I would never have to suffer again. That I would already have suffered enough for one lifetime. That I had endured misery and would never again in my life be required to endure it again. But now as I ran, I understood deep in my marrow that such bargains are not ours to make. As I thrashed through the dark trees and vines, each stumble over Xibalba vine exposed the depth of the lie I had told myself. Suffering was not and never would be meted out in any measured portion, at least not by the power of sheer human desire. Suffering was to be my constant companion. Devastation would again be mine to know. There would be no mercy. The world I knew was gone.

◙◙◙

I do not know how far or in what direction I ran, but when I opened my eyes to daylight, my person was grimy, scratched, and bruised from toe to cheek. My hair was tangled through with leaves and vines. The miasma of stale urine hung upon me as if it had become my new companion. Daylight itself looked as unfamiliar as did my person. Thin shafts of light slanted through the thick jungle canopy with scarcely enough force to reach the dank earth I lay sprawled on, spent. As my waking mind surfaced, the horrors of our courtyard slammed into my consciousness with unexpected violence.

In a flood of tears I scrabbled and grabbed at the dirt and flung it at a ceiba. I screamed at the ceiba until my throat grew raw, then pounded it and clawed furiously at its merciless bark with my fingernails, railing at its unchanged presence, its indifference. I railed at our hard-hearted Balam, the jaguar god who had failed to protect us, abandoning loyal Calumook in her time of greatest need. Again I wept into the earth, but this time my sobs were less vehement as my own self grew compliant faced with the vast, inescapable power of fate. With every tear I cried, I felt myself growing also harder, as if I were resigning myself to the paltriness of my own particular life.

Spent once more, I lay on the forest floor until my glazed and unblinking eyes fell shut.

I slept and dreamt.

I dreamt an Infant Jaguar padded up from behind the ceiba, and in my sleep I felt its raspy rough tongue licking my tear-stained cheek. I dreamt its mother too crept out from behind the same sacred tree, and shoved her more powerful tongue shoved around the skin of my face as if she had determined I was ready to shed my sorrowful aspect in favor of another. My face had come to have desperate need of her cleansing.

Howler Monkey came. He brought a gourd cup filled to the brim with cool water, which he trickled at the corner of my parched lips until they opened and I drank greedily of his gift, his gift of life. When I was finished drinking, he curled his long slender tail round the empty gourd and held it aloft. He tilted his head to the night. From the enormous, gaping black circle of his mouth, his mighty guttural laugh-howl-bark crescendoed upward to fill the air—and then he was gone.

The angry hand of Yaluk cast a jagged bolt of lightning from the sky, piercing the earth. A moment later it was answered by the deep rumble of Ah Peku, and the ground below me shuddered with dread. These gods battled in the firmament above as I trembled far below, unsure which realm I now inhabited. Never before had I been unsheltered during one of their clashes. Never before had I slept without a roof above my head. Never before had I been alone in the jungle. Never before had I been alone for so long.

My Scarlet Macaw companion spirit hung like a dull red shadow, dazed and distant in the ether, she herself uncertain of her next move.

Great Bird came. She was large and black with a long yellow beak and enormous curling tail plumes. She pried my mouth open with her shimmering beak and pushed salty chewed fish deep into my gullet. The fish became shredded pieces of a human heart. Now her beak a held single jade bead, which she also pushed down my gullet. When she was finished feeding me, she cawed *muut-muut-muut* and flew off into the shadowy jungle.

My favorite pink-purple fragrant blossom entered my hazy vision. It paused and turned its face toward me, revealing without words that there remained great beauty in the world. There will always be struggle between good and evil, it said—without a mouth to say it—and it was my task to seize the good laid before me like a perfect fragrant blossom upon the cutting table.

The carved bird figure on the end of my bone weaving pin flew past. It chirped to me a song whose words I could not decipher, even though I grasped that beneath its melody ran a darker one infused with urgency. I smelled humans.

Hummingbird whirred beside my ear and told me I must now waken, and run and run again. Owl appeared and told me I must stay hidden behind the thick jungle vines, as pursuers were fast on my trail. Even in my dream state I was uncertain who to trust: I knew Owls are messengers from Xibalba, and that those Dark Lords would like nothing more than to laugh and gloat as I paddled my canoe down through their watery cleft.

Night filled the jungle once more, and I lay beneath the shimmering light of the goddess Ixchel and the bold white glow of her waxing gibbous moon. Day and night her bright rounding orb grew. The Rabbit she held was still young. I too was still so young.

From behind the cut slits of that astral-white jade mask, the eyes of my father shone bright, then transformed into those of his ugly dwarf, and then into the dark, beady ones of his sajal. Then that sour-faced man yanked my head from the musty earth, seizing me by my hair just as he had so cruelly clutched my pet monkey so long ago—and I became his grandest prize of all.

◙◙◙

Lily Bean is crying. How long I do not know; she's been crying because I was so agitated by my narrative that I forgot her presence beside me. My old and withered person sits in daylight and safety on this wooden stool near our hut, but I had been back there as I talked, alone in that dark jungle, returned to desperation. I experienced the starkness, the terror of it again in the core of my person. I saw again that dim slanting shaft of light; Howler

Monkey and his slender tail curled round the empty gourd cup; the urging of Owl; the dank smell of the earth and the reek of my own person. It was as if I had stepped through a hole in time.

"Lily Bean," I murmur.

I hope to comfort her with this kind utterance of her diminutive name. It is what I was called as a child, long before I became Lady Winik. I reach out and pull her close, something I have seldom done. I rock this child, my arms wrapped around her, and kiss her cheek with a corner of my mouth. I dare not do it again, or with anything more than a corner. I feel awkward performing such intimate gestures of affection. I wish these gestures came more easily, as they come to other women I have known ... to Nikte', who could calm even the wildest beast. I was not raised with such affection; perhaps that is why I recoil from it. Despite the many horrors I have survived, perhaps what I dread most is that this precious lineage child will not love me.

"There, there ..." I mumble.

She uses her palm to dry her face, her perfect face. She is young and I am not. I have had to flee through the treacherous jungle and she has not. I have suffered and she has her future. I hope my comforting gestures, my consoling tone, have helped her regain some degree of composure. Keeping one's composure is a skill like any other, even if it too fails us in the end.

"Grandmother, you have endured too much. It is for you I cry, for all of your agony."

I am surprised by her words, which seem too mature for this child. Of course she is right, and I am glad she has recognized it, but what else is there to say? "Such is the nature of life, my darling Lily Bean," I tell her. "We will all endure too much. All of us."

"How have you managed?" she asks.

"Managed what?"

"Managed to continue living?"

At this question I am silent for a long while. I ponder her query as well as my response. Is living an accomplishment on my part? I had not realized it might be viewed as such. In truth I do not know how I have continued to live. I wake each morning and walk into each day.

Doubtful whether I believe it fully, I say: "What matters is how we stride through our adversity. We of the House of the

Waterlily have always been able to stride through much adversity. We know when we must be gentle and when we must be fierce." As I say these words I feel once more the grip of my Kalo'mte' grandmother's hands.

Lily Bean considers this, but distress remains on her youthful face. I recognize it. She fears she lacks this ability and will shame us.

I say, "When you need it, it will be there. You will discover this knowledge lying within."

"What of our kinspeople? Did they not discover it?"

Her question silences me once more, but then I simply whisper what I truly believe. "I don't know, Lily Bean, I don't know," I say, and I press her again to my side. Again she allows me do this, this awkward grabbing and holding, this unfamiliar demonstration of affection. She does not shy away from this withered bag of bones. As an old woman I believe I have come to understand the true tragedy of war: that innocent people, good people, die.

"I weep for them," she confesses.

"As do I, my child."

Then she asks, "Grandmother, do the bones of our kinspeople still rest at the bottom of our pleasure pool?"

"Yes, they do," I say. "Except our pool is no longer there, no longer filled with lovely water."

The next time I saw our pleasure pool it had been transformed. A thick brown sludge had settled within it, and in the places it was not, there oozed small torpid puddles of thick water. Nothing was clean, nothing clear. Chunks of bark, twigs, dry curling jungle leaves, and long scraps of vine clogged its fetid surface. A disgusting stench rose from the muck.

"Why not?"

"Because those dogs of Lalchich did not know how to care for precious things," I say. "A pleasure pool requires constant attention. Our servants skimmed the surface each day. Each month they drained it to clean the bottom and coat the sides with fresh plaster. Then they would divert fresh new spring water to fill it again, and our water priest would make offerings to Ixazaluoh, goddess of water, to purify it."

"It must have been very pleasant to dip in that pool."

"That it was. How I loved to enter it on a hot day; walk in slowly and allow the cool water to rise along the skin of my legs."

"Grandmother, you know we all dip in our little river. Why do you never join us?"

"Oh Lily Bean," I say. "I'm much too decrepit for that."

"But, I will help you get in and out. It would be so enjoyable. There is a fine flat rock right at the edge—it's easy, Grandmother, I promise."

I look at this girl, the last in the line of the House of the Waterlily, with what I hope she considers modest reticence on my part, and I smile at her. Perhaps it is wrong of me, but as I look at this child I find I lack the heart to forbid her from splashing about in the river. No, I won't spoil her watery play by mentioning that highborn must never dip our persons in a river, but only in the purified water of a pleasure pool. Now there are no pleasure pools, so we cannot dip at all. I suppose I only have myself to blame when I suffer in the heat, but rules are rules.

◎◎◎

Turmoil had descended on Calumook. With the sajal's fist clenched in my disheveled hair, I heard the din long before I saw its source. It was such an unusual clamor that at first I could not comprehend what might create a sound penetrating enough to reach so far into the jungle. The din grew louder as we mounted the sacbe toward the city, and as we did, my trepidation grew apace, until at last I beheld the abysmal scene.

Around my architect ancestor's magnificent arch swarmed men from Calumook and warriors from Lalchich. Those from Calumook stood at the monument's graceful flanks, gripping the long handles of great wooden mallets. Each man swung and hit, swung and hit, and the painted plaster crumbled to the ground. More thuds of the long wooden mallets broke and shattered more of Calumook. Thick swirls of dust churned from the devastation like the curling smoke of copal. Huge jumbled piles of grit and rubble littered our sacbe, and much swinging and hitting still remained for those dreadful wooden mallets.

As I neared the scene, the thudding grew deafening. I was overwhelmed by its sheer intensity. As I gaped, the men clambering about upon our arch reminded me yet again of leafcutter ants, except this time their methodical deeds struck me as indifferent, as now their labors had fallen under the rule of the Lalchich.

Soon after the cruel pulling of my hair, I had begun the silent intonation of our patriline chant. Now, before this woeful sight, I repeated once more the reassuring stanzas that enshrined the glory of my architect ancestor. I intoned the lyrics that expressed his great acumen, his unparalleled ability to design and calculate, to conceive and imagine. The great love he had of his people and of this place—our Calumook, nestled within the bend of our mighty river—was so great that he had presented its people with this a magnificent arch. And the people of Calumook had borne such great love for my architect ancestor that they gave him their sweat and their toil. All this I chanted again and again because I never wanted to forget.

The swinging wooden mallets now fell onto mortar and cut stone, and I winced to hear its higher-pitched clap. A well-placed strike loosened several blocks, fragmenting the old mortar that had held it in place since the hallowed era of my visionary ancestor architect. As we walked past, a plummeting mass of stones and crumbling mortar landed so close that I breathed in its dust and was gripped by a fit of coughing. Another swing, another high-pitched clap, another well-placed strike, and more blocks tumbled through air to crash upon a tall, dusty, smoldering pile of rubble and wreckage on the sacbe.

At the base of the arch, another swarm of compliant Calumook ants carried out a different set of orders from the new overlords. Some knelt, knocking off the dry mortar that clung to the arch stones. Others sorted and stacked cut blocks into organized piles, while others heaved tumplines laden with cut stone to their foreheads. Although I did not know where they were taking the stone, I believed it was destined for my father's rising temple.

Block by block, blow by blow, the work, the artisanry, of my esteemed architect ancestor was being demolished. The tragedy of the dust and the din was that the architectural heritage of our Calumook would vanish. That heritage was one of the things that defined us. Who would we be without it? If the arch of Calumook was being demolished, then wooden mallets would soon descend upon the arch at the sacbe's other end at Cenote as well, because once Calumook fell, our Cenote puppet did not have a chance.

Yes, it was our own men from Calumook—our own leafcutter ants, descendants of those who had constructed the arch—

who now labored at its flanks. They were forced to destroy it, mallet blow after swinging mallet blow.

I wonder what they thought as they swung the mallets. They must have known that the House of the Waterlily was diminished with each blow, which is why I have to believe they only swung because they were forced to swing. No, they could never be indifferent to the matter of which cross-legged men on woven mats commanded them in their toil. They must have cared about the color of woven fine-spun as much as we did, or at most only slightly less.

The victorious Lalchich warriors, now transformed into harsh taskmasters, stood around smirking on the sacbe. A haughty gleam lit up their faces when they recognized the grand prize—this person whose disheveled hair the sajal still clutched in his cruel fist.

Someone taunted me: "Oh, there's 'She of the House of the Waterlily'!"

"Out of the way, lads, here comes the charming Lady Winik! Look at her now!" another jeered.

Hair fell about my dirty face, and my filthy clothes still reeked powerfully. Scratches and bruises covered my skin, and although I had no mirror I knew my eyes were rolling wildly like those of a half-animal, a madwoman, a helpless captured beast. The cruel fist of the sajal tightened as he forced my face toward my hecklers, to gaze right at them, and as I did I knew these were the men who had slain my kinspeople. I spat at those Lalchich dogs and they laughed afresh. The traitorous sajal laughed with them.

The victors' strategy was not yet clear.

Their plan might have been to plunge a dagger in my neck that very day. If they did, they would do so at the base of our palace stair, to which my staggering legs would soon bring me. Or their plan may have been to keep me captive as had been done to me in Lalchich, hauling me out for endless rounds of torture and humiliation, this time on my own palace stair. Then again, they might have intended to send me as a concubine to the king of Lalchich, as a carnal flesh-badge of his victory over his greatest nemesis, my father.

While it may seem small cause for gratitude, I concede that I was glad I was not forced to witness the collapse of my ancestor's arch. But though my eyes were spared, my ears were not. I heard the structure fail as the final fragile rows of support stones at last gave way to the weight above. With a thunderous roar, an enormous cloud of dust, and much cheering by Lalchich voices, it crashed to the ground.

By the time it fell, I was shut in a guarded palace chamber. It was not my own chamber or even our own courtyard, and for that I was also thankful, for I did not have to gaze out at the distressing, deathly waters of our pleasure pool. For these two small blessings I was thankful, although not to any person. No, I believe these were simple oversights, given that the crushing of the spirit of Lady Winik, youngest daughter of the House of the Waterlily, would surely have been most welcome.

◎◎◎

My next appearance in public was for my wedding spectacle. It seemed my new overlords had decided they needed me somewhat more than they despised me.

It took place at the pinnacle of our palace, itself transformed. Whispers rippled through the crowd when I was led from a high palace chamber. I looked as groomed and pampered as I had always been and was wearing jade and my usual finery, so it was not the actual sight of my person that caused the stir. Rather, it was because the remaining Calumook nobility, and certainly the commoners assembled in the plaza below, had not known I still lived.

News travels fast, unfortunate news even faster.

Everyone present knew my kinspeople had died at the treacherous hand of the sajal; thus they were wise to fear him all the more. I could sense their fear despite the stony masks tightly covering their faces. They knew of my father's death as well. He was said to have been stabbed in gray restless slumber by the sharp dagger of the highest ranked lineage head of Calumook. No wonder my father had resisted sleep for as long as he could. Those were dangerous times, back then, and the web of deceit we ourselves had woven was vast and tangled.

It was with false dignity, my own stony mask firm across my face, that I stood at the pinnacle of a palace that was no longer ours. The sajal stood beside me, his hand clasped around my father's Manikin Scepter. In truth, it was this scepter that was the genuine prize of Calumook. I was merely its accompanying conjugal flesh-badge. I knew this with certainty, for the place where I stood was as foreign as it was familiar.

The new Lalchich emblem glyph was emblazoned everywhere. It screamed from their hideous cochineal-red banners and their lush red draperies and the carmine-hued swaying cloaks that teemed around me. Their disagreeable color demeaned our palace. It also demeaned the appearance of my father's heavy jade, which now hung on the person of the sajal. My father's regalia fit him poorly; I thought it made him look absurd. Upon his head sat my father's quetzal streamer headdress—a stunning symbol of royal pedigree that did not manage to transform even one drop of his non-royal blood.

As the new young queen of Calumook, I stood beside this man—the new K'uhul Ajaw of Calumook—the Pretender.

Following the loud trumpets and the drums and the marimba and the roar of the ocean conch, we descended the staircase to the clanging of our jade regalia. This time I was unable to hear within it the voice of my ancestors. As we neared the bottom rung, I noticed that two paired stelae had been erected on the sacbe. In many cities it was common for stelae to be erected in such a position, but my father had decided against it, believing it marred the visual impact of our palace. Now here they were, as if even Calumook's royal monuments now stood in betrayal of my defeated father.

The paired stelae were awaiting their public unveiling, their carved faces concealed behind ample drapes of red fine-spun.

As a king cannot play his role all by himself, and by then the Pretender of Calumook had named his own sajal. The man thus elevated was from Calumook and was himself a worm. It was clear to all that while his new title might indeed be sajal, his new station was a sham. As the months wore on, this charade became ever more obvious, and the feckless Calumook worm endured such harsh mockery that I came to feel a sliver of pity for him, despite the intensity of my resentment. This man guided me into position on the far side of the draped stelae, but I had not yet developed this pity, and I recoiled in disgust as he grasped my arm to align me.

The trumpets blared, the hollow slit log drums sounded, the ocean conch roared.

I had never before seen the new stela orator, enfolded within his fine-spun cloak, so I supposed our Calumook stela orator had met the tip of a Lalchich dagger. This new, red-cloaked orator strode forward to stand beside the draped monuments. The Pretender and I stood in perfect marital symmetry, which I deliberately marred by shifting my foot, though not far enough that I would be shuffled back into position. It was pitiful, this minuscule resistance, and I knew it even then, but it was all I could manage. If there was one truth I understood as I waited upon a stair that once was ours, it was that any authority I ever held had vanished.

Again came the trumpets and hollow slit log drums, and with a grand flourish, the orator whipped the fine-spun from both stelae at once, and my stony mask all but fell to shatter at my feet.

Never do stela orators speak after they have whipped a drape from a monument. They unveil it with dramatic flair, and then they pause. With eyes that do not move, they gauge the tenor of the assembly before them with well-practiced acumen. Through their waiting, they convey a demand that the stateliness of the carving be acknowledged and the artistry of the composition admired. They do this for the benefit of the highborn. For the illiterate throng of commoners in the plaza, their pause is meant to stimulate a demeaning sense of inferiority, for writing and art have only ever been understood by the highborn.

During the hush and the shaming, I read. As I read, such a complex mix of emotions began to roil within my person that I barely heard the booming voice of the stela orator, who stood a mere two paces from my side.

Facing the crowd, the red-cloaked man spoke without haste, enunciating each word at the utmost volume so that every last ant in the plaza below could hear. Slow, pompous gestures of his fine and noble hands indicated each glyph, each carved image. He delivered the sound-symbols with meticulous precision, expounding with eloquence upon each one.

They were lies.

No, my father had not been defeated in an ax war—he had been deceived by his treacherous sajal! No, my father had not been carried back to Lalchich and beheaded on their staircase on 9.19.18.8.6. He had been killed right here, in his sleep at Calumook, by the dagger of a lineage head in cahoots with his treacherous sajal!

The orator gestured to the B'aahk'ab title glyph: The First of the Earth. His noble hand shifted to indicate another important title glyph: Ah K'al Bak, He of 20 Captives. These were titles bestowed upon my father, and now his treacherous sajal was claiming them!

The orator gestured to the Yatan glyph, its main sign that of a mat, and I cringed. No, I had not become the wife of the Pretender under the infinitely favorable auspices of a celestially ordained union on 9.19.18.11.5, 13 Muan, 6 Chicchan. No, I would not bear him a son! No, our royal Waterlily bloodline would not be cosmically entwined with the lineage of the Pretender, and thus continue long into the future! They were all absolute falsehoods, each and every one of those carved glyphs.

Through the stony eyes of my stony mask, I glared at the red Lalchich banners around me, and at their garish upstart emblem glyph in deliberate conjunction with our venerable and elegant one. I glared at the paired stelae at my side. Yet even as the deceptions of these glyphs exposed their strategy, I also experienced a strange sense of relief.

Why relief? Because it was not the chisel of Naah Chan that had tapped these awful untruths. Naah Chan had not been forced to carve these terrible monuments. No, the hand that clasped that lying chisel had not been his, that much was certain. This carver's hand was unknown to me. Though unskilled, it did indeed show some degree of talent, though still unrefined. It was a hasty hand as well. The composition was not well balanced, and a section of lunar cycle glyphs along one side had been so poorly blocked that the dates in the last string were squeezed against one another. Naah Chan had once told me that such errors happen when a carver has rushed his composition. Obviously the carving of these paired stelae had been exceedingly rushed.

As these thoughts whirred within my person, I considered whether Naah Chan could ever have forced his chisel to tap such falsehoods. No, I did not believe he could ever have carved glyphs falsely depicting my joyous marriage to the sour-faced sajal, a man he knew I despised. True, once his chisel would indeed have carved my marriage glyphs, and he would have tapped their contours with a sense of ease, knowing I was content with my nuptial destiny. But even as anger and pride, disgust and relief all roiled at once within me, I sensed the rise of another troubling emotion: apprehension for the well-being of my beloved Naah Chan, Calumook's former master stela carver.

◎◎◎

Life in Calumook was not the same under the Pretender. Never could I have imaged how different our city might be without a Waterlily upon the throne.

After our magnificent arches fell, the Lalchich turned upon our archives, whose conflagration I was forced to witness, my stony mask a second skin against my face. It took such little effort to destroy the codices—the merest tickle of torch flame set the dry, folded pages of ink and history fast to blazing. Roaring flames licked the walls, and I breathed the scent of burning plaster. It was as if the impenetrable black smoke billowing from the door of our palace archive carried off our legacy and our wisdom, the very words of our world.

They did not stop at our books. They also assaulted the history we had carved on stone.

They did not leave the demolition of our stelae in the hands of mere ants. No, that pleasure they reserved for their own greedy selves. Thus it was the warriors of Lalchich whose hands gripped those long wooden handles, gleefully bring them down upon the beautiful symbolic stone forests of Calumook.

This time I heard not the dull thud of wood against plaster, nor even the higher pitch of wood against stone. When struck with the wooden mallets, our stelae rang out like bright bells. They rang out in disbelief that an act so appalling could be perpetrated upon something so exquisite. As the powerful blows rippled through our tall, cherished stone monuments, the slabs split, shattered into pieces, and toppled, collapsing one by one into tragic squat piles of carved rubble. This was the fate of those Naah Chan had chiseled for my father, as well as those sculpted by earlier master carvers for my father's father, indeed, for our whole long line of Waterlily ancestors. Also smashed to pieces were the two stelae not yet tapped to completion by Naah Chan's loyal chisel. One was to have commemorated the dedication of my father's Chaak temple; the other was to memorialize my marriage to the royal groom of a great and honored city. The distinct glyphs of his identity were still lacking when these too were shattered into heaps.

They moved on to our heirloom temple, the older one beside which my father's new temple had been rising. The warriors of Lalchich, proud triumphant victors, mounted the temple stair not in a deliberate ritual procession, as we of Calumook always did, but rather like a pack of ferocious wild dogs, bounding madly up it as if they'd caught the spoor of a wounded beast.

The wounded beast was us.

Our scent was inseparable from the primeval essence of the temple stones. It was enveloped by the molded clay hearts of figurines in the niches in the walls of our sanctuary. It resided in the tender, devoted embrace of painted bowls and plates upon our wooden temple tables. But most of all, the scent of our venerable Waterlily legacy was strongest within our ancestor bundles—cherished articles containing the bones of our most exalted forebears shrouded in ancient fine-spun wrappings, with our most esteemed heritage jades tucked in the sacred folds—the holiest, most precious legacies of the long and illustrious House of the Waterlily. These they defiled. These they flung to the ground, unfurling their fine-spun lengths, spreading them out to ridicule and the profane light of day, putting them to the torch, hurling them down to be gnawed by dogs. These warriors of Lalchich— they were the dogs.

Our grand ball court they kept. They played ball on it, these Lalchich warriors, under unfair rules, hauling their Calumook captives forward and forcing them to play without protective gear. No torso of flesh, however sturdy or skilled, can withstand the strike of the hard rubber ball without leather protectors and manoplas, so of course our players found themselves at the north end of the court with the dagger at the hollow of their necks.

The whole thing was a mockery of the passion play that begot our world.

What of the heroic journey of Hun-Hunahpu (and his brother Seven Hunter), who accepted that first invitation sent by the Lords of the Underworld? What of the sacred gourd-head that hung in the Xibalba tree? The conception by spittle that Little One willingly took into her open palm? The cyclical journey of her sons, Hunter and Jaguar Deer? Their nights of terror in the Houses of the Knives and the Bats? It is true that absent the preliminary ritual underpinnings, these profane acts carried little risk of celestial retribution, but I wonder nonetheless what the

Lords of Xibalba must have thought as they gazed up upon us through their cleft in the earth.

But such things I cannot know. Each one of us remains plagued by the mist the gods cast before our perfect human vision. Yet my aged eyes see this truth: evil cannot always conquer good, nor can good always conquer evil. From this truth we recognize that our burden is to continually partake of this perpetual struggle.

While there was much tearing down, there was also building. Or at least, there was an effort at building.

My sense was that construction on my father's new Chaak temple was at best intermittent, for the Lalchich victors were either occupied with their wrath and destruction against us, or else lazing and lolling about in their gluttonous conquering stupor. The traitorous sajal clearly intended to claim my father's new temple as his own. The Pretender of Calumook planned to remain on track with the K'uhul Ajaw of Calumook's schedule for the grand spectacle on 10.0.0.0.0. I knew this because I heard him speaking with his puppet sajal.

"Soon they must stop their ransacking," grumbled the Pretender.

"Yes, my lord," said that worm of a Calumook man.

"You must make them stop," the Pretender demanded, a spark of anger now his voice. My father had never allowed anger to rise in his voice.

"Yes, my lord, I will make it happen."

"You must round up the Lalchich warriors. You must take their minds off feasting and drinking and abusing the women. They have had enough. Tell them I have decreed they have had enough."

"Yes, my lord, I will do it."

"They must devote their efforts to continuing the Chaak temple. They must oversee the Calumook laborers."

"Yes, I will see to it, my lord."

"And how fare the palace maize granaries?"

"I will make inquiries in that regard, my lord."

"Make your inquiries now. Report back to me by midday."

"Yes, my lord, I will go right away."

I'm not sure what the Pretender did while his sajal investigated, but when the latter returned, the conversation continued.

"There is enough maize for many days, my lord."

"Many days?" queried the Pretender.

"Yes, my lord."

"How many days?"

"I believe there is enough for twenty days, my lord."

"Twenty days. How many mouths can those twenty days feed?"

"It depends on how much they eat, my lord."

"Of course it depends on how much they eat! Are you unacquainted with the standard daily maize ration of a stone laborer?"

"Yes, my lord, it is three gourd bowls per man per day."

"Then how many men will eat for those twenty days?"

"I'm not certain, my lord. I will need to go again to consider this measure."

◎◎◎

Throughout those tumultuous months, my body servant continued her work of grooming and pampering me. Only later did I realize how truly fortunate I was to have been permitted to retain my body servant rather than obliged to take another.

One day this woman spoke to me, something she had never done up to that time. "How do you fare, young Lady Winik, amidst such sorrow?"

I raised my head in surprise.

Except for the necessary exchange of rudimentary information, body servants never spoke to us, and even then it was with submission. Never would they presume to chitchat. After she spoke, she moved to stand behind me and began glossing my hair. From a small clay bottle she drizzled fragrant palm oil onto the strands and began the slow process of spreading it all the way to the tips.

I said nothing.

"They are too brutal, my lady," she murmured, after a long pause.

Again I said nothing. I continued to gaze at my reflection in my mirror. But then I allowed my sight to shift to the face of my body servant, whose more distant image appeared behind my own in the shiny reflective circle of polished hematite.

She was much older than I. Deep creases lined the skin around her mouth and eyes. Her nose was low and flat, and her cheeks had little character. Her graying hair was pulled back simply in the way of commoner women to form a small, unostentatious bun at the nape of the neck. As body servant to royalty, she wore an unassuming medium-spun huipil with a simple, unpretentious pattern around the neck. I was relieved this woman did not presume to meet my eye in the mirror.

I directed my gaze once more to my own reflection. Within it I distinguished the visage of Lady Winik, but it was little more than a fraught veneer.

Young I still was, that is true. And beautiful. But an undeniable hardness had worked its visible path across my brow, and for the first time I noticed a deep furrow there, incongruous on someone so young. My eyes had a somber, distant quality. I had not realized that the corners of my mouth now drew downward with such perpetual vehemence. My body servant was wise in her concern for my well-being.

"Mmmm," I murmured without conviction, not knowing how else to respond. It seemed she was merely making an effort to be comforting, so I did not wish to be unduly harsh. I appreciated her concern, but I was also confused. Should I don my stony mask as I sat on my stool? Or could I continue to sit at ease, in the relaxing privacy of my chamber as I had always done, allowing the pampering to unfold? I enjoyed the sensation of her fragrant, oiled comb gliding through my hair. Trying now to augur her intent, I paid closer attention to the feel of her draw, the tension in the fingers of her hand as it clasped the comb.

Moments earlier, I had benefited from her competent touch as she massaged the tense muscles of my strained shoulders. They had been patient and steady, those hands. Reflecting on the moments just passed, I realized I was grateful for the long familiarity of my servant's competent hands. So much else had changed, yet the constancy of her touch had not. Indeed, I had long enjoyed her touch, even if before this moment I had never as much as considered it. But her sudden words—this I did not understand. Why would she speak like this to me? It was strange even to ponder anything at all about someone like my body servant, yet I was doing it now. That, as much as anything, revealed how much had changed in our world.

"Be vigilant," she warned.

She was right. Lalchich wrought for us a new kind of destruction. Its scope and scale were disproportionate to anything our world had ever known—or at least, that Calumook had ever known. Yes, some sacking and plunder, some rapes and deaths and sacrifice had always been part of what we did to one another, but not like this. Not so much. Not for so long. Never with annihilation as our goal. But even though she was right, this was not something I would ever speak of with a body servant; therefore I did not engage in talk with her. Someone of my stature—however young and grief-stricken, however in dire need of friendship—simply did not converse with a body servant.

I also did not speak to her because I did not know if I could trust her. It was conceivable that the Pretender had told this old woman to feign affection for me. To sham her way into my heart and my confidence. To discover the plan of the revenge he must have known I was devising. Such was the confusion of my thoughts as I gazed between her reflection and mine in my mirror.

"Start slow," the Pretender would have advised her. I can envision him seated cross-legged in the seat of my father—my father's woven mat, his bench, his audience chamber, perhaps even his jaguar throne. "Lady Winik is clever. If you act too kind too fast, she will become suspicious."

My body servant would have stood before him, eyes on the floor at her feet.

"Tell no one but me. No one. If you bring me this information you will be well rewarded." I could imagine the Pretender concocting just such a scheme.

I trusted no one in those days. It was too dangerous to trust. My father's trust in my mother on the matter of my marriage had resulted in a series of miscalculations and missteps. My father's trust in his sajal had brought him death and led to the downfall of Calumook. Why would the well-being of a royal patroness and conjugal flesh-badge be of concern to a mere body servant? No, I could rely on no one but myself.

9

They spoke casually, the Pretender and that round-headed Lalchich lieutenant with the turquoise inlays. They conversed in the easy manner of close acquaintances, as if they had known one another for years.

"What news from Cenote?" inquired the Pretender.

"It remains firm in our hand."

"Ah, good, good."

"Hmm."

"And your warriors, how do they fare?"

"My men fare well. They are resting."

"Good, good," the Pretender said again.

"Yes, they are resting. Building up their strength after our taking of Becilna."

"We took Becilna more than one month ago."

Although his tone did not reveal it, the Pretender's reminder was not simply the last utterance in a string of unfettered conversation. No, a decided element of forced restraint attended his words, as did an air of impatience and worry. As he spoke them, the Pretender seemed displeased but unwilling to reveal his displeasure. Though his words took a somewhat questioning tone, they did not form a question, I reflected as I sat on my cushion in the queen's position across from the usurper and his henchman at our woven feasting mat. It was our mat that was spread across the plaster floor in the torch lit courtyard where the Pretender had resided as my father's sajal. His was a smaller courtyard than ours, but a fine one nonetheless. My father had always treated his sajal generously. Much too generously.

I had assembled a fragrant floral bundle for the center of our mat. Just one. Not in order to please the Pretender, or to decorate his mat—no, I had chosen to assemble it because I thought I might find some small consolation in once again touching the softness of petals and breathing the perfume of sweet-smelling blossoms. And indeed, standing before the cutting table, flint in hand, blooms about me, I felt the furrow on my brow become a little less deep.

"Yes, we will prepare ourselves to strike again very soon," said the lieutenant.

"Yes. Good. Another tamale?"

"Yes, thank you. What meat is this?"

"It is turkey," said the Pretender.

"Turkey?"

"Oh yes, it is turkey. You see, our hunters have become much fewer. Many people have left Calumook," the Pretender explained, his tone still measured and careful.

Everyone knew this, myself included. Many people were leaving.

The Pretender continued: "They tell me there are few good hunters among those who remain. They also report many fewer beasts in the jungle. I have heard that commoners have started hunting to put meat in their own mouths. Rumors are even being spread that our own Lalchich warriors hunt for wild animals themselves. Imagine!"

The stony set of my face did not change. I feigned inattention while listening intently from the far side of the feasting mat. I cringed to hear the Pretender refer to the Lalchich warriors as "our" warriors. I wondered how long he had been deceiving my generous father.

"Uh ..." grunted the round-headed lieutenant. He continued to eat, licking his fingers, smacking his lips in an appalling low-born manner. He was trying, I thought, to make it seem that he considered such rumors simply ludicrous, and thus unworthy of further response.

I turned to the Lalchich noblewoman beside me and, lest the men across the mat suspect me of eavesdropping, struck up a faux conversation with her. Like wearing a stony mask, listening while speaking is a skill cultivated by the nobility.

"Your floral bundle is quite lovely," she remarked.

"It is very kind of you to notice," I responded.

It seemed the round-headed lieutenant did not want to admit that his men were so poorly disciplined that they would hunt and eat jungle meat. Everyone was well aware that wild game was strictly reserved for nobility.

"In Lalchich it is not customary that we assemble such bright bundles," she admitted.

"Oh, that is unfortunate," I murmured.

The men across from me continued eating their turkey tamales. Neither spoke. The meat of the turkey—a tame, penned animal—was considerably less remarkable than the flesh of a monkey or tapir, or any other spirited, wild jungle beast.

When she did not speak further, I asked what the Lalchich used to adorn their feasting mats, and she answered that it was ferns. Of course I already knew this: as a prospective bride I had feasted on the woven mats at Lalchich, a detail this woman had apparently forgotten. "Oh, ferns," I said. "How charming."

The men were making a show for one another. They licked their fingers and smacked their lips, each hoping to fool the other into believing that nothing, absolutely nothing, was awry.

This shamming went on for some time while the Lalchich noblewoman and I exchanged further inane conversation about the heat and the flavor of the tamales and the lack of rain and the plainness of the jade ornaments of the old matron seated at the far end of the mat. Then, in a low voice, the Pretender spoke: "People cannot simply do as they please. You must see to it that order is restored in the jungle. In the city as well. There is too much lack of control. Orderliness must hold sway."

Overhearing the Pretender's words, I smirked. I cannot say why I smirked. Was it because I hated the rounded-headed lieutenant more than I hated the Pretender? Or did I too fear lawlessness, or prefer monkey and tapir to turkey? Was it perhaps because my glyphs were chiseled beside the Pretender's on the stelae at the palace stair and thus our fates were linked, even if against my will? No. None of these explanations fully accounts for my smirk, which was due to understanding at last who was in charge of whom.

◎◎◎

The round-headed lieutenant did not remain long at Calumook. We continued to eat many turkey and also duck tamales, but meanwhile it remained unclear whether he had fulfilled the Pretender's orders, though I did hear some gossip about unexpected gruff admonishments.

Had he left because he did not want to take orders from the Pretender? From anyone? I think he left simply because he was a warrior, and warriors war. They garrison for a time and then they move on. At least, some warriors in some places had begun to live lives full of slaughter and plunder. Warriors have never truly maintained order—only royalty does that. While I was often forced into close proximity to this dreadful lieutenant during his stay in Calumook, never once did I acknowledge him with my eyes—never once. Such is the real value of the stony mask. It is a skill that can be put to many uses, and sometimes it serves as our own protection better than we might ever have imagined.

Where did the lieutenant go?

There was so much fighting back then that he could have gone to many places. So great was the need for crushing and quelling, and so many the cities in upheaval, that his services were in high demand, I supposed. While the warring diminished in and near Calumook, elsewhere it grew—so ran the conversation all around the feasting mat. Like other cities, Lalchich had deposed many rulers, installed many pretenders. Holding those conquered places, however, was not so easy.

How had the House of the Waterlily managed to hold Calumook for so long? Our dynasty stretched across thirty-three generations. Thirty-three glorious and prosperous generations! Those Lalchich dogs would not hold it for even the blink of an eye before another opponent, another would-be pretender—whether from within or without—rose to challenge the throne. And even though no competitor appeared to be presently lying in wait, still they struggled to bring stable order. Without ample reason to do otherwise, people are wont to do as they please.

How had we managed?

I believe we had done so because the people loved my father. They feared the Pretender. They did not love him.

My father was beautiful, but the sour-faced Pretender was not.

My father was the Maize God incarnate, but the Pretender had not convinced Calumook of this.

My father's easy charisma drew people to him like a lodestone. The Pretender was no lodestone.

Like the hunters of Calumook, our farmers too were drifting away, aware that it was easier to make a milpa farther away. Farming close by for thirty-three generations had weakened the soil. Once more I pondered the puny, withered ears I had seen, back in that dusty milpa. Tired—the soil was weak and tired from making milpa, my father had murmured. At the time his words meant little. Chaak's rain had not come; this was undeniable. Yet how my father related those puny ears to the weakness of the dirt remains a mystery.

Every day, it seemed, another family, another drib or drab of folk, departed. Along neighborhood trails a few assorted vendors still hawked their wares in their worn coarse-spun, but gone was the hubbub of trade. Most of those who were left, it seemed, were aged women and timeworn men who came to barter their stitching and whittling—old, talentless people with little to do but stitch and whittle.

What else had held the people of Calumook? What ceased to hold them now?

My father danced with grace upon the stage in his heavy jade regalia. The Pretender could not, for it takes a lifetime of practice to dance in heavy jade; even simple folk would be unimpressed with the Pretender's fumbling and swaying. Had his person been more appealing, more elegant, it might have been possible to fool them. Our deified ancestors, however, would never have been fooled. Without doubt, my Kalo'mte' grandmother would never have interceded with the forces of the cosmos on his behalf. His own troubling lack of divine patronage was one of the many reasons he needed me as his flesh-badge.

My father had been lavish in his gifts to our lineage heads, but the Pretender was stingy.

Was the Pretender stingy? Perhaps.

But perhaps he had not been raised to observe the delicate, wordless, fluid set of invisible scales that balanced gift-giving with loyalty. Regardless of the stony mask, glad generosity was seldom easy with rivals and foes and could be difficult even between allies and friends, whose thirst time and again seemed unquenchable. Furthermore, royals and nobles had noticeably multiplied as many wives birthed many children. They all expected many feasts and gifts. At the very least, all were entitled to construction of a palace wing of their own, perhaps even a courtyard. That was how our palaces had grown to be such large and sprawling places. Eldest sons of the principal wives of the K'uhul Ajaws all demanded their own sumptuous coronation spectacles upon their own puppet thrones.

Our world had undoubtedly grown costly.

Was the Pretender stingy? Or was the problem perhaps that banditry was now so prevalent on the rivers and trails that canoes and tumplines could no longer convey jade and quetzal streamers throughout our web so easily. It was too dangerous, too unpredictable. When such thievery lurked in all places, only a reckless merchant would risk his cargo so imprudently.

The stores of prestige goods in the coffers of the Pretender would have grown meager. Fewer lavish gifts meant less support from those who had become accustomed to receiving lavish gifts. If my father, the K'uhul Ajaw of Calumook, had killed my pet monkey in fear of his rivals, what chance had the Pretender, under such immensely changed circumstances? His rivals, I thought, would hardly hesitate to shift their loyalties elsewhere.

Even the value of salt had risen. I had seen salt being boiled from seawater at the edge of the lagoon at the seaport of Somalx. The long line of peculiar pots looked as if they were on tiptoe holding hands. Merchants traded hand-molded salt cakes from fleets of sea canoes, delivering many cakes to many places. That was what they had said: Many cakes, many places. Another node in our web. Salt had struck me as quite a dull thing until I was obliged to eat my food without even a dusting of it. That long line of pots now seemed less peculiar and much more vital in its ability to produce for us something that had all at once become very dear.

Perhaps the powerful K'uk'ulkan, feathered serpent from the north, loved Somalx more than Chaak loved us? Maybe the favor of the cosmos had begun to shift. Indeed, the cosmos has always been fickle.

I recalled the trifling temple to Ek' Chuaj, patron god of merchants. It appeared Ek' Chuaj may have grown more powerful despite the temple's smallness, for the sea canoe trade of Somalx was said to have grown even more robust—not here, but elsewhere. Salt and copper bells and other goods had ceased to arrive in Calumook, the city nestled at the bend of our mighty river where our own canoes once held sway. Oh, our mighty river! It was as though its very rocks had somehow enlarged themselves to make paddling more difficult, and the need for portage more frequent. Those sea canoes did not need to worry about rocks in rivers; they were large enough to hold twenty-five paddlers. There were even tales of canoes hoisting coarse-spun sails that allowed the wind to push them from behind. It seemed so long ago, my visit to Somalx, when I had observed that city's leafcutter ants at the back of the lagoon. The salt had seemed so endless, back then. Now I know that nothing is endless, and even the seemingly unimportant can be more vital than anyone could ever predict.

◎◎◎

I knew my time had come when my back began to ache, low in the hips. I had been deep in slumber when it started with a bright waking spark of pain that grew to clench my entire person like an angry vise. Only when I could no longer bear the agony did I scream, for the presence of the Pretender's lineage midwife was no more desirable than the presence of the man himself.

The woman was as sour-faced as the Pretender himself—this most unfortunate trait saturated the blood of this family—and I pleaded with Akna, goddess of fertility, to spare the child in my womb from having to wear such a visage.

Each month the midwife intruded into my chamber to run her hands over my belly. Of course she sought a sign I was pregnant. Any indication that I was carrying a royal male heir would solidify the Pretender's hold over the jaguar throne—my father's jaguar throne. Even as the midwife chanted their patriline over my flesh, I silently chanted ours back, pleading with my ancestors to deliver me from the fate of bearing any child for this traitor line. Each month that her sour face retained its look of displeasure felt like an accomplishment on my part.

Of course the sajal often pumped his stalk within me. He performed this act despite being aware of my contempt for him—a sentiment I believe he reciprocated, though I know he found my person alluring. He would order me to remove my huipil and stand before him naked as he readied his flaccid self with his hand, all the while ogling the small tuft of hair that grew where my legs met. Then he stared at my pert youthful breasts as they bounced back and forth with his short gasping thrusts.

His drive to plant his seed in my womb was every bit as strong as my intention to deny it fertile ground, but in the end his thrusts succeeded and my belly grew round with his spawn.

Brusque and efficient, the midwife knelt wordlessly before me and pushed my legs wide, peering between them. "It will not be long," she said to her assistant. But she was badly mistaken: I labored there until the sun had crossed the sky and my mat was drenched with blood and sweat.

I held onto the wooden birthing frame and squatted on the bench. I lay on one side and then the other, my upper foot braced against the wooden frame. I wadded my mat and pushed my person down upon it. I lay on my back and curled against the hard ball of my belly. During one particularly painful contraction, I thrashed with such force that I tore the draperies from the wall, snapping the hanging rod clean through, which may have seemed a bit melodramatic. Yes, I breathed as instructed. Fast, heavy breaths, in out, in out. I barely recognized the long ugly grunts, hardly human, that emerged from the terrible twisted grimace of my mouth, and even I was astonished at the volume of my shrieking. At times I felt such despair that I cried out for my mother, even though I knew she was long dead. I believe I was crying out not for the mother I once had, but for the one I never did have— the one who would have held my clenched hand within her comforting one and whispered tender, reassuring words in my ear. I was thankful the midwife's assistant was there in my phantom mother's stead. This gentle, unassuming old woman pressed a cool, wet cloth against my forehead between my frantic bursts of agony.

She held a gourd cup to my lips so I could sip cool water. "I herbed this water under the auspices of Ajaw Chamahez, god of good health," the old woman whispered, her voice oddly hoarse. "May it soothe you."

Throughout the entire ordeal she said nothing more, although I remembered her words each time she held the cup to my lips. Even their memory brought relief. Through it all I marveled that there were people in the world at all, if this was what it took to get them there.

"One more push," urged the sour-faced midwife. "Just one more."

And then the head of the thing burst from my person in a hideous gory rush of red-pale liquid. The thing was splotched with some strange, waxy white substance, and its wet, matted head was elongated like a maize kernel as though we had already exposed it to our wooden press.

At the moment I was propped up with cushions on a mat and could see much of the pandemonium transpiring between my legs. The thing's shoulder and knee squeezed forth at the same sudden instant with another bizarre gurgle of gory liquid. With its leg bent at the knee and the knee alongside the shoulder, it very much resembled a wet frog. I had difficulty shedding that image of my son as he grew into a youth as sour-faced as his treacherous father.

◎◎◎

Soon thereafter fell the ax of Xlapan.

I knew little of that place. I had heard of it, but it had never been so prominent that we would send an emissary in the matter of my marriage. Most prudent towns and cities had sent token emissaries as a sign of deference, regardless of the impossibility that we would engage them in nuptial parley. Back then it seemed sensible to generate the impression that a long line of suitors sought a close alliance through marriage with the esteemed House of the Waterlily—so much so that even lesser places were wise to play along.

But now, in the midst of the downward spiral of our world after the fall of Calumook and the demise of my father, even meaningless places like Xlapan made reckless bids, even for great emblem-dynastied cities such as ours.

It was a time of high stakes, and of greed and betrayal. There were so many round-headed warriors and so many axes, falling on so many places. It was act or be acted upon.

The canoes of Xlapan rounded the bend in our river on a moonless night. Not bothering to enlist the element of surprise, they marched straight from the dark river bearing their daggers and swords and flaming torches, and laid straight into the first neighborhood they encountered.

That was how we knew they were coming: we heard the loud cries of slaughter. Even from our back palace courtyard we heard them. Certainly any family that remained at Calumook regretted it that night—regretted not only their inaction, which was indeed regrettable, but also their loyalty to us, if in fact they felt it.

This is what happened: The Pretender's sajal sent a Lalchich warrior-scout to gauge the strength of the invading force. Upon his return, the report was not hopeful.

"There are very many of them," the scout said, his voice urgent.

"How many?" demanded the Pretender's sajal.

"I counted at least fifty torches."

"Fifty, you say?"

"Yes, about that many," said the Lalchich warrior-scout.

"Did you see their banner? Where do they come from?"

"From Xlapan. Yes, I saw their banner. They come from Xlapan."

"Xlapan?" the Pretender's sajal repeated, unclear as to why such a backwater would be attacking a city such as ours.

The warrior-scout continued: "They appear to be staying in the neighborhood tonight. They have begun stacking weapons, organizing as if to move on the palace tomorrow."

"What is our command?" the warrior-scout asked the Pretender's sajal.

The Pretender's sajal fired back: "What is our warrior count?"

"We have thirty armed men."

"Thirty, you say?"

"Yes, thirty."

"What is our command?" asked the warrior-scout.

The Pretender strode to stand among them. The agitation in his stride was unmistakable; it was as if the ground shook with his every angry footfall. The rest of us, roused from sleep by the commotion, stood in our nightclothes before our chamber doors or huddled in small, nervous groups in the dark courtyard. Across the courtyard, my infant son was in the arms of his nurse-maid, a young niece of the Pretender.

I stood unmoving at the entrance of my chamber, clutching its curtain, terrified. Suddenly I was back in my tiny Lalchich cell, fearful of being pulled through its terrible portal. Then I was hunched in that dark recess along the winding stair, hearing the wails of my kinspeople. Again my head was wrenched to look upon the demolition of Calumook's arch. Memories rushed full force into my person, each vying for position as the greater dread. I clutched my curtain in terror. But I clutched it also in confusion, you see, for I realized I no longer recognized the face of my enemy. Was it the dogs of Lalchich I feared, or was it invaders from Xlapan?

I looked across the courtyard at my infant son in the arms of his nursemaid, and suddenly I wanted him in my arms—here, with me, in my arms. The nursemaid cleaned the excrement from his person, but it was I who gave him my breast, I who held his tiny wriggling form while he suckled. Only when I stood clutching that curtain did I appreciate how my feelings had grown for this ugly frog child, this son of the Pretender. He was my son too—my own son—and as I stood there in my beleaguered city, again suffering assault, I knew I did not want my son to die with it. No, I wanted him to live as my kinspeople had not. As my cousin had not.

Urgent strategizing voices tugged my gaze back toward the Pretender. As I watched and listened, I found I was grateful that this sour-faced man was awake and agitated, and had trod angrily to stand among those who would decide what was to be done. I hoped he would take charge and choose the correct plan of action— the plan that would save us. Clinging to that curtain, I grasped the grim truth that my captors had now become my defenders.

As I watched that small huddle of men, it became clear that the Pretender's sajal was unnerved by his king's arrival. He scratched his head with both hands, raking panicky fingers through sleeptousled hair. The poor man grew fraught when the Pretender gruffly asked, "What is our situation?"

Making a frantic effort to sound in control, the Pretender's sajal said, "Fifty Xlapan invaders are ransacking the area. They will stay in the neighborhood tonight and advance on the palace tomorrow. We have thirty Lalchich warriors."

Silence.

Then, all at once, the Pretender's sajal, not knowing what else to do, ordered in a thin wavering voice: "Take your full force and counterattack. Full attack!"

188

"Do not counterattack!" boomed the harsh voice of the Pretender.

No one in the courtyard that night could have failed to hear this command. It was so loud it echoed from the courtyard walls as if desperately seeking flight, then disappeared into the night. In the ensuing silence, no one could have failed to hear the distant sound of looting.

In a decisive voice, the Pretender told the warrior-scout: "Construct a barricade. Move fast! Topple the roof comb of the temple, use its blocks for the foundation. Destroy whatever buildings you need, assemble whatever material you can. Encircle us tightly and make it hold!"

After the warrior-scout departed with his orders, the Pretender turned to glare at his sajal, who stood trembling beside him, a dazed look upon his ashen face.

"You fool!" shouted the Pretender, and with one stab of his dagger—tucked always in his loincloth—his sajal crumpled to the ground. I suppose it is one thing to put a compliant man in a position of power, but another thing altogether to be reliant upon that same feckless worm of a man.

◎◎◎

It had begun with the bare padding feet of Lalchich warriors, and now, with the arrival of the Xlapan invaders, the city's descent into lawlessness was complete.

No longer could any Calumook commoner—any commoner foolish enough not to have slipped into the jungle by now—walk about without being harassed by our besiegers. We highborn would be safe behind our barricade for a while, but the commoners outside it were at their mercy.

The Xlapan threw them from their huts and turned their huts into barracks. They drank chicha day and night. They turned daughters and mothers into dirty limp rags. They ate maize fresh from the milpa as well as from the granaries, even down to next year's seed. They pissed on dogs for fun and then killed them because they could. They broke into the temple, the one already ransacked by the Lalchich for our ancestral bundles and precious sacred offerings—to pillage it further. While they waited for our resistance to weaken, they amused themselves by forcing the commoners of Calumook to play ball, even though they were no match for warriors—even despicable warriors from a nowhere, upstart place like Xlapan.

We heard these reports from the scouts who managed to return through our hasty barricade of rubble and stone, of wood and branches and sharp-angled spears. Lalchich sentries stood watch under pain of death by the dagger of the Pretender himself.

How did we fare behind our barricade? This is how it started:

The Pretender's older sister said, "Here is your turkey tamale. Here is yours."

The Pretender's dead sajal's wife said, "Here is your cup of cool chocolate. Here is yours."

This is what came next:

The Pretender's older sister said, "Here is your dog tamale. Here is yours."

The Pretender's dead sajal's wife said, "Here is your half-cup of cool chocolate. Here is yours."

And after that:

The Pretender's older sister said, "Here is your bowl of maize gruel. Here is yours."

The Pretender's dead sajal's wife said, "Here is your cup of water. Here is yours."

We were hungry. We were dirty and coated in sweat. We grew still more anxious and quarrelsome, having already been so for some time. Then, as it became obvious that round-headed lieutenant with the turquoise tooth inlays would not be returning, we grew desperate for our very lives.

He would not emerge from the jungle one morning and restore our rule of Calumook. He would not return to quell the vile upstart Xlapan invaders. He would not arrive, mighty club clenched in angry fist, to defeat their warriors and rescue our besieged enclave. This had been the hope of the men and women behind the barricade. The hope of the Pretender. My hope. Yes, I admit it: there were times when even I longed to catch sight of that round-headed brute. Together our mouths grew parched and our starving guts gnawed at us. I knew I was Lady Winik, but I no longer knew if I was Lady Winik of Calumook or Lady Winik of Lalchich. Anyway, the distinction had ceased to matter to any of us as we huddled behind that barricade, beseeching all the gods of our pantheon to allow it to hold.

Around that time, I began to experience a dreadful agony in my mouth. I had first noticed it some months earlier, as a mild discomfort when I chewed, but paid little heed because I felt it only sometimes. It was just here, on this left lower side, in the very back.

The pain mounted bit by bit until at last, trapped behind our hasty rubble barricade, I could think of nothing else. It stabbed and jabbed at my entire jaw with a ferocity I never imagined possible. It was an agony so peculiar that it resembled no other, which made it difficult to know how to cope. I could not eat, though to be sure, there was little to be had. It seemed unjust that amid all the tumult and chaos of the besieging of our city, my tooth would choose this particular moment to betray me.

Back then, many of us had reclined on a tooth-shaman's bench for purposes of ornamentation. Like the brutish round-headed lieutenant, many others had experienced the tiny obsidian bit and the quiet whirring as the tooth-shaman pumped a rotating drill shaft using a leather band. I had never received such inlays, as my mother considered it a vulgar look.

"They are becoming too common," she had huffed. "Even upstarts get tooth inlays now. Royals should not do such garish things to their teeth," she had instructed.

Thus, although I cannot truly estimate the pain involved in obtaining inlays, I believe it to be slight in comparison to the excruciating jabs from my back lower tooth. The pain was continuous, and continually worsening, which was why I confessed to feeling it.

"Something is wrong inside my mouth," I said. "Very wrong."

Trapped in our besieged courtyard behind our rubble barricade, we had no tooth-shaman—only an assistant was sent to my aid. He bid me lay upon a bench.

"Open your mouth," he said.

I complied without protest because by that point I was prepared to place myself at the mercy of anyone who might end my suffering. He peered inside my mouth, then poked the tooth in question with a long, thin, sharply pointed bone instrument, whereupon I leapt from the bench, sending him tumbling from his stool, and curled into a writhing ball of agony on the floor.

As I winced and wailed, I heard his words: "The rot has caused her tooth to crack. It cannot mend."

Once I had been hauled off the floor and back onto the bench, they tied my hands, feet, torso, and head with sturdy cord while the assistant tooth-shaman intoned a long series of incantations. As he chanted, he stuffed my mouth with a bitter, seeping herbal poultice. The man directed his invocations to Cit-Bolon-Tum, god of medicine, and also to my Scarlet Macaw companion spirit. His conjuring and stuffing of my mouth with bitter herbs commanded her bright plumage to wing back into my person, repairing the unhappy rupture that had enabled my tooth to crack so badly that it could not mend.

They opened my mouth and wedged a cloth-wrapped bone into the good side in such a fashion that I was unable to close my jaw.

He was not a cruel man, the assistant tooth-shaman, but neither was he a merciful one. Perhaps there can be no such creature as a merciful tooth-shaman. To complete such a task, one must be capable of inflicting enormous misery on a bound and helpless patient writhing on one's bench like a gigged fish.

When again I caught sight of his sharp bone instrument, I became terrified anew, even though the poultice's medicinal properties, along with a mighty draught of an indeterminate tincture, had calmed my nerves. Issuing little more than garbled wails, I tried to cry out when I saw the man approach with his frightful bone. Perhaps I should have kept my eyes shut as advised.

This time he pressed the sharp tip firmly against my gum while I strained mightily against my bindings. He wiggled the tip and repositioned it. He did this again, and then again, moving the sharp tip bit by bit along my gum, prying up the tooth in question by peeling back the stretch of tender gum that kept it in its socket. He introduced a different bone instrument, one with a blunt tip, to the side of my tooth. He tapped its end as though it were a chisel, and again I struggled against my restraints. Then he stuck his fingers in my mouth and grasped hold. Everything in my mouth was slippery with blood and saliva, so it was hard to maintain a firm hold, but he did manage to loosen the thing. I know this because I heard him say as much to the tight circle of keen onlookers.

Then he tied a length of cord around the tooth and popped it from my jaw with one quick snap. Having flown through my chamber until its tether stopped its journey, the bloody thing dangled in midair swinging dolefully back and forth. The assistant tooth-shaman and the onlookers alike cheered at this juncture, which I regarded as rude. However, I recall a sensation of relief as well, both because not only did my ordeal on the bench appear to be over, but the agony in my mouth might now cease—and in due course, it did.

As an old woman, I have lain upon the tooth-shaman's bench many times, each one its own misery. It is remarkable how pain can work like a sharp chisel to alter one's sense of being. It was after I lost my third cracked molar that I felt myself grow truly old. In the hang of my jaw, age made its presence known. I also felt it in the flesh of my cheeks, which drew inward at the precise locations where my teeth had once been. Mine was becoming the hollow-cheeked visage of a hag.

I would never have imagined it possible, but I have grown to appreciate soft food. The sensation of gruel upon my tongue has become an even greater comfort than the shade of a ceiba. I have surrendered to the lack of substance on which to chew because that lack is what keeps me alive. From my aged vantage point, it looks harder to be in the middle of life than at its end. I believe this is so because it is in the middle, when facility and beauty begin to wane and aches and losses start to mount, that people resist the most.

◎◎◎

My body servant roused me from slumber. Her hand was upon my shoulder and she was shaking it. "Quickly, we must go!" she whispered.

"Go?" I whispered back, groggy still and surprised I had fallen so deeply asleep with such hunger gnawing at my gut.

"Yes, we are going."

"Going where?"

"I do not know, my lady. I was ordered to waken you. They said one of our sentries spotted a Xlapan watchman with his head upon his chest in slumber. This is our opportunity to flee."

"We are leaving Calumook?"

"Yes, my lady."

"Now?"

"Yes, my lady."

"Have you packed my traveling trunk?"

"I am told there will be no trunk, my lady."

"No trunk?" I asked, more in incredulity than in displeasure, for I was honestly unable to imagine how we could depart Calumook without my wardrobe.

I was standing now. Still half asleep, my body servant was dressing me in a simple day huipil. As she worked, it occurred to me that a fancy day huipil might be the better choice if we were departing Calumook, but she was more awake than I and seemed to know more about our destination in any case. She hurriedly combed and twisted my hair, fastening it onto my head a with a few bone pins. I did not argue with any of these actions. Watching her from the corner of my eye, I half supposed I should be wondering if this wasn't all some kind of trickery.

"No trunk?" I asked—this time in irritation, and because my wondering mind had turned to suspicion. Besides, how dare she tell me there would be no trunk?

"No trunk," she replied as she led me from my chamber.

She had been my body servant for as long as I could remember. At the onset of my menses, she had instructed me on how to care for my person. She had coiffed my hair in the high-piled style of a married Calumook woman for my first formal appearance as queen to the Pretender. That day she had dared speak to me with kindness, and I had gazed at her reflection with distrust in return. Now, speaking to me for the second time, she was informing me that my trunk of finery would not be traveling with us as it always used to, whenever our entourage was in transit.

Today I marvel at that moment. How petty was my concern that my trunk be brought, and my wardrobe of finery not be abandoned. How wrong I was to speak harshly to this woman. If only I had realized that the trek before us would be long and hard. If only I had understood that we should count ourselves fortunate to creep through our barricade and scurry out of Calumook alive before the eyelids of that Xlapan watchman opened. If only I had known how difficult our lives would be in the dusty clifftop refuge we fled to. Had I known any of this at that moment, I would have hung my head in shame.

Neither I nor anyone else could carry a traveling trunk. When the Xlapan invaders first entered Calumook, some brief moments remained in which to retrieve a few splendid objects from the palace front. These we rushed to the Pretender's courtyard for safekeeping. Our barricade ran right through the palace complex, dividing front from back, one courtyard from another. It was the line between continued life and relative well-being from danger on one hand, and certain death on the other. These were perilous times, and our world was shrinking fast.

Then our world became like my father's mirror, the one propped at a perfect angle by his dwarf. Like my trunk of finery, my father's mirror, rushed to safety from the palace front, could not escape with us. It had to stay behind, abandoned in the barricaded courtyard.

This is what I imagine:

That mirror—in which my father the great K'uhul Ajaw of Calumook had observed his divine royal reflection, and in which he had gazed deep into the otherworld for divine counsel—was shattered. Once dawn arrived and revealed the truth of our flight, and after the drowsy Xlapan watchman was dead, they crushed our hasty barricade. Within it they discovered fresh booty, the greatest prize among it being my father's mirror. The Xlapan war captain, livid at the success of our unanticipated flight, raised it high above his head and smashed it hard on the courtyard stair. As it hit, my father's mirror shattered into a multitude of tiny shimmering pieces. These plunged down each hard plaster step, with each calamitous descent breaking each shattered piece into ever tinier fragments of past splendor. As befell my father's mirror, so befell our Calumook and so too our world.

◎◎◎

What of my father's new Chaak temple? His obsession? Here is what I believe.

The stone that had been pilfered from Becilna still lay in neat rows. The stone scavenged from my ancestor's magnificent arch lay beside the stone pilfered from Becilna. Our own stone, quarried and shaped by the sharp chisels of our Calumook leafcutter ants, was also there beside the scavenged and pilfered stone.

Stone was now plentiful, but the temple's construction remained incomplete. The chaos and carnage that enveloped our poor beleaguered city prevented even the strongest, most beloved ruler of the House of the Waterlily from mustering the labor to finish it. Thus, when the divine and tremendous date of 10.0.0.0.0 arrived from far below the dawn horizon, the bright shining face of K'inich Ajaw must have crossed the sky and returned to his dark earthen cave without so much as a single celebratory hollow slit log drum pounding in all of Calumook.

10

 These memories returned as I aged. I am grateful I did not remember them all at once back when I was young and in need of fortitude, because I think they would have broken me. The mind protects when it must. It also keeps hidden what it must. But with time and with age, its undisputable truths become revealed.

The echoes of the past are loudest just before I wake.

With the first song-swell of jungle parrots, my eyes flash open to the gray of early dawn, and back I am snatched, to pain and defeat, humiliation and dishonor. To the loss of my family, our legacy, a world, and a life I had only just entered before it collapsed all around me.

Always I am reminded of the helplessness of human desire. It matters not how fervently I have wished for this past to be different: it never is. I am reminded as well of the selfishness of human nature, as in unstinting disbelief I brood upon the strength of my own instinct for survival. It shifts within my veins like resin oozing from a gash in a copal tree. Each slow, bitter drop is a drop of regret, each dry sticky lump an unanswered gift to our unfathomable gods.

Whom do I supplicate? Toward whose pliable will—be it of good or of evil—does my burnt offering curl? Still that dense mist hangs before our eyes, so we petition blindly and love whoever chooses to notice our supplication.

I have been able to grow old, but my cousin was not.

It is guilt that haunts me most. It pursues the scent of remorse like a hungry rat whose thousand tiny teeth could gnaw a living heart to nothing more than a hollow red casing. When the pain grew too heavy, I hid behind a jungle ceiba and wept and wept. I decided to adopt the stony mask as my own true face, to allow its stone roots to wend deep into my grieving flesh. That mask became my ever-present shield.

It can be harder to bear the pain of those we love than to bear our own. My misshapen forearm, my mangled thumbnails, my scarred lips: these wounds of the past are nothing, compared to the suffering of my kinspeople. The obligation to atone is never fully satisfied; much like an overloaded tumpline, it must simply be carried.

The self-inflicted injuries last the longest. The time I spent crammed within that tiny recess was so short, yet it was an eternity. I could have tried to stop it. Upon hearing the rise of the first chilling wail, the first dreadful splash, I should have burst from my hiding place to slash and slash with my sharpest dagger, my bone weaving pin, my fingernails. I should have slashed and slashed those Lalchich dogs until their wretched bodies lay heaped in a pile. I was sturdy and young, and the power of my ancestors was strong from the nearness of their crypts. I could have prevailed.

And if not, then I too should have perished. My person should have swayed and gurgled its final air, as had the persons of my lifeless kin. My own faithful limbs should have come to rest in the gentle watery embrace of my kinspeople, and my own rotting head to lie beside the others on soft, proud cushions of water lily roots as the dark muck grew. It was I who should have been silenced in that tiny recess—impaled with a long, obsidian-tipped spear thrust so mightily through my person that it stuck in the painted plaster on the other side.

◎◎◎

In that dusty cliff-top town where we lived like dogs for two years, I bore my second child. The birth was much like the first, though perhaps less dramatic. Of course there was no drape to tear from my chamber wall, nor did I have a birthing frame upon whose wood I might brace myself as I pushed against the pain.

The brusque, sour-faced midwife was not there to attend me; nor was her elderly, hoarse assistant, so there was no cool gentle cloth pressed to my forehead, no offer of an herb infusion sipped from a gourd cup. Sometimes I wonder what became of that kind old midwife's assistant, who cared for me during the birth of my son. She may well have died of old age. However, this was not the likely reason for the sour-faced midwife's absence, though it never occurred to me to inquire about either of them.

This time I bore a tiny squirming daughter, and the Pretender was bitten by a rattlesnake the same day. That was my doing.

Much else was scarce, but snakes were plentiful in that rocky place. They increasingly slithered across our trail the farther we fled after escaping through the Calumook barricade and the darkness. As the day faded to twilight and we were at last sluggishly wending our way up the dry cliffs to the town, they lay about, coiled into strangely drooping piles on the sun-drenched boulders with their rattles resting on their scaly, diamond-patterned skins. We must have seen five of them. As we passed those boulders, even before I had set foot in that dusty town, I determined that this would be my means of settling scores.

You see, I was angry with myself for placing my trust in the Pretender, that night when he ordered the barricade be raised. I should have wanted a man who had so severely betrayed my family to die. Yet I had not wanted him dead: I had wanted him very much alive, so that my son and I could live.

As we approached, the coiled snakes ignored us, opting instead to simply continue their warm slumber. Only one took note of us. Raising its rattle from peaceful repose atop its scaly skin, it began to judder in brash, endless fury. So vigorous and mean-spirited was that rattle, so seemingly eager to assault us, that as we walked the trail I kept my person as far from it as I possibly could. That rattle frightened me profoundly. Though I had never heard it before, I recognized as if by instinct that any creature able to summon such terror to my heart possessed tremendous strength. The snake lifted its frightening head—an ominous, jutting triangle—and with it its entire long upper portion rose to hover menacingly above its own hideous coil. It was not the largest snake sunning on the boulders, but I imagined it was the fiercest, with the most poisonous fangs. The one most likely to strike.

It was true I had not been trained in conjuring. As I've said, I studied the glittering heavens and women's high oratory and fragrant floral bundle assembly. Perhaps in time I would indeed have studied conjuring, but opportunity to learn was not something I'd supposed we'd ever lack. Only through the fright of my body servant did I figure out what was required to command a snake to do one's bidding.

I heard her from inside our tiny hovel of a kitchen in the back. This was where she cooked, along with several other servant women. Rats had not only begun devouring our maize but were also, it seemed, frightening her. We never had rats in the palace of Calumook, so I could well imagine she was justly fearful of their black beady eyes and ugly twitching snouts. So was I—that's how I knew it was fright that caused her to utter the words of the incantation.

"Rat, Rat!" she called, in a supplicant, ritual tone I had never heard her employ. "Rat, Rat, of the long hairless tail! It is I, we of the humans, descendants of the Twins! The Twins who singed your tail of its hair!"

At once I knew the meaning of these words. She was conjuring a creation-era power that held sway far beyond our visible world.

It had been Rat who revealed to Hunter and Jaguar Deer the hiding place of their father Hun-Hunahpu's (and his brother Seven Hunter's) ball game equipment. Their grandmother had hidden it so her grandsons would not play ball. So there would be no loud slap of hard rubber on plaster, there above the cleft in the earth. So the Lords of Xibalba would not perk up their ears. So her grandsons would not journey through the cleft of Xibalba, never to return.

"Rat, Rat! I command your will!" my body servant called, still in her supplicant ritual voice.

It had also been Rat who foiled the magic of Hunter and Jaguar Deer. The Twins accomplished an entire day of slashing milpa with a single swing of the axe, and then lounged in the shade of a ceiba for the rest of the day. Along with Deer and Rabbit, Rat undid this magic during the night, and the next morning the Twins arrived at the milpa only to discover all the trees back up upon their stumps.

The angry Twins caught Rabbit and Deer by their tails, seeking revenge. But the tails broke off when Rabbit and Deer ran away, which is why deer and rabbits have short stubby tails. Rat they caught as well, but he could not escape. As punishment, the Twins put his tail in the fire, singeing away its fur, which is why rats have hairless tails. But while writhing in pain, and in exchange for mercy, Rat revealed a wonderful secret: That their grandmother had hidden their father's (and uncle's) ball game equipment. They would find it tied to the rafters inside the thatch of the roof.

Then my body servant cried out, "Rat, Rat! Leave this kitchen or I will finish what was started! I will singe away all the ugly gray hair from your entire form!"

Hunter and Jaguar Deer sneaked Rat into their hut during the evening repast. They asked their grandmother if she would spice their food with chilies, and she did. Then they asked for water to cool their spicy-burning mouths, and their Grandmother went to fetch it. But because they had drilled a hole in her jar, the water was gone by the time she returned, and she had to go again. With their Grandmother thus occupied, they sent Rat to gnaw the ropes that bound the ball game equipment to the rafters. Once he gnawed them through, the long-hidden gear dropped into the open, waiting arms of the Twins, and fate continued its advance.

If the will of creation-era rats could be commanded with words of entreaty, I reasoned, then the will of snakes might be likewise commanded.

I waited for the next almanac day associated with snakes—the day of Chikchan—to cycle fully round. When it did, I walked along the path to the sun-drenched boulders where I had seen snakes lying, coiled in their droopy piles. I was disappointed to find no snakes resting there, but nonetheless I placed a lump of burning copal upon the rock, believing they might be hiding in the brush close by. As the smoke curled into the sky, I raised the pitch of my voice and called on the patron deity of cosmological snakes to hear me and do my bidding.

"Chikchan!" I cried. "Hear me, Chikchan! I call to you in petition!"

I waited for a sign, and when I heard the brush rustle from the movement of some creature on the ground, again I cried, "O Chikchan! Send forth the slight but ferocious one!"

Not twenty days had lapsed before the Pretender limped into our courtyard, a rag bound tight above his knee. I was sitting on the stoop before my tiny chamber, my belly round and hard, the fetus within just then deciding to consider its departure from my womb.

Yes, the Pretender was limping, badly. His ankle was purple and had swollen to the size of his thigh, and it clearly pained him a great deal. A man clutched each arm to carry some of the weight the Pretender could not bear on his bitten ankle. They took him to his chamber, and I did not see him for many days, though we all knew how he fared, which was not well.

Did I regret my role in his snakebite? No, I did not. Was I pleased? No, I was not. I would have done it again, to be sure, but I confess that seeing him wounded and limping offered little joy, even though I had thought it might gladden me.

I was told he sweated profusely as he lay in his own chamber across the tiny courtyard. So did I, laboring in my chamber. A shaman of that cliff-top town—we no longer had our own—came to lance his wound and suck and spit the vile venom, just as a cliff-top midwife attended my birthing. His breathing became hoarse and labored, as of course mine was when ugly non-human grunts again emerged from my grimacing mouth. But whereas his ankle swelled to the size of his chest, the taut roundness of my belly shrank with the slithering wet arrival of my daughter. His ankle grew black and putrid, I was told, despite the shaman's chanting and sucking and burning of copal as he sought to command the spirits to expel the raging malice and heal the suffering man. I believe he experienced intense pain, and of that I am not proud. But to this day I regard myself as having exacted a small measure of retribution for all he had done against us.

◎◎◎

Lily Bean has been listening intently. I admire her ability to listen and regard it as a sign of maturity that bodes well for our future.

Then she asks: "What of Naah Chan? I have been waiting to hear, but you have not told me what became of him."

"Ah, my precious Lily Bean," I say, and then I fall silent. I consider which to tell her—what I know, or what I hope—and I decide I will tell her what I hope is true, for that is the story I tell myself of Naah Chan.

Naah Chan was one of the lucky ones. He was lucky because he was clever. His alert ears heard the bare feet of those Lalchich dogs alight along our sacbe. His attentive eyes saw long lines of evil shadows pass beneath the moonlight. He knew why they came. He knew they brought death.

Naah Chan roused his father and mother and his sisters and brothers from slumber and bade them pile in one basket the essentials they would need for a new life. Moving from shadow to shadow, he led them toward the river. Behind them in the distance he heard the rising cries of terror and slow wailing, and he bade his kinspeople run faster. They did, no longer trying to stay hidden among the shadows.

Once at the river, he saw Lalchich sentries standing guard over their canoes. Soon, he knew, they would be piled high with booty plundered from our city. Naah Chan told his family to keep their bodies low and their voices mute as they moved far from the sentries, skirting them in the darkness. They ran downstream, following the flow of our mighty river, the river that for thirty-three generations had brought such prosperity to Calumook.

He spotted a small dugout tied to a tree that angled hard from the bank and led his family to that low, dark silhouette bobbing on the water. One by one, with soundless, tiny splashes, he hoisted them inside. Naah Chan did not get in. No, he swam, rope slung in mouth, guiding their tiny craft.

The water was cool. It glinted in the moonlight. It smelled of escape, and of a new, simple life far from civilization as well as from fear and chaos. Without haste, he moved the dugout down river and then across it, hoping that any Lalchich eye that should spot it floating on the water would suppose it had merely gone adrift. What Lalchich warrior would care about an empty dugout adrift on the river, when there was so much booty to be had in a city so grand?

Far downstream from the pandemonium that by then was engulfing our poor Calumook, the family of Naah Chan abandoned the dugout. From there they went on foot into the dark jungle, still moving in silence, but now with speed. For many days they ate nothing but fruit from the trees. At last they arrived at a hamlet that was home to a distant relation of Naah Chan, a place they would be welcome and safe.

There, in the quiet countryside, he lived in a thatch hut with his family. He made milpa each day and fed his family. He learned to carve wood rather than stone. No one in the hamlet built houses of stone or needed to boast and brag on carved stelae, but everyone needed of a bench or a stool.

I picture him with a wooden handle in his hand. It is not the handle of a chisel he is holding, but an ax with a strong edge of beige chert. He swings it hard against a tree. Thunk-pause, thunk-pause, its sharp edge bites the living wood and the tree falls to the ground. He leaves it in the shimmering heat for many days, until it is as dry as a parched, splintery bone. Again his ax bites the wood, which now is crisp and white. Crack-chip, crack-split: it becomes firewood for his mother's three-stone cooking hearth, there in the smoky kitchen of their thatched hut. Firewood is plentiful here.

From his mother's hearth, he carries a small ember tucked in a tiny clay pot. He blows on the ember to bring it aglow and touches it to one dry bit of tinder, and his slash bursts into flame. It whips and roars as it spreads, devouring the thirsty brush until it turns to white ashes and black nourishing char. For days it smolders, hot sooty stumps festooned with white cinders rearing up from the hot land.

Once cool, Naah Chan and his kinsmen arrive with their digging sticks. They have made milpa forever.

Their wide-brimmed hats, plaited of palm fronds, shade their faces and eyes from the brightness and the burn of the sun. Coarse-spun sacks encircle their waists. They move in unison, one slow, measured foot at a time. They chant the digging song, the planting song, the soil song, the growing song, songs to B'olon Tz'apa, patron of seeds and harvest.

They have made milpa forever.

Naah Chan pushes the end of his digging stick into the earth. The stick is smooth and worn from use. It opens a shallow hole, into which he tosses last year's dried seeds: maize, beans, and squash. His calloused hand never misses as the tossed seeds slide from his gently guiding fingers. Then his rough sandaled foot nudges soil over top, and soon the darkness and moisture and offerings to the *aluxes* and ceremonies to Yum Kaax will cause sprouts and thin root tendrils to reach into the earth. Naah Chan makes milpa with those who have made milpa forever.

◎◎◎

He sees her near the cave with the other girls. Like them, she carries a water jar in the crook of her elbow. Like them, she wears a simple coarse-spun huipil, but hers is woven well, adorned more with more care, he thinks, than any of the others. She wears her huipil with confidence, now kneeling beside the slight spring. She takes her turn, dipping the yawning black mouth of her empty clay jar to catch the slight flow. She waits as it gurgles full. She straightens to standing, then hoists the jar to her hips and, swiftly bending her knees, smoothly guides the heavy, wet vessel to rest upon her head. Nestled into a cloth, the jar is held steady by her practiced hand.

She sees him at work near his hut. He is leaning forward, bent at the waist, this newcomer, and clasping a chisel's wooden handle tight in his hand. She notices the strong muscles glide beneath the skin of his back as he works. He is tapping a simple leaf-spiral pattern on the legs of a bench. His attention is directed to the wood. He notes its grain, its strength, its beauty as he tap-taps his chisel in the shade of a tree. He is the only one in this hamlet that has ever carved leaf-spirals on the legs of a bench.

◎◎◎

The newborn, aged a mere fleeting handful of moments, lies on its mother's chest. The midwife has washed this tiny thing and cut its tangled purple cord, having tied it in a tight, close knot. He is strong and well formed, sweet as new honey.

"Here is your son," says the wife of Naah Chan. She hands the baby to his father, who cradles it in his arms.

"Coo-coo-coo," he whispers. "He is beautiful."

She smiles, still weary from the labor of birth.

The baby burbles and babbles and waves his tiny fist in the air, swinging it wildly and without purpose. Naah Chan laughs and kisses the crinkled little forehead, still pink and new and full of promise. Then he reaches his strong carver's hand to stroke his wife's cheek, which is still flushed with her recent exertions. "You are beautiful," he tells her.

She smiles. "He looks like you," she says.

"I think he looks like you."

"He will grow to be a strong man."

Naah Chan smiles. "Yes, he will."

"Will you teach him to work wood?"

"Yes, I will teach him."

"Soon we will have another," she says. She closes her eyes, happy to sleep after the long and tiring night.

"Yes, we will have many more," Naah Chan says. Again he strokes her cheek, then lies down beside her on the narrow bench of their thatch hut. He nestles the tiny baby between them.

◎◎◎

Lily Bean smiles. She seems pleased with these fables.

I am silent for a time as these visions spin and swirl. Where did they come from, these fables? From my memory, or from my imagination? Perhaps they come from aged confusion. Whatever their source, they are my truest wishes for Naah Chan. I hope he escaped, whether by dugout on the dark flowing river before dawn, or by jungle trail in daylight. I hope he was able to carry his family to safety. I hope he married a beautiful woman. I hope they loved one another, as he and I would have, had I been born that commoner girl at the base of the palace stair, and not Lady Winik of the House of the Waterlily.

Yes, yes—again I was thinking of her—of that commoner girl who witnessed my father kill my monkey at Calumook, so long ago. That is the kind of girl Naah Chan would have married. I remember her eyes, full of grief at my loss. I hope she bore him many strong children. I choose to imagine a very old, very content Naah Chan, still carving leaf-spirals on benches and stools.

◎◎◎

I can tell no such fable about Calumook's master astronomer. Whatever Naah Chan's fate truly was, I wish I did not know what befell my kind-hearted astronomy teacher.

After that worm of a man, the puppet sajal of the Pretender, guided me into position on the bottom rung of our grand palace staircase, but before the red-cloaked Lalchich stela orator had whipped the drape from those paired stelae with dramatic flair, our astronomer was dragged from a lower palace chamber. Two Lalchich men gripped each thin, humble, learned elbow. The only sound on the stair was the scuffling of feet. They forced him to his knees before the paired, red-draped stelae.

I believe he died because he refused to risk celestial wrath by confirming the falsehood that 9.19.18.11.5, 13 Muan, 6 Chicchan presented favorable auspices, under which the Pretender and I were wed. The auspices were not favorable in the least—of that, I believe our dark cloak was certain.

He loved his art. He loved to gaze upon the glittering heavens from the dark observatory rooftop in the deep hush of night. He loved to teach our youth to love those same glittering heavens, to instill in them the discipline and patience needed to measure the divine movements of our celestial bodies with precision, and to augur their esoteric messages. No, this humble astronomer would rather have his head severed from his neck with the tip of a dagger than go against the infinite wisdom of the cosmos. This was the truth I witnessed as I stood beside the Pretender and his red-cloaked orator on the palace steps before those red-draped stelae. My eyes met those of my kind-hearted astronomy teacher in the briefest flicker of shared anguish.

◎◎◎

Only once did I have a chance to kill him.

One son was not enough, so as soon as the proscribed number of months had lapsed following his birth, the Pretender was at it again with his wretched stalk. I submitted. By then my fecundity was the sole reason I remained alive.

He had pumped his stalk in his fist, staring at the dark tuft of hair at my legs. He had entered me and soon had finished his exertions.

Upon ending, he would commonly separate himself from me and depart my chamber. On this occasion, however, he must have been weary, for he remained sprawled upon my person in a most undignified manner. I first felt his slumber in the slump of his person, but soon he began to snore, his mouth gaping open beside my ear. I thought I might suffocate from his profound and unexpected heaviness.

Trying to breathe I shoved his person from mine in one swift motion, tossing him over on his back amidst the mats and cushions of my bench.

I was certain this movement would rouse him from slumber, and soon a blow would land on my cheek ... but it did not. After a few rasps and grumbles, his snoring resumed the same tenor it had had when he lay sprawled upon me.

There he lay. Slumber had taken him far away.

His chest was bare, his arms haphazardly flung wide. His chin jutted forward, and his sour cheeks were oddly slack. His eyes raced back and forth beneath their lids, and for a moment I wondered if he dreamt of a life different from the one he was living. His lips flapped and fluttered with snores from time to time. For a long while I lay watching the Pretender and pondering the opportunity presented like a priceless gift by his deep sleep on my bench.

My long bone weaving pin, the one with the tip carved into a bird figure, lay amidst the cotton skeins in a basket near my loom. The basket was only a short distance from where we lay. I would not need to move far to stretch out my arm, clasp the edge of my basket, slide it gently toward me, reach my hand inside it and fumble about until it found my sturdy bone pin. I could plunge it through one eye and then the other before he even had a chance to cry out.

Without shifting my gaze from his face, I stretched my arm to its full length and clasped the edge of my basket, sliding it gently toward me. I reached my hand inside and fumbled about until I found my sturdy bone pin. Then I paused. I gripped my pin, still staring at his sour, sleeping face. I placed my thumb firmly upon its decorative carved end—I would need to hold it thusly during its plunge.

But my arm remained stretched to its full length, my hand at the rim of my basket. I could not bring myself to pluck the pin from the basket and plunge it into his eye. As he lay there overtaken by oblivion, all the malice had fallen from this man, who now resembled a mere sleeping child, a small, innocent, vulnerable thing. I could not do it. I could not move the hand that clasped the pin; I could not plunge it through his eye to let loose the flow of his wretched blood upon my mat. A venomous fang—that I could indeed command—but however much I despised this man, I could not, with my own hand, kill even a man as vile as this while he slept.

When I awoke the Pretender was gone. My arm was still stretched out across my mat, my hand across the rim of my weaving basket.

◎◎◎

We lived like dogs in that dusty cliff-top town. We were fugitives, deposed royals with no home—or I was, at any rate. The Pretender was still a pretender.

We seized the lodgings of their elite and lived within their tiny courtyards and cramped chambers, where shabby threadbare curtains sagged from doorways and walls bore the brushstrokes of talentless countryside painters. Likewise, their clay pots were poorly shaped and festooned with the egregious glyphs of the barely literate scribes of this cliff-top town.

I still recall the first clay cup I held. Upon our arrival, cool water was offered our hot and weary party. After quenching my thirst, I looked at the cup in my grimy hand. I knew to conceal my bewilderment as I read, or attempted to read, the glyphs painted on it. They might have seemed oddly amusing, had we not been so reliant upon the people and things of this sorry place. Due to our circumstances, however, they were nothing of the sort.

As we had done around our barricade at Calumook, we posted sentries on the land side of the town and at the entrance to our courtyard. No human could scale the cliffs, so there was no need to post a sentry there. The Pretender said this was lucky because we had few men to spare, and I believed him.

He also told me I was fortunate to have retained my original body servant. I had no reason to doubt this statement. I cannot know where our other servants and slaves went, but they no longer attended us. My fan servant had been gone since the night the barricade went up. Now no one had a fan servant, and all were familiar with the sticky feel of sweat. And as we neither hosted nor attended spectacles, there was little need for grooming and pampering, and in any case I had no trunk of finery. My body servant also now cooked in our tiny kitchen and was moreover obliged to work as a charwoman, bent sharply at the waist with a tied twig broom in her hand.

Mostly I sat resting on the shady stoop before my modest chamber. There I suckled my infant daughter as my son toddled around the tiny courtyard. Some time back we had begun applying the wooden press, but at this moment it was not on him, which may explain why he felt so cheerful. His skull had begun to accept a lovely maize-kernel form, and thus far the sour look had not set in with meanness. As I watched him from the stoop, my son seemed perfect.

Several days earlier he had begun to toddle about on his own little feet instead of crawling around on hands and knees. How I grinned at his delightful little arms, bent at the elbow and held a bit away from his chubby little belly. Moving one foot and then the other, he tottering about, still not fully confident in his astonishing newfound ability. It was easy to see he knew he was doing something unusual, as from time to time he glanced back at me both for praise and reassurance. His nursemaid was gone, so my body servant now performed her chores as well, wiping the excrement from both my children's tiny persons.

I was sitting idle, looking at the disgracefully old, cracked plaster of the courtyard floor and observing my body servant as puffs of dust rose from each quick sweep of her twig broom, when the Pretender, now fully recovered from his snakebite, came striding into our courtyard.

It was not unusual he should stride into our courtyard. Here I saw him far more often than I had in Calumook, largely because we did not have a front palace and a back palace. In this place we did not have a palace at all.

He held his audiences and strategy meetings in a small room off the adjoining courtyard. It too was tiny, so I heard his voice more than I actually saw him, which, as I have noted, was often. Yes, he was often in our courtyard: as a fugitive Pretender in a dusty cliff-top town, he had little to do once the complaining and empty threats and eager, useless scheming in his cramped audience room had run their course. Anyway, how could a spare handful of men of middling intelligence sitting cross-legged on ragged woven mats engage in lengthy and riveting discussion of our dire situation?

We had no visiting dignitaries to entertain. Had such guests arrived, we had little food for them to feast on. Like so much else, my supervision of the palace kitchen—a female task that is frequently invisible—was no longer a daily task, as our Calumook cuisine had long since vanished from the mat. As with so much else back then, we struggled with food. The distinctive preparation and display of food incorporating the unique ingredients and flavors of our cuisine was just one of many such quiet battles. Meanwhile, up in that dusty place we felt fortunate even to drink a cup of cool chocolate. There was no chance at all that we would mount any spectacle, for we lacked the drums, the ocean conch, the trumpets, and all else a spectacle demanded. There were no ball games, and even if any of our party had wanted to play for amusement or sport, we had no court upon which a ball could bounce. We had little tribute to accept, in public or in private, beyond what we could eke from the emaciated leafcutter ants of this place. What did arrive came in small, simple bundles of inglorious, tattered coarse-spun tossed at the feet of our sentries.

During those two years, only one carved stela was erected. It heralded the glorious Pretender, his glorious victories over his rivals in glorious wars, his glorious reign in this glorious city. The message was every bit the farce that the carving itself was, with its tiny glyphs squeezed into a corner of the final panel by a carver who ran out of room. The hand that wielded the chisel would generously be described as inept.

Because of all this, the Pretender spent considerable time lounging in our tiny courtyard, on the other side of which I also lounged.

I had seen him reclining on a shady mat during the day during his recovery from the snakebite. I think that perhaps only then did he realize how agreeable relaxation could be—his work as my father's sajal had been quite demanding, I admit. Here he had little to do. Oddly, even though we knew we were fugitives trapped on those cliffs—frightened, hungry, and so much less pampered—I sometimes recall those two years as strangely pleasant.

From my view as an old woman, I believe the Pretender may have felt the same.

His ambitious drive to grandeur had failed, and miserably so. His time on the throne of Calumook had been brief and not at all grand. It had been he who lost our city to the Xlapan. As the successor to my dead father, it was he who had failed to hold a grand spectacle atop his newly completed Chaak temple. Like my father, I suppose, the Pretender had imagined the stanzas that might have been composed, words telling of the glorious establishment of a new royal dynasty. But no scribe would ever dip his stylus in an ink-filled conch to color and adorn any folded paper codex. No blue for images, no red highlights, no black glyphs would soak into white bark paper to convey his eternal legacy. It is possible the Pretender may have struggled with emotion beneath his stony mask, but he gave no evidence of such as he strode into the courtyard that day.

An angry purple blotch still visible on his ankle was the only sign of his recent brush with a venomous death. Even his limp was now gone, and from my vantage point across the tiny courtyard, he seemed strangely relaxed. I sat on my stoop, my daughter now fast asleep, a long strand of milky drool dangling from the corner of her mouth.

The Pretender's stride was unhurried, and once had entered our courtyard from its far corner, he just stopped. A low, rumbling sound emerged from deep in his throat, a sound I had never heard before. The sound grew louder. Then, all of a sudden, he stooped low and scurried toward of my son. My body servant, twig broom in hand, straightened from her bent position, and she and I both gaped at this oddly scurrying man. I believe we were both uncertain as to the Pretender's intention, and though we may both have been alert to the need for some rapid protective measure, there was no chance to take one: the Pretender had already swept my son off his tiny tottering feet.

"Well, aren't you just a big boy all of a sudden," the Pretender said, pushing his own face up against the tiny one.

At first my son appeared startled, and it seemed as if he was about to cry. But then his chubby little face widened into a grin and cackled at the Pretender. It was a strange, high-pitched gurgling sound, this cackle.

"Ha-ha-ha-ha!" the Pretender cackled back at him.

"Giggle, giggle," my son responded.

Tucking my son under his arm as one might tuck a ball, the Pretender jogged all the way around the courtyard before swinging him into the air and catching him so that again, their two noses touched. He jiggled the tiny boy from side to side, those little legs swaying wildly in midair.

"Ha-ha-ha-ha!"

"Giggle, giggle."

"Ha-ha-ha-ha!"

"Giggle, giggle." And then, in his tiny infant voice, my son cried, "Again!"

The Pretender's eyes grew wide with delight. "Did you just say again? You want to do that again?"

This time his cheerful request was unmistakable: "Again!"

The Pretender moved to tuck him under his arm again for another jog around the courtyard, but by then I was on my feet and rushing in their direction.

I do not know why I rushed like that, or what I intended to accomplish other than to be there, right there beside my son, even if that meant willingly standing side by side with the Pretender. To be sure, he and I had been side by side many times as king and queen, and as public personae on the royal stage of our defeated city, but always I had held anger in my heart during such appearances, and we parted ways when they were over. Since the birth of our second child he had ceased to mount me as often as before, and for that I was grateful. I wish it had been otherwise, but I admit I was also thankful he had taken charge on that confused night of the Xlapan invasion and saved us, my infant son and me.

Perhaps I really do know why I rushed like that. While I had been the one to witness my son's first smile and first tentative steps, it was the Pretender who had just evoked his first intelligible word, and I wanted to be there to witness it. Where that tiny child had learned to say "Again!" I will never know.

That moment—standing beside the Pretender, both of us agog at that chubby face laughing against a backdrop of blue sky and rustling leaves—was the only time, ever, that I thought of my son as our son, and of the Pretender as my husband. It was also, I think, the sole moment in which he and I shared an awareness that we might, after all, have a few wishes in common.

It is not a moment I recall with joy. Rather, I remember it with considerable disappointment. In whom? In myself, because I trod perilously close to disloyalty to my father by discovering even this small speck of joy with the man who had so grievously betrayed him.

Why were we in that dusty cliff-top town?

We were there because we were hunted. My son, my daughter, and I, as the last living blood descendants of Calumook's House of the Waterlily, were hunted. Even the Pretender was hunted, not for his blood but for his haughty chiseled-in-stone claim to my father's jaguar throne.

Lurking in the jungle, lying in wait, biding their time—strategizing, scheming, conjuring—were the warriors of many petty kings and ambitious upstart chieftains. Such men were wont to imagine their persons seated cross-legged on our Waterlily jaguar throne. They saw the tall quetzal streamer headdress on their own heads, felt their persons dance in heavy jade upon the pinnacle of our palace. Any palace. All our palaces. Oh yes, they were lurking.

We heard reports of war.

We heard rumors of ascensions and overthrows as well. Of defeats and victories, betrayals and slaughters, suffering and deprivation. Shifting loyalties had always been a risk, but now, with the demise of dynasties that had endured for scores of generations, these shifts spurred dangerous instability. Ours was not the first dynasty to fall, or the last. And with each new downfall came the hunting—hunting to claim titles, hunting to extinguish bloodlines, seize thrones, destroy histories. Once kept tight in check, puppets and minions, rival lineage heads and upstart war captains all now vied for jaguar thrones.

We were not safe here. We were not safe anywhere.

That was why she spoke to me again, my body servant. She had not spoken to me since that confusing night in Calumook, when we fled through our makeshift barricade without my trunk. That night seemed so long ago.

She was wiping my daughter's bottom when she spoke. "My lady," she said, "our sentries are not strong."

I knew this. Still, I remained silent for the same reasons as before, chiefly that I was simply not accustomed to conversing as an equal with my body servant. Even here, even then, careful rules of status comportment held sway.

"We are not safe here," she warned. After a pause she continued: "*You* are not safe here," she said, her voice low and ominous.

I said nothing.

We were in my tiny cramped chamber. It was early in the morning, and the air was still cool. The day's new light was soft and hopeful. She was wiping my daughter's bottom. I was combing my hair, preparing it for the public eye. The public may have consisted of just our tiny courtyard, but still this had to be done. Grooming my own person was a gift I had offered to ease my servant's burden. But even then we had not spoken: one day I had simply picked up my comb and arranged my own hair. It was a very simple coif, to be sure, but I had done it with my own hands. Of course she had noticed me doing it, and each of us noticed that the other had noticed. As of that day I coiffed my own hair each morning, and I knew she was grateful—even though, as I said, we never spoke of it.

"My lady, the townspeople talk of many warriors in the jungle. They say they are assembling fast, and soon will strike."

Despite all that had happened, despite the many years she had groomed my person, despite her additional work—as wiper of my small children's excrement, cook, and now also charwoman, sweeping our floors with her tied twig broom—I remained hesitant to converse with her so openly.

Tradition is strange. We cling to it as a known and proper thing, even when we no longer should. Sometimes it plays tricks on us; sometimes it helps us survive. Change is hard, I know with certainty. Change can also sometimes trick us into doing something we later regret. Tradition and change: both can deceive, and both can offer opportunity, but it is hard to know which is happening at any given moment. When my servant spoke to me that morning in my tiny chamber off our tiny courtyard, I did not know whether to finally abandon tradition or to cling to it all the more.

More warriors assembling in the jungle?

The Pretender and his men seldom told me such things, but I was practiced at eavesdropping and heard them regardless. This I had not heard, however. Was she trying to trick me? To what end? Now, here, after all that had happened, there seemed very little to gain by doing so.

11

What the townspeople said was true. Warriors had been massing in the jungle, and for some time. My body servant was correct on another matter as well: Our sentries were not strong.

How could they be, that ragtag assembly of second-rate warriors?

Among those warriors were the young, untested Lalchich fighters who had not proven their mettle in the attack on Calumook. Unimpressed with their skill with sword and shield, the round-headed lieutenant had left them behind when he advanced to wreak destruction on other cities. Why should I insist my strongest share their booty with the weakest? Better to leave the weakest behind. I imagine that was the rationale for doing what he did.

A score of Calumook men were also among our warriors. These unfortunates had no kin in the countryside and thus nowhere else to turn. Their families had died in the ransack in Calumook following its fall to Lalchich, or had survived it only to perish during the Xlapan invasion. Or by ill fate the men had little family to begin with—and then none at all. What else were they to do? All the danger and disruption had made milpa near Calumook all but impossible; besides, as my father had said, the dirt itself had weakened. The odds of capturing booty were slim for these mediocre warriors, but the odds of living without whatever meager ration of combatant gruel they might receive apparently seemed even worse.

Our fighting force also included a handful of speculators from the cliff-top town who learned too late that loyalty to our fugitive royal party was not the wisest pledge.

As I imagine it, the lure, the legend of emblem-dynastied Calumook—its grandeur, the assurance of wealth and status upon the K'uhul Ajaw, Pretender-in-exile's rightful reinstatement to the coveted jaguar throne...this vision was enticing in comparison to the reality of otherwise exceedingly uncertain circumstances.

Within the warrior ranks were factions that split along these predictable lines, and more personal, internal lines as well. All in all they were undisciplined, second-rate, self-interested losers and chancers, each one of them. Such a ragtag hodgepodge could never be strong, but it was all we had up there on the cliff-top.

What did the Pretender think of all this?

A man with his capacity for organization and scheming would have been acutely aware of every weakness in our situation. He must have realized how dire it was. How could he have lain in the shade of the courtyard ceiba, enjoying the fresh cooling breeze, under such grim circumstances? How could he have played with my son like that, bouncing him about in our courtyard, tucking him under his arm like a ball? He even mounted me on occasion, though with much less urgency.

Of course I'll never know the thoughts of that sour-faced man, but he likely realized his days were numbered and nothing he could do would alter that truth.

When did he realize this?

Was it when he heard—or imagined he heard, for by then we would have been far away—the sound of my father's mosaic pyrite mirror shattering? Was it when he lost my father's Manikin Scepter? Where had it gone? Had it been overlooked in the frantic gathering-up of regalia from the front of the palace? Did someone steal it from behind our barricade? Might there be a traitor to the traitor? Or perhaps he realized his quest had ended when the Katun ending of 10.0.0.0.0 came and went? Or when he saw the pathetic stela erected in his honor in that dusty cliff-top town. In earlier times, its pitiful, talentless carver might have met a dagger for what would be perceived as effrontery. But now? The Pretender may simply have given up and chosen to take pleasure in whatever days fate might still allow.

I became aware of a hand upon my shoulder. In my dream, I believed it was the tender hand of Naah Chan.

Naah Chan was stroking my shoulder. It was bare, and my person responded to his touch. I smiled in my sleep and turned my face to his. Musty shafts of sunlight shone upon the green vine of our jungle curtain. I am not certain how long the hand was on my shoulder, as in slumber time passes at its own peculiar pace. Soon, though, I realized the hand was shaking me, and then my body servant whispered, "Lady Winik, you must awaken," and I did awaken, though reluctantly. I did not want to emerge from my dreamy life with Naah Chan.

"Lady Winik, we must go," she whispered.

Confused, I thought I was back in Calumook—that the rubble barricade still encircled us and the Xlapan still besieged us and the eyes of an enemy watchman had just fallen shut in the hours before dawn. But I was not behind the rubble barricade in Calumook. Nor was I with Naah Chan behind our green vine.

"Go?" I mumbled.

"Yes, we must leave."

"Leave?"

Then I remembered where I was. I was in my tiny chamber in the tiny courtyard of the dusty cliff-top town. "Where?" I asked. "Why?"

"My lady, the townspeople say they will strike this night. All of us are leaving. All of his servants are leaving." I knew whom she meant when she said "his." She meant the Pretender.

Still more softly, in a whisper filled with regret and humility but mostly decisiveness, she added: "I am leaving with them."

Despite the darkness, I knew the look on her face as she said, "I am leaving with them." Hers was a flat, expressionless face, and an aged one. Even if I had been able to see the deep creases around her mouth and eyes that night, they would not have changed at this flagrant admission. The small bun at the nape of her neck had not changed throughout all the years I had known her. Morning and night it was the same, always a tight gray knot of hair pulled taut, hair so thin you could see the pale shiny skin of her scalp.

I had not given her permission to leave. But of course we both knew she did not need my permission. She did not need it because that era was gone. It had been drawing to a close for many years, and now it was over. It was over the moment she said, "I am leaving with them."

She was abandoning us highborn to the fate of the spears and the daggers of the warriors massed in the jungle. She was rousing me from sleep to tell me goodbye. She loved me enough to want to tell me goodbye before she escaped to freedom and I did not.

I stared up at her dark face hovering above me, her hand still resting on my shoulder. I noted the continued presence of this hand.

A body servant touches only out of necessity, after which the touch ceases as if silently apologizing for having had to occur at all. The continued presence of my servant's hand also defined the end of our era, or more precisely, the end of our pretense that this era had not ended. As I stared at her, I could see only a small glint on the wet of one of her eyes. Although an admission like "I am leaving with them" might have sent those eyes dashing nervously from side-to-side, I could see they did not dash. They were still and steady and gazing into mine, despite the darkness. She had served me long and well. I did not resent her departure. I did not begrudge her her life.

"Goodbye," I told her, still groggy from sleep. "Fare thee well, and with you go my wishes for safety." These were the kindest words I ever said to her, and while I had not expected to say them, I meant them nonetheless.

Silence prevailed for a brief moment, and then she said: "My lady, no. You are leaving with us."

I peered again into the shadows of her dark face, uncertain I had heard her correctly. In the darkness, I said nothing.

"You cannot stay here—you are coming with me. Your children also. You will live with me in the hut of my aunt. It is far from here, far from everything. It is in a small village. We will be safe. You will live with me in the hut of my aunt."

I had trouble grasping the meaning of her words. And as ridiculous as it sounds, I truly had never before considered that my body servant might have a family. A mother, a father, an aunt. Was there, or had there ever been, a husband? Did she have her own children, children whose excrement she had wiped away?

I raised my person to sit on the bench and, still uncomprehending, reached out a hand to clasp her arm. She did not shrink from my touch, but merely waited for my comprehension to grow, and though it may seem odd, it was the honest feel of her unassuming arm that first revealed to me the sincere and loving nature of this soul. Her arm felt like bliss.

I whispered, "Yes." And then I said it again, louder this time: "Yes. We will leave with you."

"You will be safe."

Then I said, "Thank you, thank you."

Moments earlier, I would never have imagined such words—words of genuine gratitude to a body servant, even one who had loyally served me for as long as my memory stretched— would ever cross my lips.

Together, carrying my children—I my daughter and she my son—we padded barefoot through the dimness of the tiny courtyard. No mention of the Pretender, no mention of traveling trunks, not even a woven cloth sack slung over a shoulder.

Again we trudged through the night. We trod on paths so narrow and obscure that had I not kept my eyes trained on her back, I am convinced I would have lost my bearings and been devoured by prowling jaguars. Even as we walked and walked, I knew that never, as long as I lived, would I again consider this woman my body servant. Instead, Nikte' became my dearest friend, and more of a mother to me than my own mother had ever been.

◎◎◎

Scarcely had we begun the painful shaping of my son's head into the form of a delicate maize kernel, when we had to shape it back into that of a ball. We had taken no wooden press when we fled from that dark cliff-top town, so we fashioned something similar and fastened it on the top of his little head, and again crying ensued. I felt sorry for my son, not only because he had to endure two rounds of such agony, but also because he would never possess a head as beautiful as mine, a head that had been molded to the perfect lovely form of a maize kernel.

Soon after my son's skull resumed its round shape, I noticed the sourness creep onto his face. At first I supposed it might be the result of molding a head twice, which had never been done— who could guess what otherworldly repercussions might follow?

But as he grew from a toddler into a boy, I realized it was the blood of the Pretender that soured his face. The sour look then attacked the face of my daughter as well. I confess that I found it a challenge to love my children, with faces such as those.

Nikte' wrapped my own head with a long swath of coarse-spun.

"It looks ridiculous," I complained.

"It will save you," she said.

"Even the birds will laugh at this silly turban."

"Let them laugh all they want."

"It looks like I'm wearing a bandage because someone struck me on the head."

"You are," she answered.

"What do you mean?"

"That is the story I will tell the villagers."

"Really?"

"Yes, you were struck a very hard blow, which is also the reason you can't speak properly."

I was sincerely puzzled. "What do you mean?" I asked.

"Winik, the words that come from your mouth are words that no one in this village has ever heard. They will sound very strange. I will tell them it is because you lost the ability to form proper words when you were struck on the head. They will believe it."

I started to laugh, and Nikte' began to snicker, something I had never heard her do. Soon we were both giggling so loudly that her aunt stuck her head around the corner to see what was so funny, which made us laugh all the more. I laughed to think that people might believe that a knock on the head might make someone speak in a different way. I think Nikte' might have been laughing because she had not laughed in a very long time. It must have felt good to toss back her head and let laughter loosen a face that had been rigid so long it might have forgotten how to allow itself to be free.

Her plan proved a good one, and she was right; the villagers did believe it. "People here don't want to attract attention," Nikte' said. "They don't want to suggest to any bird or insect that wealth might be hidden in this place. Milpa," she explained. "That is what we do here. We want nothing more than to make milpa."

I did not want her to know it, but I also laughed because I thought these country bumpkins must be very naïve to civilized ways if they were so easily fooled. Only much later did I learn how mistaken I was: the villagers had known of my pedigree all along, but it was far safer for everyone if we all professed to believe the silly tale about a knock on the head.

I confess it took some time to become accustomed to her calling me Winik and not "my lady," which she did as soon as we departed that tiny courtyard. Never again did she address me as a lady, which of course I was not.

There still lived highborn with maize-kernel heads, but none besides myself lived in this village or anywhere near it. There still were towns in our world where nobles lived in fine stone houses, but few great cities remained, and even fewer great palaces and temples. Nobles in fine-spun lived, yes, but the very few living royals had either fallen or soon would. In time, all our cities would be devoured by the encroaching jungle, and vines would conceal the grand stages where we danced gracefully in heavy jade. Our cities became places of wreckage and ruin, of ceiba sprouting in ball courts, weedy piles of rubble, and mocking lowborn inhabiting the courtyards of royals, putting on airs. Soon enough, only dogs would stride, and snakes slither, the length of our crumbling sacbe.

It was her village that I lived in. There I lived in peace, raised my children in peace. And there old Nikte' died in peace.

She grew ancient, as I am now. Most of her teeth fell from her head, as mine now have. She grew infirm. But her face, once expressionless, had altered with our arrival in the village.

Though I would never have called her jolly, she took to laughing more and sometimes even jesting somewhat with her aunt and me, and certainly with my children. She fashioned toys of cloth and whittled delightful little wooden marionettes whose arms and legs moved with the tug of a string. She taught them how to roll clay between their palms and coil tiny pots, then fire them in the cooking hearth. We both cared for my young children, wiping their excrement from their persons. Together we mothered them, and of that I was particularly glad—glad that I could share them with her, for she had never married or birthed children of her own.

This is what Nikte' told me:

"When I was young I was shy and serious, and neither pretty nor bright. No boy wished to marry me, nor did I ever wish to marry. But work, work I could do, and without complaint. After my parents died, I was sent to Calumook in service to a noble household of my lineage. I became your nursemaid, Winik, because I was loyal and I could work, and because my lineage head gifted my service to your mother upon your birth. It was I who clasped you by the arm after your father killed your pet monkey and you squalled the long way down the front palace staircase before all the eyes of Calumook. That was a dreadful day."

"That was you?" I asked.

"Yes, that was me," she said.

"That was you," I said again, this time more as a reflection than a question. She had been with me that long.

"Yes, Winik. Inside, I felt your sadness with you. I had seen it all, the capture of your monkey in the sajal's tight fist. Your father's decision when he knew he had to act in the face of Calumook's lineage heads, mine among them. Those men were always cantankerous and squabbling, Winik. He had to do what he did. But still I cried for your pain, for I knew how much you adored your monkey. I knew as well that soon you would begin your training on how to don the stony mask, a necessary skill for a woman of your rank. I knew the discussions had already begun on the matter of your marriage—long before your grand Ixchel Moon celebration, in fact. I felt pity for you, their beautiful rag doll whose future was for sale through haggle and pact. But I only ever thought of you as a little girl who adored her monkey."

When Nikte' told me this, I wept.

I wept because suddenly I remembered everything about that terrible day. Not for a very long time had I thought of it, and so much had happened since, it was as if I was again experiencing that same wrench in my gut at the sight of my monkey's scruff clenched in that cruel fist. Again I saw the tight slits of his little eyes and heard the tiny muffled crack as my father twisted his neck. That frightful sound stirred deep sorrow in my heart. And I wept because I loved my father—the memory of my father—and refused to concede that I had ever only been a rag doll for his scheming. No, that part could not have been true.

I also wept because I remembered something I had almost forgotten about that day—the young commoner girl about my age whom I had seen standing at the base of the palace stair. Like Nikte', she had witnessed it all. Like me, she carried a pet monkey astride her hip. I remember my nursemaid—now I know her name was Nikte'—clasping her palm across my bawling mouth, whisking me away to our back palace courtyard. That commoner girl with her monkey had watched it all. I saw them both through tear-filled eyes—prisms of sorrow and envy.

Yes, envy. I remember yearning for that girl's simple life—her coarse-spun huipil, her bare feet, the feel of her monkey's arms lovingly draped about her simple, lowborn person. I wanted to be her, to live her humble life. The death of my monkey, the flinging of its limp corpse into the jungle—at that moment, the loss of my innocence began.

Then Nikte' said, "It was then that I pledged to do what I could to protect you. You see, Winik, at times a simple body servant can have clearer grasp of the world than a royal girl who understands only what she is told."

For a time I sat there blank-faced, perched upon a low stool near the hearth of our thatch hut kitchen.

"Yes," I said at last, tears welling. "Thank you. Yes. I thank you from every tiny corner of my person."

She moved her head in one slight bow, then continued: "When the Lalchich surprised us on the trail from Somalx, I was helpless to protect you. I too was rendered a dirty limp rag. I too was tied round the neck with their rough rope. I was much further down the rope than you. I watched as they tied you in. I heard the sobs of your mother, heard her awful confessions. I too hated the Lalchich. I was fortunate: I later managed to escape when a distant lineage woman took pity on me and set me free. I guided our Calumook warriors, your liberators. I instructed them on where to find the tiny cell deep within an inner palace courtyard where you were held prisoner. I knew you still lived."

Again my eyes brimmed with tears, this time also because I was ashamed. I had never known one thing, never asked one thing, about my nursemaid, my body servant, my charwoman, my cook. Not for one instant had I considered this woman's fate at the brutal hands of the Lalchich, nor did I even have any recollection of her presence in Somalx. I supposed it must have been she who soothed and salved me following my brush with a watery death in that sudden ocean squall. Despite her own suffering in bondage, her concern for my well-being had never faltered. She had saved my children's lives and my own by bringing us to this village, and for that I had come to love her. Now that I knew all of this, I loved her all the more. All the gentleness I had ever sought to conceal came rushing over my person, spilling forth across the strong carapace I had had to grow. It was finally safe to allow this gentleness to reappear. I knew it from looking at Nikte', looking into her flat, plain face.

As I gazed at this woman, I felt as if I was meeting someone new, not speaking with a person I had known my entire life long. I now understood how deeply selfless the soul of Nikte' was, how loyal and valiant her heart. She had also had to don the stony mask, but her mask had been affixed far more closely than mine. A mere body servant was obliged to don it even before the child she loved.

◎◎◎

Old Nikte' died in peace. I was at her side as she lay upon her ragged mat, her failing hand cradled in mine. When her person breathed no more, it was I who cleaned it.

I cleaned it with a coarse-spun rag. I cleaned it with a heart brimming with both sorrow and love. I cleaned it with a coarse-spun rag. I cleaned it of its death liquid. I cleaned it chanting her patriline chant. I cleaned it chanting ours as well, so that she might be greeted by my Kalo'mte' grandmother. I cleaned it as my heart overflowed with grief and love. I cleaned it with a coarse-spun rag.

◎◎◎

After Nikte' died, my daughter bid me move again, to the village of her husband. My daughter and I had spoken of this before. This had been our conversation:

"Mother, move to my husband's village with me."

"No, Daughter, I am happy to remain here."

"Why? There is nothing in this place. My husband's village is better."

"That is not true. For me there is much in this place."

"What is here, Mother?"

"Nikte' is here."

"You would choose that old hag over me, your own daughter?"

"Watch your mouth. Nikte' is not an old hag. She saved us all when you were just a nursling at my breast."

"Yes, Mother, I know. But that was long ago."

"Yes, it was long ago, but that makes no difference. I will remain here with Nikte' until she dies. After that we will see."

"But she is so old she does not even know who you are."

"But I know who she is."

My daughter has always been selfish. She has been sour-faced for so long she does not know any other way to live. The sourness crept up on her. It began to reveal itself before she could even totter about on her own tiny feet. First it was only a small, disagreeable scowl at her brow, but then it grew to infest the entire surface of her face. My son was able to totter long before the sour-ness seized his face, and he is a better person for that. At least he was capable of accepting my feelings for Nikte', even if he did not share them. I believe a sour face may well be a sign of disloyalty.

But after Nikte' died, I did move to the village of my daughter's husband.

My daughter had spoken truly; his was a better village. It had easier access to water, more firewood closer in, and a better, breezier lay of the land. By then my daughter had birthed two children, Lily Bean and her brother. The boy's face bears a trace of the sour—only a trace, to be sure, but enough to render him lacking. But Lily Bean's face has remained perfect, and now that she has almost reached menarche, the sour will not set in. I am certain it will not set in.

⊙⊙⊙

I moved to this village to be with my daughter, but also because it was closer to Calumook. Unlike the village where Nikte' was born, people here knew how to speak properly. Had highborn lived here—which they did not—they would have thickened their cool chocolate beverage with fine white maize meal.

My chance to visit Calumook was finally drawing near. It had been many years since I had seen my beloved natal city, the place that birthed the House of the Waterlily. Travel was safer now. The violence in the jungle had calmed, and trails were once more passable in the daylight with far less risk. Rain had begun to fall as well, and the maize in many of our milpas had taken on a healthy, vibrant green hue. The ears we broke and tossed in our tumpline baskets were much larger than the puny, withered ears I had seen with my father.

When it rains I reflect upon our Maize God.

Although I cannot surely know, I do not believe any K'uhul Ajaw now dances his dance. No regal foot is lifted in the air with poise; no dwarf spins as his ugly counterpart. There is no pounding of hollow slit log drums, no blare of long trumpets, no mighty roar of ocean conchs. Gone as well is the graceful clanking of heavy jade. Perhaps that is why the voices of our ancestors seem so distant.

Does the Maize God think we have forgotten him?

Back then, we remembered him often with scattered drops of our own precious blood, and also the blood of our captives. Did the Maize God regard these offerings as paltry? Should we have given more? After all, he never did command Chaak to send us rain. If he considered our gifts so paltry back then, why is he not angry with us now, when we offer him so little? Why would the Maize God order Chaak to pour his rain upon our milpas now, but withhold it before, when our offerings were so splendid? Chaak's grand temple was never completed—that cannot be disputed. No magnificent dedication spectacle honored his generous creation-era gourd-head sacrifice. No one cried his name from the lofty summit of a Calumook temple. Or from any summit of any temple.

In some towns, I have heard, kings who are not holy mount the steps of tiny temples to make trivial offerings. How can the Maize God not be angered by such charades? I brood over the possibility that back then, so much blood was shed that the Maize God drank his fill, and now his thirst is sated.

If this is so, then might his tongue parch once again?

I cannot claim to comprehend these enigmas—as I've said, such things are not for mere humans to know. Dense mist still hangs before our eyes, suspended there by our creator gods to obscure from us the mystical workings of the cosmos. Our role is to cherish them as they require, call out their names, and offer up our maize dough sustenance.

◎◎◎

I gaze once more at the young face of my granddaughter. It is indeed perfect.

Like mine, her nose has a pleasing bony arch. The curve of her eyebrows is firm but delicate; her skin is olive in hue. That the sour visage of the Pretender, my father's betrayer, is nowhere to be seen is another sign that the restoration of the House of the Waterlily is near. My survival has atoned for our avarice and vanity. We paid a heavy price for our misdeeds. My kinspeople lifeless at the bottom of our pleasure pool. The destruction of our magnificent arches and all of Calumook. The death of my father, whose bones lie I know not where.

As for me, I have atoned for my own transgressions as well. I endured the wretched stalk of the Pretender. I suffered the sight of my children's sour faces, withstood the indignity of his traitorous blood coursing through their veins. I toiled in the dirt of a milpa, sweat upon my royal person, in order to eat. In order for my children to eat. For Lily Bean. My little cousin should have ascended the throne. Now, this perfect girl has appeared. I have been patient. I have waited and watched the blood of the Pretender diminish, seen his stain washed from our lineage like filth from cloth.

I know such things take time. Her patience will be tried, as will her wits. She may not succeed, but our only hope lies with this perfect child. Soon she will be the custodian of our Waterlily chant.

"Grandmother?" she asks.

"Yes, my child?"

"You have taught me our patriline chant."

"Yes, that is right. You have learned it well."

"But I'm mixed up. How can you and I be of the same patriline? You are my mother's mother. Should she not be of the Pretender's lineage? And me, should I not be of my father's?"

I frown as I consider my response. Pedigrees can be confusing. How to describe the complicated paths of blood and heritage, of celestial involvement, of the difficult shifting intertwine of patriline and matriline, knowing there are exceptions to every rule when circumstance compels?

This is what I say:

"When it happens that the woman is the superior figure, we can choose to reckon descent through her. This is the case with us, you see. I was by far the superior figure to the Pretender. Because she is my daughter, your mother is the superior of her low-born husband."

"But, why me and not my brother?"

"Of course he is of our patriline. But, you, Lily Bean, your face is perfect, which means you are the superior figure. Lily Bean, you will lead the House of the Waterlily back to glory. You, without question."

◉◉◉

Only several months after arriving in my daughter's village was I finally able to visit Calumook. Not long after I stepped from the jungle trail, there I stood before the ruined entrance to my father's palace courtyard. I had not stepped over our threshold since that long-ago night when I escaped across it, my damp nightdress reeking of urine and of death. I was a mere girl.

As I looked upon the weeds and the ceibas springing from the rubble that once had been our painted walls, I felt far older than I was. Looking to the sky of day, I saw Ixchel hanging there in the guise of a thin, pale, waning sliver. She had long since begun spilling the water of life from her big clay jar.

My father's courtyard had witnessed my birth and my childhood, and it had later continued the taking of my innocence.

As I stood before its threshold, the persistent wails of my kinspeople reached me. I heard the cries as their Waterlily necks were slit, their lifeless corpses tossed like rubbish into our pleasure pool. I heard that single tiny, muffled crack below my chin.

But this was not why I had come. I had not come to step across this derelict threshold. I had not come to mourn my lost youth, or to yearn in vain for a life never lived. I had not come to listen yet again to those wails or that muffled crack. I have heard these hideous sounds long enough. Longer than I ought. For these, I have finally atoned.

Already I stood before the threshold of the Pretender's courtyard.

This deserted place was where my son was born. I remember the drapery I tore from my chamber wall during his delivery. I remember the kindness of the midwife's assistant, the sweetness of the cool herbed water in the gourd cup she gave me to sip from. I recall the agony of that birth, but the passage of time has rendered it distant and abstract, like so much else. Even overgrown with weeds and vines, I was able to discern the hasty rubble barricade that had encircled us during our long, hungry siege. I found myself pondering the death of that Xlapan watchman whose fatal slumber allowed our survival.

But that was not why I had come, either. I did not come to think about the Pretender or of my son—I have thought of them enough. But I do think of Lily Bean. Always I think of Lily Bean.

I traced the path along which Nikte' whisked me to safety, palm over my bawling mouth so long ago. Here fell my tears. Here fell our feet. This was when she first loved me.

Even though it was full of rubble and grit and tall weeds, and no longer covered with smooth plaster as it had been back then, I walked our long-ago path with reverence. As I put one foot before the other, I thought of humility.

I stopped near the front palace stair, the place where sacbe and palace joined. Our sacbe ran inland, away from the flow of our mighty river, which once brought wealth to our city nestled within its bend. Upon this sacbe I once strode arm in arm with my father, my little cousin astride my hip. Those cheerful days were long in the past. Gazing upon the union of our sacbe and palace, I perceived it as a place fraught with betrayal.

Our once-grand city was empty, abandoned but for grasshoppers and the long dragging tails of iguanas. Ceibas sprouted and clinging vines crept from the rubble that once was our palace. As I stood amidst our familiar but emptied world, I reflected on the life I never lived. Instead of that life, I worked milpa beneath the brim of a braided palm hat. I pulled weeds and broke off ears of maize and piled them in my basket. The sudden jump of grasshoppers grew ordinary.

I stood before our palace, peering upward along its collapsing stair. Gone were our green flapping banners. Gone also were the red ones. I do not know if the Xlapan invaders ever hung banners. Back then, highborn like me knew our places on this stair and played our parts in the endless spectacles that kept the universe in motion and our world in balance.

Until it fell apart.

Hillocks with dark doorways stood amid the weedy palace rubble. These were once our palace chambers—audience rooms of the lineage heads, my father's rooms. In these rooms cross-legged men had sat on woven reed mats and begun to parley on the matter of my marriage. The negotiations had concluded in these rooms as well, when a different group of cross-legged men determined that I, as a flesh-badge Waterlily prize, would wed my father's treacherous sajal. Gone were the awnings that brought shade, gone were the bright woven buntings and curtains, and gone as well were the cross-legged men upon their mats and benches.

I smiled to see that the twin stelae carved by the deceitful chisel of someone other than Naah Chan were no longer standing. Broken at the butts, they were. As I surveyed their jagged ends, it was as if I heard the faint, ringing echoes of the mighty blows of long wooden mallets. But not even their scattered carved pieces could be seen. I searched in the rubble but could find nothing, which I took as another sign that my shame—our shame—had ended. No glyphs carved in stone remained to record my inauspicious marriage to the Pretender on this, our grand palace stair.

A lost history is not always cause for regret.

◎◎◎

The longer I remain in this place, the more I recall the feel of fine-spun on my shoulders.

Persisting within my hands is the memory of guiding my bone weaving pin, the one topped with the carved bird figure. Once more my young fingers tug and coax, bend and pull the colored wefts. Soon intricate designs appear, prominent among them our lovely water lilies—stylized green pads and the white petals of blossoms with golden yellow hearts. The tiny, pale jade beads I once wove into the neckline of my huipil feel cool in my palm.

I sip cool chocolate from a painted clay cup. I smell the aroma of grilled venison. My skin is smooth, and the nails of my feet and hands are trimmed and even. My plaited hair hangs maiden-long down my back.

But neither did I come here to loll in the remembrance of youth and luxury.

Why did I come?

For a moment, my timeworn mind does not recall. I am confused by the memory of fine-spun against my skin, the lavish glossing draw of a comb through my hair. I have been spending so much time in these tales that they have begun to blur with the present. My grasp of what was then and what is now and what were my own concocted fables—all of this has become tangled and uncertain. On occasion my memory collapses in upon itself entirely, and I forget why I have walked to the shelf near the door. I know I intended to fetch some item, but I cannot remember what it was. I stand and peer about, my thoughts snarled and anxious.

Sometimes I think I hear the voice of Nikte'. Sometimes it is my father's voice I hear.

When I hear them, the nighttime glow of embers in the hearth seems very dim. As I watch its gleam fade to sooty black, I know my time is short, and I know how my death will be.

From beyond our hut I will hear the din of night grow loud. Within it, the lazy call of an owl. The guttural laugh of Howler Monkey will rise from the jungle. The cave of night will move in around me. In the inky sky, the glittering dance of stars will continue, and Itzamnaaj's three glowing hearthstones will remain in their place. But I will not. Ixchel will hang in the sky, this time deep in wane, like me. Her clay jar will tip its last drops of water, and from within her aging crescent, Rabbit will beckon. Theirs is a tug more powerful than the tug of the blue-green ocean.

◎◎◎

At last I remembered why I had come back to Calumook. I came on a quest for guidance.

I turned to face the front of our old palace. I saw crumbling ruined walls and thick jungle vine, but also I saw the bright sun, the resilient rays of our still-faithful K'inich.

Raising my hands to my mouth, I cried out: "Ah Ciliz! Ah Ciliz!"

I called in the supplicant ritual tone I had learned from Nikte'. I called the name of the god of solar eclipses in the supplicant ritual tone I once used with Chikchan, the cosmological snake, who sent a venomous rattler to sink its fangs into the man who betrayed my father.

I called to Ah Ciliz in honor of my astronomy teacher. That kind-hearted man died here, on this desolate, abandoned stair. I was standing there, he was standing here, and our eyes met in a flicker of shared anguish before he ceased forever to gaze into his beloved starlit heavens. I imagined him living somehow amongst his constant celestial companions.

"Ah Ciliz! I have returned! I am Lady Winik of the House of the Waterlily! I have returned!"

I listened as the wind rustled through the leaves of the ceiba, blowing its green boughs low and then bringing them back to where they had been. I watched a bird flit from one branch to another, then disappear amidst the vines. I smiled as the low, guttural scream of Howler Monkey—patron god of the arts, step-brother of Hun-Hunahpu—roared from the jungle to greet me.

"Ah Ciliz! This loyal daughter has returned to her ancestral home! She has survived!"

My supplicant tone seemed fitting in this strange uninhabited realm. Our once-proud emblem-dynastied city lay forsaken, filled only with ghostly echoes, my own now reverberating amongst them in this world of rubble.

"Ah Ciliz! I have returned to honor my ancestors, to honor my ancestor father, the K'uhul Ajaw of Calumook!"

The loud echo of my cries dissipated into this world of memories and was replaced with silence. Motionless, I waited for a sign. I thought about our world.

"Ah Ciliz! I have returned to our home to honor my Kalo'mte' grandmother! I pledge to her I will undo the wreckage wrought by our enemies! I will create for us a new ancestor bundle!"

At this I held up to Ah Ciliz my length of fine-spun cloth.

For many months I had labored to spin an entire skein and weave this small bit of cotton cloth. I was proud of my toil with spindle and loom—standing before our ruined palace, I felt even prouder than I had when I was weaving it. I had endured the derision of my sour-faced daughter to create this soft cloth with my stiff old fingers. The unassuming length of fine-spun was no labor of frivolity, but rather one of redemption.

In a loud, portentous voice of supplication, I cried out my true reason for returning to Calumook. "Ah Ciliz," I cried, "Guide me to the remains of my father!"

Silence followed as my petition reverberated throughout the empty city. My arms were held as high as I could raise them. I proffered my length of fine-spun, holding it out for Ah Ciliz to see. There I stood, cloth in hand, wide toothless expanse of mouth beaming in anticipation.

My father was stabbed with a dagger while sleeping in a front palace room. But my father had used many chambers, and I did not know the front palace as well as the back. I had returned to seek out some possession—some tiny bone, a small jagged piece of carved stone with his glyph, any minor token of him. This I would wrap in my fine-spun. With this I would create for the House of the Waterlily a new ancestral bundle.

An iguana appeared.

His movement drew my attention when he lifted his heavy reptile head from behind a gray rock. He heard me. He lifted one sharp-clawed foot, then the other, dragging his slow scaly form across the rubble to stop before one of the dark doorways that used to be a palace chamber. He turned his long scaly neck and head, and stared into my eyes. A long, low hiss emanated from his mouth. Still he stared.

He made a loud clicking noise, and still he stared.

I understood his words. "Lady Winik? Is that you? You have returned?"

I called back to him, "Yes, it is I! I have returned!"

"Welcome back to your home, beloved Daughter of Calumook," Iguana hissed.

Tears rushed to my eyes. I called back: "Yes, I have returned!"

"We have mourned your absence for too long!" Iguana hissed.

Then he turned to gaze toward the dark doorway of the rubble of the room before which his scaly form lay. I turned my head, following his gaze with my eyes.

Why this chamber? I would not have expected to find what I sought on the first story of our palace, but who was I to question such guidance? Perhaps what I sought was indeed hidden within this unpretentious room. Ah Ciliz, a god who has the power to bite the sun, can know many things.

As though in a trance, I moved toward this dark doorway. With each slow step, Iguana followed my passage with his eyes and his scaly turning head.

Is this where my father died? Do his bones rest within this modest room? I could not fathom why my father might conceal even a single possession in this unassuming first-floor chamber.

As I slowly crossed the rubble, one foot after the other, I considered whether my father might have suspected the Lalchich were coming after all, or realized his sajal was not as trustworthy as he had assumed. Had my wise father secreted his finest possessions in a humble place where no one would think to look? Had he safeguarded them here until his loyal surviving daughter could muster her wits and her command of the spirit world to return at last and claim them?

I entered the shadows of the chamber and waited for my eyes to adjust to the low light. Soon I was able to make out the wreckage strewn about during the last ransack, the one by the Xlapan. Broken shards of pottery, smashed and rotting wooden chests, corners thick with cobwebs. A ramshackle pile of mildewed mats on a bench, chewed on by rats and bats. The stink of their dank, musty feces.

A rat, startled by my presence, scurried from beneath the pile of old mats. Rapt, I watched him scurry around the corner of the room and out the door. I was reminded of Rat, who once revealed to Hunter and Jaguar Deer where their father's (and uncle's) ball game equipment was hidden. It was hidden in the thatch, tied to the dusty rafters of their grandmother's hut. Then the realization struck me: something was hidden here in this ruined chamber as well, hidden by my father, and Rat has shown me where to look.

I cautiously lifted a corner of the musty old mats, fearful that more tiny beasts would emerge. Like Nikte', I was frightened by their beady black eyes and ugly, twitching snouts. But no more rats scurried forth, and so I lifted the mats higher. Then I saw it.

There, in the plaster of the bench, was a patch. Someone—a person, not a rat—had burrowed into the bench and then covered the hole over with fresh plaster. I knew this from the thin crack that formed there; new plaster will always shrink away from the old a bit. It is true that looters know of such hiding places, and also of such telltale signs, but apparently they missed this one in their careless, greedy chicha stupor. My wise father must have concealed something within this bench—this unassuming bench, within this unassuming first story chamber—to better ensure its safekeeping.

Perched on rubble outside the door, Iguana watched me. His tongue curled slowly out and then slowly back into his mouth. Suddenly I understood that Iguana had stood sentry before this patched bench, helping to conceal its surface from the greedy vision of the ransackers.

I found a broken wooden stave that had once been part of a carved chest. I snatched it up and used it to pound and dig at the plaster patch. With each blow I intoned the words of our patriline chant, near-forgotten stanzas that had not crossed any lips in Calumook for many long years. I also chanted the patriline chant of my beloved Nikte', because her memory remained dear to me. I looked to Iguana, who continued to observe my every move—and then I punched through to the dark void inside the bench.

I could only just see inside it. I removed the jumble of rocks one by one and brushed away the dust and grit of crumbling plaster. My hands searched and then lit upon something firm yet soft, something neither rock nor plaster. I ran my hands over it to make out its dusty form. It was long and almost as wide as my waist. It had the texture of fine-spun material like the lengths that wrapped our ancestral bundles. I pondered whether this might be such a bundle, but as I removed it from the void I realized it was far too long. I could not fathom why a bundle would be hidden inside a bench in a first-story palace room. Such was not its proper place.

Like the precious gift of Ah Ciliz that it was, I carried the bundle over the crumbling threshold of the doorway to peer upon it in the light of day.

As I emerged into the sunlight, the scream of Howler Monkey, patron of the arts, step-brother of Hun-Hunahpu, rose up to greet me. By instinct I scanned for enemies, for intruders, for anyone—but there was no one. I was the sole living person in all of what was once our Calumook. Iguana, still perched on his rubble mount, continued his watch. Brushing away dust and remnants of plaster, I noted that the wrapping was well woven and finely decorated, and my heart began to beat faster. I unwrapped one long edge and then began turning and unwrapping, turning and unwrapping, chanting all the while. Suddenly there was a flash of bright green, and I removed the last of the fine-spun wrap to find before me, uncovered and brilliant in the bright Calumook sun, my father's perfect quetzal streamer headdress.

The End

Afterword

It would be wrong to suggest that water lily motifs abound in Maya art, but they are not uncommon. They most frequently appear on ceramics; the Maya Vase Database contains forty-six vessels featuring such imagery. While such motifs can be found on plates and carved vases, they more typically occur on polychrome vases. When their provenance is unknown, intact polychrome vessels are usually understood to have come from looted elite burial sites. In several instances, holes were deliberately made in vessels with water lily motifs, presumably as part of Maya funerary ritual.

Water lily motifs take many forms, with various associations. Common elements include two long stems, one connected to one or more lily blossoms and the other leading to one or more lily pads. The stems usually emerge from the top of a skull. These skulls are interpreted as existing in a watery world because they are associated with conchs, long-legged water birds, and fish—occasionally the fish are even nibbling on the lily blossoms. Sometimes the skull contains dripping water iconography that situates it in a cave or other seeping-water location. Taken altogether, such imagery points to a "Waterlily Monster" residing in the underworld, Xibalba, as accessed through a watery entrance.

Beyond identifying the flower's watery setting, other associated motifs offer additional clues to the meaning of water lilies in ancient Maya thought. K5941 depicts the Maize God, Hun-Hunahpu, and the Tonsured Maize God (Hun Nal Ye) dancing underwater as two slightly different Waterlily Monsters emerge from the bottom of the scene. K7185 depicts the Maize God emerging from the head of a Waterlily Monster. Such scenes suggest that water lily imagery is linked with death, rebirth, and maize sustenance.

In other instances, either the Waterlily Monster emerges from the open maw of a vision serpent (e.g., K5541), or is itself a vision serpent (e.g., K8649). Vision serpents are understood as the vehicle by which visions of royal ancestors are summoned through ritual bloodletting. K7146 depicts a dwarf blowing a conch shell while lying on a bed of water lily pads, all of which sit atop a Waterlily Monster. Dwarfs and conch shell trumpets are also commonly associated with royalty.

K7287 depicts a Waterlily Monster inside a turtle carapace. Above his head he holds a very large femur bone throne. Turtles are associated with both watery settings and the three hearth-stones of creation. This large, raised throne may suggest that a leader's rule is supported by, or emerges from, the bones of ances-tors. Associated glyphs sometimes offer further information. As examples, glyphs on K7146 indicate noble title, while those on K7185 mention the ruler Yoaat Bahlam. Inscriptions on the Art Institute of Chicago's Water-Lily Vase—the first on a Classic Maya vessel to be deciphered—identify its artist as Ah Maxam (Lord Flint Face). That text further states that the artist is a member of the royal lineage of the kingdom of Naranjo. Glyphs for Ah Max-am's mother and father also appear on the vessel, as well as on stone monuments from the region.

Taken together, at least as evidenced through a sample of the vessels in the Maya Vase Database, water lily imagery was linked with death and rebirth and maize substance and ancestors and rule. My use of Waterlily in this novel encompasses all of these possible meanings bundled together, albeit non-specifically.

I would like to comment as well on the House construct. Mayanist readers will know that the social construct of the House is not commonly used for the Maya; instead, the hieroglyphic re-cord of their words gives us "dynasty" or "family." I find compel-ling, however, Susan Gillespie's 2000 *American Anthropologist* article advocating the utility of House, particularly because her model allows House and Lineage to coexist side by side. I like her discussion of how the physical dwelling (house) is closely re-lated to, but not the same as, the social construct (House), which is physically and conceptually bigger than a physical space. The construct is based on the often sprawling, archaeologically visible residential groups, but it also allows for a wide variety of relationships among its less visible human occupants. In Gillespie's model, various kin and affines, fictive kin, extended family, hangers-on, members from distant lineage branches, courtiers, slaves, and servants are seen as possible members of a large cadre of social affiliates. Her inherently fluid and elastic social construct retains patrilineage as its core but allows for non–kin-related expansion, as lineages subtly (or not so subtly) competed for loyal supporters. I think of it as a "big tent" vision of Maya social order.

How societies evolve and change—and how and why they decline—is a matter of interest and importance for scholars and the public alike. The Maya were living in small farming villages by at least 1500 BC; shortly thereafter, at least at some sites, they were building small- to medium-sized temples and buildings that many archaeologists believe reflect the existence of chiefdom-scale societies. By AD 250, most Maya cities had constructed very large temples and sprawling palaces, and stela carvers were chiseling Long Count dates on stone monuments. Populations had grown quite large in many areas, trade in elite prestige goods was in full swing, and powerful divine kings had founded great dynasties, many of which would be very long-lived.

The archaeological record clearly reveals that in the ninth century, great societal decline and transformation occurred everywhere in the Maya world. By the end of that century, nearly all Maya city-states had fallen, marking the end of over six hundred years of wealthy and powerful divine dynasties. The collapse of the fictional Calumook is set prior to the turn of the year AD 830, the planned dedication date of the king's grand Chaak temple. Under "normal" circumstances, the Classic Period Long Count Katun ending (10.0.0.0.0) that corresponds to AD 830 would have been occasion for great celebration, including the dedication of many dated stelae. But it was not: in the Southern Lowlands, the year AD 830 is important year where the Maya Long Count record falls silent in many places.

For other cities the glyphic record ends much earlier, as at Bonampak, Mexico, in AD 792; or much later, as at Toniná, Mexico, in AD 909. The earliest cities to fall were in the Southern Lowlands, where the collapse of the Maya world was most violent, and where I placed the fictional Calumook. Maya city-states were never politically unified, and the south's experience of collapse was not representative of the rest of the Maya world. In the Northern Lowlands—at Uxmal and Chichén Itzá, for example—the "collapse" was much less dramatic and occurred some 150 years later.

Explanations for the collapse of individual Maya cities varied greatly. Just as timing differed regionally, so too did the causes. In the Northern Lowlands, drought and overpopulation appear to have been significant factors. Evidence from Copán, Honduras, points to overpopulation and increased environmental pressure, as farming on steep hillsides led to heavy soil erosion. The nature of Maya kingship itself was also a factor. Rivalry among and within cities was constant. Noblemen's ability to marry multiple wives meant growth of a non-food producing segment of the population whose expensive lifestyle demanded increasing levels of tribute from commoners. Such a system was costly to maintain and clearly unable to withstand the multiple and complex challenges of the Late Classic. In *House of the Waterlily* I have brought all these factors to bear on fictional Calumook, though a city need not have experienced all of them simultaneously. While I have intentionally painted this story with a broad brush, I hope readers might nonetheless recognize the substantial variability in how and when and why any individual Maya city may have fallen.

Even though the Maya world changed radically in the ninth century, very many Classic Period cultural foundations survived. They were no longer living in their grand Classic-era cities, but Maya people were alive and well when the Spanish began arriving in the early 1530s. However transformed, they never disappeared. Today the Maya are some seven million strong and occupy a socioeconomic spectrum ranging from traditional milpa farmer to highly educated urbanite.

In closing, I observe that fiction often succeeds because it can draw out recognition of human commonalities. In this novel, the Classic Maya world and its decline form the cultural backdrop for personal human stories unfolding on a smaller scale. In this light, I hope *House of the Waterlily* offers not only something from which readers can learn, but also an opportunity to relate to the Maya as fallible human beings like the rest of humanity, people who experienced joys and sorrows like the rest of us and, also like the rest of us, did the best they could for the era in which they lived. Where academic discourse fails to impart recognition of this commonality of lived human experience, creative writing can offer a solution.

A Brief List of Additional Resources

Additional Reading

Coe, Michael D. *The Maya,* 8th edition. Thames & Hudson, 2011.

Coe, Michael D. and Mark Van Stone. *Reading the Maya Glyphs.* Thames & Hudson, 2005.

Diamond, Jared. *Collapse: How Societies Decide to Fail or Succeed.* Penguin Books, 2005.

Harrison, Peter. *The Lords of Tikal: Rulers of an Ancient Maya City.* Thames & Hudson, 1999.

Martin, Simon and Nikolai Grube. *Chronicle of the Maya Kings and Queens,* 2nd edition. Thames & Hudson, 2008.

McAnany, Patricia A., and Norma Yoffee, editors. *Questioning Collapse: Human Resilience, Ecological Vulnerability, and the Aftermath of Empire.* Cambridge University Press, 2010.

Webster, David. *The Fall of the Ancient Maya: Solving the Mystery of the Maya Collapse.* Thames & Hudson, 2002.

Recommended Websites

Foundation for the Advancement of Mesoamerican Studies, Inc. http://www.famsi.org/index.html
Contains great resources such as searchable image databases of Mesoamerican/Maya sites, maps, pottery, drawings, and a wide variety of other artifacts.

http://www.mesoweb.com/welcome.html
Contains a wealth of searchable articles, drawings, and photographs; an encyclopedia; and many other resources.

Reading Response / Classroom Assessment / Discussion Guide

1. Try your own "chisel" at Maya Long Count Glyphs!
   Find help at http://research.famsi.org/date_mayaLC.php
   a. Draw the Long Count glyphs that Naah Chan was busily carving to dedicate Calumook's new Chaak temple.
   b. Identify each glyph using its Maya name.
   c. Identify the number of days in each glyph's temporal unit.
   d. When did the Classic Maya Long Count begin?
   e. On what date in our calendar would Calumook's new Chaak temple have been dedicated?

2. Why did the Classic Maya Period end? How are the causes represented in *Waterlily*?
   Offer five paired responses below. I'm looking for one concise sentence for each specific cause, and a second concise sentence for each specific *Waterlily* representation.

   2.1. Cause:

   Waterlily:

   2.2. Cause:

   Waterlily:

   2.3. Cause:

   Waterlily:

2.4. Cause:

Waterlily:

2.5. Cause:

Waterlily:

3. How did Maya economic/political/social/religious life change from the Classic to the Postclassic? Offer five paired responses below: approximately one concise sentence for each specific change, and a second concise sentence for each specific *Waterlily* representation.

3.1. Change:

Waterlily:

3.2. Change:

Waterlily:

3.3. Change:

Waterlily:

3.4. Change:

Waterlily:

3.5. Change:

Waterlily:

4. Integrating specific examples from *Waterlily,* discuss the purpose of Maya sacrifice. One typed, concise paragraph.

5. "Free Write": In one double-spaced page, comment on something specific (and not addressed above) that in your opinion stood out in *House of the Waterlily.*

Discussion Questions

What did you learn about the Maya that you didn't previously know?

What is a K'uhul Ajaw?

Do you think the K'uhul Ajaw of a Maya city actually romped and played with his children in his palace courtyard, roamed neighborhoods for pleasure, or personally visited the rural milpa of a lineage head?

In what ways were the ancient Maya like contemporary Americans? In what ways were they unlike contemporary Americans?

How—and why—does Lady Winik's personal perspective on life change? How is this reflected at the time of her death?

What is the main driving goal or motivation of the elderly Lady Winik as her time grows short? Why do you think she wants it so badly? What other motivations might she have, and why?

Acknowledgements

My most recent on-site research for *House of the Waterlily* was made possible through participation in the National Endowment for the Humanities Summer Institute, *Revisioning the Ancient Maya World: New Directions in Teaching and Scholarship,* during the summer of 2011. I thank the American taxpayers for my participation in the NEH. Any views, findings, conclusions, or recommendations expressed in this publication do not necessarily reflect those of the National Endowment for the Humanities. As well, generous support was provided through a 2012 Artist Enrichment Grant from the Kentucky Foundation for Women, an organization whose mission promotes feminism and social change. *House of the Waterlily* fits these criteria because it highlights the role of women in antiquity, and because it considers human contributions to environmental harm.

The image of the Waterlily Monster on the title page was originally created by an unknown ancient Maya artist, from an unknown Maya site. The codex style image was painted on a ceramic vase (with dimensions of 10 cm in height, a diameter of 9.5 cm, and a circumference of 26.5 cm. See *Painting the Maya Universe,* page 86 and *Maya Book of the Dead,* page 113). The image was electronically traced by graphic artist Alyssa Brandt, from the rollout photograph of vessel K5961 in the online Maya Vase Database. Thank you Alyssa, and also Dr. Justin Kerr, with whom I corresponded in regard to using his K5961 photograph.

For reading drafts and offering thoughtful insight and resources and other great ideas, I thank Ann Stebbins, Jim Keller, Greg Partain, Mick Lewis, Willard Carmean, Kim Carmean, Jerry

Sabloff, Tom Jamison, Cynthia Kimball, Alice Spielberg, Tom Hakansson, Tom Krause, Ryan Kelly, as well as several anonymous peer reviewers. All of you improved the manuscript in innumerable ways. Thank you, all of you.

Lightning Source UK Ltd.
Milton Keynes UK
UKOW01f1422290917
310128UK00001B/13/P